Barb and J. C. . . . . f Boulder, Colorado, clo . . . . cky Mountains. He teaches English for the Metropolitan State College of Denver, and she teaches for the University of Colorado at Denver. Barb's short fiction has appeared in numerous genre magazines and anthologies. She is the author of the novel *Blood Memories*. J. C.'s poetry, non-fiction and short fiction have also appeared in many genre magazines. Although they have worked together as a writing team before, *Dhampir* is their first novel-length collaboration.

Find out more about Barb and J. C. Hendee and other Orbit authors by registering for the free monthly newsletter at www.orbitbooks.co.uk

DHAMPIR

Barb & J. C. Hendee

orbit

An *Orbit* Book

First published in Great Britain by Orbit 2005

A CIP catalogue record for this book is available from
the British Library.

ISBN 1 84149 364 3

Typeset in Bembo by Palimpsest Book Production Limited
Polmont, Stirlingshire
Printed and bound in Great Britain by
Mackays of Chatham plc, Chatham, Kent

Orbit
An imprint of
Time Warner Book Group UK
Brettenham House
Lancaster Place
London WC2E 7EN

For Jaclyn, our little starving artist
raised by two starving artists

Prologue

The village appeared deserted but for thin trails of smoke escaping clay chimneys to drift up and dissolve in the darkness. All doors were barred, all window shutters latched tight until only the barest wisps of light from candles or lamps seeped between their cracks. There was no one in the village's muddy center path to see the night-shadowed object flitter toward a cottage near the tree line.

The shadow stopped, hesitating next to the cottage. Slowly, its form shifted and expanded as it ceased to consciously hide itself. Nothingness became booted feet and reaching arms, a tall and slim torso, and a head with two pinprick glimmers for eyes. It scaled a tree rapidly and jumped onto its goal.

Settling upon the thatched roof, it slid on its belly to crawl headfirst down one wall. Then it stopped, poised at the top of a shuttered window. One finger extended to slip a clawlike fingernail between the shutters. Prying and pulling, it worked at the shutter until the latch finally gave with a sharp snap. The figure paused, waiting, listening for any answering sound from within the room. When none came, it pulled the shutters open.

On a bed inside lay a small, old woman. Long silver hair, tied in a braid, rested next to her head across a yellowed linen pillow. A faded patchwork quilt of carmine and teal squares covered her.

The creature hung its head down through the window. Its voice sounded like an echo across a vast plain as it whispered, 'May I come in?'

The old woman moved slightly in her sleep.

Again the voice asked with a touch of yearning, 'Please, old mother, may I come in?'

She moaned and rolled, her face turning to the window. On her wrinkled brow was a small, white scar half smothered by the creases of aged skin. Her eyes remained closed in sleep as she murmured in reply. 'Yes . . . yes, come in.'

The visitor reached one arm through the opening and upward to set its fingernails in the wall. It crawled over the upper edge of the window, letting its feet swing inward, then dropped soundlessly to the bedroom floor. Crossing to the bed, it quickly reached out with one hand and clamped it down over the old woman's mouth.

She woke, eyes wide and frightened, but only for a brief moment. Then she stared with an empty gaze into the eyes above her. The night visitor relaxed its grip, lowering its head to her throat. All in the room became still and quiet and timeless.

Then its head swung up to stare at the open window. A dark stain covered the side of the old woman's throat. The visitor began to lower its head again to the old woman, but paused. With an owl-tilt of its head, its gaze returned to the window as it listened.

Outside, someone was walking the village path. The visitor moved to the window.

Strolling along the village path was a young woman wearing studded leather armor and high, soft boots pulled over earth-colored breeches. In one hand she held a short pole, and in the other a long knife with which she worked at sharpening the pole's end into a crude point. At her side hung a short falchion in its worn leather scabbard. The night was too dark for most eyes, but as the woman passed between moon-shadows of cottages and nearby trees, the visitor saw her dark hair with hidden shimmers of red that offset smooth, young skin little more than two decades of age. No true fear or wariness showed in the woman's posture as she moved through the village, fashioning the wooden short-spear.

'Hunter,' it whispered to itself with amusement.

The pathetic humor of what it saw was too much to hold in, and it laughed under its breath as it leaped out the window to spider-walk up the cottage wall onto the roof. The dark form shrank and vanished into the night forest.

1

Long past sundown, Magiere walked into another shabby Stravinan village without really seeing it. Peasants lived the same way everywhere. All their bleak, shapeless huts began to blur together after six years, and Magiere only noted their number as a gauge of population. No more than a hundred people lived here, and perhaps as few as fifty. None showed themselves this late in the night, though she heard the creak of a door or window shutter as she passed by, someone peeking out when she wasn't looking. The only other sound was the scrape of her hunting knife on hard wood as she sharpened the end of the short wooden pole no longer than her arm.

Darkness didn't frighten her. It suggested to her none of the fear-conjured threats that made these peasants shudder behind their barred doors. She checked her falchion in its sheath, making sure she could draw it out easily if needed, and continued her stroll toward the far end of the village. A drizzle of rain began, which soon matted down her black hair, smothering any crimson tint it might have shown in the light. With her pale skin, she must look as baneful to the villagers as their visions of the creature they'd hired her to eliminate.

Not far outside the village she stopped at the communal graveyard to survey the fresh mounds of earth, each surrounded by tin lanterns put there to keep evil spirits from seizing the bodies of the dead. There were no headstones or markers as yet on these new graves – they had been buried in haste before such could be prepared. She turned back through the village again, studying the buildings more closely this time as she looked for the one most likely to be the common house.

Most of the peasants would be gathered in some communal building, seeking safety in numbers. She glanced around for anything large enough, but all the huts looked the same – drab, weatherworn timbers with thatch roofs and clay pot-chimneys. They were dismal and silent, like everything else in this hope-abandoned land. Garlands of dried garlic bulbs hung across the few windows. The only signs of life were the few streams of smoke rising into the night sky. Slight tinges of iron and char scented the wet air. An unattended forge must be smoldering somewhere nearby. People dropped everything at dusk in times like these.

Movement caught Magiere's eye. Two shivering figures ran across the muddy road. Their tattered rags exposed filthy skin. Magiere absently slipped her knife into its sheath, then gathered her own warm cloak a bit tighter. The figures scurried toward the graveyard, trying to keep the gusting breeze and rain from snuffing out their lanterns.

'Hello,' Magiere called out softly. They both jumped and whirled toward the sound.

Thin, wretched faces twisted in alarm. One of them backed away, and the other jerked up the wooden pitchfork he was carrying. Magiere remained still and let them see what she was, but she gripped the wooden pole a little tighter. Understanding the mentality of these people was a large part of her job. Very slowly, beneath her cloak, her free hand settled on the falchion's hilt, ready to draw. It paid to take care around panic-stricken peasants.

The man holding the pitchfork peered uncertainly through the rain at her studded leather armor and pole. The fear on his face changed into a vague semblance of hope.

'You are the hunter?' he asked.

She gave a slight nod. 'Have you more dead?'

Both men let out a slow breath of relief and stumbled forward.

'No . . . no more dead, but the zupan's son is close.' The second man gasped, then beckoned with his hand. 'Come quickly.' The peasants turned and fled back up the muddy center path.

She followed, stopping when they did at a door with a small sign above that had been worn unreadable long ago. This rough building had to be their common house, since the village was far too remote to have an inn catering to travelers. 'Zupan' was their name for a village chief. He, along with some of the villagers, would be waiting inside for her.

An expectant sigh slipped through her lips as she wondered what this zupan would be like – a cold, hard sell she hoped. The ones who fawned over her, in hope that she wouldn't suck the village dry, were the most repulsive. It was easier when they resisted, until she made them realize there was no other reasonable prospect than to pay her price or wait to die. The quietly agreeable ones were the most dangerous. Once the job was finished, she would have to watch for unexpected company in the shadows on her way out of town, ready to reclaim their payment with a harvest blade or shearing knife through her back.

'Open up!' one of her escorts shouted. 'We have the hunter with us.'

The door creaked inward. The orange-red glow of firelight spilled out, along with an overwhelming stench of garlic and sweat. Magiere glanced down into the eyes of an age-stunted woman clutching a stained shawl, face drawn and sallow as though she hadn't slept in days. At the sight of Magiere, the woman's expression altered to one of desperate hope. Magiere had seen it too many times.

'Thank the guardian spirits!' the woman whispered. 'We heard you would come, but I didn't . . .' She trailed off. 'Please come in. I'll get you a hot drink.'

Magiere stepped into the thick heat of the small common house. One thing she hated most about her vocation was all of the traveling in the cold. Eight men and three women were crowded into the tiny room. On a table to one side lay an unconscious boy. At least two people at any given moment hovered close to the boy in case he died.

A superstitious lot, these peasants believed that evil spirits sought out the bodies of the newly dead, using the corpses to prey upon and feed off the blood of the living. The first thirty-six hours were the most critical for a malevolent spirit to enter a corpse. Magiere had heard all the other legends and folk stories; this was just one of the more popular. Some thought vampirism spread like a disease, or that such creatures were simply evil people cursed by fate to an undead existence. The details varied; the results were the same – long nights spent shivering from fear more than the cold as they waited for a champion to save them.

A huge, dark-haired man, like an ancient grizzly with a gray-stubble beard, stood at the table's head, watching the boy's closed eyes. It was a long moment before he lifted his gaze to Magiere and acknowledged her presence. His clothing looked similar to everyone else's, perhaps with one or two less layers of grime, but his bearing marked him as the zupan. He pushed through the overcrowded room to face her.

'I'm Petre Evanko,' he said in a surprisingly soft voice. He motioned to the woman who had greeted Magiere. 'My wife, Anna.'

Magiere politely nodded, but didn't introduce herself. Mystery was part of the game.

Zupan Petre stood for a moment, taking in her appearance, one that Magiere had carefully tailored long ago for her work.

Studded-leather armor marked her as warrior too much on the move for anything heavier or bulkier. The volume of her cloak made it uncertain what might be hiding beneath. Her thick black hair with its red accents was bound in a long, plain braid, sensible and efficient. Around her neck hung two strange amulets no one would be able to identify, and which she only left in view when working a village. She carried a short, pointed pole made of wood, with a leather-covered handle.

Magiere swung the pack off her shoulder, its top flap swinging open as it settled at her feet. Zupan Petre looked down at the mixed contents of unlabeled jars, urns, and pouches, some of which were filled with strange herbs and powders. These were all the accoutrements expected for someone who battled the undead.

'I'm honored, Zupan Petre,' Magiere said. 'Your message reached me two weeks ago. I regret my delay, but there are so few hunters and so great a demand.'

His expression changed to gratitude. 'Don't apologize. Come and see my son. He's dying.'

'I'm not a healer,' Magiere quickly interjected. 'I can remove your undead, but I can't cure the damage already done.'

Anna reached out to touch her cloak. 'Please just look at him. You may see something we cannot.'

Magiere glanced at the boy, and then moved closer. The other villagers shuffled out of her way. She was always careful to explain her limitations and give no one open cause to accuse her of making false promises. The boy was pale and barely breathing, but Magiere grew puzzled. There were no sores or fever, no sign of injury or illness.

'How long has he been like this?'

'Two days now,' Anna whispered. 'Just like the others.'

'Were they all young boys?'

'No, one older man and two young women.'

No pattern. Magiere stared intently at the sleeping boy and then turned to Anna. 'Take off his shirt.'

She waited quietly for Anna to finish before examining the boy's arms and chest. Then she inspected the joints of his limbs. His flesh was intact but so pale it seemed almost blue, even in the amber firelight from the hearth. She lifted his head. Her eyes narrowed slightly at the sight of two oozing holes under his left ear, but she kept her expression guarded.

Her gaze shifted quickly to Zupan Petre's face. 'Have you seen these?'

The zupan's bristly brows wrinkled in a frown. 'Of course. Is that not the way of a vampire, to bleed its victim through the throat?'

Magiere looked back at the holes. 'Yes, but . . .'

The holes were large, but perhaps it had been a large snake or some kind of serpent. Powerful venom could account for the pallored skin and shallow breathing.

'Has someone been with him all the time?' she asked.

Petre crossed his arms. 'Anna or myself. We would never leave him like this.'

Magiere nodded. 'Anyone else?'

'No,' Anna whispered. 'Why are you asking such questions?'

Magiere checked herself and quickly salved their uncertainty. 'No two undeads kill in exactly the same way. Knowing the details will help me prepare.'

The old woman relaxed visibly, looking almost sheepish, and her husband nodded in approval.

Magiere returned to her pack by the door. Two villagers, who'd been carefully peering over its contents, quickly stepped back. She laid down her pole and from out of her pack pulled a large brass container, its shape somewhere between a bowl and an urn, with a fitted hard-leather lid. All over the lid and bowl were scratches and scribbles of unintelligible symbols.

'I need this to catch the vampire's spirit. Many undeads are spirit creatures.'

Everyone watched in rapt interest, and when she knew she had their complete attention, she changed the subject. It was time to talk about price.

'I know your village is suffering, Zupan, but the costs of my materials are high.'

Petre was ready and motioned her to a back room. 'My family went door-to-door last week for donations. We are not rich, but all have helped by giving something.'

He opened the door, and she glanced inside at goods piled upon a canvas quilt spread over the dirt floor. There were two full slabs of smoke-cured pork, four blocks of white cheese, about twenty eggs, three wolf pelts, and two small silver symbols – perhaps for some deity who had not answered their prayers. All in all, it was a very typical first offer.

'I'm sorry,' Magiere said. 'You don't understand. Food is welcome, but the quilt is of no use to me, and the rest won't cover my costs. I often work and gain no profit, but I can't work at a loss. Without enough coin, I at least need goods I can sell to cover what I spend to make ready for battle. Most of my materials are rare and costly to acquire and prepare.'

Petre turned white, genuinely shocked. He apparently had thought the offer quite generous. 'This is all we have. I sent my family out begging. You cannot let us die. Or are we now to bargain for our lives?'

'And what good would it do the next village if I left here unable to prepare for their defense?' she returned.

This exchange was customary for Magiere, though Zupan Petre appeared to be more intelligent than other village leaders she'd dealt with in the past. She kept her expression sympathetic but firm. Villagers almost always had some little treasure hidden away where tax collectors couldn't find it. It might be a family heirloom, possibly a small gem or some silver taken off a dead mercenary, but it was here.

'You've come all this way, and you'll do nothing?' The flesh beneath his eyes was turning gray.

Anna reached out and touched her husband's shirt. 'Give her the seed money, Petre.' Her voice was quiet, but quivered with fear.

'No,' he answered sharply.

Anna turned to the others, who so far had watched in silence. 'What good is seed if we are all dead before spring?'

Petre breathed in sharply. 'How long will we live with nothing to eat next year? How long will we live in the lord's dungeons when we cannot pay the tax?'

Magiere stayed out of this predictable bickering. They would go back and forth, for and against, until their fears began to win over. Then would follow the hope that if they could just overcome this terror, something would come later to see them through the next year. She knew these peasants too well. They were all the same.

A short flurry of arguments ensued, but Magiere busied herself inspecting the contents of her pack and ignored the discussion, as if the outcome was obvious. Those in favor of keeping the seed coins and taking a chance with the vampire were soon squelched. The argument faded so quickly it would have been startling, had Magiere not heard it so many times before.

At first no one spoke. Then a lanky, middle-aged man stepped from the corner of the room to face the zupan squarely. From the char smudges on his leather apron, he was likely what passed for a blacksmith in a village of this size.

'Give her the coins, Petre. We have no choice.'

Petre left the hovel and shortly returned, panting. He stared at Magiere with burning eyes, as if she were now the source of their suffering and not the one summoned to save them.

'Here is what's left after this year's taxes.' He threw the bag to her, and she caught it. 'Next year there may be no crop.'

'You are free to watch,' she replied, and several villagers cringed back into the room's shadows. 'I will control the undead. Stay in your homes and look through the shutters to see how well your seed coins are spent.'

The hatred in Petre's eyes faded to be replaced by defeat. 'Yes, we will watch you destroy the monster.'

The rain had subsided slightly. Magiere knelt in the center of the village path, illuminated by two torches, hafts stuck in the ground to either side of the path. She placed the brass urn firmly on the wet soil and twisted it a few times until satisfied it was securely settled and would not tip over. Beside it she set a small wooden mallet.

Anna and two village men were watching from narrow openings in the common cottage's shutters. A few other eyes peered from window shutters in hovels and huts around the village. But the zupan would not be satisfied with a voyeur's view. He stood within shouting distance, just outside the door where he'd surrendered the future of his village to a killer of the undead.

Magiere took a bottle from her pack and poured a fine white powder into one palm. She then sifted it back and forth between her hands. With a sudden flourish, she threw the handful high in the air and waited. The tiny particles didn't fall but hung in the air like a vaporous cloud, creating a wondrous glow all around her as the particles caught the torch light. Gasps from the peasants reached her ears.

From another bottle, she poured red power into her hand and threw that aloft as well, with a wilder flourish of her arm. It danced between the white particles, contrasting and moving like sand-grain fireflies.

Magiere stood in silence, eyes closed for a moment. She opened them again without looking at anything particular. Amid the hovering powders, her pale skin and dark hair made her seem a wraith of light, unliving, as if she were transformed to something kin to the night creatures she hunted. Each time a swirl of red power in the air drifted by her head, its sparkling reflection of the torchlight echoed in her tresses with streaks of crimson. She reached down and picked up the stake, holding the leather grip tightly.

'The red calls the beast, like blood,' she shouted. 'It can't resist.' She lowered herself to a crouch, braid falling forward over her left shoulder, and stared up the path where she knew the creature would come.

A pale flicker darted between the buildings.

Her finger pointed to a decrepit hovel ten paces down the path ahead of her. 'There! See, it comes!'

With the fingertips of her free hand, she flipped the lid off the brass urn and grabbed another bottle of red powder, flinging the contents into the air around her.

Without warning, something solid collided with her back, knocking her forward with enough force to daze her. Behind her, Anna screamed. Magiere spit out mud and spun on the ground out of the attacker's way. She scrambled back to a crouch, turning in all directions to see what had hit her. The path lay empty.

For long moments she turned from side to side, watching between the huts of the village for any sign of movement. The zupan had backed up against the common cottage door, eyes wide, but he remained outside, watching.

'What in—'

It hit again from the side, pitching her back down. Water soaked through her leggings and washed over her armor as she skidded across the mud, until her shoulder struck the haft of one torch stuck in the ground. The torch toppled and sizzled out.

Magiere was up again, searching. The shadows around her deepened with only one torch still burning.

She could hear window shutters slamming closed amid shouts and wails as the villagers panicked. A passing glimpse as she spun about showed that even Petre had now stepped inside the door, ready to slam it shut if need be. The zupan shouted, 'There, to your left!'

A blur appeared in the corner of her sight, and she ducked a swinging arm. She made a grab for it as it passed. 'No more games,' she hissed under her breath.

Her hand closed over woolen material, and she jerked back.

There came a sharp tear as her own force strained against that of her attacker, but the fabric held. Unable to keep her balance, her body twisted to the side as she and her opponent both spun about when she refused to let go of its garment. They hit the ground together, each scrambling in the mud for a foothold. She turned on one knee to face it and readied the stake. Its head lifted in the torchlight.

Thin and filthy, its flesh glowed as white as the first of her floating powders. Silver-blond hair swung in muddied tendrils around a narrow, dirt-splattered face with slanted amber eyes and slightly pointed ears. The cape she had managed to grasp hung in rotted tatters around its shoulders.

Magiere scuttled back two steps, still gripping the leather-handled stake, and tried to find better footing without taking her eyes off the white figure.

It charged again, moving fast. A claw hand slipped inside her guard and snatched the tail of her braid. They were both soaked in rain and mud, making all movements slick and desperate. She fell to the ground, on purpose this time, and rolled. When their tumble finished, Magiere came up on top and rammed downward with her stake, holding it as tightly as possible.

Blood sprayed upward from its chest as it thrashed on the ground, screaming in a keening wail. Magiere bit down on her own tongue by accident in an effort to hold the thing down, stake securely in its heart.

The creature thrashed wildly, clawing at the stake. Its torso arched, half lifting Magiere off the ground, and a guttural scream came up from deep in its throat. Then its body went slack and splashed back down in the mud.

Magiere held on until the creature was completely still, then quickly scrambled to the brass urn. Picking it up, she snatched the mallet and swung it hard against the container's side.

A piercing clang reverberated in the air. Magiere dashed around to the far side of the body, striking the container again and again. Standing in the cottage doorway, the zupan clapped his hands over his ears against the painful clamor. As the last clang faded, Magiere slapped the lid tightly over the brass jar, sealing it. She stood there, the village quiet except for her own panting.

Zupan Petre started to rush forward, perhaps to see the monster close up, or to offer some assistance, but she held out her hand to keep him back.

'No,' she gasped, weaving back and forth in exhaustion. 'Stay where you are. Even slain, they can be dangerous.'

'Hunter . . .' Petre searched for words, his expression a mix of emotions. 'Have you ever seen such a beast?'

Looking at the blood-soaked form on the muddy ground, Magiere shook her head. 'No, Zupan, I have not.'

As the zupan watched in stunned silence, Magiere pulled a rope and dusty canvas out of her pack. The canvas was mottled with dark stains long dried into the fabric. She wrapped the corpse in it, tying a rope loop around the ankles of the bundled body. Then she quickly gathered her equipment into the pack and slung it over one shoulder. The sealed brass jar was cradled under her arm.

'It is over then?' asked Petre.

'No.' Magiere took hold of the rope. 'Now I must properly dispose of the remains and send its spirit to final rest. In the morning, you will be free.'

'Do you need help?' Petre Evanko seemed hesitant to ask, but would not let his fear hold him back.

'I must be alone for this,' she answered bluntly, making her answer a command to be obeyed. 'The spirit will not go willingly. It will fight to live again – fight harder than what you've seen here – and should there be another body nearby to take for its own, all of my efforts will be wasted. No one enters the woods until morning, or I won't be responsible for what happens. If all goes well, we will not see each other again.'

Petre nodded his understanding. 'Our thanks, Hunter.'

Magiere said nothing more as she headed into the woods, dragging the corpse behind her.

Mud had seeped into every available opening in Magiere's armor and clothing. The grit against her skin, combined with the long walk hauling the body and her equipment deep into the woods, put her in an irritable mood. She stepped out of the trees into a small clearing and looked behind herself once more. It would be a shame to have to kill some foolish villager, but she saw no sign of anyone and could hear nothing but the natural speech of the trees in the wind. She dropped her burdens.

A low rumble of a growl came from the bushes at the clearing's far side, and Magiere stiffened. Leaves shivered, and a huge dog stepped out into the open. Though he was tall and wolfish in build and color, his grays were a little bluer and his whites a little brighter than any wolf's. Strange eyes of near silver-blue glittered back at Magiere. With a low grunt, the animal looked toward the bundle on the ground behind her.

'Oh, be quiet, Chap,' she muttered. 'After all this time you ought to know my sound.'

Magiere's spine arched suddenly as she felt two feet slam into her back. Her eyelids snapped wide open in cold surprise and she slid across the clearing's wet mulch floor, thumping up against the base of a maple. She scrambled to her feet. Across the clearing, thrashing its way out of the stained canvas, stood the white figure with the stake through its heart.

'Damn you, Magiere! That hurt.' He reached down to grip the butt of the stake. 'You didn't oil it properly, did you?'

Magiere rushed across the clearing and kicked his feet out from under him. The slender figure dropped on his back with a grunt, and she was on top of him, pinning his arms to the ground with her knees. Both her hands wrapped tightly around the butt of the stake.

Anger swelled up inside her like a fever. Strands of muddy, rain-soaked hair clung to her face as she glared down at the white figure beneath her. She jerked the stake up.

'You irritating half-wit!' she snapped. 'If you'd stuck to the plan and not sent me rolling around in the muck, maybe the sheath wouldn't have jammed with grit.'

Where there had once been a point on the stake, there was now nothing. The stake stopped at the bottom edge of the leather-wrapped butt. Magiere gave a quick glance into the hollow bottom of the stake, then banged it against an exposed tree root. There came a sharp *snap-knock* as the pointed end sprang out of the hollow and back into place.

'What were you doing back there?' She grabbed the front of his shirt. 'You know better than that, Leesil. We do it the same way every time. No changes, no mistakes. Just what is your problem?'

Leesil's head dropped back to the ground. He stared up into the canopy of trees with a melancholy sigh that was far too exaggerated for Magiere's taste.

'It's the same thing all the time,' he whined. 'I'm bored!'

'Oh, get up,' she snapped, and rolled off her companion. She tossed the stake down by her things and reached under a bush to pull out a second pack and a tin lantern. The lantern was still lit – by Leesil before he came into the village for their performance. She opened the shutter, turned the knob to extend the wick, and the light increased a small portion.

Leesil sat up and began opening the front of his ragged shirt. Below the neckline, the true color of his skin showed – not corpse white but a warm tan. He itched at the white powder on his throat. Across his chest was strapped a burst leather bag still dripping with dark red dye. It was caked with a mound of wax that had held the collapsed stake in place on his chest, giving the appearance that he'd been impaled. He winced as he untied the twine holding the assemblage in place.

'You're supposed to attack from the front, where I can see you.' Magiere's voice rose slightly as she rolled up the stained canvas and rope she'd used to drag Leesil out of the village. 'And where did you learn to skulk like that? I couldn't see you at all at first.'

'Look at this,' Leesil answered in astonished disgust, wiping the dye off himself with one hand. 'I've got a big, red welt in the middle of my chest.'

Chap, the large hound, strolled over to sit by Leesil. Sniffing at the white powder on his face, the dog let out a disgruntled whine.

'Serves you right,' Magiere answered. She stuffed canvas, rope, and brass urn into her pack, then lifted the bundle over her shoulder. 'Now pick up the lantern and let's leave. I want to make the bend in the river before we camp. We're still too close to the village to stop for the night.'

Chap barked and began fidgeting on all fours. Leesil patted him briefly.

'And keep him quiet,' Magiere added, looking at the dog.

Leesil picked up his pack and the lantern and started off after Magiere, with Chap ranging along beside, weaving his own way amongst the undergrowth.

It seemed to take them little time to cover the distance, and Magiere was relieved when they approached the bend of the Vudrask River. They were now far enough from the village to safely settle for the night and build a fire. She turned inward, away from the open bank of the river, and picked a clearing in the forest that was still well hidden by brush, out of plain view. Leesil immediately headed back to the river's edge to wash up, with Chap following along, and Magiere remained to build a small fire. When Leesil returned, he looked more himself, though not exactly normal by most standards. His appearance was something Magiere had grown accustomed to, even before he'd told her of his mother's heritage.

His skin was indeed a medium tan, rather than the white of the powder, and made Magiere feel pale by comparison. But his hair was another matter – so blond as to seem pure white in the dark. There was little need to powder it for a village performance. Long tresses with a yellow-white sheen hung to his shoulders. And then there was the slight oblong shape of his ears, not quite pointed at the top, and the narrow suggestion of a slant to his amber-brown eyes beneath high, thin eyebrows the color of his hair.

Magiere had noted several times how much the lithe man was like a negative reflection of her own appearance. Most of the time, Leesil kept his hair tied up out of sight in a scarf wrap that also hid the tops of his ears. His mother's people were so rare in this part of the land that he and Magiere felt his mixed heritage might create undue attention – which would not be good considering his role in their profession.

Once settled around a comfortable fire and half-wrapped in a blanket, Leesil reached into his pack and pulled out a wineskin.

Magiere glanced at him. 'I thought you were out.'

He smiled. 'I picked up a few necessities in that town we passed through a day back.'

'I hope you used your own money.'

'Of course.' Leesil paused. 'Speaking of money, how did we do back there?'

Magiere opened the small bag and began counting out coins. She passed over two-fifths of the take to Leesil, keeping the lord's share for herself. Leesil never argued, since Magiere was the one who had to deal directly with all the villages. He tucked his coins into a pouch on his belt, then tipped his head back for a long guzzle, squeezing the wine sack as he swallowed.

'Don't get drunk,' Magiere warned. 'It's not long until dawn, and I don't want you sleeping until noon when we should be moving.'

Leesil scowled back at her, then belched. 'Calm down. This is the best of it, money in our pockets and time to relax.' He scooted back from the fire to lean against the remains of a toppled tree stump and closed his eyes.

The fire crackled and popped. Chap lay down close to Leesil. Magiere settled back, allowing some of the tension in her shoulders to ebb away. In moments like this, she couldn't remember how many nights had passed since the first such evening. If she actually took the time to count it out, they couldn't have been at the game for more than a few years. She rubbed an aching muscle in the back of her neck. This was a better life than the one she'd been born to – which would have consisted of a quick old age from being worked to death on the farm. Still, Leesil's unexpected change of strategy and his 'playfulness' tonight seemed like an omen, leaving her fearful about her carefully planned future. A future she had not yet mentioned to him. It dawned on her that she was being as foolishly superstitious as the peasants she scorned, but the uneasiness would not fade. Perhaps it was just the way she had been raised.

Born in the nearby country of Droevinka, Magiere never knew her father, but throughout her childhood she learned bits and pieces about him. As a transient noble vassal, he ruled the peasants for the lords and collected rents due on land plots, staying in one place for months or sometimes years, but eventually always moving onward to wherever his higher lord sent him. Few had seen him except on early night collections, after daylight faded, and everyone could be found in their hovels and cottages, retired from labor. Her mother was just a young woman from a village near the barony house. The nobleman took her for his mistress, and she remained mostly out of sight for nearly a year.

Rumors of her mother's fate were whispered about

the village, but the little-known truth was all too
mundane. Some told tales of glimpsing her on the manor
grounds in the evening, pale and listless. It was during
the later half of her stay at the barony house that some
noticed she was with child. She died giving birth to a
girl child, and the nobleman was ordered onward to a
new fief. Not wishing to be burdened with an illegiti-
mate daughter, he gave the infant to her mother's sister
and disappeared. It was this aunt who had named her
Magiere, after her mother, Magelia. None of the villagers even knew Magiere's father's name. The chasm
between classes was wide. He had power. They did not.
That was all anyone needed to know.

Aunt Bieja tried to be kind and treat her as family,
but the other villagers were not so inclined. The fact
that her father was noble and had simply taken one of
the village's few pretty young women – simply because
he could – was cause enough for people to want
someone, anyone, to punish. He was gone, and Magiere
remained. And yet there was more to it than simple
resentment.

Whispers, fearful stares, and rude calls were frequent
whenever she walked past the other villagers. They
would not let their children have anything to do with
her. The only one who had tried – Geshan, a goatherder's
son – ended up with a severe beating and warnings to
stay away from the 'dark-begotten' child. Something
about her father had frightened them, something more
than just his position of dealing legal life and death. At
first, she wanted to know everything, to know what had
been so frightening about him and why they all shunned
her so.

Aunt Bieja once said with sympathy, 'They fear your father was something unnatural,' but that was as far as she'd go.

Finally, Magiere grew less curious about her parents, and she began to hate the villagers for their superstitions and their ignorance. With the passing of years, little enlightenment came and hostilities toward her increased. In the end, she cared nothing for her past and grew hard toward those around her.

When she turned sixteen, Aunt Bieja took her aside, pulled a locked wooden box from under the bed, and presented it to her. Inside the box was a bundle, wrapped in oilcloth against the wet climate, which held a falchion, two strange amulets, and studded leather armor suitable for a young man. One of the amulets was a topaz stone set in pewter. It was simply hung on a leather string. The other amulet was a small half-oval with tin backing that held what seemed to be a chip of bone with unrecognizable writing carved carefully into it. Unlike the other, this one was strung on a chain that passed through the squared side of the amulet, so that its oval half hung down with the bone side always outward.

'I suppose he expected a son,' Aunt Bieja said, referring to Magiere's mysterious father. 'But you might be able to sell them for something.'

Magiere lifted the falchion. It was exceptionally light for its look, and the blade gleamed even in the low candlelight of the room. A small glyph like a letter – but from no language she knew – had been carved into the base of the hilt. The shining metal suggested that Aunt Bieja had kept it polished over the years, but there was a thick coating of dust over the box it had been stored in, which indicated the contents had not been disturbed in a long time. The blade might bring a good price at market, but Magiere's thoughts began to run a different course from that night onward. It was a late spring night when she slipped out of the village, never once looking back.

There had to be something better in the world . . . something better than stepping outside each day to see faces filled with hatred, or people who pretended they didn't see her. She cared neither for her unknown past, nor any kind of future with such a wretched lot. Loneliness would be bearable if she were actually alone.

The following years had been hard, moving from town to town, working at anything to stay alive, and learning the things she wanted to know – how to fight, where to hunt for food, and how to turn coin from the foolish and unwary. There was little work for a young woman on the move, and she nearly starved to death twice. But she would not go home. She would never go back home.

Her hatred of superstition never faded. She became even more aware of how superstitious the people of the land were and how common from place to place. It was easy in the end to choose the specific things to exploit. Most of all, people feared the dark and death, and more so anything connected to both. The idea for 'the game' didn't just come to her suddenly. It developed in stages as she began to realize she might make a living by playing on fear, the same kind of fear which had once ostracized her.

At first, she worked alone, convincing peasants that vampires were often spirit creatures that could be trapped and destroyed. The elaborate display of floating powders, fake charms and incantations made ignorant villagers actually believe she could trap undeads in the brass urn. She even worked out the trick of the dye in the wine-skin, so that she could terrify her customers with sudden bleeding wounds as she wrestled with invisible attackers. In the areas she traveled, she would set up a place in one town for messages, usually a well-patronized tavern rife with gossip, where her exploits would be passed quickly on a wave of whispers. Outside just such a place was where she'd met Leesil for the first time. He was very good at what he did. So good, she really shouldn't have caught him.

Walking away from a tavern in the evening, she felt a sudden trembling itch at the small of her back run up her spine and into her head. The whole night around her appeared to come alive as her senses heightened, and she *heard* rather than felt the hand digging in the cloth sack over her shoulder. When she turned and snatched the wrist, ready to deal with this thief, there was complete surprise on his face – a strange, tan face with glittering amber eyes beneath high, thin blond eyebrows.

Magiere couldn't remember exactly what they said to ease out of that tense moment. Perhaps it had been a mutual recognition of their special talents. Leesil's unusual appearance mingled with the schemes in her thoughts. She'd never actually seen an elf before, as they were not known to travel and lived far to the north. The combination of his human and elven blood created an exotic look in face and form. They spent a wine-soaked evening of conversation, during which he took off his head scarf and allowed her to see his ears. The next morning, they left town together, along with a strange wolfish dog Leesil had with him. That was four years ago.

The fire cracked again. Chap lifted his head and whined, staring into the darkness.

'Stop it,' Leesil slurred, halfway through his flask by this point. 'There's nothing out there.' He scratched the back of the dog's neck, and Chap turned to lick at his face until he had to push the animal's muzzle away.

Magiere leaned over and looked out into the forest. Chap didn't usually fuss about nothing, but still, he was a dog. More than likely he'd just heard a squirrel or a hare.

'I don't see anything,' she said, and turned back to the fire. In the red light, she remembered the dimly lit common cottage and the two unexplainable oozing holes in the neck of Zupan Petre's son. Her head began to ache. She dreaded the discussion she'd planned to have with Leesil. For a month, she'd been putting it off, always waiting for a better time. But this last job made her wonder how much longer she could stall. She was getting tired of it all, and Leesil was getting careless. Things were becoming a little too unpredictable.

'Before you drink too much, we need to talk,' she said quietly.

'I never drink too much, always just enough.' He squirted another mouthful from the wineskin. He was about to take another gulp, when the tone of her voice made him stop halfway. He lowered the wineskin. 'What about?'

She reached inside her pack and took out a folded

parchment, slightly crumpled. 'There's a bank in Belaski where I put money when we pass through, and where I have messages sent to wait for my next visit.'

Leesil's expression went blank. 'Messages? What are you talking about?'

She held out the folded parchment to him. 'This is from a land merchant.'

Leesil took the parchment, slack jawed with surprise. 'You've been hoarding money away?'

'He's been looking for a certain kind of tavern for me, somewhere along the coast . . . seems he's found one.' She paused. 'I'm buying a tavern in a Belaskian town called Miiska.'

Leesil blinked as if he didn't understand a word. 'What?'

'I didn't want to tell you until the right place was found. I never planned to run the hunter game forever, and I'm tired.'

'You saved money?' Leesil shook his head. 'I don't believe it. All I've got is what's in my pouch.'

Magiere rolled her eyes. 'That's because you drink it all, or waste it at a card table.'

Then she heard him suck in his breath and the words began to flow.

'Just like that?' he nearly shouted, ignoring her answer. 'No warning. Not even a "By the way, Leesil, I've been saving for a tavern." And you never mention it. How much have you been putting . . . no, never mind. We're in this together. I say we do four or five more villages and then talk about quitting.'

'I'm done,' she answered softly. 'I want something of my own.'

'What about me?'

'You'll like the town,' she rushed in. 'We just head for the coast and turn south. It's ten leagues down the coast from the capital city of Bela. I'll handle the drinks. You can run the gaming. I've heard you talk about running a faro table . . . every time you lose your last coin at one.'

Leesil waved her off with his hand and a disgruntled scowl.

'Chap can watch over things,' she continued, the dog lifting his head at his name. 'We'll sleep inside every night and stop taking all these risks.'

'No! I'm not ready to quit.'

'You'll be the card master . . .'

'It's too soon.'

'. . . a warm bed, plenty of ale and mead . . .'

'I don't want to hear any more.'

'. . . and mulled wine from our own hearth.'

Leesil became quiet. She could see him working his thoughts, examining the possibilities. He wasn't stupid, quite the opposite. Finally, he let out an exasperated grunt, or perhaps it was a burp.

'Can we talk about this in the morning?' he asked. Still sulking, he took another long drink.

'Yes, if you like.'

And with that, Leesil rolled his back to the fire. Magiere leaned over, snatched up the parchment he'd never even bothered to look at, and tucked it away again inside her vestment. As she settled down, Leesil suddenly sat up and looked about as if lost, startling Chap to his feet.

'How could you have saved that much money?' he blurted out in confused exasperation.

'Oh, shut up and go to sleep,' Magiere snapped.

Leesil rolled over again, grumbling under his breath.

Sleep wouldn't come quickly enough, and Magiere felt restless and anxious. Leesil wasn't going to easily give in to this sudden change of plans. That much she'd expected, but he was at least thinking about it now. It wouldn't be too hard, she hoped, to push him the rest of the way, though it might take a little while. Waiting until he had coin in his pocket was the best time. With an empty purse, he would have been more resistant, wanting to wait for another ill-gotten windfall.

Magiere watched the small fingers of fire dancing before her. She noticed Chap had not curled up next to Leesil as he usually did, but sat a little ways apart, looking off into the trees. Finally fed up with watching him watch nothing, she closed her eyes. She didn't see him shift his place, taking position to the side of the fire, equally near both Leesil and herself.

Out in the thickness of the forest, something moved. From tree trunk, to bush, to snag-fall, to tree trunk, it darted closer to the wisp of firelight. It settled behind an aging oak with scales of fungus sprouting from its sides and peered into the clearing where two forms slept quietly. Between them was a dog, its body somehow shimmering too brightly in the watcher's vision for a normal hound. But the hidden watcher gave the animal no more notice when it focused its eyes of pinprick lights close upon the woman lying beneath a wool blanket.

Her pale skin now glistened in the firelight, and highlights of blood red ran in her dark hair.

'Hunter,' it whispered to itself and choked back laughter with a swallow as fingers tickled their claws down the bark of the oak.

2

Chap lay with his long head down, nose just shy of his paw tips. His half-open eyes rarely blinked as he stared relentlessly into the darkness around the camp. Above the whisper of leaves and grass in the breeze came Magiere's light breathing and Leesil's soft, drunken snore.

The fire burned low in the late night, a pocket of molten-colored embers sprouting the occasional flicker of flame. The camp was well flanked by large trees in a black forest wall. Not far away, sounds of the Vudrask River, swollen with spring rains, gurgled as water splashed against rocks in its steady, ceaseless flow. Magiere rolled over on her blanket with a low murmur. Wisps of her hair loosened from its braid and caught in smudges of leftover dried mud on her face. Chap glanced at her once and then resumed his vigil.

Movement flashed between two trees a half dozen leaps outside of the camp.

Chap raised his head and growled for the first time since his companions had settled down to sleep. Silver-blue and gray hairs rose on his neck, and his jowls wrinkled until teeth showed between his lips. The rumbling growl swelled into a snarl. Magiere struggled in her sleep, but didn't awaken.

Another quick blur passed in the darkness.

Haunches, shoulders, and leg muscles tensed. Chap

dropped his head down again, growing silent, and inched forward along the ground.

A white face with eyes like glistening stone appeared above a bush two leaps out. It stared at Magiere.

Chap launched forward with a high-pitched snarl. In the time it takes to lick a muzzle clean with the tongue, the forest wall covered him from sight.

Magiere woke in a panic and thrashed off her blanket in time to see Chap's rapidly moving body disappear into the forest. She jerked her falchion from its sheath in confusion, still heavy with sleep as she wondered what noise had broken through her exhaustion.

'Leesil, wake up,' she said quickly. 'Chap is gone . . . after something.'

The dog rarely barked unless threatened. He never attacked unless ordered to do so by Leesil, and in the years Magiere had known him, the hound had never abandoned camp.

An eerie, hate-filled cry floated through the forest from somewhere near the river. It was nothing she could imagine coming from a dog's throat.

'Leesil . . . did you hear me?' She got to her feet. 'Something is out there.' Her amulets brushed against her companion's shoulder as she leaned over him and snapped, 'Get up!'

He murmured something and rolled away from her. The wineskin lay empty beside him.

'You drunken sot,' she said in frustration.

Another raging cry echoed low through the trees, and this time she knew it was Chap. She hesitated for a moment as she considered whether or not she should leave Leesil alone. Then she charged into the forest toward the sound.

Something had spooked the dog so badly that he'd attacked without orders or even bothering to wake the camp. Visions of Stravinan wolf packs tearing him apart pushed Magiere to move faster. She smashed through low-hanging branches and underbrush, the sound of the river growing stronger ahead.

He wasn't even her dog, but he'd thrown his own body between hers and danger enough times that the thought of him being hurt bothered her more than she expected. The strange wailing snarl she'd heard earlier mingled with Chap's usual growling bark, but the closer she got to the river, the more the gurgling rush of water made it difficult to get a bearing on the dog's location.

Magiere called out as she ran, 'Chap, where are you?'

She had no torch, but the nearly full moon gave just enough light to distinguish some passage through the forest. Twice she tripped, catching herself with her free hand while gripping the falchion tightly with the other. The earlier bungled fight with Leesil had left her muscles sore. She cursed the overzealous hound, from both frustration and concern. Through the trees she caught the glitter of moonlight on rippling water.

'Chap!' she called again, rushing forward.

A flicker of white passed through the left corner of her vision and she stopped. From the same direction came the sound of Chap's chopped barks. Magiere ran toward the sound, only to have it move off to the right, again toward the river. The forest broke into a small clearing upon the river's shore. What she saw caused her legs to freeze. Even from behind Chap, she could see the dark stains around his neck and shoulders. She moved wide to his left, not wanting to startle him.

His muzzle was smeared and dripping, and though it was too dark to tell the color, she knew it was blood. Whatever fur on his body wasn't matted and wet stood straight out, making him look even larger than usual. The lips of his muzzle were pulled back, showing teeth in a shuddering snarl. Magiere's head turned slightly toward the dog's quarry, trapped against the river's edge.

Man-shaped, it crouched in the mud and gravel, hands placed flat on the ground as if it could move on all fours if it so wished. Shreds of a shirt hung from its torso where Chap had torn at it. Trickles of blood ran from wounds down the arms and chest of this moon-colored man. The dark hair hanging to his shoulders appeared out of place, as if he'd been carved from pale wood with blackened corn silk placed on his head as an afterthought. The stringy hair shadowed his face, but his eyes shone as if reflecting a nonexistent light. He lifted one ema-ciated hand to stare at the gashes of teeth marks ringing his wrist. Small gnarled nails, like misbegotten claws, extended from each fingertip.

'Not possible . . . just dog . . . but its touch burns.' The man's voice was filled with surprise. 'Filthy mongrel . . .' he hissed in anger, 'could not hurt Parko, not like this.'

Glowing eyes turned away from his wounds as he became aware of Magiere's presence. The man's head began to tilt to one side, then farther and farther still, until it nearly rested upon his shoulder like an owl as he stared at Magiere. Hair fell away from his long face, and she tightened her grip on the falchion.

Sunken cheeks and eye sockets made dark pockets in

skin as white as a cave grub's. Some illness had wasted him away to thin muscle and bone.

'Hunter?' he said with a sharp intake of breath, voice sweet and tonal. His head tilted farther sideways, then crow-chatter laughter erupted from his throat. 'Hunter!'

Magiere felt cold and fearful at that word. The man knew of her, or at least knew why she'd come to this place, yet she had never seen him before.

He dodged left, springing from all fours.

'Chap, stay back,' Magiere ordered, but not quickly enough.

Chap mirrored the man's movement, but before he landed, the white figure reversed direction in a forward leap to the right. Chap's front legs gave in the loose gravel as he tried to twist back. He toppled, skidding in a clatter on the river's rocky beach. Magiere saw the man's movement, right then left, then her eyes flicked toward Chap as the dog fell. She blinked.

The man was in the air coming down upon her.

Magiere ducked and rolled forward along the ground, passing under the airborne arc of the man. There was no time to ponder how he moved so fast or leaped so far. She spun and came up with her back to the river in time to see her assailant twist in the air, already facing her again. His feet barely touched the ground before he lunged at her.

Magiere swung the falchion in a fast, short slash between herself and her attacker. It was a feeble attack, but she hadn't intended it to strike home. All she wanted was to scare him off. It would do no good to kill a local villager now, after she'd successfully worked her way out of Leesil's little impromptu performance.

The white man ducked and hopped to the side, avoiding the blade. She took advantage and shifted the opposite way to get her back away from the river. The man's disturbing laugh echoed off the surrounding trees.

'Poor hunter,' he moaned playfully, raising fingers with stained nails and straightening from his crouch.

Magiere took a step back. 'I just want the dog. I don't want to hurt you.'

He laughed again, eyes half closed until their glow resembled sparkling slashes in his face.

'Of course, you don't,' the man said, his voice as hollow as his cheeks.

Then he sprang.

It was the same dream, but this time wine-soaked slumber couldn't wash it away.

Leesil, only twelve years old, squatted on the floor of the dark room beneath his parents' home, listening to his father's lesson.

'Here—' his father pointed to the base of the human skull in his hand – 'is where thin straight blades can be applied while the individual is distracted. This will cause instant and silent death in most large-skulled humanoids.'

Father rolled the skull over to expose the opening where the spine would have been attached.

'It is a most difficult stroke. If you fail to execute it correctly' – he scowled briefly at Leesil – 'a hard side stroke on withdrawal may save you before the target can make any sound. Always use the stiletto or similar thin strong blades for this – never a dagger or knife. Wide blades will jam in the base of the skull, or be deflected by the top vertebrae.'

The man stared at his son. A thick, peppered beard hid the lower half of his thin angular face. He held out the skull. Young Leesil looked at it, but mostly noticed how slender and almost delicate his father's hands were, so graceful in everything they did, no matter how vicious.

'Do you understand?' his father asked.

Leesil looked up, the stiletto in his own hand a little too large for a boy. In waking hours, he remembered nodding silently in answer to his father's question, but the dream was always different than memory. He was about to take the bone skull, but hesitated.

'No, Father,' young Leesil answered, 'I don't understand.'

Out of the shadows rose a second figure, seeming to sprout from the dark ground in the corner of the room. She was tall, slightly more so than his father, and delicately slender, with skin the honey-brown of Leesil's own, though smooth and more perfect than any person's he had ever seen. Long hair and narrow, feathery eyebrows glistened pale gold like threads of a sunlit spiderweb. The points of her ears rarely showed from beneath those polished tresses. Her large amber-brown eyes slanted up at the sides, matching the angle of her brows.

'The proper answer is yes, Leesil,' she said in her sweet voice, a loving mother's admonishment for misbehavior.

Her eyes looked calmly down at him and made him ache inside for want of pleasing her, even when it made him sick inside to do what she asked.

'Yes, Mother . . . yes, Father,' he whispered. 'I understand.'

Leesil rolled over in his sleep and moaned, pulled

suddenly awake, but uncertain what had interrupted his slumber. For a moment, he was grateful for whatever had roused him. His head hurt from exhaustion and too much wine. He'd drunk too little to block out the dream on this night, yet barely enough to achieve slumber. With his vision blurred, it took several moments for him to realize the camp around him lay empty.

'Magiere?' he called. 'Chap?'

There was no answer. Fear began to clear the alcohol daze from his thoughts.

From a distance came a wailing he couldn't call human or animal. Leesil pulled himself to his feet, shoved two stilettos up his sleeves into wrist sheaths, and staggered through the forest toward the sound.

Magiere shifted away again, holding her assailant at bay with short swipes of her blade, which wouldn't break her guard. Her breath was coming harder now from exhaustion, but all her feints and maneuvers hadn't discouraged her opponent. He ducked and dodged each swing, grinning one moment, or letting out a short, cackling laugh as he hopped and danced. Her foot brushed something low to the ground, a bush or a downed branch, and she realized he'd maneuvered her back toward the trees.

Panic rose in her throat. She'd barely managed to keep him at bay, not taking her eyes from him for fear he'd make another leap that she couldn't stop. If she had to concentrate on not losing her footing in the forest, she'd either stumble and fall or, worse, get distracted and lose her guard.

'Hunter, hunter,' the white man sang as he leaped to

her right, landing in a crouch, all fours poised together. 'Come catch your prey!'

Panic became tinged with anger.

Playing his game was a losing battle, and she began to suspect that this fever-maddened villager somehow knew more of her occupation than he should. Still, she preferred to avoid killing him if at all possible. A madman babbling about a charlatan hunter of the dead would be a questionable accuser. A dead body cut down with a sword on the night she'd passed by would raise many questions, perhaps enough for the villagers to insist that the local lord hunt her down. Magiere settled herself, waiting for him to move again and looking for an opening to bludgeon him unconscious with the flat of her blade.

A whining growl came from the riverside, and she remembered Chap tumbling hard to the ground. Reflexively, both Magiere and the man glanced to the side, then back quickly enough to see the other's mistake. He lunged, hooked fingers aimed for her throat. Magiere had no time to think and acted on instinct. She brought the falchion down in a sharp slash.

The claw-hand missed its mark, slamming into her chest. The sword blade smacked against his collarbone. Fingernails scraped across leather armor. Sharp steel slit away tattered cloth and bit into white flesh.

Magiere felt the ground jerked from under her feet as she was knocked backward. Her head and back slammed against a tree trunk, and she tumbled dizzily to the side, landing hard on the ground. Her heart pounded one beat as she waited for the weight of her opponent to land upon her, but it didn't come. Magiere looked up, trying to will her vision to clear.

The white man stood over her. His wide eyes stared down at the shallow wound running across his chest as if the thought of the blade harming him had never entered his thoughts until that moment. Sickly humor vanished as his face twisted into a mask of anger.

'Not possible . . .' he murmured.

There was no more hope for not killing the man. Magiere tightened her grip and tried to lift the falchion to protect herself. Before she could finish, the man jerked from his stupor and fell upon her. One bony hand grabbed her throat, pinning her neck to the ground. She tried to swing the falchion at his head, but he caught her wrist and smashed it down as well.

'You cannot do this to me,' he snarled at her. 'Not possible!'

Magiere's vision blurred again as his hand squeezed tighter around her throat.

'You cannot hurt Parko.' It was a denial more than anything else.

She could feel the dizziness growing from lack of air. With the spinning of the forest came the sensation of cold seeping into her flesh. The fingers around her throat seemed to squeeze the heat from her body.

Magiere struck out with her free hand, at the oval haze of the man's head. Her fist stopped on impact, and the blow sent a jarring shock through her arm that made her shoulder ache. His head barely moved. She wrapped her hand across the blurred face and pushed as hard as she could.

His flesh felt as unyielding as the bone across which it was stretched, and a cold sensation seeped into her again through her hand.

Terror rose in Magiere as the white face faded completely from view and she knew she was not far from unconsciousness. The cold burrowed deeper until she felt it in her chest, until even her fear wavered and was smothered in the sensation. The chill seeped in from her throat as well, and the wrist of her pinned sword arm.

A twinge inside her answered the growing cold.

It didn't come from the life fading from her body, but instead wormed out of some hidden place inside her, moving through her restlessly. It stirred a rising fever that slipped from bone to muscle to nerve, leaving tingling heat behind wherever it passed. Finally settling in her stomach, heat turned into a knot of growing ache even the cold couldn't blot out, then spread up her throat. A hollow opened inside of her, waiting to be filled.

It made her . . . hungry.

Magiere felt starved. A desire built on mounting rage sought a way to end the hunger. Crushing the life from her attacker would end that hunger.

She pushed against the man's head. This time, it gave just a little.

Hunger spread out from her stomach, worming its way through her limbs until it seared away fatigue and fear, consuming the chill from the man's touch. She tried to lift her weapon arm and felt her wrist slowly leave the ground against the pressure of the white man's grip. In her darkness, she heard a frenzied hiss escape her assailant's lips as he released her throat to pull at her grip on his face. Magiere gasped in air, filling her lungs.

'No . . . no . . . no!' he screeched. 'You are no match for Parko.'

Straining against his grip, she could neither swing the blade, nor force her other hand back to his head. His body began to jerk forward, accompanied by a strange snapping sound. As her vision began to return, she made out the blurred oval of his head surging toward her face – *click* – then back and in again – *crack* – straining against her own pushing force. The sound was an animal's jaws snapping closed.

She realized what he was doing. With their grips meshed, he was desperately trying the only thing left to break the deadlock. He was trying to bite her.

Magiere arched her back, pushing her face up and away out of reach, then shoved hard with both arms. A vicious snarl came from her left, and her body was suddenly dragged along the ground for half a foot. The white man let out a wail of anger as his grip on her wrists faltered, and Magiere lost her concentration in trying to understand what had just happened.

She caught sight of Chap flying in from her left, striking the man and rebounding away. The man's body jerked hard to the right, and again Magiere felt herself dragged across the ground with him. The snarling blur came again, and Chap struck the white man in the side. Both dog and man tumbled off Magiere and across the ground into the darker night shadows of the trees, their snarls and growls indistinguishable one from the other.

Magiere hurried to get off the ground and between the two of them, worried that Chap was no match for this opponent. She stumbled, catching herself against the limbless trunk of a tree. The strange hunger gnawing in her belly was still there, but had grown weaker. Light-headed and dizzy, she found her footing unsteady as she stepped toward the scuffle, trying to distinguish man from dog.

The white man spun toward her, but he was still out of her reach. Chap lunged at the man's leg, and the man swung his hand back at the animal. The dog was too quick, and a squeal of pain stabbed Magiere's ears as Chap bit down on the man's wrist.

In that moment, sound and feeling and sight flickered from Magiere's mind. Dog and man seemed far away, too great a distance for her to reach. Her throat still felt half constricted and her breath came hard.

The squeal of pain had barely ended when she gripped the falchion with both hands and slashed out sideways, throwing her whole body behind the blow. She aimed high but blindly, unsure of her target but knowing the man would likely rise up to pull his arm out of Chap's jaws. The swing overbalanced her and forest shadows blurred together, spinning.

Magiere's head thumped off the soft mulch of the forest floor when she fell. All the hunger washed out of her in a sudden flood. Trying in panic to find which way was up, she rolled before the man could descend again to finish her. But he didn't come.

She gave up and lay still, unable yet to sit up, let alone stand. As the spinning night settled into a heavy pain inside her skull, she heard the sounds around her. There was the gurgle of the river moving across its rocky bed, and the light chatter of tree branches in the breeze. She heard the rasp of her own desperate breathing, and the crackle of fallen pine needles and leaves beneath her as she shifted her body, trying again to get up.

And that was all. All the tiny sounds, the night sounds, slipped from her attention and between them was only silence. When the shadows above her started to focus again, changing from muted blurs into branches and stars in the sky just above the treetops, she rolled heavily to her side.

Two glistening eyes stared at her.

Breath caught in her throat until she made out the shape of the stained muzzle and canine ears. Chap looked at her expectantly.

On the ground at his feet lay a tumbled form of white flesh and tattered clothes. Chap looked down at it, and his jowls wrinkled with a low growl that ended in a whine of discomfort. He hung his head, panting.

Magiere crawled across the ground on all fours. Her body felt as though she had run a league without pause. As she drew near the man's body, she lifted the falchion, barely keeping it up in the air, ready to strike. There was no movement from the man.

'Chap, get back,' she said, her voice cracked and dry.

She reached out to poke the man with her blade, but still there was no movement. When she crept closer, it became obvious why he hadn't moved.

Where his head should have been was only the stump of his neck. She slumped back, her sword dropping heavily to the ground.

So many villages had come and gone that she couldn't remember them all. But each time there had always seemed to be a rational reason for the villagers' deaths. This village was no different. The man's cold skin and white complexion were obvious signs of illness, and it would not be the first time that was the real reason why mothers and fathers, spouses and siblings gathered by their dead to pray for lost spirits. Illness often brought madness, as it had done in this man. And she had killed him.

The burning hunger was gone. The madman's cold in her flesh was gone. Remembering those alien sensations made her skin quiver and stomach lurch, but there was no time to puzzle over it. She'd killed one of the villagers, and that was as bad as things could get. She slumped, head dropping in exhausted despair, when a small, pale light caught her attention.

To her bewilderment, she looked down and saw her topaz amulet. She thought she'd remembered tucking it away, but there it dangled loose on top of her studded leather vestment. It glowed so softly, it might have gone unnoticed had she not been looking directly at it. She watched until it faded and then wondered if the odd light were merely an illusion – another result of fatigue and lack of air.

She looked at the dog sitting nearby, watching her expectantly. She had to push the words past her constricted throat.

'Come here, Chap.'

Chap trotted across the short distance and sat in front of her. It was an effort to lift her hands to inspect him. The dog didn't seem to have any serious injuries, just a few small gashes on his shoulders and sides. The blood matting his throat came from a shallow cut of no serious concern. Relief washed through her. He'd be stiff and sore tomorrow, but she'd expected worse after such a fight.

Rubbing at her neck, it felt as if the bruises were

already developing. Chap made a sudden lunge at her, and his tongue shot out to slap wetly across her chin and cheek.

'Stop it,' she snapped. 'You can save that for your drunken master.'

Chap darted away and paced back and forth near the fallen body. He let out a short, low bark, then darted through the trees toward the river.

Magiere couldn't understand what had set him off again, but looking toward the water did bring her back to the immediate problem. The skyline was growing light. Dawn was approaching. Something had to be done with the body.

There was no time to bury it, and even a hidden grave might be stumbled across before she could get far enough out of the area. She had no idea how far the villagers normally ranged from their homes and fields, foraging for firewood or whatever else the forest yielded. Without a way to carry the body off, the river was her only choice. Magiere began dragging the corpse by the feet down to the shore.

The shirt was too tattered to work with, so she quickly rolled wild grass into rough twine. She used this to tie the pants legs closed and then loaded them with rocks. All the while, she avoided looking too closely at the body. Touching its flesh made her sick inside. It was chill, as if it had been dead longer than the short time that had passed. When finished, she turned to go back to the forest and hunt for the head. A rush of nausea swelled up in her throat at the sight before her.

There was Chap, the dead villager's head swinging from his mouth, its hair gripped in his teeth. He came up to her, dropped his burden at her feet, and sat staring at her, waiting expectantly.

She couldn't decide what revolted her more, the sight of the severed head, eyes open in the last moment of shock, or the dog's calm disposition at handling the grisly object. Nausea faded to another chill through her blood as she remembered how Chap paced by the body and then ran for the river shore. She stared into the dog's silver-blue eyes.

He'd known what to do even before she'd thought of it. But he was only a dog.

Magiere leaned down to take the head, her gaze not leaving Chap until she knelt by the body. There was no time to ponder this uncanny development. With no other method available, she used the long hair to tie the head onto the corpse, knotting it several times around the pants' belt. She dragged the body into the river, wading out thigh deep in the cold current, and pushed it under and out as far as she could.

It bobbed for a moment, floating down current. Then it finally sank beneath the surface. A metallic clatter from behind made her twist about in the water.

On the shore sat Chap. His ears pricked up as he looked at her. This time at his feet lay the falchion she'd left behind in the trees.

'Stop it!' she snapped at him in frustration, sloshing out of the river. She grabbed up the weapon. Bending over made her head spin with dizziness again. She paused to steady herself. 'Stop doing these things.'

Chap let out a whining grunt, and cocked his head as he watched her.

There was still a dark stain on the blade. With a glare

at the dog, she went to the forest's edge and wiped the blade off in the grass. As she finished, someone came out of the forest clearing and stumbled across the river's rocky shore. Leesil.

He looked back and forth. Spotting Magiere, he rushed down the shoreline, tripping twice, but never quite falling on his face. Chap ran up to him, circling the slender man with his tail whipping back and forth.

'I heard . . . and you were gone,' Leesil spit out between pants of breath. 'What's going on? Why are you . . . ?' He looked at Magiere's messed up clothes, grass and leaves caught in her hair, then down at Chap, and saw the bloodstained fur. His eyes widened. Leesil quickly inspected the dog, and when he found no life-threatening wounds, he looked back at Magiere. 'What happened?' he asked more clearly.

Magiere looked away from his bloodshot eyes. The sun was somewhere just below the horizon, and the clouds were tinged with red. The day had not really begun yet, but her entire life had shifted course. If she were a super-stitious peasant, she would have called it an omen.

'I'm done, Leesil,' she said. 'All of it is over with.'

Leesil's white-blond eyebrows furrowed together over his wide eyes, a mix of surprise, bewilderment, and anger.

'What's wrong?' he yelled. 'We were going to talk about this.'

Magiere's gaze drifted toward the water. The corpse had submerged, but the river might change that. She thought of the lifeless body being dragged along beneath the surface, unable to resist the power of the current.

'I'm leaving for Miiska,' she said. 'Are you coming?'

★   ★   ★

In the small coastal town of Miiska, a waterfront warehouse bustled with activity, even though dawn had not yet arrived. The huge main floor between the unfinished plank walls was stocked with ale casks, wheat bundles, and wool on the import side, and dried fish and a few crafted goods on the export side. Crates, barrels, and twined bundles were carried in and out, noted by clerks. Even with the doors open, the warehouse had the jumbled odor of oil-treated rope, weathered wood and metal, sweat from livestock and workers, and whatever had washed up on the shoreline in the last day or two. A small waif of a boy in an oversize faded green shirt, with a mop of dun-colored hair on his head, continually swept the wooden planks under everyone's feet, trying to control the constant buildup of dust and dirt. Workers were busy preparing cargo for a barge leaving at dawn. In spite of the busy fury, few people spoke to each other.

To the right of the dockside doors, which were wide enough for a wagon to enter, stood a tall man watching over the work with careful detachment. He gave no orders and rarely checked on anything, as if knowing all would be carried out to his satisfaction. His daunting physical height made it appear he was accustomed to looking down at others, even those not shorter than himself. Long muscular arms, inside a deep green tunic, were crossed over his chest, but his arrogant bearing suggested he hadn't built those arms by lifting crates himself. Close-cropped hair the color of blackened corn silk looked even darker around his pale features. Crystalline blue eyes, nearly transparent, watched everything at once.

'No, Jaqua,' a voice said from behind. 'I ordered twenty

casks of wine and thirty-two of ale. You've confused the figures.'

His gaze shifted to the back of the cavernous room. A brown-haired young woman, only two-thirds his height, scolded the head receiving clerk.

'Miss Teesha, I'm sure you—' Jaqua began.

'I know what I ordered,' she said calmly. 'We can't possibly sell all this wine right now. Send twelve casks back. And if the barge captain tries to charge us a shipping cost, tell him we can find someone else to do business with.'

The tall overseer left his place by the door, moving toward the argument.

'Is there a problem?' he asked evenly.

'No, sir.' The clerk, Jaqua, drew back. His face became flat without expression, but his fingernails whitened as he gripped his scribe's board tight with both hands.

Teesha smiled with tiny white teeth. She looked up without concern at her towering partner.

'No, Rashed. Just a mistake in the wine order. It'll be taken care of.'

Rashed nodded, but didn't move, and Jaqua scuttled off to correct his error.

'He's confused several orders lately,' Teesha said. 'Perhaps he's been sampling the wine himself a little too often.'

Rashed was incapable of returning her smile, but this did not seem to bother her. Few would call her beautiful, but she possessed a brightness in her doll-like face that caused men who met her to think of marriage one breath later. Rashed knew her exterior was only a sweet garment covering the truth, but still her appearance was as pleasing to him as it was to anyone – perhaps more so. Her company itself pleased him as well.

'If you don't like Jaqua,' he said, 'replace him.'

'Oh, don't be so harsh. I don't want him replaced. I just want . . .' She stopped in mid-sentence, staring at him.

Rashed stared at the north wall of the warehouse, clutching his throat tightly with one hand. He felt a cold numbness rush downward through his body. Years had passed since he'd felt pain, and its return amazed him. His thoughts clouded, fading away before they could completely form in his mind.

He stepped closer to the wall, and turned around to lean back against one of its timbers for support. The cold line across his throat ran all the way through to the back of his neck.

Teesha grabbed his arm, first gently, then her slender fingers squeezed.

'Rashed . . . what's wrong?'

'Teesha,' he managed to whisper.

Her childlike hands grabbed his tunic firmly, steadying him. When he began to slump, he felt her arms shove him back up to his feet again. She was as strong . . . stronger than any man in the warehouse, though no one else knew this. She put an arm around his waist, supporting him, and hurried him out a side door away from suspicious eyes. Outside, he struggled to help her by remaining on his feet. He felt her hands touch his face, and he looked down into her worry-filled eyes.

'What is it?' she asked. 'What's wrong?'

Sorrow washed over him in a wave, and then anger. A white face with sunken eyes and cheeks glowed in the dark of his mind's eye. Then it snuffed out and vanished. He found himself staring out over the tops of buildings to the forest and skyline in the northeast.

'Parko's dead,' he said in a hissing whisper, too shocked to speak loudly, too angered to voice it clearly.

Teesha's smooth brow wrinkled in confusion. 'But how do you know this?'

He shook his head slightly. 'Perhaps because he was once my brother.'

'You've never felt such a strong connection to him, even before he left us for the Feral Path.'

Rashed lowered his eyes to hers, anger taking hold above all other sensations.

'I felt it. Someone cut his head off and . . . something wet . . . running water.'

She stared at him, frozen in the moment, and through her hands he could feel the shudder run through her small frame. She quickly pulled her hands from his face, as if repulsed by what he'd described, then leaned her forehead against his chest.

'No. Oh, Rashed, I'm sorry.'

His eyes lifted again toward the northeastern skyline, and a chill like cold water over living flesh washed through him again. It was unsettling in a forgotten way, as it had been decades since he'd felt anything akin to cold.

'We have to find out who did this. Where is Edwan?'

'He's nearby.' Teesha closed her eyes for a moment. 'My husband says he is sorry, too.'

Rashed ignored the sympathies.

'Send him out. Tell him to find whoever did this and bring me a name. Tell him to look northeast.' He raised his gaze inland again. 'Tell him to hurry.'

A soft glimmer wavered in the air near the two, almost nothing more than the light cast from a lantern's cracked shutter. Teesha's face turned in its direction and her lips moved as if speaking, but not a word was heard. The light vanished.

3

'We'll have to stop soon,' Magiere, said tiredly, running a hand across her face. 'It's getting dark.'

The sun was setting over the ocean off the coastal road of Belaski, illuminating the land with a dusky orange glow that made it appear less gloomy and hopeless than in full daylight. Leesil always liked dusk, and he stopped for a moment to watch the fading light over the water. The coastal road they followed south from Bela, the country's capital city, was reasonably fast and clear, much easier traveling than the five days' trek west out of Stravina.

It had been twelve days since the death of the mad villager, and Leesil had yet to ask any hard questions about what had really taken place that night on the shore of the Vudrask River. Magiere had provided scant details about what had happened to her and Chap. There still remained the puzzles of why Chap had attacked without orders, and why Magiere appeared so enraged and shaken. It was something beyond the killing of the villager. Neither of them broached the subject, even when they stopped at a village to purchase a donkey and cart to carry Chap – which should have raised questions about the reason for the dog's injuries. His wounds appeared mostly healed by then, but Magiere insisted he needed rest.

'Let's make camp,' Magiere said.

Leesil nodded and strolled off the road. He watched

Magiere run her hand across her forehead again, trying to push a few strands of hair dulled with road dust off her face. He knew she hated being dirty.

'Maybe we should slip down to the shore,' he said. 'Seawater's not the best bath in the world, but it'll do in a pinch. Though it's no good for washing out clothes, unless you like wearing salt crust.'

She turned a suspicious glare on him. 'Since when did you care about clean clothes?'

'Since always.'

'Stop trying to humor me.' She let out a short, sarcastic laugh. 'I know what you want, and you'd better forget about it. We're not going to swindle even one more village. I'm through.' She started to follow him off the road, then paused and looked back.

'What's wrong?' he asked.

'I'm not sure.' She shook her head. 'Since dusk, I've had an odd feeling that someone is . . .' She trailed off.

'Someone is what?'

'Nothing. I'm just tired.' She shrugged. 'Don't put us too far from the road. It's too hard to get the cart through the brush.'

Leesil's own cloak was beginning to feel thin in the rapidly cooling air, and he quickly chose a clearing in the trees. Magiere unpacked a dented cooking pot, loose tea, dried meat, and apples, while he cleared a space of ground and got a small fire going.

Despite his outer calm, his thoughts were still troubled. Once again, they had fallen into simple routine, going through daily motions without really talking, and there were several subjects beyond tonight's dinner that he wished to discuss.

'Do you need help getting Chap?' Magiere asked suddenly.

'No, he can walk on his own.'

Leesil went to the cart and wrapped his slender, tan arms around the dog's neck. 'Hey, there. Time to wake up and eat something.'

'How is he?' Magiere called.

Chap's eyes opened instantly, and he whined before lifting his silver-gray muzzle to lick Leesil's face. He pulled free of Leesil's arms and hopped out of the cart, heading toward the cooking fire.

'See for yourself,' Leesil answered. 'And I think he's about as bored as he could get with riding in the cart.'

Leesil always found her attitude toward Chap a bit odd. She never petted the dog and rarely spoke to him, but always made sure he ate and was well cared for with what little comforts could be offered. Leesil, on the other hand, enjoyed the dog's companionship immensely. But in the days before Magiere, Chap had often hunted up his own supper because his master simply forgot.

Leesil unhooked the donkey and tied it in an area with sufficient grass, then returned to the fire.

'We passed a side road half a league back,' he said absently, taking a waterskin off the ground and pouring water into the cooking pot for tea. 'Might lead off to a village.'

'If you wanted to stop, you should have said something,' Magiere answered just as casually.

'I didn't want to . . .' Finally angered by his partner's polite front, he snapped, 'You know exactly what I mean! Maybe this isn't Stravina, but the nights are just as dark in peasant villages here. We're passing profit by for no reason other than you don't feel like working. You want to buy a tavern? Fine, but I don't see why we have to leave the game nearly coinless.'

'I'm not coinless,' Magiere reminded him.

'Well, I am!' Her serene attitude infuriated him. 'I've only a share from one village, and you didn't give me any warning. If I'd known we were backing out, I would have made some plans.'

'No, you wouldn't have,' she said, not looking at him, her voice still calm. 'D'areeling red wine is expensive, or if it wasn't wine, you would have found a card game somewhere or a pretty tavern girl with a sad story. Telling you earlier wouldn't have changed anything.'

Sighing, Leesil searched his mind for a way to convince her. He knew she was thinking a great deal more than she said. They'd been working together a long time, but she always kept an invisible wall up between herself and everyone else. Most of the time he was comfortable with that, even appreciated it. He had his own secrets to keep.

'Why not one more?' he asked finally. 'There's bound to be other villages along—'

'No, I can't do it anymore.' She closed her eyes as if to shut out the world. 'Pushing that mad villager's body into the river . . . I'm too tired.'

'All right. Fine.' He turned away. 'Tell me about the tavern then.'

The enthusiasm in her voice picked up.

'Well, Miiska is a small fishing community that's doing good business on the coastal sea route. There will be plenty of workers and a few sailors looking to drink and gamble after a hard day. The tavern has two floors, with the living quarters upstairs. I haven't thought of a name yet. You're better at things like that. You could even paint a sign for the door.'

'And you want me running the games, even though you know I lose half the time?' he asked.

'I said *running* the games, not playing them. That's why the house wins, and you always end up with an empty purse. Just run an honest faro table, and we'll go on being partners just like always. Things aren't changing as much as you think.'

He got up and put some more wood on the fire, not knowing why he was being so difficult. Magiere's offer was generous, and she'd always been straight with him. Well, as straight as she could be with such a tight lip. No one else in his life had ever included him in their every plan. Perhaps he just didn't like the unknown risks that might be hiding in so much change.

'How far is this Musky place?' he asked.

'Miiska.' Magiere sighed heavily. 'It's called Miiska, and it's about four more leagues south. If we make good time, we might make it there by late tomorrow.'

Leesil pulled the wineskin from his pack as Chap circled the camp, sniffing about. His mind began to truly consider Magiere's plans for the tavern, and the possibilities gnawed at him softly. A bit of quiet and peace might put an end to his nightmares as well, but he doubted it.

'I may have a few ideas for a sign,' he said finally.

Magiere's mouth curled up slightly, and she handed him an apple. 'Tell me.'

* * *

At the edge of the camp, a soft glimmer hung in the forest. Most would have taken it for the fading light of dusk, except where it moved through the shadows of trees. It moved closer, pausing each time the armored woman or fair-haired half-breed spoke, as if listening to every word. It stopped behind an oak at the edge of the fire's reaching light and settled there.

Rashed paced inside the back room of his warehouse. Tonight, he didn't wish to go outside and observe the giant glowing moon, as was his custom. Nervous tension lined his pale face as his booted feet clomped across the wooden floor. Personal appearance was important to him and, even in crisis, he'd taken the time to don black breeches and a freshly laundered burgundy tunic.

'Pacing like a cat won't make him return any faster,' said a soft voice beside him.

He glanced down at Teesha in mild annoyance. She sat on a hardwood bench cushioned with paisley pillows, sewing impossibly tiny stitches into a piece of tan muslin. Her work-in-progress was beginning to depict a sunset over the ocean. He never understood how she could create such pictures with only thread and scraps of material.

'Then where is he?' Rashed demanded. 'It's been over twelve days since Parko's death. Edwan is not fettered by physical distance. It could not possibly take him this long to gather information.'

'He has a different sense of time than we do. You know that,' she responded, breaking off a piece of blue thread with her teeth. 'And you didn't exactly give him much to work with. It could take time just to find and confirm whomever or whatever he might be looking for.'

Holding the needlework with delicate hands, she examined her stitches as if this were just another night – although usually she could be found absorbed in some ancient text after sundown. In one of the lower rooms, her shelves were filled with books and scrolls they'd paid good coin to acquire. Rashed did not fully understand why words on parchment were so important to her.

He wished her calm could infect him, so he sat down next to her. Candlelight reflected off her chocolate-brown hair. The beauty of those long, silk curls held his attention for only a short time. Then he was up and pacing again.

'Where could he be?' he asked no one in particular.

'Well, I'm getting sick of waiting,' a third voice hissed from the corner shadow. 'And I'm hungry. And it's dark now. And I want out of this wooden box you call our home!'

A thin figure emerged from the corner of the room, the final member of the strange trio living in the ware-house. He appeared to be about seventeen years old, though perhaps small for his age.

'Ratboy,' Rashed spit the nickname out as if it were a joke told one too many times. 'How long have you been skulking in the corner?'

'I just woke up,' Ratboy replied. 'But I knew you'd be *upset* if I went out without saying hello.'

Everything but his skin appeared brown, and even that had a slightly tan cast from months' – possibly a year's – old filth. Plain brown hair stuck to his narrow, pinched head above plain brown eyes. Rashed had heard many terms in his life to describe different shades of brown – chestnut, mahogany, beige – but the dirty figure of Ratboy brought no such words to mind. He played the part of the street urchin so well, the persona had become part of him. Perhaps that was one of his strengths. No one ever remembered him as an individual, just as another grubby, homeless adolescent.

'You don't need to worry about my anger, unless you give me reason,' Rashed said. 'You should be concerned for yourself.'

Ratboy ignored the warning and sneered, his upcurled lips exposing stained teeth.

'Parko was mad,' he answered back. 'It's one thing to revel in our greater existence and senses, but he lost himself. Someone was bound to kill him sooner or later.'

Hard words froze in Rashed's throat. Although his voice was soft and calm, his expression betrayed him.

'Needless killing is another subject you should not criticize.'

Ratboy turned away, shrugging slightly. 'It's the truth. He may have been your brother once, but he was mad with love for the Feral Path, obsessed and drunk with the hunt. That is why you drove him out.' He picked at a fingernail with his teeth. 'Besides, I already told you, for the thousandth time . . .' His voice trailed off like a falsely accused child facing a disbelieving parent. 'I didn't kill that tavern owner.'

'Enough,' Teesha said, looking at Ratboy like a scolding mother. 'None of this is helpful.'

Rashed paced rapidly across the small room again. He owned the entire vast warehouse, but this room had been designated for private use a long time ago. Several trapdoors in the walls and floors led outside or to lower levels. Teesha had decorated it herself with a mix of couches, tables, lamps, and elaborately molded candles in the shapes of dark red roses.

With the exception of their unusually pale skin, both he and Teesha passed easily for human. Rashed had worked hard to set up their life in Miiska. It was important that he find out what happened to Parko, not only for revenge, but for the safety of all of them.

'I'm sick of waiting every night,' Ratboy said petulantly. 'If Edwan doesn't come soon, I'm going out.'

Teesha's mouth opened to answer him when a soft, shimmering light appeared from nowhere and began gaining strength in the center of the room. She simply smiled up at Rashed.

The light grew dense and swirled into the shape of a ghastly form floating just above the ground. A transparent man stared at Teesha.

He wore green breeches and a loose white shirt, the colors of his clothes vivid in the candlelight. His partially severed head rested on one shoulder, connected by a remaining strip of what had once been flesh. Long, dark-yellow hair hung down his blood-spattered shoulder and arm with the illusion of heaviness. His appearance was exactly the same as at the moment he'd died.

'My dear Edwan,' Teesha said. 'It has been lonely without you.'

The ghost floated toward her as if the small distance between them was too much.

'Where have you been?' Rashed demanded instantly. 'Did you find Parko's murderer?'

Edwan's movement stopped. His body half turned until his sloping head faced Rashed, and he stayed there in a long silence.

It was unusual for the ghost to appear visibly like this. His own appearance embarrassed him, and he did not like to see horror, revulsion, or even simple distaste in the eyes of others. Normally, he only appeared to Teesha, who never showed any sign of discomfort. But lately he'd taken to materializing in the most grisly detail whenever Rashed was present.

Rashed kept his expression emotionless on purpose. 'What have you learned?'

'It was a woman called Magiere.' Edwan's hollow voice echoed. He turned to face his wife as if Teesha had actually posed the question. 'She hires herself out to peasant villages seeking to rid themselves of vampires and their like.'

'I think I've actually heard that name,' Ratboy chimed in, perking up now that his attention was stimulated. 'It was a traveling peddler. He mentioned something about a "hunter of the dead" working the villages of Stravina. But it has to be nonsense. There aren't that many of our kind. Not enough to make a living off of, if anyone was good enough to try. She's a fake, a charlatan. She could not have killed Parko.'

'Yes, she did,' Edwan answered, his words like whispers from the past traveling down an endless hall. 'Parko rests in the Vudrask River, his head . . . his head . . .' – he stuttered briefly before continuing – 'his head severed from his body. She cut his head off. She knew what to do.'

Ratboy scoffed under his breath from the corner.

Teesha simply sat listening and thinking. Rashed began pacing again.

He'd himself heard much about the occasional 'hunter' traveling the lands, calling themselves by fanciful titles such as 'exorcist,' 'witchbane,' and 'hunters of the dead.' Ratboy was correct on one count. They were always cheats and mountebanks merely seeking profit by preying on peasant superstitions – regardless of whether those peasant fears were based on a hidden truth. But Rashed knew something more had happened this time, and Parko had died because of it. It was difficult, almost impossible, for a mortal to kill a vampire, even one who'd abandoned his intellect to run wild through the nights, lost to the Feral Path.

'And more,' Edwan whispered.

Rashed stopped. 'What?'

'She's coming here.' The ghost now turned completely to face Rashed. 'She's purchased the old tavern on the docks.'

At first no one moved, then Ratboy rushed forward, Rashed stepped close, and even Teesha was on her feet. Their questions barraged the spirit, one upon the other.

'Where did you hear . . . ?'

'How can that be . . . ?'

'Where did she find out . . . ?'

Edwan's eyes closed as if the voices hurt him.

'Quiet,' Teesha snapped. Both Rashed and Ratboy fell silent as she turned back to the ghost, speaking calmly and quietly. 'Edwan, tell us anything you know about this.'

'Everyone in Miiska knows the owner disappeared months ago.' Edwan paused, and Rashed turned a suspicious glare in Ratboy's direction. 'I listened to her talk with her partner. The missing owner owed money on the property to someone in Bela, so the tavern was sold off low just to pay the debt. This false hunter now holds the title to the tavern, free and clear. She will arrive late tomorrow and intends to settle here to run the tavern.'

Rashed lowered his head, murmuring to himself. 'Perhaps she is not such a charlatan. I didn't kill our master and leave our home just so we could end up as some hunter's bounty.'

The others remained silent, lost in their thoughts.

Finally, Teesha asked, 'What should we do?'

Rashed looked back at her, examining the lines of her delicate face. He wasn't about to let a hunter anywhere near Teesha. But other thoughts also troubled him. 'If the hunter makes it into Miiska, we'll have to fight her here, and we can't afford that if we're to maintain the secrecy we've established. Another death in town' – he glanced at Ratboy – 'could ruin everything we have here. She must not reach Miiska.'

'I'll do it,' Ratboy said, almost before Rashed had even finished.

'No, she managed to destroy Parko,' Teesha said, her expression changing to concern. 'You might get hurt. Rashed is the strongest, so he should go.'

'I'm the fastest, and I blend into anything,' Ratboy argued, eagerness in his eyes. 'Let me go, Rashed. No one on the road will ever remember I passed by. People always remember you. You look like a nobleman.' A hint of sarcasm slipped in for only a blink. 'That hunter will never even see me coming, and this will all be over.'

Rashed weighed the possibilities. 'All right, I suppose your bad habits might serve us this time. But don't toy with her. Just do it and dispose of the body.'

'There's a dog.' Edwan began speaking, then his words lost coherency. 'Something old, something I can't remember.'

Ratboy's pinched face wrinkled into a frown. He let out a grunt of boredom. 'A dog is nothing.'

'Listen to him,' Rashed warned. 'He knows more than you.'

Ratboy shrugged and started for the door. 'I'll be back soon.'

Teesha nodded, her eyes a bit sad. 'Yes, kill her quickly and then come home.'

Ratboy stopped only long enough to roll up a canvas tarp that he could tie to his back and to put some of the dirt from his coffin into a large pouch. He brought no weapons. No one saw him exit the warehouse out into the cool night air.

Thoughts of the hunt consumed him. Rashed's obsession with secrecy meant that little or no killing was ever allowed in Miiska. The three of them commonly erased the blurred memories of their victims while feeding. While this nourished the body, it did not feed Ratboy's soul nor the hunger in his mind.

He loved to feel a heart stop beating right beneath him, to smell fear and the last tremble of life as it faded from his prey and was absorbed into his own body. Sometimes he killed outsiders, strangers, and travelers in secret and hid the bodies where no one would find them. But those were too few and too far between. Occasionally, he had gone too far and caused the death of someone who lived in Miiska and then tried his best to hide the body. Of course, the one time someone truly noticeable had disappeared, the old tavern owner, it hadn't been his doing, but Rashed still didn't believe him.

Tonight, Rashed had actually given him permission, and he would make the most of it, enjoying every slow moment. He felt the hunger rise up again, begging and demanding as he realized that he still had not fed this evening.

A quarter of the night passed as he worked his way along parallel to the road. Now and then, he stopped to fully test the night with his senses. Sniffing the night air, he picked up nothing at first. Then a thin whiff of warmth reached his nostrils. He crawled through the trees and brush to the edge of the coastal road from Bela, and heard the faint creak and scrape of a wagon, its axle in need of grease.

Ratboy waited patiently beneath a wild blueberry bush. Peering through the leaves, he could see the wagon rolling closer. The horse looked old and tired. A lone driver sat with his head nodding now and again as he drifted in and out of sleep. This was certainly not the one he'd been sent to find, but it seemed a waste to let the opportunity pass. And catching the hunter while he was fully fed and powered would be best.

'Help me,' Ratboy called out weakly.

The driver's head raised up, awake. In his well-worn, purple cloak, he looked to be a half-successful merchant, probably one who traveled a great deal and wouldn't be missed for a full moon. Ratboy fought the urge to lunge.

'Here, please. I think my leg is broken,' he called in mournful agony. 'Help me.'

His face awash with nauseating concern, the merchant began climbing down instantly. Ratboy did so enjoy this.

'Where are you?' the merchant asked. 'I can't see you.'

'Here, over here.' Ratboy kept his voice soft, plaintive, as he stretched himself out on the ground.

Heavy footsteps brought the smell of warm life running to Ratboy's side. The merchant knelt down.

'Did you fall?' he said. 'Don't worry. Miiska is not far, and there we can get you some help.'

Ratboy snatched the man's cloak collar and jerked downward while rolling, until the two had switched places. Staring down into the surprised face, Ratboy could not help mouthing the word, 'Fool.' Hands like bone manacles pinned the merchant to the ground. In panic, the man pitched wildly, trying to throw off his attacker. It did no good.

Pain stopped humans from exerting their bodies too far. Ratboy felt no pain, not as mortals did, and had no such limitations. The struggles of his victim amused him. A flash of pleasure coursed through him as he saw surprise turn to fear in the merchant's eyes.

'I'll let you go if you can answer a riddle,' Ratboy whispered. 'What am I?'

'My wife died last summer,' the man said, panting, fighting harder to free himself. 'I have two young sons. I must get home.'

'If you're not going to play, then neither am I,' Ratboy scolded, pinning the merchant harder against the ground. 'Just make one guess. What am I?'

His victim stopped struggling and simply stared up at him in what appeared to be a mix of disbelief and confusion.

'Sorry . . . too late.'

Ratboy bit down quickly in the soft hollow below the merchant's jawline.

The blood in his mouth was nothing compared to the life warmth filling his body as he fed. Sometimes he liked to rip and tear while his prey was still alive. Tonight the hunger was too strong for such playfulness. The heartbeat slowed in his ears, the taste of adrenaline and fear rose in the merchant's flesh, then both faded.

Whenever it was over, there always followed a moment of melancholy for Ratboy, like a child's last moment at a carnival, when lamps were snuffed out, the acrobats retired, and tents closed for the last time – until next year. He lifted his gaze to the road north. The hunter was out there, traveling toward him. It was just a matter of time.

4

Just within sight of the coastline road, Ratboy traveled swiftly, slipping through the trees and constantly smelling the air for any hint of his prey, even though he knew she was still hours away. Just what did a charlatan vampire hunter smell like? Taste like? In an endless existence, anything new, any new experience was a rare and savory thing.

As night slipped away and the first streaks of dawn appeared over the ocean, he grew concerned, but not about where he'd sleep that day. Sea caves were easy enough to find, and in desperation he could always burrow under the forest mulch beneath the canvas tarp roped to his back. But what if she passed him while he slept? Indeed, she would pass him. He'd hoped to come across her camp while she slept, but the scent of few travelers drifted to him and none with the fragrance of a woman. What should he do?

He realized he may have underestimated normal human speed. So how far away was she? And when she awoke, how far could she travel in a day? He frowned, knowing the need for cover was becoming imminent. The road next to the tree line lay empty in both directions.

Ratboy crossed through the trees to the shoreline and looked around for a deep-looking cave or pocket in the cliff wall. Dropping over the side of the cliff, he scaled downward like a spider and disappeared into an ancient hole, crawling back and away from the light with no fear of darkness or whatever might already be living inside. He laid the pouch of coffin earth on the cave floor and curled around it on his side in the scant space. Then he pulled the loosened canvas over himself against any stray lance of sunlight that might somehow find him.

Logic told him that although he'd only traveled for half the night, she would not be able to cover the distance to Miiska left to her in one day. He'd sleep and then back track. One way or another, he'd intercept her and then bring her head back to Rashed as a taunting gift. Every time anyone in Miiska disappeared, Rashed blamed him. In truth, sometimes he was to blame, but not always, and certainly not for the tavern owner. Some grizzly old drunk offered little temptation to a killer like himself.

His eyelids grew heavy, and he lost his train of thought.

By late afternoon that day, Leesil's narrow feet hurt, and his partial excitement about seeing their tavern began to wane. Even the beauty of the coastline and the sea running out to the horizon no longer filled him with awe. Such frantic hurrying seemed unnecessary. The tavern would certainly still be there no matter when they arrived. Magiere never pushed them like this when they were on the game. No, the three of them had simply traveled at a comfortable pace until reaching their intended target. He was getting sick of her constant nagging: 'Leesil, hurry. Leesil, not far now. If we keep going, we'll make it tonight.'

Even Chap looked tired of his cart ride and whined softly, eyes tragic with boredom, but Magiere wouldn't allow the dog to walk yet. The old donkey looked near death. What was Magiere thinking? This sudden desire to be an honest businesswoman had changed her in unpleasant ways. Close to exhaustion – or at the moment what he decided would count enough for exhaustion – Leesil noticed the sun's bottom edge meet the ocean horizon.

'Enough's enough,' he announced loudly.

When Magiere, walking ahead of the donkey and cart, showed no sign of hearing him, Leesil stumbled theatrically to the roadside and dropped on the grass.

'Come here, Chap,' he called. 'Time for a break.'

The elegant, gray-blue head of his dog jerked upward in hope, ears poised, eyes intently fastened on his master.

'You heard me. Come on,' Leesil repeated loudly.

Magiere heard Leesil's shout this time and turned her head just in time to see Chap bounding out of the cart and back down the road to where Leesil sat. Her normally stoic jaw dropped slightly as she stopped in the road. The donkey and cart moved on without pausing.

'What in . . . not again,' she stammered, then caught sight of the escaping cart. She grabbed the escaping beast's halter and pulled it to a stop. 'You elven half-wit,' she called back to Leesil, dragging donkey and cart back to where he sat. 'What are you doing?'

'Resting?' he said, as if asking for confirmation. He looked down at his legs stretched out comfortably on the ground, then nodded his head firmly. 'Yes, most assuredly. Resting.'

Instead of lying down, Chap sniffed around the rough sea grass, stretching his limbs, then bounded off into the brush nearby. Leesil took his wineskin and slipped its carrying strap off his shoulder. He popped its stopper, then tilted it up and over his open mouth for a long, satisfying drink. The dark D'areeling wine always tasted slightly of winter chestnuts. It comforted him in ways he couldn't describe, and that was likely all the comfort he'd get, unless Magiere stopped driving all of them with her stubbornness. But two could play that game.

Magiere stood dumbfounded, glaring at him, covered in road dust and in need of a wash.

'We don't have time to rest. I've practically dragged you since midday as it is.'

'I'm tired. Chap's tired. Even that ridiculous donkey looks ready to keel over.' Leesil shrugged, unimpressed by her apparent dilemma. 'You're outvoted.'

'Do you want to be traveling after sundown?' she asked.

He took another drink, then noted he, too, was in need of good bath. 'Certainly not.'

'Then get up.'

'Have you looked at the horizon lately?' He yawned and lay back in the grass, marveling at the tan-colored, sandy earth and salt sea smell in the air. 'We'd best make camp and find your tavern in the morning.'

Magiere sighed, and her expression grew almost sad and frustrated at the same time. Leesil felt a sudden desire to comfort her, until the ache in his feet reminded him what a pain in other regions she was being. Tomorrow would be – should be – soon enough, even for her. Let her stew over it if she liked, but he was not moving another step down the road until morning.

He watched Magiere's gaze turn toward the ocean, noting the clean lines of her profile against the brilliant orange of the skyline. She glared out at the horizon as if willing the far edge of water to deny the sinking sun access and hold it there. Her head slowly dropped, just enough for her hair to curtain her face from view. Leesil heard, just barely, the soft sigh that came from her lips. He gave an exaggerated sigh of his own.

'It's better this way. You don't want to wake the caretakers up in the middle of the night.' He paused, waiting for acknowledgment or rebuke, but Magiere remained silent. 'What if the place looks bleak and depressing in the dark? No, we'll arrive like true shop-folk at midday or so and assess the place in broad daylight.'

She looked back at him for a moment, then nodded. 'I just wanted to . . . something pulls me like a puppet.'

'Don't talk like a poet. It's annoying,' he retorted.

She fell silent, and once again they took up their familiar routine of setting up camp. Chap continued to sniff at and dig in the sand, thrilled to be released from his rolling prison.

Leesil occasionally glanced over at the sun. Perhaps they had been in the gray, damp world of Stravina too long. There was a definite difference between wet and damp. Wet was thin salt spray blowing inland from a fresh sea, with an offshore breeze to gently dry you off. Damp was shivering in blankets that brought no warmth in some mountainside hut and watching the walls mold.

'Will we see this every night in Miiska?' he asked.

'See what?'

'The sunset . . . light spreading across the horizon, fire and water.'

For a moment, her forehead wrinkled as if he spoke a foreign language, then his question registered. She, too, turned toward the sea. 'I expect.'

He snorted. 'I stand corrected. You are no poet.'

'Find some firewood, you lazy half-blood.'

They made camp on the far side of the road that divided them from the shoreline. In reality, it was quite a distance down to the water, but the enormity of the ocean created an illusion of closeness. The last hint of daylight dropped below the horizon, and thick, wind-worn trees provided cover from the evening breeze. Leesil was digging through burlap bags in the cart for leftover apples and jerky when Chap stopped sniffing playfully about and froze into a stance of attention. He growled at the forest in a tone that Leesil had never heard before.

'What's wrong, boy?'

The dog's stance was rigid, still and watchful, as if he were a wolf eyeing prey from a distance. His silver-blue eyes seemed to lose color and turned clear gray. His lips rose slightly over his teeth.

'Magiere,' Leesil said quietly.

But his partner was already staring at the dog, and then at the forest in equal intervals.

'This is like what he did that night,' she whispered, 'back in Stravina near the river.'

They'd spent a number of nights in Stravina near a river, but Leesil knew which night she meant. He pulled his hands out of the cart and put them up his opposing sleeves until he grabbed both hilts of the stilettos sheathed on his forearms.

'Where's your sword?' he asked, keeping his gaze fixed on the trees.

'In my hand.'

Ratboy's eyes flicked open, and the black, damp walls of his tiny cave disoriented him for a moment. Then he remembered his mission. The hunter. Time to backtrack.

As he emerged into the cool night air, he rejoiced in the feeling of freedom the open land offered. This was a good night. Yet part of him already missed Teesha and the odd comfort she created in their warehouse. 'Home' she called it, though he couldn't remember why any of their kind needed to make a home. It was her idea, with Rashed to back her up. Still, no matter how much he liked the open, he'd grown accustomed to the world they'd built in Miiska. Best find the hunter quickly so he could take his time killing, draining her, and then return *home* before dawn.

Below the cliff, the white sandy beach stretched in both directions, but he quickly turned away and scaled upward to the cliff's top, fingers gripping the rough wall of earth and rock effortlessly. The beach might be faster traveling, but it was too open. Reaching the top edge, he swung himself up and was about to gauge his bearings when the scent of a campfire drifted to his nostrils.

His slightly tapered head swiveled, and at the same moment, he smelled a woman, a man, and a donkey. Then his nose picked up something else. A dog? Edwan had made some ridiculous comment about a dog. Ratboy hated Edwan almost more than he hated Rashed. At least Rashed offered valuable necessities – a place to sleep, a steady income, and the shielding disguise of normality. Edwan merely sponged up Teesha's time and gave nothing in return. All right, so he had located the hunter and her companions, but that was a small thing. And what could he, Ratboy, have to fear from a dog, a tamed one traveling with its masters?

Quivering elation rippled through him. Had he found his prey so easily? Could this woman be *the* woman? Had she literally made camp within sight of his sleeping den?

Orange flames from the fire were just visible through the trees, and he wanted to get a better look. He dropped down to his belly and cast about for some way to cross the road unseen. The road offered no possibility of cover, so he decided to simply cross it quickly. In a blink, like a shadow from flickering firelight, he was across the hard dirt path, blending into the trees and brush on the far side. He crawled closer to view the camp.

The woman was tall, wearing studded leather armor, and looked younger than Ratboy expected. She was almost lovely, with a dusty, black braid hanging down her back as she poured a flask of water into a pot near the fire. Her companion was a thin, white-blond man with elongated ears and dressed almost like a beggar, who stood digging about in the back of a small cart and then . . .

A silver-gray dog, nearly the height of Ratboy's hipbone, leaped to its feet and stared right at him, as if the foliage between them did not exist. Its lips curled up. The growl escaping its teeth echoed through the quiet forest to Ratboy's ears. Something in the sound brought a strange feeling into his chest. What was this feeling? He hated it, whatever it was, and it made him pull back behind the thick trunk of a tree.

Edwan had said something about a dog.

A dog was nothing. Peering out again, he saw the woman grab her sword, and he smiled.

'What's wrong with him?' Leesil asked.

Chap's low snarling continued, but he stood his ground, not attempting to advance in any direction.

'I don't know,' Magiere answered, for lack of anything better to say. And in truth, she didn't know, but she was beginning to suspect the hound harbored some extra sense, some ability to see what she could not. 'Get the crossbow from the cart and load it.'

For once on this trip, Leesil didn't argue and moved quietly and quickly to follow her instructions.

Chap's growls began rising in pitch to the same eerie sound he had made that night by the Vudrask river. Magiere moved toward the dog, reached down, and grasped the soft fur at the back of Chap's neck.

'Stay,' she ordered. 'You hear me? You stay.'

He growled in low tones but did not move from his place. Instead, his locked gaze shifted to the left and his body turned to follow.

'It's circling the camp,' Magiere whispered to Leesil.

'What?' Leesil looked about, foot in the crossbow's stirrup and both hands pulling on the bowstring to lock it in place. 'What's circling the camp?'

She looked at her partner, at his narrow face and wispy hair. At least this time he wasn't drunk and had the crossbow loaded, but now she wished she'd told him more about killing the mad peasant. How strong the pale man had been, how terrifying . . . how she'd felt the strange hunger suddenly grow in the pit of her stomach. Afterward, the whole occurrence had seemed too unreal, and she'd passed it off as just her own mind mixing up all the trappings and tricks of playing the game too long. A bad encounter had made her slip into believing her own lies for a panicked moment.

And now she had no answer to Leesil's question.

Chap's white-and-silver muzzle rose, and she expected him to start wailing. Instead, his gaze started moving up and across, up and across, up and up.

'The trees!' she called out, crouching low behind the cart for fear of what a skulker might do from a high vantage point. She reached over the cart's side, pulling Leesil's belt until he crouched low. 'It's up in the trees.'

The dog's ability to follow his position was becoming more than a mere annoyance to Ratboy. There was no way to try a flanking or head-on attack, so he worked his way over and above his target through the tree limbs. He inched along carefully.

'I'm going to bring your skin home for a rug, you glimmering hound,' he whispered, making himself feel better picturing the animal's bloody silver fur draped over his own shoulders. Teesha might even like the unusual, soft color.

But who to kill first? Ratboy had seen a few half-breeds in his time, and this male certainly carried some elven blood. The crossbow was little to worry about. It would hardly slow him down, even if the half-blood could shoot straight.

He could snap the dog's neck quickly enough, landing on it first, but that would give the other two time to set themselves for a fight. No, first priorities were best put first – disable the hunter; then kill the dog and the half-blood. That way he could play with the hunter as long he wanted.

From his position on a sturdy branch, he focused on the hunter and leaped.

There was no warning. Leesil caught a glimpse in the dark, the blur of a faceless form passing overhead and down.

A wiry, brown-headed figure dressed like a beggar slammed into Magiere, knocking her to the ground. Leesil expected the attacker to tumble to the ground himself but, to Leesil's surprise, the man did not fall, but landed firmly on his feet. And on impact, his fist was already in mid-swing downward.

'Magiere!' Leesil shouted. He barely finished spinning around to aim the crossbow when a loud crack sounded as the attacker's fist struck Magiere hard across the cheek-bone. Magiere's head bounced against the earth in recoil. Leesil fired.

The quarrel struck low through the beggar's back, point protruding from his abdomen, but he responded with only a quick shudder and turned toward Leesil.

A cry, high pitched enough to be human, burst from Chap's throat as he launched himself into the beggar. Both figures rolled across the camp and over the fire in a mass of rapidly moving teeth and fur that scattered half the burning wood and kicked sparks up around them.

Magiere lay on the ground unmoving, as Leesil leaped

out the back of the cart. By the sound of the blow, he knew she was likely to be unconscious. For a moment he was caught between stopping to check on her and following his dog to help finish off the intruder. Between a crossbow quarrel and Chap's ferocity, the foolish intruder had only moments to live anyway. Still, he couldn't afford to be caught with his back turned. He pulled another quarrel from the crossbow's undercarriage, readying to reload as he started around the scattered fire, then skidded to a stop before he'd gotten halfway.

Dog and intruder had separated. The wiry little man – or perhaps teenage boy – dropped low as Chap charged again. The dog was in mid-air when the intruder lunged forward from his crouch, one hand swinging up with hooked fingers to snag Chap's belly fur. Chap lost his trajectory.

Perhaps it was the dark or scattered ash floating in the air, or the flickering half-light of the nearly snuffed fire playing mock images upon the fight in the scrub grass. But Leesil could swear the little man somehow reversed direction while Chap was still in the air. Whether he had landed in a blink to turn back, or never actually left the ground, Leesil couldn't be sure.

The filthy beggar's feet kicked upward into the dog's side, adding force to momentum. Chap snarled as he arched across the clearing, head over tail, and yelped in pain as he grazed the base of a tree and tumbled across the sandy ground. He was instantly on his feet again.

Leesil pulled the bowstring, trying to reload the crossbow, and nearly losing his grip when startled by a shout from behind him.

'Chap, no!'

Leesil turned his head just enough to see, but still keep the beggar boy in his view. Magiere was up, falchion in hand, though somewhat unsteady on her feet.

'Get back, Chap!' she shouted again.

Chap trembled and snarled, but kept his distance. Every muscle under his fire-singed fur tensed in protest, as if her order was not only unfair but incorrect.

No one moved.

The young intruder held up his hand and stared at the canine teeth marks on it.

'I'm bleeding,' the boy said in puzzled astonishment. 'It burns.'

His dull brown eyes grew wide and uncertain. He was shaken for some reason, seeming to not have expected pain or injury. He looked no more than sixteen years of age and was built as if he'd spent half that time in near starvation. Calm appeared to settle upon him, but there was still apprehension in his stance as he shifted his weight lightly from foot to foot, perhaps caught between fight and flight. He grabbed the quarrel protruding from his abdomen, and pulled it out with a quick jerk and only the slightest flinch.

Taking in all of this at once made Leesil momentarily forget about reloading the crossbow. This strange youth should be dead, or near enough to it, and Magiere should be lying unconscious on the ground. But his partner stood beside him, gripping her falchion, knees slightly bent in a half-crouch, expression tense and purposeful. And the intruder who stood well out of reach across the fire was considerably less worse for wear than he should be.

'What's your name?' Magiere whispered though the darkness.

'Does it matter?' the boy asked.

Leesil could see that neither of them even noticed his presence anymore.

'Yes,' Magiere answered.

'Ratboy.'

Magiere nodded in answer. 'Come and kill me, Ratboy.'

He smiled once and leaped.

Leesil dropped and rolled. He heard the thump of feet landing right behind him and glanced back in time to see Magiere spin on the ground, coming up behind her attacker with the falchion already in motion. The boy twisted to dodge, but the blade still cut a shallow slash across his back, and he screamed out.

The voice was impossibly loud and high. Leesil flinched.

Ratboy started to fall, but caught himself on the cart with both hands. He propelled himself around to face Magiere. She rushed him before he fully regained his balance and kicked him in the upper chest. Ratboy's body arched over backward, feet leaving the ground, and Magiere's blade came rushing down at him while he was still in the air.

Leesil couldn't imagine the strength of an ordinary kick whipping someone's torso over in the rapid manner he saw. And Magiere was maneuvering faster than he'd ever seen her move before. But Ratboy's speed increased to match hers.

The blade cut deep into the ground where Ratboy should have landed. Instead, he now stood to the right of the fire, hissing and groping with one hand at his back where Magiere's falchion had cut into him.

'It burns,' he screeched, astonished and angry. 'Where did you get that sword?'

Magiere didn't answer. Leesil pulled himself up from the ground and glanced at his partner.

Her eyes were wide, locked on Ratboy. Her lips glistened wet as her mouth salivated uncontrollably. Leesil wasn't sure she could have spoken if she wanted to.

Magiere's breath was long, deep, and fast, and the smooth features of her face twisted, brow furrowing with lines of open hatred. Her skin glistened with a sweat she hadn't worked enough to build up.

Chap circled in beside her. A low tremble ran through his body that showed in the quiver of his pulled-back jowls. In his savage state, the resemblance between dog and woman was impossible to ignore. As Magiere's lips parted, her mouth looked like the snarl of the canine beside her. Her eyes refused to blink and began to water until small tears ran down her cheeks.

Leesil could not turn his attention fully back to Ratboy. He held his position to keep Magiere in his field of view as well. This was not the woman he'd traveled with for years.

Dog, boy, and woman all stood motionless, tense and poised. All watched for the first sign of movement. Leesil couldn't stand it all any longer and cocked the crossbow.

Ratboy feigned another charge, then darted away at the last second, absorbing the sight of Magiere and Chap, she armed with her sword and the dog with his claws and fangs. Ratboy's back and arms were bleeding badly now and the fear was plain on his face.

'Hunter,' he whispered and then bolted for the tree line.

Leesil raised the crossbow and aimed at the fleeing figure, not believing it would do much good. Somehow Magiere's sword and Chap's teeth had been more damaging than a quarrel through the body at close range. Before he could fire, Ratboy was gone in the dark. Leesil stepped quickly around the campfire to put its waning light at his back, but there was no sign of the fleeing figure. Chap started to trot in the direction of the trees, but Leesil called the dog's attention with a snap of his fingers and shook his head. Chap whined and sat down with his attention still fixed out into the dark.

'Leesil?'

The sound of her voice was weak, barely a whisper. Leesil turned about, almost as on guard as when facing the vicious beggar boy.

Magiere breathed heavily now, as if exertion and injury had suddenly caught up with her all at once. Her features smoothed as wrinkles of rage faded, and her eyes cast about in confusion.

'Leesil?' she said again, as if she couldn't see him. Then she sank to her knees, the falchion's blade thumping against the ground.

Leesil hesitated. A small fear knotted in his chest. One unknown danger had fled the camp only to leave him with another he'd unwittingly kept company with for years. He'd seen a boy move with impossible speed and strength and his own dog savagely rebound unscathed from vicious attacks. He'd seen his only companion of years get up from a blow that might have downed most anyone, then slowly twist into something . . . someone he recognized only in the barest manner.

Magiere slumped over, head halfway to the ground. She'd dropped the sword entirely. Her weapon hand bent backward against the ground, unable to turn over to properly brace her weight.

Leesil had never touched her, except during their mock battles for money. The thought of stepping nearer to her now made his insides tense. Instinctively, he lifted the crossbow, holding it tight and pointed at Magiere.

How many times had she been the last one to sleep as he drank himself into slumber? How long had he wandered from theft to gambling table before he'd tried to lift her coin purse by mistake? How many people had he known in his ambling life willing to let him share their dream, even if it wasn't one he particularly wanted? And he'd never before seen her need anyone.

He rushed over, dropping the crossbow as he caught her before she collapsed fully to the earth. Magiere crumpled and her weight was more than Leesil could hold in his half-crouch. He fell backward on the seat of his breeches, and Magiere's shoulders and head toppled back against his chest, nearly knocking him flat.

'I've got you,' he said, pushing himself up as he steadied her, one arm around her shoulders. 'It's all right.'

He knew it was a lie. There was something very wrong with Magiere – about Magiere – and *he* was certainly not all right. Nothing was all right anymore. Now what was he to do? Would she come completely out of this – whatever it had been – by morning?

The heat of fear and fight was draining out of him,

and the night air felt suddenly chill. He felt Magiere shudder, then go limp as she leaned against him.

As he sat there, trying to pull an old woolen blanket out of a pack and across her shuddering body, he thought he noticed a soft glow on her chest just below her neck. When he finished with the blanket, he looked again, but found nothing but the dangling amulets she wore half tucked into the top of her leather vestment.

Ratboy didn't remember his journey back to Miiska. He only remembered growing pain and weakness, and wild bewilderment. Too injured to think or even rationalize, he felt the energy of his existence slowly dripping down his back and from his arm, weakening him. He'd been able to focus his will and remaining energy to closing the quarrel wound, but not his other injuries. The sword wound and teeth marks refused to close.

He'd been injured before, yet had never had a wound leech his strength like this, and lack of understanding only fueled his fear. Stumbling, he fell against the timber wall of a building, not even aware of what part of town he had entered. If he lost the last of his strength before reaching shelter, the sun would rise upon him.

In this early time before the day, the town lay silent. Rows of small weatherworn houses stretched out on both sides of him. He needed to get under cover before dawn, and he needed strength and life. He needed to feed.

A light feminine humming caught his attention, and the sensation of nearby warmth, flesh, and then blood filled his nostrils. Hunger and longing pulled him from his stupor, and he scrambled on all fours to the nearest corner of a house. There was also the smell of horse dung and metal, as well as coal and wood ash. It took a moment for him to piece together what his eyes saw. There was a woodpile to his right, and to the left around the corner were stable doors. In the rafters of the overhang hung horseshoes waiting for fitting.

Ratboy's eyes widened as recognition came upon him. He was outside Miiska's only blacksmith's shop. Following the humming voice, he crawled to the woodpile with a fence behind it. He was as careful as possible while climbing the stacked wood to peer over the fence.

A girl of about fifteen years knelt by the family wood stack on the opposite side of the fence, her silky, mouse-brown hair tousled as if she'd risen from bed only moments ago. She wore only a white cotton night shift that Ratboy would have found enticing at any other time. Now all he needed was life, blood to strengthen him until he could find some way to close the wounds caused by the hunter and the dog.

The girl hummed gently again and then said, 'Misty, come out of there. You're the one scratching at my window to be let in. Stop playing games and come in the house.'

A soft meow answered her and a young tabby popped its head from out of the woodpile on the girl's side of the fence. Ratboy saw her make a mock frown at the cat, trying hard to seem angry.

He did not weave into her thoughts with his voice, lulling her into forgetfulness so he could take what he needed and then disguise the teeth marks. Instead, he lunged.

The cat hissed and retreated into its hiding place.

Ratboy was over the fence and on the girl before she saw him at all. With one hand, he snatched her hair and pulled her head back to expose her neck, and with the other he held her body up against his. His open jaws snapped across her throat and bit down, tearing through the skin. Any cry she might have made was cut off as he crushed her windpipe. There was no time for her to struggle. Her hands merely shook, unable to act.

The first few seconds of warmth and life did not register, but soon his mind began to clear.

Red liquid covered his face and hands and shirt, but he didn't care. The only thing on his mind was the pain in his back and wrists fading to a dull soreness as he dropped the dead carcass on the ground, leaving her there.

Cold never bothered the undead, but the luxury of warmth inside after feeding was a pleasure he never grew tired of, no matter how many times he felt it. It burned through him now, filling him up. It was more pleasure than he could ever remember, even when he'd been alive. And it washed away the hunger, killed the burning of his wounds, and he no longer felt his strength seeping from his body.

Sated and euphoric, he nearly lost track of the time, until a less pleasant tingle ran down the back side of his body across his skin.

There was a glow above the skyline to the east away from the ocean. Sunrise was coming.

Ratboy fled along the dock side of the town toward the warehouse. There would be a lot of explaining to do. Perhaps a little lying as well.

★   ★   ★

Leesil had managed to toss stray pieces of wood into the fire and kick it together, but it did little more than sputter a few small flames for the rest of the night. He couldn't afford to drink now, so that also meant no sleep. Not that he could sleep, as this night's events had been almost as unsettling as his never-ending dreams. It was not a hardship, as he'd gone as long as three sleepless nights before fatigue caught up with him. He remembered his mother could go even longer when the need arose, and likely his own ability was inherited from her. Something to do with her elven heritage that she'd so seldom discussed.

Chap had changed quickly back into his cheerful self, as if nothing out of the ordinary had happened. Having found a comfortable spot on the ground near his master, he'd spent the night silently grooming himself and napping for short periods, only to stir occasionally at the forest sounds only he could hear.

Sitting quietly with Magiere sleeping in his lap, Leesil passed long, tense hours in the dark before he could look at her face without imagining it transformed into what he'd seen earlier that night. He had checked her for wounds, but she was uninjured as far as he could detect. By the time he could look at her face without flinching, morning twilight was just beginning. There should have been a black-and-blue patch and conceivably split skin with dried blood on the side of her face. He now saw only a light bruise on her left cheek. Instead of relief, he felt another surge of fear and confusion. As the sun rose just high enough that he could feel its warmth on his back, Magiere's eyelids quivered and opened.

'Are you all right?' he asked quietly.

'Yes,' she answered hesitantly, then added, 'My jaw hurts.'

'I'm not surprised,' he said. Then he remembered she hadn't been hit in the jaw but on the side of her face.

Before he could ask another question, he felt her body tense. She blinked wide as she stared up at him, apparently now realizing she lay in his lap.

'What's going on?' she asked.

'Good question,' he said, raising his eyebrows. 'I like that question. I might even ask it myself.'

Magiere rolled to sit up as quickly as she could without leaning on him for support, but her scowling eyes stayed fixed upon Leesil.

'You dropped in a heap last night and started shaking,' he explained. 'I didn't want you to get chilled in the night from exhaustion.'

'I'm not exhausted,' she muttered angrily, then climbed to her feet.

Her hand went instantly to the side of her face, and she wavered slightly where she stood. Leesil retrieved his wineskin and, taking a tin cup from his pack, he filled it with red wine.

'This is all we have for the pain. Drink it. All of it.'

Magiere seldom drank anything besides water or spiced tea. She grabbed the cup too roughly and slopped part of it on to the ground. She sipped it, winced, and then rubbed at her jaw. Leesil watched suspiciously.

'Do you want to tell me what happened last night?' he asked.

She shook her head. 'What is there to tell?'

Leesil crossed his arms. 'Well, let's see now. We were attacked without reason. I shot him, and he pulled the quarrel out as if it were a splinter. Then he acted like Chap's bite was a mortal wound. Not to mention he seemed surprised that your sword could actually hurt him. And then you . . .' He paused only a moment, waiting for a response, but none came. 'Let's see . . . loss of the power of speech, kicking a man into the air and onto his back almost faster than I could see . . . not to mention your drooling maniacal expression. What exactly do you think—'

'I don't know!' she shouted at him.

Magiere dropped to the ground next to the cart and leaned back against its wheel. Her head drooped until Leesil could no longer see her eyes. She let out a deep, angry sigh. Then a second sigh, weak and heavy.

In the years he'd known her, many words occurred to him that would have adequately described Magiere – strong, resourceful, heartless, manipulative, careful – but never lost or vulnerable.

'I don't know what happened,' she said, almost too quietly for him to hear. 'If I tell you something crazy, Leesil, you mustn't laugh.'

'I wait in suspense,' he said, not understanding why he suddenly felt angry instead of more sympathetic. He was worried about her, but still angry. Perhaps it was the long, edgy night of sitting with no answers.

'I think we've been on the game too long.' She lifted her head, but did not look at him. 'What's real and what's false are becoming blurred in my head. I don't want to fight anymore . . . or at all or . . . I don't know. All of this can stop if we just make a peaceful life. We'll run an honest business, keep to ourselves, and this will all go away.'

'That's it?' Leesil's frustration was quickly fueling his anger.

'That's all I know.' She finally looked at him, then away, shaking her head. 'I don't know what else it could be.'

That was no answer, just another evasion. She'd told him nothing. Or had she? Leesil's past had erased all desire to protect anyone besides himself. He wasn't certain now if he felt protective or simply puzzled. He only knew that Magiere's demeanor was at least changing back into the cold and moderately pleasant countenance he'd come to know and depend on. Perhaps it was just the years of living in lies and playing games that had finally caught up with her. That would have to be relief enough for now. But there would be more questions when another opportunity arose.

'All right,' he said, throwing up his arms and letting them drop. 'If you've no secrets to tell, we'll mark this one as another mad thief on the road. By midday, we'll be in Miiska.'

'Yes.' She half smiled. 'Good enough for a new life.'

'I'll make the tea,' he grumbled, kneeling down to collect and fan the last embers of the fire. He looked at her and nodded. 'A new life.'

At the break of dawn, Rashed dragged Ratboy's bloody, struggling form into the underground drawing room and threw him up against a wall.

Teesha's eyes rose from her needlework in near alarm. 'What is going on?'

'Look at him!' Rashed spit.

Half-dried blood covered Ratboy's chin and upper

torso. Although Rashed thought the youngest member of their trio to be an impatient upstart, he'd never considered him a complete fool – until now.

'This witless whelp left a dead girl lying in her own yard with her throat torn open!'

Teesha stood and smoothed her blue satin dress. Her chocolate curls bounced slightly as she approached Ratboy, who was sprawled against the base of the room's back wall. She looked him over, and her head tilted ever so slightly to the side as her small face took on a disappointed expression.

'Is this true?' she asked.

'While you're staring so hard, take a look at my back,' the dusty urchin answered, finding his voice. 'That blackish stuff isn't human blood. It's my own.' He held his wrists out. 'And these scars were open wounds not long ago. You ever see one of our kind get scars before?'

'Impossible,' Rashed hissed, but his brow wrinkled when he leaned over for closer inspection. Jagged white slashes resembling teeth marks covered Ratboy's forearms. 'How?'

'That hunter!' Ratboy screeched back at him in frustration. 'She truly is a hunter. I've seen few of our own kind move so quickly, and her sword sliced my back as if I were living flesh.'

'Nonsense,' Rashed said in open disgust, stepping back. 'The charlatan used her earnings to buy some warded blade, that's all. You obviously rushed in with your usual naïve confidence and failed. You got cut for your own recklessness and ran away like a coward. And to make matters worse, you didn't bother thinking about us, did you? Instead of coming back here to face the slow process of healing, you consumed a young girl to death not twenty houses from your own and then left her body to panic the town.'

Ratboy's jaw dropped as if Rashed's accusations were too outrageous for defense. 'But I have scars!'

Rashed paused only a second, then turned away in disgust.

'You sent him,' Teesha said gently, eyebrows raised with her eyes half closed, as if to spread the guilt properly. Her tiny red mouth set in a position of chastisement. 'He isn't experienced enough to battle a hunter, charlatan or legitimate, and you know it. And none of us were certain how real or false she was. You should have seen to this matter.'

If Ratboy had made such a statement, Rashed would have shaken him like a rag doll, but Teesha's words rang true. The tall leader glared down at Ratboy again, but did not continue his assault.

'When will she reach town?' he asked.

Still petulant, Ratboy answered, 'Sometime today. She's traveling with a half-elf and . . . that dog.' He turned to Teesha. 'Edwan was right about the dog. His teeth burned me. I wasn't ready! If I'd known, I could have won. I would have broken that hound's neck in the first blink.'

The wax rose candles flickered around them, and Teesha patted Ratboy's shoulder. 'We need to go down to the caverns and sleep. Take off those rags and let me see your back. I'll find you another shirt.'

Teesha's attention washed all the anger from Ratboy's face, and he allowed himself to be led away like a puppy.

Rashed frowned at their backs. Ratboy's injuries were

his own fault, scars or not, and Teesha's motherly kindness only encouraged further carelessness. That little leech of an urchin should sleep all night in his own crusted blood.

But for now, such petty thoughts were minor concerns. Rashed had built this home out of nothing. His small family had reasonable wealth and safety, the likes of which normally came to only the older of the Noble Dead after years of planning and manipulation. While he slept this day, a hunter – charlatan or no – was coming to take it all away. She must be removed quickly and quietly. Teesha was right. He should have handled this affair himself.

Rashed began snuffing out the candles, one by one. Keeping the situation away from Miiska was no longer possible. Parko, his fallen brother, must have let something slip before he perished, otherwise why would this hunter come here? There was no question she came looking for the three of them. So he would wait, perhaps a night or two, and allow this hunter to become comfortable. And then he would deal with her personally.

5

Magiere caught her first glimpse of Miiska late that morning and felt a twinge of uncertainty. She had literally banked everything on finding peace in this small port town, and dreams by a campfire were often a far cry from reality.

Leesil showed no similar apprehension. 'Finally,' he said, and his step quickened until he moved out ahead of her. 'Come on.'

Like him, she had become fond of clean, salty air. Unlike him, she could not express such appreciation. His habit of speaking exactly what he thought often confused her, but now she hurried to follow, jerking on the donkey's bridle. She was glad of Leesil's open curiosity. He might make this easier.

Chap no longer rode in the cart, but trotted along beside Leesil, head high as if he knew exactly where he was going, a hound on his way home after the morning run. After so many years trying to perfectly fit their parts in the 'hunter of the dead' game, Magiere was struck by just how peculiar looking a trio they were. She wondered what the townspeople would think of them.

'I wish we could have cleaned up first,' she said.

'You look fine,' Leesil answered, sounding ridiculous in his torn, oversize, untucked shirt and dirty breeches. He hadn't bothered to don a scarf or even to tie up his hair so that the tightened, smooth sides of his ponytail would cover the tips of his ears. Perhaps now that he was arriving at his new home, he didn't see the need to blend in anymore.

The distance to the town closed quickly, until Magiere felt as if she had stepped across an unseen boundary to enter its domain.

People bustled around the main street where it opened into a small marketplace at the near end of town. Smells of warm milk, horse manure and sweat and, most of all, fish assaulted her as she passed the first cluster of hawkers' shacks and tents. A candle maker measured out dye into a pot of melted wax. Nearby, a clothier emptied a cart and hung up multipatterned cloth that would give a harlequin fits. From beyond the buildings and toward the docks came a shrill whistle and the sound of a taskmaster's voice cracking dockworkers into motion to empty the belly of some barge just into port. And, of course, there were the fishmongers, each trying to out shout the other for their fresh, dried, cured, or smoked catch for sale. This was not an outback village of superstitious peasants but a thriving community.

'Not bad.' Leesil smiled, watching a wagon rock by toward a small warehouse, its back filled with wooden wine barrels. 'I could grow accustomed to this.'

They passed a small tavern on the right where a stout woman swept last night's dirt and leavings out the door. By its look and place in the town, Magiere knew it wasn't the one she'd bought, but she had a moment's hesitation, wondering if she'd need to jerk Leesil back before he slipped through the open door.

Even in the mill of activity, heads turned toward them. Magiere kept her back straight and her pace even.

Newcomers would be common in a port town. However, only one or two other people openly carried any weapon, and she now wished she'd stowed her falchion in the cart. Hopefully, there would be no need of it here.

The scent of fresh bread caught her attention, and her gaze wandered about until she spotted the aroma's origin. She walked up to a table in front of a small cottage. Through one shutterless window she saw the clay ovens and realized it was an actual bakery.

'A loaf of black forest and a loaf of rye,' she said to a balding, plump man in an apron.

The man hesitated, and Magiere felt immediately conscious of the way she must look, armored and armed. There was an awkward silence.

'Do you have any sweet rolls?' Leesil grinned at the baker, stepping up to the table and examining everything. 'I'm hungry enough to clean you out.'

The man's eyes widened a bit at Leesil's high eyebrows and blunt-point ears peeking through sliver-yellow hair, but Leesil's smile inevitably proved infectious. He could come across as the most carefree, harmless creature. Magiere knew better. She also knew when not to disturb Leesil's influence on people.

'I have some cream pastries inside,' the man suggested.

'Cream pastries?' Leesil let out an ecstatic gasp. 'Fetch me three before I drop right here at your feet!'

The baker both scowled and smiled at Leesil's dramatics and disappeared through the bakery door with a throaty chuckle.

'You'd be lost without me,' Leesil whispered to his partner, clearly pleased with himself.

'You just keep on believing that,' Magiere muttered, but she was secretly relieved.

Upon the baker's return, Leesil fussed sufficiently over the pastries and then tossed one to Chap, who swallowed it whole with hardly a snap of his jaws. When the baker's face went flat with indignant shock, Leesil realized his mistake and covered it with a politely dismissive manner.

'Oh, he's one of the family. Loves cream, and' – Leesil gave the baker a quick conspiratorial wink – 'I only give him the best. Say, do you know where we could find Constable Ellinwood, the town bailiff?'

'Constable Ellinwood?' the man asked, wiping his hands on his apron with an expression of worry. 'Is there trouble?'

'Trouble?' Leesil pitched his voice to sound surprised. 'No, we've purchased a tavern here in town, down near the docks. We just need to present the deed and find our property.'

'A tavern . . . by the docks? Oh, you bought the old Dunction place. Why didn't you say so?' The plump baker called out to a clean-faced boy chopping wood at the bakery's far corner. 'Geoffry, run and fetch the constable. He'll be eating his midday meal with Martha about now. Tell him the folks who bought the Dunction place are here.' Then he turned back to Leesil. 'Come, come,' he motioned with one thick hand. 'I'm Karlin. I've some tables around the side, so you can sit and finish your pastries. The constable will be right along.'

Feeling simultaneously embarrassed and relieved at how well Leesil was managing, Magiere followed along silently. She would rather have gone to find the tavern herself and looked it over in private before tending to formalities, but things were proceeding smoothly enough. And she found herself hungrier than expected when faced with fresh bread – and something more comfortable to sit on than dirt. Moments later, she sat with Leesil, tearing off hunks of rye bread to dip in a bowl of honey the baker had brought, and waiting for the proper authorities to come directly to her. Apprehension faded just a little, now that they were out of the main street and away from so many curious eyes.

'I don't think this town sees many strangers come in by the road,' she commented.

Leesil nodded. 'You should have stowed that falchion.'

Magiere glared back at him but said nothing. He was probably armed to the teeth with his little knives, which were easier to conceal in his clothing.

Despite her nervousness, Magiere did like the look of constant business around her. These people seemed to live with more purpose than guarding against their own superstitions. They had affairs to tend to, with family and friends around them who didn't watch each other with a suspicious eye, waiting for some curse to pop up from their own imaginations. She might not get to know any of them, but they would be her customers, and she was determined not to despise them.

That determination wavered when young Geoffry, the baker's son, came running back, followed by a behemoth of a man, who strode among the townspeople as if each was his personal servant. At the sight of him, distaste settled in Magiere's stomach. She put down the pinch of bread she was about to dip in the honey. She'd seen his kind before.

Dressed in a purple brocade tunic and forest-green sash, he'd garnished his matching purple cap with a white feather. Although his attire must have cost what Magiere earned in three village jobs, the sash only accented the size of his protruding belly rather than helping him appear distinguished. He looked like a grape ripened too long on the vine. His face was filled with the overly forced sternness common to those who took their position – but not their duties – too seriously. This would be Constable Ellinwood.

Karlin the baker respectfully ushered the constable to her table, and Magiere's distaste grew. Constable Ellinwood possessed a dour, fleshy countenance, and small, piglike eyes that suggested he thought daily free tankards of ale and fleecing the townsfolk at every opportunity were his rightful due. She doubted he had bought that expensive double-felt tunic with his own wages, from what Magiere knew of the pay for such positions.

Inwardly, she realized the hypocrisy of her contempt. But although she and Leesil had probably done worse in their time, at least they struck a village once and moved on immediately. They didn't remain to drain the townspeople like some bloated leech.

Karlin, on the other hand, seemed pleased with the constable's presence and began introductions.

'These are the folks,' Karlin said, and Magiere noticed how the baker's skin glowed with health next to the pasty rolls of Ellinwood's flesh.

'You bought the Dunction place?' Ellinwood asked Leesil, repeating what he'd been told.

'I don't know who owned it previously,' Magiere interrupted. 'But I have a deed for a tavern near the docks.' She unfolded a worn sheet of paper.

Leesil leaned back quietly, comfortable enough with the change of roles now that he was stuffing himself and washing mouthfuls down with an occasional sip from his wine sack. Turning his attention to Magiere, Constable Ellinwood's fingers reached down to grip the deed, exposing two heavy, etched-gold rings on his fingers.

'I'll show you where the place is,' he said, after a cursory read, 'but I can't stay to get you settled.' Even his voice sounded thick and sluggish to Magiere. He puffed up importantly. 'One of the local girls was found dead this morning, and I'm beginning an investigation.'

'Who?' Karlin gasped.

'Young Eliza, Brenden's sister. Found in her own yard.'

'Oh no, not another . . .' Karlin trailed off as he glanced toward Leesil and Magiere.

'Not another what?' Magiere asked, looking not at Karlin but at the constable.

'Nothing to concern yourself about,' Ellinwood said, puffing up even more. 'Now, if you want to see the tavern, follow me.'

Magiere withheld any further comment. If Ellinwood really considered the dead girl none of their business, he wouldn't have announced it so blatantly. And Karlin knew the victim, though that was not a great surprise. Miiska was a healthy-size town, but not so big that most people wouldn't know each other, at least casually. Magiere's mild distaste for the constable turned to revulsion.

Down near the docks, the ocean scent blew stronger, filling Magiere's lungs with salt-laden comfort. The view of the ocean's horizon with its thin trailing clouds was breathtaking. A small, treed peninsula shot out south of the town, and to the north the shoreline hooked seaward briefly before heading up the coast. The dark blue of the water in the small bay told her the drop-off was steep and a perfect place for a small port town to crop up, offering commerce and a safe stopover for barges and smaller ships traversing the coastline.

The tavern, on the other hand, was not all she had hoped. When they passed down to the far end of town, they found a small two-story building tucked back against a few trees toward the base of the short peninsula.

Dingy, weatherworn, and possibly in need of a new roof, the sight made Magiere hesitant to step inside. The outer walls looked old and hadn't been re-stained in years, turning mottled brown and gray from years of weather wear in salt air. At least the shutters were still intact. One of them banged softly against a window in the light breeze. Leesil stepped forward and touched the wood next to the entrance.

'It's quite solid,' he said excitedly. 'Wonderful. A bit of stain, a few shingles . . .'

'What did the previous owner call it?' Magiere asked Ellinwood.

'I don't think he ever gave it a name. Folks just called it Dunction's.'

'Why did he sell it?'

The constable puckered his lips. 'Sell it? He didn't sell it. He just ran off and left it one night when no one was watching. I suppose he didn't own it outright, because I received formal notice from a bank in Bela that they'd reassumed possession. It was all in order.'

'The owner ran off?' Magiere asked. 'Was business that bad?'

'No, this place was filled to the brim every night. The dockworkers and bargemen have missed it fierce. So have I, to be honest.' He rapped his knuckles once on the door before opening it. 'Caleb?' he called. 'You home? New owners are here.'

Ellinwood didn't wait for an answer and opened the door to step inside, waving Magiere and Leesil after him. Chap slipped in last before the door could shut. With pleasant surprise, Magiere found the inside much better cared for than the outside. The wood floor was swept and clean, if a little worn. To the right in the main area, respectable-looking tables were positioned to fit as many as possible, with room enough for the passage of serving staff handing out tankards and bottles. A huge stone fireplace, large enough to crouch in, dominated the end of the room beyond the tables, offering warmth and a welcome.

The bar on the left was long and made of stout oak turned dark and shiny from years of polishing and the oil of patrons' hands as they leaned their way through the evenings. Behind its far end was a curtained doorway that probably led to the household kitchen or stockroom, and beside it was a stairway leading up to the second floor where the living quarters would be.

Overall, the inside was far better than Magiere had hoped. As little as she had paid for it, she'd wondered some nights what she could expect sight unseen. And for some reason she couldn't explain, the hearth was more important to her than anything else. It was sound and looked strong.

'This is perfect,' Leesil said, as if he didn't quite believe it. He moved past her, turning around in amazement, running his slim hand over a table as he walked through the room right up to the hearth Magiere was still eyeing. 'I'll set up the faro game by the front window nearest the fire. We might have to sacrifice a table or two to make room.'

She suddenly noted he had not directed one word or acknowledgment in Ellinwood's direction.

Hearing footsteps, she turned toward the staircase. Descending slowly were an old, stooped man, an old woman, and a little blond girl about five or six years old.

'Oh, there you are, Caleb,' Ellinwood said, rubbing his hands, apparently deciding his business here was finished. 'These are the new owners. I must get back to work.'

He bid Magiere a good day, ignored Leesil, and left.

Uncertain of exactly what was going on, Magiere turned back to the old couple and child. The old man was half a head taller than her, with straight ashen hair pulled back at his neck. His face was wrinkled but smooth of expression, his eyes dark brown and steady. He wore a plain muslin shirt that matched his wife's tan skirt, both clean as the well-swept floor. The old woman was tiny as a sparrow, her hair pulled up in a neat bun.

'We're the caretakers,' Caleb said upon seeing Magiere's bewilderment. 'This is my wife, Beth-rae, and my granddaughter, Rose.'

Chap trotted over to the old lady, who pulled the little girl out of the way. The dog's ears popped up straight as he looked at tiny Rose, his nose reaching out little by little, sniffing, until the child held out a tentative hand.

As a rule, Chap didn't like being petted by anyone but Leesil, and Magiere tensed, ready to reach out and jerk the dog back by the scruff if he growled. But Chap licked at the small fingers and the child giggled as his tail began to switch. Magiere experienced a wave of instant good will toward these three that washed away the bad taste Ellinwood had left.

'Oh, look, Caleb.' Beth-rae brushed back a loose strand of gray hair. 'They have a dog. Isn't he beautiful?' She leaned down and scratched Chap gently behind the ear. Chap whined with pleasure and pushed his great head into her side.

'He's a dear thing, but fierce, too. I can tell,' Beth-rae said. 'It will be good to have him standing guard.'

Little Rose thumped both her hands across Chap's back and laughed.

'His name's Chap,' Leesil said, also puzzled by the dog's unusual friendliness with strangers.

'Come to the kitchen, Chap,' Beth-rae said. 'We'll find you some cold mutton. But don't get too accustomed. It's fish for us most days.'

As Beth-rae and Rose and Chap left the room, Magiere again looked at Caleb as if to question his presence.

'We're the caretakers,' he repeated, meeting her gaze. 'When Master Dunction disappeared, the constable commissioned the bank in Bela to keep us on until the place could be sold.'

While wondering about Caleb's use of the term 'disappeared,' Magiere turned her attention to a new dilemma.

'Do all three of you live here?'

Leesil came over to join her. 'Of course, they live here. Who do you think has been keeping the place up?'

Magiere crossed her arms, shifting from one foot to the other. Taking on a tavern was one thing; supporting a family of three she'd just met was another. Leesil must have read the expression on her face, for he cut in before she could speak.

'We're going to need help anyway,' he said. 'If you're running the bar and I'm running the games, who's going to serve and cook and keep the place up?'

He had a point. Magiere hadn't given much thought to food, but most patrons coming in for ale would probably want to eat as well.

'What did Dunction serve?' she asked Caleb.

'Simple fare. When the place was still open, Beth-rae baked bread all morning, then cooked different types of stew or fish chowder. She's good with herbs and spices.' He paused. 'Come upstairs, and I'll show you the living quarters.'

Although his tone remained casual, Magiere sensed a cautious tension in the old caretaker, as if there was more going on here than he indicated.

'How long have you been here?' she asked, following him up the staircase.

'Nine years,' he answered. 'Rose has been with us since my daughter . . . left us.'

'Left you?' Leesil asked. Then he muttered under his breath, 'Seems like people keep leaving this place.'

Caleb didn't respond. Magiere held her tongue as well. The old man's affairs were none of her business.

The upper floor was as well tended as the lower. The

top of the stairs emptied into the center of a short, narrow hallway. First Caleb showed her a large bedroom at the left end of the hall, somewhere above the common room downstairs, and proclaimed it to be hers. There was another room for Leesil at the midpoint of the hall, just across from the stairs, and a third small room at the right end of the hall. The last had likely been used for storage or other purposes. There was a sagging bed tucked into the corner, two pillows at its head, and a little mat on the floor.

'This is where we stay, Miss,' Caleb said. 'We don't take up much space.'

For the second time that day, Magiere sighed in resignation. Leesil was right; they couldn't manage everything by themselves. Besides, she had no idea how to make spiced fish chowder and no time for tasks like cleaning the hearth if she was to learn how to run this place.

'What arrangement did you have with the bank?' she asked.

'Arrangement?' Caleb's brows gathered.

'What does the bank pay you?'

'Pay us? We've just been living here, tending the place, and were careful not to use up all the stores before the new owner arrived.'

Magiere didn't know whom she despised more at that moment, the very poor or the very rich. The bank was able to arrange free caretakers, taking advantage of two people suddenly left without an employer.

'All right,' she said to Caleb. 'You two work for me, and I'll pay you a twentieth share of the house's profits, plus room and board.' She pushed past Leesil down the hall and away from the small room. She stopped at the top of the stairs and looked back at them. 'And I don't need that big bedroom. We'll switch places later this afternoon.'

Leesil stared at her, then looked at Caleb and shrugged. A flicker, just a hint, of astonishment passed across Caleb's face, but he nodded as if such an offer was commonplace.

'That will be just fine,' he said calmly. He moved down the hall past her and went quietly back downstairs, no doubt to inform his spouse of the changes to come.

Magiere stepped into the doorway of what would be Leesil's room and leaned against the jamb. Leesil strolled over to stand in the doorway next to her, pretending to examine the near-empty space. There was nothing to look at except the bed and an open-shuttered window in the far wall that looked out toward the ocean, its view only slightly obscured by the branches of a nearby fir tree. Magiere willed him to be silent.

'How uncharacteristic,' he finally said.

'If you disagreed, you should have spoken up.'

'I don't disagree.'

Neither spoke for a short while. Between the two of them, they'd likely starved out entire villages for the price of her services. Magiere finally said, 'I want a new life.'

Leesil looked at her out of the corner of his eye, loose hair exposing his ears. He nodded and smiled.

'I suppose it's a start.'

By sundown that night, Magiere's personal appearance and her world had altered considerably. Beth-rae arranged for a long, hot bath in the kitchen so she could scrub every bit of mud from her hair and skin. While she bathed, her clothing miraculously disappeared and was replaced by a muslin dressing gown. Still planning too many activities that night to remain in what she considered nearly nightclothes, Magiere went back upstairs into her small room. What was once a mere closet for three would do well enough for one.

Furnishings had been moved from one room to another, and all the comforts of a home surrounded her. Where there was once a bed barely large enough for two now stood a bed for one with a plain-posted canopy of faded curtains dyed a deep sea green. It seemed the previous owner had either been single or slept alone. Someone had entered while she bathed and placed a thick down comforter on the bed. And on top of that lay her pack and knife and the sheathed falchion.

Heat from the kitchen fire traveled up the stone chimney in the corner and helped warm the room, though her bare feet still felt a little chill on the wood floor. A wardrobe of dark wood stood against the wall across from the bed. Replacing Rose's mat was now a small table with one chair and two stout, white candles that flickered throughout the dark room. She opened her pack to empty its contents on the bed.

From the bottom of the pack, she pulled a canvas-wrapped bundle. Tied with twine, the rough material had sharply creased after years of storage in its place. It had been so long since she'd opened it that Magiere was forced to cut the twine with her knife, as the knot would not uncinch. Inside was a dark blue brocade dress with black laces on the bodice. Aunt Bieja had given it to her years ago.

Magiere put it on quickly, fumbling a bit with the laces before tying them securely. She absently fingered the metal chain of her bone-and-tin amulet, then dropped it to let it rest between her breasts near the topaz stone. Meaningless trinkets that merely added to her persona as the hunter, she had no idea why she kept them on now, but it seemed too odd to take them off after so many years.

There was no mirror in which to view herself, but when she looked down at the drape of the skirt, it felt odd and alien not to see her own breeched legs or booted feet. She felt a sudden urge to pull the dress off, but with her everyday clothes missing and having limited other clothing in her pack, there was little else to wear at the moment. She turned instead to putting away her things.

Her worn blanket and teapot and few spare undergarments made the wardrobe look barer than before she'd placed anything in it. The small size of the room was actually a relief, since she had so few personal belongings with which to fill it.

'By all the dead deities,' came Leesil's voice from behind her. She quickly spun about. 'What did you do to yourself?'

Bathed as well, he stood with a hand on the open door latch, wearing a dressing gown similar to the one she'd just taken off. His wet, shoulder-length hair, pulled back over his ears, looked like beach sand in the low light, but he still looked himself. He stared at her as if she were some stranger who'd sneaked in unannounced.

Magiere felt acutely aware of her own appearance, the tightly laced gown and how her black hair hung loose to her shoulder blades. She suddenly wished she'd left on the oversize dressing gown.

'Beth-rae took my clothes to wash,' Magiere snarled at him. 'And you might take care. She'll probably burn yours, by the state they were in.'

'Where did you buy that?' he asked, stepping into the room.

She noticed that when they were both in their bare feet, he was perhaps a little taller than her.

'Don't you knock, or has sleeping on the ground rubbed out all your manners?' she replied. 'And I didn't buy it. My aunt gave it to me a long time ago.'

That comment halted his line of questioning immediately. Talking about their pasts was something they both made a point of avoiding.

'Where's Chap?' she asked.

'In the kitchen.' Leesil rolled his eyes. 'He's fallen in love with Beth-rae. Every time I see them, she's feeding him something. That's got to stop. What good is a fat guard dog?'

He still eyed Magiere up and down, and it was starting to irritate her even more.

'We'll search the place tomorrow, take a look at the cellar or whatever passes for storage, and get an inventory. If there are enough ale casks down there, we might be able to open for business tomorrow evening. If you need anything else for the games, let me know.' She picked up the falchion and turned to place it inside the corner of the wardrobe while Leesil plopped down in the chair, watching her. 'In the afternoon; we'll go back to the market, and maybe the docks to see what's in the warehouses that we might want or need. There's not much money to spend, but it'll get us by until business builds up.'

A shift of shadows outside the doorway caught Magiere's attention from the corner of her eye, and instinctively she knew it wasn't Caleb or Beth-rae. Leesil turned as well, staring at the door he'd left open, and a stiletto appeared in his hand.

Magiere didn't stop to ponder where he'd hidden that in his dressing gown. She slipped the sheath of her falchion, letting it drop to the floor.

There was no light near the door, and even the candles didn't show who was there. A deep voice came into the room, gentle, even soothing.

'Don't be alarmed.'

Darkness seemed to follow the figure as he stepped forward into the doorway, then the shadows drained away, or perhaps he'd just shifted forward into the reach of the candles' light.

'How did you get up here?' she demanded, wondering why Chap hadn't alerted them to an intruder.

The man was about forty years old, of medium height and build. His peppered-brown hair lay carefully combed back. Perfect white patches at both temples framed even features that were striking rather than handsome. There was a slight widening bump at the bridge of his nose. His clothes were hidden beneath a floor-length, mahogany cloak. Only the rounded points of well-made boots were visible. He did not appear to be armed, but there was no way to tell what might be hidden beneath that cloak. His hands were clasped in front of his chest, and she noticed the top half of the little finger on his left hand was missing.

'Answer up!' Leesil snapped. He was now on his feet and had somehow produced a second blade in his other hand.

The man stared for a moment at Magiere's falchion, as if studying it, then he looked her over with as much concentration. His eyes stopped to rest on her amulets. She wanted him to stop looking at her and quickly tucked the amulets inside the dress, out of sight. While shoving them beneath her bodice, she noticed the topaz stone seemed brighter than normal, but she turned her attention back to the stranger. He gave no notice at all to Leesil.

'My name is Welstiel Massing. But you're the one, aren't you? The one who kills vampires?'

Magiere couldn't think of a response. The man spoke so blatantly, without any pretense, as if it was a common thing to ask a stranger.

'We don't know what you're babbling about,' Leesil answered. 'But we aren't open to customers yet. I suggest you come back tomorrow.'

Again this Welstiel Massing acted as if no one had spoken, his attention centered on Magiere.

'You are not what I expected, but you're the one.'

'I don't do that anymore,' Magiere answered.

Something about this stranger frightened her — as much as anything ever frightened her. She wanted nothing to do with any aspect of her own past, and his presence disturbed the recently gained balance of her new life.

'I doubt you can avoid it here,' Welstiel said. 'I just came to warn you.'

'Get out,' she said coldly, losing her patience, 'or I'll throw you out.'

Welstiel backed up, not in fear, but as if he were a creature with impeccable manners. 'Forgive me. I simply thought to warn you.'

'Well, now, you have,' Leesil spoke up, 'and I'll show you the front door.' He moved forward.

For a moment it appeared this night visitor was not going to move. Then his eyes rolled casually toward Leesil. He turned and headed down the hallway as if leaving was his own idea.

Both Leesil and Magiere were caught in their own surprise for a moment, and then Leesil bolted out the door to 'escort' Welstiel Massing down the stairs. Magiere followed in time to see her partner standing at the top of the stairs, wide-eyed. She heard the tavern's door downstairs close. Leesil looked back at Magiere with an expression on his face as if he'd come in on the tail end of a bizarre conversation that he couldn't quite figure out.

'He's rather quick for an older man,' Leesil said quietly, then added, 'I'll be back.' And he scrambled down the stairs out of sight.

Magiere returned to her room and sank down onto her bed. Whatever this visitor had come for, she would not be dragged back into the old game – not for money, not for anything.

Leesil appeared again in the doorway. 'Chap, Caleb, and Beth-rae are all asleep in the kitchen. I told you she was feeding him too much.'

'I'll speak with her in the morning.' Magiere nodded, glad to focus on tasks at hand again, anything to distract her. 'But wasn't the front door locked?'

'I'm not sure. I just assumed so. Caleb and Beth-rae

don't seem the types to leave the place wide open.' He was about to leave again, but stopped, turning to Magiere with serious intent on his face. 'Don't let that lunatic bother you. We'll keep him out of the tavern. We don't have to do business with anyone we don't want to.'

Magiere laid her falchion back down, watching candlelight reflect off the shining blade.

'That's not necessary. I think he's harmless, but he's out on his ear if he starts talking about vampires again.'

'How do these people find us?'

She looked at him with a little annoyance. They'd spent years spreading every possible rumor across the countryside about her, just so people *could* find her.

'Yes, right,' Leesil added. 'Stupid question.'

She shook her head. 'We'll try to open for business as soon as possible.'

'Have you come up with a name?'

'I thought you'd do that when you painted the sign.'

'How about "The Blood Pie Inn"?'

'You're not funny.'

He laughed and stepped out, closing the door behind himself.

6

Two evenings later, a somewhat refurbished tavern named 'The Sea Lion' opened shortly before dusk. Leesil had never lived close to the ocean before, and watching a herd of sea lions swim along the cresting waves heading north had sparked inspiration for a name that suggested location and strength. At first he hadn't even known what to call the creatures he saw, until he asked one of the sailors down at the docks. Magiere knew she possessed little imagination with words, but Leesil usually expressed enough words and imagination for both of them

Most of their patrons were sailors far from home, or unmarried dockworkers. A few young couples showed up as well. There were also two middle-aged women shopkeepers claiming to love Beth-rae's fish chowder, who came trundling in behind the main crowd. After eating, the pair took eager interest in the new attraction of Leesil's faro table and sat chatting comfortably with the nearby sailors as Leesil flipped the cards.

Ironically, the old caretakers, especially Beth-rae, seemed like gifts from the heavens. Before arriving in Miiska, Magiere had never really given thought to serving food, but now realized her shortsightedness. Everyone who sat about talking and drinking and playing cards ordered something to eat, sooner or later. They came for the food almost as much as the ale. One pair of dark-skinned dockworkers even ordered spiced tea. Magiere discovered she didn't have any such thing in stock, but when she told the two men, they looked at her as if a house special they'd ordered for years had suddenly disappeared from their favorite place. She ran upstairs and blended something from her leftover travel rations, then handed it off to Beth-rae to brew as an 'on-the-house' replacement until she could purchase the proper blend. Other than this one free offering, the money was coming in. It was not a fortune, and it might take weeks or more to make as much as she and Leesil had taken from a village or two, but it was certainly a more comfortable way to make a living. Caleb had helped establish the price of served goods, based on what the previous owner had charged, and that was as good a place to start as any.

Magiere returned to her favored post behind the bar and watched as Caleb served out drinks and delivered orders of delectables from Beth-rae's kitchen. She leaned back against an ale keg on the rear counter and relaxed just a little, feeling clean and comfortable. Beth-rae had washed out her old black breeches the night before, and Magiere wore them now, along with a loose white shirt and unbuttoned russet vest she'd picked up at the open market. She wore her amulets tucked inside the shirt, as was her custom. In spite of the many life changes of late, the dress Aunt Bieja had given her simply didn't feel right, so she'd decided to stick with habit in her attire.

She looked around the room in satisfaction. Every-thing appeared almost exactly as she had imagined. Chap sat by the fire, his usual attentive self, watching for trouble. Leesil laughed and joked while dealing cards, taking bets, and managing his trick of putting everyone at ease with his lighthearted nature. She hadn't seen him drunk in three days, although he looked haggard in the mornings, his eyes more bloodshot than usual, as if he'd needed the wine to get to sleep all those years. She'd slept beside him on the open ground enough times to know about his difficulties with nightmares. The few times they'd run out of wine between towns she'd woken in the night to hear him mumbling and thrashing, sometimes shouting unintelligibly, in his sleep. She never mentioned it to him.

Little Rose sat near the fire behind Chap, who occasionally checked on her while she drew with charcoal on some faded parchment Leesil had bought for her.

Every time the door opened, Magiere couldn't help anxiously glancing over to see if it might be the intrusive visitor, Welstiel, from their first night here. As the evening wore on with no sign of him, she stopped eyeing every person who walked through the door and relaxed just a little more. If this was the first of many such nights to come, she might actually find the peace she'd imagined.

She did not hear the door open, but rather felt the wind and heard Leesil call out a ritual welcome. When she turned from an ale barrel, her first glance told her something was out of place.

He wasn't a merchant, not like those she'd seen in town. Nor was he a dockworker or bargeman, though his build would have made such work no strain at all. A sailor or even captain was out of the question, for his skin was so pale it hadn't seen a full day's sun in a long while. He stood across from her on the other side of the bar, unusually tall with a heavy bone structure and cropped black hair. A well-tailored burgundy tunic did little to hide the tight muscles in his arms. His eyes caught and held hers. Clear blue, almost transparent, they reminded her of Chap's. He bore himself like a noble, but if that were true, what was he doing here in a dock-side tavern?

A low rumbling sound took a moment to register in Magiere's awareness beneath the din in the room. It pulled her attention mostly because she wasn't sure why she could hear it at all amidst the chatter of the patrons. But it was familiar in an unsettling way. Her eyes shifted toward its source.

Chap was on his feet in front of the hearth, lips quivering just short of a snarl. He was growling.

Her gaze clicked back to the man in front of her, then back to the dog – and little Rose, who sat round-eyed in surprise behind the hound. Chap had not reacted once all evening to any other patron.

'Quiet, Chap,' Magiere snapped loud enough for the dog to hear.

He stopped growling but remained rigid, even when Rose began pulling on his tail.

Magiere turned her full attention back to the nobleman. 'What can I get for you?'

'Red wine.' His voice was hollow and deep.

This new habit of forming rapid impressions of people was beginning to bother Magiere. Ever since she'd come to Miiska, certain inhabitants had caused her to reach quick assessments, or perhaps she'd never before spent so much time around so many people. She distinctly experienced immediate dislike for Constable Ellinwood, an uncharacteristic goodwill toward Caleb and Beth-rae, an unexplainable fear of Welstiel, and now a new emotion created by this nobleman – caution.

She poured wine from a cask into a tin goblet, then set it on the bar. The man held out three copper coins. He knew the price and so had been here before under the previous owner. For some reason, she wanted him to lay the coins on the bar rather than take them from his hand. Nonetheless she reached out and snatched the coins. The nobleman didn't touch his wine. His gaze remained on her face, as if he were memorizing each feature.

'A fine place,' he said. 'Nothing like the taverns in Bela, but very comfortable for Miiska. I have some friends I'd like to bring sometime.'

'Any good patron is always welcome,' she answered politely with a courteous nod.

He nodded in return without smiling, and then his expression grew even colder. 'You're the one, aren't you?' he said. 'The one who hunts Noble Dead?'

The buzz of laughter and chatter all around her grew faint as a dull throb pounded in her ears. She couldn't help letting her gaze slip quickly around the room to see if anyone had heard. Noble Dead – she'd never heard that expression, but his meaning seemed clear.

'I don't do that anymore.'

'You are a killer,' he said quietly. 'I have seen one or two true killers before. They never stop. They can't.'

'There's faro in the corner, if you care to play cards, or find a table and order some food. I have customers to attend.'

Magiere turned back to the wine casks, wanting to dismiss him and yet suddenly nervous about exposing her back. She heard Chap's growl again, but when she looked back this time, the nobleman was gone. Chap was no longer by the hearth but sniffing at the closed tavern door, his lip still curling just short of a snarl. She let out a slow exhale.

'Come away from there,' she called, to the dog.

Chap didn't move, watching the door until little Rose came between the tables to drag him back to the fire as if he were a giant wooden pull-toy. The dog reluctantly followed her.

Magiere enjoyed no more of the pleasant sounds around her that night and continued drawing ale with numb hands until the last guest left. She had suspected this might happen eventually. It was always a possibility that someone who knew of her previous life would stumble across her. She simply hadn't expected it to be so soon – and twice within the first week, so perhaps the gossip was already spreading. And both occurrences seemed less a query or recognition than a challenge for denial.

'What a night,' Leesil said, still looking down at the cloth-covered faro table with the thirteen ranks of spades laid out. Copper coins, and one silver, were piled highest on queens, tens, and threes for some reason.

Magiere pulled out of her own thoughts. 'How'd we do?'

'Fine,' he answered. 'A little less than a fourth above the starting pot, but I was gentle with them. We'll make enough on food and drink, so best not to scare them off by emptying their pockets too quickly.'

Surprise at his clarity of thought almost cut away her black mood, but not quite.

What had that nobleman wanted? She had never seen him before, and yet he'd seemed to recognize her on sight. He'd done no searching of the room when he entered but came directly to her. Then again, perhaps others in town were talking about her. She tended to stand out some, and there certainly weren't any other armed women strolling through town on their first day with a half-elf and oversized dog in tow. But what was going on? And an unexplained death the night before her arrival didn't help matters. It was too close to the pattern of the game she and Leesil had played for years.

'So . . . Magiere?' Leesil said, sounding a little annoyed for being ignored. 'What's your problem? Been sampling the casks too much tonight?'

The large empty room suddenly felt more enclosed than when filled with people. She thought of the dead girl Ellinwood mentioned and Karlin's reaction. Had there been other murders in this small coastal town?

'Caleb,' she asked, 'who is Brenden?'

The old man was wiping out tankards and hesitated as though wondering about her question.

'The blacksmith,' he answered simply. 'His shop's near the market at the north end of town, on the shore side.'

'I need some air,' Magiere said, grabbing her falchion from under the bar and strapping it on, not caring what anyone thought, including Leesil. 'Can you clean up by yourselves?'

Her partner blinked. 'Do you want company?'

'No.'

She practically fled the tavern, sucking in cool gulps

of salt air after closing the front door behind herself. All around, Miiska lay sleeping, but in a few hours some of the fishermen would rise well before dawn to prepare their nets and lines. Not allowing herself to think, Magiere walked down rows of cottages, houses, and shops without really seeing anything. She took no notice of the very few street torches and lanterns still burning or the stragglers stumbling from another tavern or inn as it finally closed well past midnight. She just wanted to clear her head of all the plaguing thoughts running through her mind.

Scents began to register in her smothered thoughts – horse dung, charcoal, and soot. The blacksmith's shop and stables. Magiere stopped in the middle of the street, uncertain and wavering between directions.

Ellinwood had said the murdered girl, Eliza, was the sister of someone named Brenden. Brenden the blacksmith.

It seemed no one in this town said anything straight out, but there had been more than one mention of citizens disappearing. Karlin the baker had been more than startled by the announced death; he'd tried to keep himself from blurting out something about others. And now at least two people knew exactly what her past profession had been, or thought they knew.

Magiere hadn't even realized she was walking again until she reached the end of the street and heard horses stirring in the stables. Around the bend was the smith's work area and behind that a long, chest-high stack of cut wood against a fence. Just beyond she could see a small cottage out back. A thin trail of smoke curled up from its pot chimney in the moonlight.

She slipped quietly around the far end of the fence, careful to check that the front door was closed, and she saw no sign of anyone awake inside. There was only one curtained window to duck under on the cottage side facing the trees. She stepped around back.

There was something of a back porch and a failing flower garden to one side. Another garden patch, likely for vegetables, was farther back behind the stables. A second woodpile lined the cottage side of the fence. It wouldn't look good to be caught prowling on her first week in her new hometown, so she kept a watch on the back door as she looked about. Of course, the body was long gone, but there might be other telltale signs left behind.

A dark patch on the woodpile caught her attention. At first she thought it was just a space between the cut and split logs, but as she moved closer she could see it was not a hollow. Some of the ends of the stacked firewood were stained darker than the others. In two places, it appeared the dark fluid had dripped and run down. She knelt near the base of the stack.

Earth near a shore was usually damp, but looking carefully now she realized that the coastal earth she had seen while traveling was light colored, close to the gravely sand of the shore itself. On the ground here she found more dark spots, like the stains on the wood. One large one was surrounded by others, smaller and smeared. The ground was a mess of footsteps, likely from Ellinwood and his so-called guards. Beyond that, she could find no other signs of chase or struggle.

She ran her fingertips through one dark patch. Though mostly dried to the semi-damp state of the shore earth, some did stick to her fingertips. She lifted it to her nose, then tasted it lightly with her tongue.

Blood.

Magiere closed her eyes and then opened them quickly as the backs of her lids conjured up images of what the killer may have done to his or her victim to spill so much blood. Yet it was all in one place, as if the girl had not been able to run, struggle, or fight for her life.

'I thought you no longer concerned yourself with such, *dhampir*?' a voice said from behind her.

She whirled around to her feet in one motion, gripping her sword. At first she could see nothing, and then she spotted a waver of shadow beneath a tree on the yard's seaward side.

Welstiel stood there, dressed exactly as before in his long, wool cape. He stepped out from the trees to the edge of the yard, and moonlight glinted off the white patches near his temples. She found herself glancing at his hands, and although she couldn't quite make them out, she remembered the missing end of his finger and wondered how he had lost it.

'Are you following me?' she asked angrily.

'Yes,' he answered.

That silenced her for a moment. When confronted with that question, most people denied it.

'Why?' she finally asked.

'Because this town is plagued by Noble Dead,' he said, 'who survive by feeding upon the living. This girl is not the first, and you know that. And no one in Miiska can stop them but you.'

'And how would you have any idea what I know?'

Her words were more a retort than a question she expected to be answered. And no answer came. Magiere's stomach knotted sharply with pain from anger and anxiety.

'What does that mean?' she asked. 'Noble Dead?'

'The highest order of the dead, or rather, undead,' he answered. 'The Noble Dead possess the full presence of self they had in life, their unique essence, so to speak. Vampires are but one type, as well as liches, the more powerful wraiths, and the occasional High Revenant. They are aware of themselves, their own desires, intents and thoughts, and can learn and grow through their immortal existence, unlike the lower-ranking undead, such as ghosts, animated corpses, and the like.'

'You are no foolish peasant,' she said softly. 'How can you believe such things? There are no vampires.' She turned back to stare at the stained earth and woodpile. 'We have enough monsters of our own kind.'

'Yes,' he said quietly. 'Of our own kind.'

She heard him step toward her into the yard, but did not look back at him.

'Undeads who drain life do exist,' he said. 'And they have made this place, this town, their own. Such creatures may be more . . . exclusive . . . than most peasants believe, but they exist just the same. You know all this. You are a hunter.'

'Not anymore.'

'You won't be able to avoid such tasks here.'

'Really?' She turned on him, eyes narrow with anger. 'Just watch how well I avoid this, old man.'

He wasn't quite that old, but he acted like some superstitious village elder. She thought of their first meeting and another question came to her mind, something he'd said tonight.

'What did you call me . . . *dhampir*?'

'It is nothing.' He turned to leave. 'An ancient and little-known word in my homeland for one specially gifted and born to hunt the undead.'

She did not stop his departure. She watched him fade between the trees, heading toward the shore.

In spite of his possible intent to rattle her, his wild statements made her feel better, not worse. A few nights ago, she feared he wanted something from her that she was unwilling to give, but now he seemed like just another superstitious fool, albeit a well-dressed one. Yes, there was a murderer loose in town, a sick and twisted one at that, but Ellinwood and his cronies were paid to deal with such things. She was a barkeep now, not a hunter, even if a few townsfolk had heard about her past. In a year, maybe two, that reputation would wash away with the tide until she was only Magiere, owner of The Sea Lion tavern.

She wiped her fingers off in the sandy soil, then brushed off the dirt against the thigh of her breeches, feeling her breathing slow and the tightness in her stomach relax. She walked away from the backyard, the woodpile, and the stains on the ground without looking back

Only a handful of steps down the street, she spotted Caleb walking toward her.

'What are you doing out here?' she asked in confusion.

'Streets at night aren't always safe. I came to find you.'

'I can guard myself well enough.'

But his concern touched her a little, especially since

he appeared so tired. The last few days of stocking and preparing to open had not been easy for him, not to mention waiting on tables half of tonight. She was about to start for the tavern again, waving him on, but Caleb was staring back toward the stables and the smith's cottage.

'Why was Master Welstiel here?' he asked.

Magiere turned her head stiffly toward Caleb.

'You know him?'

Caleb shrugged. 'He is new to Miiska, but he came to the tavern often when Dunction was owner. The two of them enjoyed each other's company, and Master Welstiel was always welcome.'

Perhaps this new detail explained Welstiel. If he was very fond of the previous tavern owner, he might be concerned about finding answers, even after such a while. And he might well have heard some idle rumor about her past, if others were talking about her – like that pale nobleman in the tavern earlier in the evening.

He might also just be guessing about what he thought she knew of events in Miiska.

Any one thing by itself was easy enough to dismiss. Even two could be dismissed as the ways of a madman. But all of it was beginning to mount up, one thing upon the other.

'We should get some sleep, Miss,' Caleb urged. He reached out to tug at her shoulder, and only then did Magiere turn away from staring back to the stables, the cottage, and the stained woodpile. She headed down the road silently, Caleb by her side.

As Magiere and Caleb started for home, a faint light behind them slipped from the shadows, brightened to nearly the glow of a coal ember as it hovered in the road where the two late night walkers had just been standing. It floated after them for a while, then turned down a side alley and disappeared.

Constable Ellinwood arrived at his rented rooms shortly past the midnight hour, glad to finally be home.

Although he was known to sit drinking ale with his men at any one of Miiska's various taverns late into the night, he found these 'duties' more and more difficult as time passed. He felt that it appeared normal, even proper, for the town constable to patronize Miiska's drinking establishments with his guards. He would listen to his men tell boring stories about their families, the arrest of some cutpurse, or breaking up an argument between hawkers at the market. He would smile and nod and attempt to show interest.

But ale did little to fill his mind with dreamy comfort, and lately, it had grown more difficult not to leave early from the guardhouse, where he completed much of his work, and flee home to his lavish rooms in Miiska's finest inn, The Velvet Rose. Once alone in his rooms, he could sit and mix yellow Suman opiate powder with his hidden stores of Stravinan spice whiskey. The combination created a powerful tonic for his troubled thoughts and allowed him to sit in bliss for hours and hours, floating in a perfect state of existence.

Although he'd learned of the elixir years ago when a traveling merchant gave him his first taste, he hadn't indulged much in the past, as the cost of both components was exorbitant. Particularly the powder, which came from across the sea on the far continent, south into the Suman Empire and its kingdom of il'Mauy Meyauh. And even there, it was grown in secret and had to be smuggled out of the country. The price was often too much for him – except of course on special occasions when he was able to extort an unusually high fine for a criminal's release. He found it quite unfair that a man in his position, who earned one of the largest stipends in Miiska, should not be able to afford simple comforts after a hard day's work. Of course, he didn't have to live in the Velvet Rose, but his plush rooms also brought him great pleasure, and a man of his stature needed to keep up appearances.

Then nearly a year ago, a miracle occurred and he could afford all the Suman opiate and spice whiskey he desired. And 'home' was a lovely place to be at night.

Ellinwood laid his cloak on the silk comforter covering his bed and went to his polished cherry wood wardrobe to unlock the bottom drawer. He took out a large glass bottle full of amber liquid and a silver urn, smiling in anticipation.

A knock sounded on the door.

His smile faded, and he decided not to answer. Anyone calling at this hour had no decent business. If there were some town emergency, his first lieutenant, Darien, could handle it. He himself deserved a rest.

The knock sounded again, and a cold voice said, 'Open the door.'

Ellinwood flinched. He knew the voice. He placed the bottle and urn back in the drawer and hurried to open the door. In the hallway stood Rashed, the owner of Miiska's largest warehouse. The constable was at a loss for words.

'Um, welcome,' he managed to say. 'Did we have an appointment?'

'No.'

Any contact with Rashed unnerved the constable, but they had such a mutually beneficial relationship that he was determined not to jeopardize it.

'Then, how can I help you?' Ellinwood asked politely.

Rashed entered the room and closed the door. He was so tall that his head nearly touched the low ceiling. He'd never come to the constable's rooms before, and Ellinwood's typical feeling of 'nerves' grew to anxiety. An oval mirror in a silver frame reflected the constable's fleshy visage – completely decked out in shades of green velvet. He could not help briefly comparing himself to the perfectly constructed creature now sharing the room with him.

Rashed glanced around briefly. 'There's a hunter in town, and if she bothers me or mine, I'll kill her and anyone who tries to assist her, including your guards. Do you understand?'

Ellinwood stared at him and sputtered, 'Who do . . . the new owner of Dunction's? Oh, you've been listening to town gossip. She did not strike me as impressive on any level.'

'She is a hunter, and if she hunts here, there will be bloodshed – hers. And you will look the other way, as always.'

The constable tried to draw himself up. Although he and Rashed had a clear agreement that any disappearances or dead bodies found would be shabbily investigated, this was the first time Rashed had spoken so openly about shedding blood. And he'd certainly never felt the need to relay such information before the fact.

'Why are you consulting me?' Ellinwood asked.

'This is different. I don't know when a confrontation will occur, but I prefer not to have any of your guards in the way.'

'I'll handle my guards. But you will be discreet? She is new in town and few know her.' He paused a moment, trying to find something that might be a suitable explanation for future use. 'Perhaps the business, or a sedentary life, didn't suit her as well as she thought it would. There would be little interest if she and her partner simply disappeared one night.'

Rashed nodded. 'Of course. No bodies.'

'Well, then. Do whatever you think is best.' Ellinwood's eyes strayed to the bottom drawer of his wardrobe. 'Now, if you will excuse me, it has been a long day, and I would like to rest.'

Rashed's crystalline eyes followed and rested on the drawer as well. Mild disgust passed across his face, and he tossed a bag of coins on the silk comforter.

'For your trouble.' He turned and left the room.

The constable slumped in relief, his breath coming quick and short. Perhaps he should have stipulated that if Rashed wished to speak again, he should arrange a meeting at the warehouse, as was their usual custom. He had no wish to be alone with a vampire in the close quarters of his room ever again. But these creatures who owned Miiska's main warehouse certainly served his needs, and even had other uses from time to time.

Ellinwood had first encountered Rashed's kind about a year ago. He had been returning home after an evening of ale with his guards, and as he cut through an alley, he stumbled across the sight of a filthy street urchin with his mouth on the throat of a sailor. When Ellinwood realized the urchin was draining the sailor's blood, he cried out in alarm. The killer actually looked up, hissed at him, dropped the sailor, and moved forward to attack. Three of his guards, who were just leaving the tavern after him, heard their superior call out and came running to investigate. The urchin vanished down the alley.

As he himself had been in mortal danger, Ellinwood set guards to searching the town with vigor. A few of Miiska's citizens had come to him in the past swearing that night creatures had taken a loved one. The constable had not put much stock in such accounts until he'd seen this twisted little thing in the alley drinking human blood. Stories of monsters and demons were common among the sailors and merchants who traveled up and down the coast, passing through strange and foreign lands. And didn't most myths come from some grain of truth? The constable was determined to track down this murdering, possibly unnatural, urchin.

The next night, a message arrived at the guardhouse – an invitation. Ellinwood gave in to curiosity and went down to the warehouse. Rashed greeted him and took him to a plush room of low couches, embroidered pillows, and exquisite little rose-shaped candles. But Ellinwood did not take too much time admiring the décor.

Even in the room's soft light, the constable could see something was not quite right about his host. His skin was too pale for someone working a warehouse on the docks of a port town, as if he'd not been in the sun for months. And the man's eyes were almost colorless. His countenance seemed to express no desires, no hunger for pleasures, no emotions at all.

Then a pretty young woman with chocolate-brown curls and a tiny waist entered. She introduced herself as Teesha and smiled at Ellinwood, exposing dainty pointed fangs. When Rashed looked at her, his empty expression changed completely to one of longing and fierce protection, and the constable decided to remain quiet and see where this meeting would lead.

Rashed offered Ellinwood twenty shares of the warehouse – a virtual fortune – to look the other way if one of Miiska's citizens simply disappeared or was found dead in some unnatural state. He related that such occurrences would likely never happen, but then amended his comment to 'very infrequently.' In order for this exchange to take place, he did not try to hide what he or Teesha were. And while it took the constable a moment to absorb the fact that he was speaking with two undead creatures, he did not flinch. He was no fool and did not snub opportunity. Rather, he viewed himself as quite shrewd. If he did not agree, he'd never leave the room alive. But as long as he kept his position as town constable, he could keep Rashed's secret and merely pretend to investigate disappearances or strange deaths. Not only would he retain his stipend for living expenses, but he would also receive enough money to keep his supply of Suman opiate and Stravinan spiced whiskey constantly filled. It was a perfect arrangement.

Now Ellinwood reminded himself to clarify something with Rashed. Meetings must take place in the warehouse. After all, he must retain some privacy. Yes, he must clarify this at the first opportunity.

Feeling more at ease, the constable opened his wardrobe drawer again. He mixed the opiate from the urn with the whisky in a long-stemmed crystal glass and began to sip. Not long afterward, he was sitting in a damask-covered chair, infused with pleasure, his mind drifting into bliss.

7

Teesha waited patiently down near the docks for the right drunken sailor to pass by. The wonder and enormity of the ocean never ceased to please her, especially at high tide. The shore was a wall between worlds that guided the movement of all things between water and land along its lapping edge. She walked in bare feet, occasionally digging delicate toes into the sand, not caring if the hem of her purple gown dragged slightly and became soiled.

Many years ago, before her arrival in Miiska, one of the docks had collapsed due to rotted support poles. On its way, it had pulled down a small two-masted ship that couldn't be untied in time. Workers had dragged some of the remnants from the water, and the remains of ship and dock lay a short way down the shore. Perhaps they'd once thought to salvage materials from the accident, but nothing had ever come of such plans. Now, piled high on the shore out of the tide's reach, dock pillons and ship's struts stood up in the dark like the remains of a beached sea monster left to rot away to the bones. Weatherworn, but still partially solid, they offered a perfect haven. Teesha strolled calmly around the columns, listening to the dark rather than seeing it and periodically sniffing the breeze.

Then came the scent of warm flesh nearby. She tensed in anticipation and slipped behind a thick wood strut that could have been an old dock support or maybe a ship's beam. Only appearing to the solitary, she would pull back into the shadows if a pair or group approached. She peeked out carefully into the wind.

A lone sailor made his way along the shore toward the harbor. Canvas breeches with ragged unstitched hems hung to just below his knees, the salt-stained garment held up with a rope belt. On his feet he wore only makeshift sandals strapped at his ankles with leather thongs. His skin was dark from the sun, but his face looked soft, with only the wisps of an adolescent beard.

Teesha did not rush into view but relaxed by the pole, waiting for him to come nearer and see her. When he did, his step slowed only for a moment before he turned his course toward her. No more than five arm's lengths away, he stopped, staring at her pretty face, wild brown hair, and bare toes.

'Are you lost?' she asked him in a soothing tone that hummed behind the sounds of light wind and waves. 'You must be lost. Where is your ship?'

For an instant he frowned in puzzlement, thinking she was the one lost or confused. Looking into his young face, Teesha could see her words playing over and over in his mind until he wasn't sure if she or he had asked the question. A haze crossed his eyes as his frown deepened.

'Lost . . . lost?' he stuttered. Then he asked more urgently, 'Yes, where is my ship?'

'Here,' she said in the same soothing voice, the same humming tone. 'Here is your ship.' And her delicate fingers slid lightly down the side of the wood pillar at her side.

The words seemed to push at his mind, not unlike an erratic breeze in the sails after a long calm at sea.

'Come and I'll show you the way,' she urged.

Teesha held out her hand to the young sailor, and he took it. She urged him to follow her as she stepped back into the aged wreckage of dock and ship. She never even looked over her shoulder to find her way, but kept her eyes always on him as they moved. And he followed her willingly under the makeshift roof of broken poles and old bleached planks, back into the shadows.

'Here it is.' She smiled with perfect teeth.

The sailor was indeed young, maybe seventeen, with a hint of ale on his breath, but not enough to make him drunk. That didn't matter either way. He looked about uncertainly.

'Yes, you're home again,' she said, laying her free hand on one of his, the one she held gently to guide him. 'This is your ship, your home that goes with you.'

His features softened. Teesha heard a sigh of relief escape his lips.

'Come sit with me.' And she guided him down to the sand.

She ran her fingers through his uncombed hair and kissed him gently on the mouth. Feeding had never been difficult for her, once she'd learned her own way to hunt.

His hands reached out and grasped her arms so he could kiss her back, and she tried to shift upward to her knees. He was stronger than he looked, but obeyed when she whispered, 'Shhhh, not yet,' and pulled his head against her shoulder. When his neck was fully exposed, she wasted no time.

Sometimes she fed from their wrists, sometimes from the vein at the inside joint of the elbow. Whatever worked best in the moment. But tonight, she punctured one side of the sailor's throat, gripping his head tightly, both to support his weight and keep him from reflexively jerking away. His body bucked once. Then he was lost in his dream again.

She took what she needed, no more, and drew her fangs away without tearing his flesh. Taking a small dagger from her sleeve, she precisely connected the punctures on his neck but made certain the cut was shallow and slightly ragged. She could have just cut him and drunk from the wound, but that wasn't enough for her. The touch of warm flesh on her lips, slipping around her teeth, was so much more pleasing than the aftertaste metal left in the first drops of blood.

Laying him back in the sand, she untied his purse – not that she needed money, but this was also part of the deception. She placed one hand on his sleeping brow and stroked his eyes closed with the other. Her lips brushed against his ear as she whispered. 'You were walking to your ship tonight, home once again, and two thieves came. You fought them, but one had a knife . . .'

He flinched in reflex. One hand rose sluggishly, trying to reach for his own neck, but she gently pushed it back down.

'They stole your purse, and you crawled back here to hide, in case they returned, and you slept . . . now.'

When she heard his breathing deepen, Teesha rose quickly and left. He would be safe there. But if anything happened to him after their encounter, that fate did not concern her.

In this same manner she had fed for years. And she always tried to pick the ones who'd not be around for long. Miiska was such a perfect place, with sailors and merchants coming and going. Occasionally, she killed one by accident when need and hunger overbalanced her careful control, but that had not happened in a long time. And if need had caused her to choose a local citizen of the town, she always buried the poor unfortunate, and Rashed blamed Ratboy whenever some mortal went missing. She saw no need to alter his perception.

Now she ran lightly along the shore, feeling the warmth and strength of the sailor's blood, glad for her own innate ability to sometimes put the past and future from her mind and to live only in the moment.

'Teesha?'

She stopped in surprise, looking at the water and the wind in the trees above the shore.

'My love?'

Edwan's empty voice echoed from behind her, and she turned. He floated just above the sand, his green breeches and white shirt glowing like white flame through a fog. His severed head rested on one shoulder, and long, yellow hair hung down his side all the way to his waist.

'My dear,' she said. 'How long have you been there?'

'A while. Are you going home . . . already?'

'I wanted to check on the warehouse and see if Rashed needs anything.'

'Yes,' he said. 'Rashed.'

Edwan's visage changed subtly, as if the corpse image were no longer freshly dead, but had been lying in decay for a week or two. The glow of his skin was now sallow, whitened, with the hint of bruises from stagnant blood beneath his tissue.

Teesha lost the moment's joy of strength and heat. She stepped lethargically up the shore and wilted to the ground against a leaning tree.

'Don't brood. We need Rashed.'

'So you tell me.' Edwan was by her side, though she hadn't actually seen him move. 'So you told me.'

Together, they listened to shallow waves lapping at the beach. Teesha did not know how to respond. She loved Edwan, but he lived in the past, as did most spirits among the living, barely able to grasp the present. And she knew what he wanted. It was always what he wanted. He was the hungry one now, and with no true life to live, memories were all he had.

But it drained her so much, depressed her to do this for him. Every time he needed, and she relented, for the next five or six nights, it destroyed her ability to live only in the delicious present.

'No, Edwan,' she said tiredly.

'Please, Teesha. Just once more,' he promised – again.

'There isn't enough time before sunrise.'

'We have hours.'

The desperation in his voice hurt her. Teesha dropped her chin to her knees and stared out to where the water disappeared into the dark.

Poor Edwan. He deserved so much better, but this had to stop. Perhaps if she showed him the sharpest of memories, played out to the end, he might be able to accept their current existence – her new existence.

She closed her eyes, hoping he'd someday forgive

her for this, and reached out to him with her mind, reached back. . . .

High in the north above Stravina, snow fell from the sky more days of the year than not, and it seemed the clouds continuously covered the sun. Day or night made little difference, but Teesha hardly cared. In her tightly tied apron and favorite red dress, she served up mugs of ale to thirsty patrons and travelers at the inn. The place was always warm with a burning hearth, and she had a smile for whoever came through the door. But that special smile, as welcome as a break in the clouds when she could see the sun, was only for her young husband, working somberly behind the bar, making sure all was right and not one guest had to wait for an ordered drink.

Edwan seldom smiled back at her, but she knew he loved her fiercely. His father was a twisted, violent man, and his mother had died of fever when he was just a child. He had lived in poverty and servitude. That was all Edwan could remember of childhood, until he left home at seventeen, traveled through two cities, found a job tending bar, and then met Teesha, his first taste of kindness and affection.

At sixteen, Teesha had already received several marriage proposals, but she'd always declined. There was just something not quite right with the suitor – too old, too young, too frivolous, too dour . . . too something. She felt the need to wait for someone else. When Edwan walked through the tavern door, with his dark yellow hair, wide cheekbones, and haunted eyes, she knew he was her other half. After five years of marriage, he still rarely spoke to anyone but her.

To him, the world was a hostile place, and safety only rested in Teesha's arms.

To her, the world was songs and spiced turnips and serving ale to guests – who had long ago become close friends – and spending warm nights under a feather quilt with Edwan.

It was a good time in life, but a short one.

The first time Lord Corische opened the inn's door, he remained standing outside and would not enter. The cold breeze blowing openly into the common room was enough to set everyone to cursing, and Teesha ran to shut the door.

'May I come in?' he asked, but his voice was demanding, as if he knew the answer and was merely impatient to hear it.

'Of course, please,' she answered, mildly surprised, as the tavern was open to all.

When he and a companion entered, and Teesha could finally shut the door, everyone settled down again. A few people turned to look in curiosity, then a few more, as the first curious ones did not turn back to their food again.

Nothing about Lord Corische himself stood out as unusual. Not his chainmail vest and pieces of plate over padded armor, for soldiers and mercenaries were seen often enough. He was neither handsome nor ugly, large nor small. His only true distinguishing features were a smooth, completely bald head and a small white scar over his left eye. But he was not alone, and it was not Lord Corische the tavern guests stared at in any case. It was his companion.

Beside the smooth-headed soldier walked the tallest,

most striking man Teesha had ever seen. He wore a deep blue, padded tunic covered in a diamond pattern stitched in shimmering white thread. His short hair was true black against a pale face with eyes so light she wasn't certain of the color, like the smoothest ice over a deep lake.

The two men walked to a table, but the bald soldier still hadn't taken his gaze off Teesha.

'Can I bring you ale?' she asked.

'You'll bring me whatever I find pleasing,' the soldier answered in a loud voice, enjoying the moment. 'I am Lord Corische, new master of Gäestev Keep. Everything here already belongs to me.'

When the villagers around them heard Corische's announcement, hushed murmurs began, but all words were kept low enough not to be heard.

Teesha held her breath and dropped her eyes. Over a year had passed since the previous vassal lord had died of a hunting wound. No word of a new lord arriving had reached them in all that time.

'Forgive my familiar manner,' she said. 'I did not know.'

'Your familiar manner is welcome,' Corische said quietly.

He did not look remotely noble to Teesha, but then she had rarely seen a noble in her life. Corische did have a look about him that fit these mountain lands, cold and possibly cruel to the unwary. But if either one of these two strangers were a lord, Teesha would have thought it his companion.

Corische's striking companion did not speak. He even appeared detached, not listening to their conversation. After a slow gaze at the crowd, as if gauging for possible dangers, he settled back and ignored his surroundings.

'This is my man, Rashed,' Lord Corische said, without motioning to his companion. 'He's from a desert land far across the sea and despises our cold weather, don't you, Rashed?'

'No, my lord,' Rashed answered flatly, as if this were a ritual simply to be completed.

'May I fetch ale, my lord?' Teesha asked politely, wanting some reason to move away from the table.

'No, I came for you.'

The answer stunned her into confusion. 'Beg pardon?'

Corische stood up and pushed his cloak back. His skin was pale, but his shoulders and upper arms were thick beneath the armor.

'I have already been in the village a few nights, watching you. Your face is pleasing. You will come back to the keep with me and stay while I'm detained here. A few years at most, but you'll want for nothing.'

Fear hollowed out Teesha's stomach, but she smiled as if his request were an ordinary flirtatious remark.

'Oh, I think my husband may object,' she said, turning to go back to her work.

'Husband?' Lord Corische's brown eyes moved beyond her and settled knowingly on Edwan – fragile, fierce Edwan, who was tightly poised, ready to jump over the bar.

'This is not the time, my lord,' Rashed said quietly.

A long moment passed. Then Corische nodded to Teesha, stood, and left without a word. Rashed got up and followed.

That night in bed, Edwan begged her to pack her belongings and slip away with him.

'To where?' she asked.

'Anywhere. This isn't over.'

The small northern village was her home, and she foolishly insisted they stay. Two nights later, a local farmer that Edwan once quarreled with over the price of bread grain was found stabbed to death behind the inn. When Lord Corische's men came to investigate, they found a bloody knife hidden under Edwan and Teesha's bed. Rashed was there, seemingly overseeing the search, yet all he did was enter, sit at a table before the hearth, and wait. When the knife was brought out by Corische's soldiers, neither surprise nor anger registered in his transparent eyes. He simply nodded shallowly, and the guards proceeded as if their orders had already been given.

Teesha was too stunned to cry out when soldiers dragged her husband from the inn in shackles. She saw Rashed's eyes, and how empty they were, except for a twitch she couldn't be quite sure of before it was gone again.

Before Teesha could lunge after Edwan, a third guard snatched her by the arms from behind. Lord Corische then entered the inn and stood patiently in front of her, waiting for her to give up her struggling.

For the first time, Teesha began to believe his crude appearance and rough speech were a disguise to mask some hidden self. There was no life in his face, no feeling at all.

'What will happen to him?' she whispered.

'He will be sentenced to death.' Corische paused. 'Unless you come to the keep with me tonight.'

Had she been stupid or just naive? She had heard stories around the inn about nobles and their abuses, destroying the lives of others without concern. She thought such tales were merely exaggerations.

'If I come with you, he will live?' she asked.

'Yes.'

He did not let her pack so much as a spare dress. She was escorted outside to two bay horses held at the ready by one of Corische's men. Corische mounted one, and Rashed the other. Edwan was nowhere to be seen.

'Rashed is your servant as well now,' Corische said. 'He will protect you.'

Rashed leaned down and gripped her under the arms. He lifted her in front of himself as if she were parchment. Although horror prevented her from taking note of the moment, it came back to her many times later. On that night she was still Teesha the serving girl, who loved her husband and believed life consisted of songs and spiced turnips, Teesha the serving girl who couldn't understand where her Edwan was or what was happening to him. Sitting sideways on the saddle, she leaned back and clung to Rashed's tunic as his horse jumped forward.

The ride to Gäestev Keep took forever. With no cloak, the freezing air cut through her dress. Rashed did not verbally acknowledge her presence, but after she shivered once, he rode with both his arms covering hers to shield her from the wind. Corische rode on ahead, with his remaining soldiers bringing up the rear of the procession.

And still there was no sign of Edwan. Had he already been dragged off to some damp cell?

The keep loomed ahead, and her fear shifted to her own fate. It was an imposing construction of stone, a squat and wide tower with a stable and guardhouse built against its sides. When Rashed lifted her down, she considered running but had no notion of where to go, and she feared what would happen to Edwan if she did run.

The inside of the keep looked as bleak as the outside. No welcoming fires burned, and the bitter wind was exchanged for the bone-chilling cold of air trapped within stone walls. No pictures or tapestries hung on those walls. Old straw covered the main floor. Stone steps running around the inner wall led to the unseen upper levels. The only furniture visible was a long, cracked table and one massive chair. Two small torches on the wall burned to provide light.

Lord Corische did not notice her chattering teeth and walked past her to lay his sword on the table. Torchlight glinted off his smooth head.

'Ratboy,' he called out. 'Parko.'

The timbre of his voice dropped to an echoing, angry growl. Skittering, running feet on the stairs made Teesha unconsciously pull back behind Rashed. Two strange men – or creatures – entered the room.

The first looked like a street urchin, covered with dirt down to the surface of his teeth. He could have been a boy or a young man. Everything about him was brown except for his skin, which she glimpsed beneath smudges of grime. The second figure, however, terrified her instantly, even more than Corische.

An emaciated white face with bestial eyes that sparked in the torchlight looked as if it were carved from bone. Strands of filthy black hair hung down his back beneath a tied kerchief that she guessed had once been green. But it was his movements that frightened her most.

Quick as an animal, he darted into the room, springing off the steps before reaching the bottom. He caught himself on the table and used his hands to propel himself around, smelling at the air.

His eyes settled in her direction, and he lunged across the room, stopping halfway, neck swiveling and craning as he tried to see her behind Rashed.

'You do not wait to greet your master?' Corische said coldly.

'Forgive us,' Ratboy answered in a lilting tone. 'We were preparing the woman's room as you asked.'

His polite voice belied the hatred and mischief in his eyes. Parko dropped low to crouch on all fours and did not turn to face Corische.

'Woman,' Parko said, nodding.

The numbness of Teesha's emotions faded as she looked about at the pit into which she'd been cast. These were the kind of men who served her liege lord? Where were the fires? Where were the guards and the casks of ale and the food?

Rashed stepped forward, exposing her to view. He crouched down to Parko's level.

'You cannot touch her, Parko. Do you understand? She's not for you.'

The odd, gentle quality in his tone surprised Teesha.

'Woman,' Parko repeated.

'He does not need your warnings,' Corische said, removing his cloak, 'and you forget your place.'

Rashed stood and stepped back. 'Yes, my lord.'

Corische then turned to Teesha. 'I am not cruel. You may rest for a night or two before taking up your duties.'

'Duties? What are my duties?'

'Acting as lady of the keep.' He paused for a moment, then laughed as if he'd finally understood some elusive joke. The sound brought Teesha's dinner to the base of her throat.

'If I am to be lord here,' Corische continued, 'I must have a lady, even a floor-scrubbing tavern wench like you.'

That was her first hint that Corische harbored no desire to play lord of Gäestev Keep. Most feudal over-seers were assigned fiefs as gifts from nobles wealthier than themselves or from their own liege lords. But what did Corische want from her? She knew nothing of ladies or playing at nobility. She looked again at Ratboy and Parko in confusion. If Corische surrounded himself with lowly creatures in order to feel more important, then why enlist someone like Rashed? And why bother with a woman to play at being lady of the house?

She was locked in a filthy tower room that night and left to shiver with no fire and only a thin, moldy flannel sheet as a blanket. No one came all the next day, but the following night, she heard the door unlock and was caught between relief and terror. Rashed entered with a tray of tea, mutton stew, and bread, and he carried a cape over one arm.

'It's freezing in here,' she said.

'Put this on.' He held out the cape as he set the tray on the floor in front of her. 'The keep is ancient. There are no hearths, only a fire pit in the main room. I found wood and lit it. Some heat might rise, but do not go down there without the master or myself.'

She couldn't tell if he was being kind or just instructing her in one more rule of the house. Then she realized it didn't matter. He seemed the closest thing she had to a friend in this vile place. Unwanted tears ran down her cheeks.

'What about Edwan?' She stood, taking one step closer to Rashed. 'Will he be released soon?'

Rashed was silent for a moment, not moving, his eyes staring at the wall behind her.

'Your husband was sentenced this morning and executed at dusk.' He said it without any change of tone in his voice. He turned toward the door, preparing to leave. 'Do you wish to sit by the fire?'

A kind of madness tickled Teesha's brain.

'Do I wish to . . . ?' She began laughing. 'You bastard.'

For nothing – she'd come to this nightmare pit for nothing, and Edwan, who deserved a peaceful life more than anyone she'd known, was dead simply because some twisted lord fancied his wife. The vicious comedy of it all became more than she could bear. Death was far preferable to this existence.

She bolted past Rashed, running down the short hall. She didn't know if Rashed pursued her or not as she ran down the stone steps to the main room. Lord Corische sat at the cracked table writing on a scroll with a feather quill. Teesha ignored him and ran for the great oak doors.

As she reached out for the iron latch, Parko sprang in front of her as if sprouting from the earth, snarling and sucking in her scent. She staggered back in reflex, but did not turn around, her eyes focused watchfully on the disheveled figure in front of her.

'Let me out of here!' she ordered Corische. She had nothing left for him to take, nothing that mattered to her, and so no more reason for fear.

Then she saw the enormous iron bar across the door. She hadn't even noticed it while rushing to escape. It was wider than her own upper arm and so thick and heavy it didn't seem possible that any one person could have lifted it alone. It was most certainly impossible for her to do so by herself.

'Take this down,' she said, her back still to Corische. 'Our pact is over.'

'Rashed put that bar up. Even I would have difficulty removing it. Did you enjoy dinner?'

Hatred was a new emotion for Teesha, disorienting, and it took a moment to think through Corische's insulting chatter.

'If you wanted a lady for your house, why didn't you find one? Are you afraid she would detest your crude manners and lowborn airs? No, you wanted someone beneath you that you could lord over' – she looked at Parko, no longer frightened by him, then caught sight of Ratboy hovering in the corner – 'like the rest of your wretched little mob.'

She heard something slam down on the table hard enough to make it slide and grate on the stone floor. He was easy to anger. Good. She turned about to face him and saw clean, unmasked rage.

'You live at my mercy,' he said, 'at my whim. Do not forget that.'

'Your mercy?' The madness in her laugh matched Parko's eyes. 'And what makes you believe living has anything to do with this? You murdered my Edwan, and I will do nothing to bring you pleasure. Do you understand me now? I will not grace your table nor entertain your guests nor do anything you desire. I will try to escape every day until I succeed or you tire of it and kill me.'

Corische appeared stunned into silence.

Teesha only blinked once, reflexively, and he was suddenly across the room at her side.

His hand lashed out and grabbed her arm. The stale smell of him filled her with revulsion, but his grip hurt so badly she couldn't help crying out.

'You *will* do as I say,' he hissed. 'I am master here. This keep may be a pathetic hovel, but I am still lord and you will obey.'

'No,' she whimpered. 'You murdered my Edwan.'

Corische swept the floor with one foot, kicking aside the straw to reveal a worn wooden hatch with an inset iron ring. Before Teesha could resist, he jerked up the hatch and shoved her inside.

Teesha expected to fall straight down, but instead she tumbled along stone steps in the dark. When she reached bottom finally, her head banged against a stone floor she couldn't even see in the half-light spilling down from the open hatch. A hollow thud echoed through the chamber as the hatch slammed closed, leaving her in complete darkness.

She sat up, feeling along her limbs for any wounds greater than bruises or scrapes. At least now she was away from him for the moment.

A savage grunt came from the dark.

'You will do whatever I ask,' a voice said, 'because you won't be able to stop yourself.'

Corische had come down the steps behind her and was somewhere in the chamber.

Teesha slid back from his voice. Finding the bottom

stair with her hand, she turned to scramble upward to the hatch. Something tangled in her hair, jerking her back, and she felt fingers coil tighter just before her head was slammed to the floor.

She couldn't be sure if she'd lost consciousness for a moment, but she became aware of someone large crouched over her, pinning her down. The smell of Corische's breath hit her in the face. His hand was still in her hair, pulling hard enough to hurt as her head tilted back. She tried to thrash free and cried out instinctively. Her scream was cut short as she felt canine teeth bite down on her throat.

Teesha gasped in panic, wondering from where the animal had come, and became rigid with shock when she realized it was Corische. Air became harder and harder to take in as she heard him suck her blood through his teeth. As he continued to drink, the dark around her began to tingle on her skin. Her head swam, her breath grew shorter and shorter, until she could barely feel the air move in and out through her slack mouth.

He pulled back suddenly, and she wheezed in a lungful of air just before she felt herself jerked up to sitting position. Her arms were still pinned to her sides by Corische's thick legs. Both his hands clamped across the back of her head, and he crushed her face into his chest.

The stink of his flesh made her gag, but his skin felt chilled. And there was something wet smearing against her face.

She opened her mouth, trying to breathe, and the wetness spread across her lips. A coppery taste hit her tongue. The liquid was as cold as his skin, but she could still recognize the taste from the times she cut a finger

or thumb while preparing food in the inn's kitchen –
and she'd raised the small wound to her mouth, trying
to stop the drops of blood.

Corische pressed her face tighter against his chest
until she could not breathe at all, only feel and taste
the slight bit of his blood escaping into her mouth.
Every sensation in the dark became unreal and distant
until all feeling in her body faded and her breath stopped
altogether.

Teesha awoke on the stone floor in the dark. Had it
been hours or days? It felt . . . somehow felt even longer.
There was light in the room, yet the hatch above was
not open. Rashed knelt over her, a small oil lamp in
his hand. Something flickered across his cold features.
Pity? Regret? She sat up to look about anxiously, but
Corische was nowhere to be seen. A heavy wooden door
with an iron slide bolt was set in the wall opposite the
stairs that led up to the hatch. Otherwise, the room was
empty.

Rashed stood and opened the door to expose a long
hall angling downward into the earth. Along its sides
were other doors like the first, each with a slide bolt,
but also looped steel at the jambs where the door could
be secured with a lock.

'This used to be a dungeon of some sort,' he said.

Teesha was too weak and confused to either question
or object when he scooped her up in his arms, lantern
still in hand, and carried her into that hallway. He did
not stop at any of the doors but walked to the end of
the passage, and placed his free hand firmly against the
end wall, careful not to drop her. The stone under his

hand gave, sinking into the wall, and he reached inside to some hidden pocket of space. Teesha heard something akin to grinding metal, then the grind of stone as the hall's end pivoted open to reveal a set of stairs angling farther downward. Rashed slipped through and descended.

He walked on and on until finally he reached an end chamber. Within it was nothing more than five coffins. Four were of plain wood and little more than long boxes, while the fifth appeared to be of thick oak with iron bindings, crafted for the final rest, yet without any handles on the outsides of its lid.

'This is where you must sleep now,' he said, 'in a coffin with the dirt of your homeland. If you go out into the sunlight, you will die.' He set her down in one of the four wooden coffins. 'You will rest here near my own. I've already prepared it for you.'

And so Teesha, the carefree serving girl, was gone, and something else was born in her place.

She learned many things over the next few nights: That she could not refuse the wishes of her master, that she needed blood to exist, that Rashed's coffin was half full of white sand, and that she was undead. Rashed taught her everything with his endless dispassionate patience, and although she sometimes wished for the rest of true death, hatred for Corische kept her rising every night.

He was more than lord of the keep. He was a master among the Noble Dead, those beings among the undead who still retained their full semblance of self from life in an eternal existence no longer subservient to the mortality under which the living grew old and weak.

They were the vampires and liches who possessed physical bodies, their own memories, and their own consciousness. The Noble Dead were the highest and most powerful of the unliving. The only weakness for vampires, however, was that they were slaves to the one who created them. Corische's master, his own creator, had somehow been destroyed, and so he was free to create his own servants.

Teesha found that when he gave a verbal order, she could not refuse him. Internally, she could despise him, fantasize about seeing him scorched in flames, and think whatever she pleased. But when he spoke, she could not stop herself from obeying. Neither could Rashed, Parko, or Ratboy – not that Rashed would have refused anyway. The tall, composed warrior seemed honestly loyal to his master. This revolted Teesha, as Rashed was clearly superior to Corische on every imaginable level.

Rashed taught her how to feed without killing, harmonizing the thrum of her voice to the exertion of her will, until the victim became pliable and docile.

When she asked Rashed why he cared so for mortals, that he did not wish to kill them, his reply was coldly practical.

'Even a heavily populated area like this one cannot support four of us recklessly. We must be careful or lose our home and our food supply.'

She came to understand that their kind developed different levels of power. Rashed thought her mental abilities were quite pronounced. His own and Ratboy's were adequate. Parko couldn't express himself well enough for the others to gauge his abilities, yet his senses were highly acute, even beyond the average heightened senses of a Noble Dead, and he was a constant trial for Rashed to control. Corische's telepathic skills were so limited that Teesha sometimes wondered how he fed.

Most of the Noble Dead developed mental abilities, but these often were dependent on the individual's inclinations in life. Teesha had always loved dreams and memories, for her life had been filled with the best of them, and so she eventually found she could easily reach into the mind of a mortal and project sweet waking dreams and alter memories.

The first time Rashed took her hunting was a revelation. They rode his bay gelding together for a while and then dismounted and tied the horse to a tree. Slipping through the forest, she realized they were hiding in the shadows on the outskirts of her home village. A farmer came out of the tavern and stepped into the trees to relieve himself. Teesha recognized him. His name was Davish.

'Watch me,' Rashed said. 'This is important.'

He stepped out of the shadows. 'Are you lost?' he asked Davish.

The farmer started slightly at the sound of a strange voice, and then he looked in Rashed's eyes and seemed to relax into a kind of confusion. 'Lost? I . . . ? I'm not sure.'

'Come. I will help you home.'

Davish appeared to be frightened, but not of Rashed. He kept looking around as if he should know where he was but did not. Rashed reached out as if to help him, but then gripped his arm, pulled him over, and wasted no time biting down on his throat. Teesha watched in fascination.

Rashed did not drink much and then pushed the dazed farmer toward her. 'Feed, but not too much. You must not kill him. You'll be doing this on your own soon enough.'

Teesha grabbed Davish and began feeding, unable to stop herself, and surprised by how right the act felt. She was not repulsed at all. Then she realized how delicious his blood tasted, how warm, how strong she felt. Pure pleasure seeped through her. She could not stop.

'That's enough.' Rashed pulled her off. 'Don't kill him.' He laid Davish out on the ground and then used a knife to connect the holes made by his teeth, but he did this carefully and did not cut too deeply. He leaned close and whispered, 'Forget.'

'What did you do?' she asked.

'You simply reach inside their thoughts with your own. Force the fear, the moment, the emotion to fade.'

And so she learned that Rashed was able to manipulate emotions, and able to create a blank space in his victim's memory. Teesha herself learned to create dreams and manipulate more complex memories.

Ratboy, on the other hand, hunted through his ability to blend. No one noticed him. No one remembered him. He did not hunt with finesse or by creating dreams, but he was able to feed by mentally intensifying his own innate ability to be forgotten. That was all.

Parko quite often killed his victims, but they were mainly peasants. As master of Gäestev Keep, Corische was responsible for looking into these deaths so, of course, little investigation took place.

Teesha hunted either alone or with Rashed. His forethought and consistently rational manner impressed her.

He wasn't exactly predictable, which would have made him mundane, but rather, he was constant. His intelligent, calm nature was the only thing she could count on besides herself in this new existence.

Corische, on the other hand, exhibited mood swings she never learned to understand. One night, her choice of dress might please him, and on the next night, the same dress would disgust him and give him cause to humiliate her. The unwashed state of his armor and his yellow teeth sickened her. True hatred was a new emotion for Teesha, and because of this, she did not question how often it consumed her. She began to wonder about the nature of his control and to consider how she might be forced to obey her master and yet thwart him at the same time. Since she was only compelled to obey him when he gave a verbal order, a subtle approach seemed the only possibility. The answer took a month but was simple enough in the end.

She would become exactly what he claimed to want.

Half a year passed, and Teesha made only small changes at first. She took up fine needlepoint and hired a talented local woman to come three times per week for lessons. She asked Corische for money and ordered fine dresses in the styles that most often seemed to please him. And he began to smugly revel in her efforts.

Since her master was masquerading as a feudal lord, he could not completely ignore his duties. A good portion of land profits remained in his purse, so he collected rents and even occasionally sat in judgment over peasants who were accused of petty crimes. But in that first year, he had a new barracks built on the north side of the keep, and afterward forbade any of the soldiers to enter his home. A competent middle-aged soldier named Captain Smythe, along with Rashed, handled the typical workload required for overseeing a fiefdom with four villages.

One night, when Corische and Rashed were leaving to collect rents, Teesha watched Rashed lift the iron bar off the door. He was physically the strongest creature she had ever known, an immortal incarnation of bone and muscle. But she had also begun to see through his cold dispassion, catching him at times staring intently at one of her needleworks or the small items she'd ordered for the making of a proper noble household. Rashed hungered for the trappings of the living. She saw no shame in this, and knew she could use his hunger to her advantage. Teesha decided that night to accelerate her plans.

First, she had every room above the cellar cleaned by hiring a temporary housemaster, allowing him to believe she and Corische were a pair of lazy nobles who debauched all night and slept all day. She ordered tapestries, braid carpets, and muslin bedding for the two small guest rooms, a chandelier with forty candles, silver goblets, and porcelain dishes. Every night, she had a roaring fire laid in the pit to create an illusion of life and warmth. Although she told herself this was all simply a ruse for Corische's benefit, she began to see layers of herself she'd never realized before. Weren't taste and style simply learned skills that the wealthy taught their children? Isn't that what she'd always believed? Back in the tavern with Edwan, Teesha cared for nothing beyond warmth, love, and the friendship of others. She'd worn one dress in the summer and another in the winter.

Why had that never bothered her? Why hadn't she seen how much more there was to desire? She hated Corische, but part of her appreciated how his curse had opened her eyes.

Corische watched with a growing arrogant satisfaction as day after day she slipped deeper into the role he expected of her. And she watched Rashed's fascination grow as the cold keep slowly changed into a living place. She even found that she derived some comfort from pleasing him. And he was the only one she entertained any interest in pleasing.

Eventually, Corische stopped taking notice of all the things she did. She was doing what he wanted, and he made little or no comment on it. Rashed, on the other hand, could not hide his growing approval, which seeped out for a blink or two to wash away the grim coldness of his features. He'd ask where she'd found the latest tapestry or how she would use the strangely shaped flowered vase. Once, he even complimented the knotted pattern she was stitching into a pillowcase.

Then one late evening, when Corische was out, she slipped downstairs to spot Rashed alone in the main room, unaware of her presence. A wrapped and tied bundle of new cloth she had ordered was sitting on the table, and he was trying to peek inside without leaving any trace that he'd been inspecting it.

For a moment, Teesha forgot about Rashed's place in her half-formed plans and stood entranced by his bizarre obsession with mortal trappings. A forgotten softness filled her briefly while she watched him. Firelight almost gave his face color, and he looked so handsome standing by the table, as curious as a boy about her bundle. Then she remembered herself and shook off the feeling. She must think of him as a tool. He would be her instrument, and she could not let emotion sway her from using him.

In another month, Corische began to invite guests to the keep – at first only a nearby lord from a neighboring fief, then a few others as the visits were a success. Teesha could see he sought to improve his social standing and rise in mortal political ranks. After the year's end, she stepped up her studies, using house accounts Corische put at her disposal to order scrolls and books.

She studied history and languages on her own. Lord Corische knew she was trying to improve herself and did not interfere, but neither did he take an active interest, seeming to shy away whenever she was entranced in some text. Rashed, however, openly approved of her efforts and, to her surprise, started teaching her mathematics and astronomy. He showed little interest in most of her books, but was apparently educated, instructing her from memory alone. It was the most she'd learned about his origins somewhere in the great desert lands he referred to as the Suman Empire. Her ability and interest in academics gave her more cause to appreciate her new life – should she call it life? There was so very much to learn and study and absorb, and she'd never given any of it a moment's thought. She'd never known that anything beyond her small world of spiced turnips and Edwan even existed. How droll, how sad.

Although she studied astronomy and languages diligently, Teesha learned little about the other household members. Parko grew more difficult to speak with as time passed. Often he would be out at night, only appearing when Corische wanted him for something.

He seemed to have an awareness that told him when his master would expect his presence. On the other hand, Ratboy would annoyingly pop out of dark corners whenever he felt like it. She caught him watching her intently several times, only to have him turn away with dramatic disinterest when discovered. He was always polite but bored and discontent – something of which she took careful note.

Throughout that second year, Corische began to make guests in the house a regular event, at least once per month.

In the third year, a caravan came through the village. She hurried out early after dusk in time to purchase a large piece of rich, dark burgundy brocade and silver thread before the merchants closed their tents for the night. For the next month, she worked in secret, sewing Rashed an exquisite tunic. She finished it early one evening and sat waiting in the main hall, knowing he would be along sometime soon, as always.

'Here,' she said. 'I thought you could use something new in your limited wardrobe.'

He offered no response when she handed the wrapped bundle to him. He took it with only a slight twitch of puzzlement in his left eyebrow, wasted no time snapping the binding strip, and unwrapped the muslin to display the tunic.

Rashed looked at Teesha once, quickly, then back down at the tunic, staring for a long moment. He said nothing to her as he turned away, but his hands shook slightly as he carefully refolded the muslin around the tunic and then walked toward his own chamber. It was not until later in the year that she would realize why he didn't start wearing it immediately. He would only wear it on the rarest occasions when expected to look his best for guests, and when he did, he was conspicuously concerned with anything that might cause the slightest stain or smudge on the fine fabric.

But that evening, Teesha sat quietly satisfied as Rashed disappeared down the side hall, her gift in his hands. He thought himself so guarded, but he was so easy for her to read. She told herself the gift was only meant to sway him further to her side. But he had looked pleased, hadn't he?

It took a moment, distracted with Rashed as she was, before she sensed the eyes watching her. She turned her head slowly with a scowl, expecting to catch Ratboy lurking in the corner again, but she couldn't have been more wrong.

The sight that met her eyes would have made anyone else, even one of her current household, back away – but not Teesha. She froze, unable to speak, and perhaps experienced a moment's fear. Then her eyes grew forlorn as if her heart had been shattered all over again. No tears fell, for the dead no longer had the ability to weep. She tried and failed three times to speak, then stumbled halfway across the room to stop short. A smile finally came to her lips.

Edwan stood at the foot of the stairs in his hideous, transparent form.

Perhaps she'd been living in a nightmare so long that seeing the ghost of her dead husband did not strike her as traumatic. Perhaps death was too intimate a thing for her to be repulsed by his visage. She smiled wider, cutting short a small laugh of relief.

'How long have you been here?' she asked.

'Since . . . beginning,' Edwan said, though the sound didn't quite match the movement of his sideways lips speaking from the half-severed head upon his shoulder. 'I saw . . . he did to you.'

Teesha's smile faded. 'And you left me alone?'

Language seemed difficult for him, but she could still read his familiar face, pale and bloodless as it was.

'You have not been alone,' he said, almost petulantly, his words growing clearer. 'I was afraid to show myself. I exist at the moment of my death.' His body turned, for he couldn't move his severed head and it was the only way to pull his closing eyes away from her.

Teesha stepped close, glancing quickly about to make sure no else was there. She reached out to touch him, but her hand only passed through his chest without even a tingle on her flesh. Edwan's eyes opened.

'You are beautiful to me,' she said, and she meant it.

'Then leave this place. I am bound to you, and if you leave, I can follow.'

She was astonished. 'Edwan, I can't leave. I'm bound to my master.'

'Is that why you've changed yourself? Why you work to make this place and yourself so beautiful for him?'

For a moment, she thought he spoke of Corische, then she caught the quick twitch of his eyes toward where Rashed had left just moments ago. She couldn't find any way to make him understand the years that had passed. There wasn't enough time before someone would come in and discover him, so she comforted him with soft words.

'We will be free, my Edwan. I have planned it.'

Another year passed. Sometimes Teesha could feel Edwan nearby, even when others were present. None of them appeared to notice the spirit, only she. She studied and never once let pass even the smallest opportunity to do some kindness for Rashed. She bought special irons to heat, so she could curl her hair elaborately before pinning it up. Her dresses became simpler and darker in color but more elegant. Occasionally, Rashed would knock on her door and come in to find her primping or trying on some gown. After he left, Edwan would reappear in thinly disguised agitation, and Teesha would parade for him, telling him all she had worked for and how it would soon be time to leave. She did not allow herself to dwell on the unwanted thought that Rashed's opinion of her gowns was the only one that mattered.

During this phase, she actually had little to do with her master. He never touched her and rarely sought her company unless they had guests. He even stopped reveling in her obedience and simply took it for granted, as he did with Rashed. Then one night, Corische invited six lords and their ladies from southern Stravina for roast pheasant and aged spring wine.

Both Corische and Teesha had become skilled at pretending to eat. Consuming food wasn't impossible for the dead. It simply provided no sustenance, and only raw foods, particularly fruits, had any real flavor for them. Cooked flesh tasted bland and nearly repulsive. Wine was at least tolerable, sometimes pleasant.

While Corische tried to draw one of the noblemen's attention to an exquisite tapestry that Teesha had ordered from Belaski, she politely interrupted and asked the gentleman a question. She phrased it in the old, little-known Stravinan tongue spoken mainly by nobles with too much free time and too high an opinion of their bloodline. It was easy enough for her to snatch the surface thoughts from the gentleman's mind to perfect her accent by the time she finished her first sentence.

The nobleman smiled in delight, thumping his glass down as he responded. Everyone at the table suddenly switched to conversing avidly in the nearly dead tongue – everyone, that is, but Lord Corische. He sat in mild discomfort at first, perhaps a bit nervous that he had no idea what was being said around him, and then Teesha caught his eye.

She looked at him with all the disdain she had amassed in the years with him, and it flooded through her gaze to wash over him.

Realization dawned on Corische, and his discomfort turned to barely contained outrage. Teesha felt the initial sweet bite of satisfaction, a unique blend of triumph and revenge. The culmination of her plan was coming soon.

Shortly before dawn, after all guests were safely in bed, Corische found her by the fire. Lately, he had begun to dress like Rashed and now wore well-tailored breeches and a dark orange tunic, his chain mail abandoned.

'Do not forget your place, *my lady*,' he said sarcastically. 'I was displeased at supper.'

'Truly?' She raised her perfectly plucked eyebrows and watched him take in the sight of her low-necked, black gown and plaited chocolate hair. 'That is because you are not noble and could not share in our discussion. You are not even ancient.' Her tone remained even and polite. 'I know Rashed believes you to be old, but his good heart is easily fooled. What were you in life, *my lord*? A mercenary? A caravan guard? However did you escape your own master?'

Her goading struck a chord, and he stepped back, voice ragged. 'You will not speak to me this way.'

'Yes, *my lord*.'

She could not disobey, but she would now openly despise him.

It took a little more time for Corische to fully grasp what she had become, and in turn, he began losing his contentment. More often than not, his frustration caused him to behave like a mannerless thug. Teesha, so much the noble in all things that mattered now, made him look coarse and low when they were seen together. No matter how he tried, he couldn't catch up on the few years she'd spent training herself while he played at his rank like an uneducated soldier. He reacted with anger, threatening her into submission, which she readily gave because she knew it wormed into him even sharper. If she altered herself and began looking and behaving like Teesha the serving girl again, how would his noble acquaintances respond? She was the only true hold he had upon his place in rank and society.

He changed tactics and began anew. First came the compliments whispered in her ear at feasts for guests – and all watching saw the eagerness in his eyes and the revulsion in hers, mixed with a touch of well-played fear. Then came the gifts, such as a pearl necklace shaped like petals he presented her at a holiday dance given by a neighboring lord. She flinched with a shudder as he put it around her neck, her eyes like a doe's running from the hunter. And last, and only once, in private he tried to confess how fond he'd grown of her – how deeply fond – and was answered by her flat and cold expression.

Corische began going on long hunts, sometimes staying out all night, only to arrive home in time to beat the dawn.

If Teesha felt even the slightest sorrow regarding her existence, it only involved Edwan, who watched somewhere unseen. But she hid it away carefully, especially when she began to play seriously with Rashed.

By now, it was no secret to any in the household that he adored her in a white knight manner. For all his passionless ways, Teesha had made it so. She sewed him fine clothes, comforted him with kind words, and took over mundane tasks like arranging for his laundry. She made a point of seeing to his needs first. Stepping up the process, she began to sometimes approach him as he worked on accounts, placing a tiny hand on his shoulder while speaking with him. As always, she pushed aside thoughts about the solid feel of his collarbone and reminded herself that he was her tool. When she was alone again, Edwan appeared in her room, on the verge of despair.

'Why are you doing this?'

'Doing what?'

'Seducing that desert man.'

'We need him, Edwan.' She spoke flatly and calmly, without anger or sorrow. 'Can I drive a stake through Corische's heart? Can you? Can you lift the bar from the doors?'

Her husband moaned and vanished in a flash. She

regretted his pain, but the situation couldn't be helped. They needed Rashed.

The next night, her master rose and left at full sundown. She sat by the fire pit, sewing. When Rashed walked in, she smiled at him. He nodded, turned to leave, and then stopped.

'What are you doing?' he asked.

'Sewing a table runner.'

Rashed shook his head as he stepped up to stand in front of her, knowing she was well aware of what he meant.

'I know you despise Corische. But there are aspects of him you don't know. He is glorious in battle. That is where his power lies.'

'Is that why you followed him?'

Rashed looked hard at her, perhaps finally suspicious. 'Do you honestly want to hear this? I thought you cared little for the past.'

'Certain aspects of the past are quite important to me. I'd like to know how someone like yourself became a slave to a low-born creature unfit to kneel at your feet.'

Stunned by her bluntness, Rashed paced for a moment, his face filled with puzzlement.

'I was fighting near the west of il'Mauy Meyauh, a kingdom of the Suman Empire across the sea. My people were at war with a group of the free tribes of the desert. I don't know where Corische came from, only that his own master died by accident in a fire. I did not understand at the time, but now wonder how one of our kind could ever fall to an accident. Once free, Corische wanted to secure himself by creating his own pack of servants.

He was careful, and only chose men easy to control like Ratboy . . . and Parko, my brother.

'Parko disappeared from our camp one night. I followed his trail and found Corische. We fought. Even as just a mortal, I made him earn his victory. In the end, he pierced my heart. As I bled to death, he made me an offer. At that moment, all I could think of was that Parko would never get along without me. Strange, foolish thought. When I awoke, I was Corische's servant. He took my inheritance and forced us all to travel north. We crossed the sea into Belaski. In Stravina, he found patronage under a powerful mortal lord. The master and I distinguished ourselves in battle for him. In five short years, we were appointed here, to Gäestev Keep. After the warmth of the south, this place was a frozen prison until . . .'

'Until I came and made it beautiful?' Teesha finished, almost impishly.

He nodded silently.

Teesha could see him slipping into the relief he'd gained since she'd started making changes in the keep, but this time she wasn't going to allow him that release.

'This isn't our home,' she hissed, and Rashed backstepped once in surprise at her sudden change of tone. 'No matter what I've done to it, it's *his*. We merely exist here. And that's all we'll ever have!'

Rashed stared at her for a time longer than any silence Teesha could remember between two people. His eyes were no longer filled with suspicion. He was confused, and Teesha's long careful nurturing of his desires began to take hold.

'What would you have us do?' he finally asked.

'Leave, go southwest to the coast, make our own home.'

'You know we can't,' he said gently. 'He will always be our master.'

'Not if he's dead . . . finally dead.'

Now it was Rashed who changed his demeanor, voice cold, hushed, and almost vicious.

'Don't say such things.' He dropped to sit on the bench, glaring at her, but his eyes shifted about as if he was looking for Corische to suddenly enter the room.

'Why not? It's true,' Teesha retorted. 'You serve him, but I see the anger under that cold mask you wear. You bought his rise in power with your family's money and your own skills. Yet he treats you – all of us – like property, nothing more, and we will never escape until he is gone.' She slid off the bench and knelt, touching his leg, her voice low to match his. 'If I stay with him much longer, I'll find a way to end my existence.'

Rashed pulled back but continued to stare down at her. 'If he were gone, would you leave this place with me?'

'Yes, and we'd take Ratboy and Parko. We could make our own home.'

Rashed finally stepped completely away and walked toward the heavy front door. He stopped and half turned, but he did not look at her. His jaw clenched.

'No, it's not possible.' He jerked the door open with both hands. 'Don't speak of this again.'

But the seeds were properly planted. Alternately kind and cruel to Corische, Teesha easily managed to keep him home more often. Sometimes she flattered him, and he drank and fed upon her words. Sometimes, out of Rashed's presence, she would quietly insult Corische, making cutting guesses about his low birth. Behaving more and more like a fool of desire, he restrained himself from lashing out, shrank back, and sought some new way to solicit her approval. He never gave her verbal orders. She became the master and he the slave, and she despised him all the more for it.

Corische may not have let his anger out at Teesha, but it still burned inside him. In a fit of rage and frustration one night, he broke the handle off a broom and beat Parko with it. Such an action could never have harmed one of them, but Rashed came running in to see why his brother yelped out in fear. He did not interfere, but Teesha saw clouds darker than disapproval pass over his desert warrior's face.

At every opportunity, Teesha drove Corische to desperation, especially when Rashed was nearby, seeking to portray their master as a petty abuser – which he was – and Ratboy, Parko, and herself as the abused. Rashed's expression grew more grim each night. Teesha bought a painting of the seacoast and hung it above the hearth as a less-than-subtle reminder, one that Corische wouldn't comprehend. She managed to quietly call Rashed's attention to it whenever possible. Large and well-crafted, the painting with its dark, cresting waves was a physical image of what they did not have – freedom to leave and see new places.

There finally came a night when she knew Rashed was on the edge. She tried several times to engage him in conversation, but he refused to respond. It was time for the last step. And Teesha waited until the following evening, when all five of them had barely arisen after dusk.

They were gathered in the main room, busy with mundane activities, and she leaned in close to Corische's ear, and whispered, 'I believe I met your mother a few nights ago. She was a gypsy hag working in a caravan tent, selling herself for two coppers per man.'

All her other jibes had been callously elite, copied from the manner with which she'd seen nobles insult the lower classes and carefully played so that Corische's ego might construe them as possibly goading instead of contemptuous. But this base comment was a lewd, open barb, the like of which had never passed her lips.

Corische's nostrils widened and for a moment he was stricken into stillness. He struck her across the face hard enough to knock her from the hearth bench and smash her small body into the stone wall.

Teesha blinked in pain. Her head pounded, and the room appeared to grow dark. One moment, barely a blink, stretched itself to a length she couldn't measure. All she could hear in the darkness inside her head was a ringing that played in her ears. Not a word from anyone. She had made a mistake in judging Rashed's mood. Corische would not be played with this way ever again, not after what she'd just done.

Finally, some of the darkness cleared. Corische stood over the bench, his arm just finishing its swing. Behind him, Rashed was lunging across the center oak table. His face was twisted in rage, his mouth wide with extended fangs, and a fierce growl ripped from the back of his throat. His right hand swept down to snatch the hilt of Corische's sheathed sword lying upon the table.

Corische turned at the cry of rage behind him. His eyes did not grow wide in surprise but narrowed like an angry dog's, cornered down an alley. Mouth open, his voice started to issue a command Rashed would not be able to refuse.

Rashed drew back his arm and flicked his wrist in a blur. The sheath slid up the sword's blade on his backswing, and before it even cleared the blade tip, the weapon swung forward.

Teesha heard a slight cracking sound when the blade cut through Corische's neck. His head bounced off the hearth's mantle, a spray of black liquid spattering the wall.

The sheath finally clattered to the floor.

Teesha crumpled down against the wall. Rashed landed on the near side of the table as Corische's body collapsed where it stood. The head rolled across the floor to bounce off Ratboy's boot.

Teesha blinked again. That was all the time it took.

After years of preparing moment by moment, everything changed in an instant. Teesha watched the near-black liquid, too dark for living blood, pour out of the corpse's neck stump onto straw-covered stones. It was the only movement in the room.

Parko was the first to disturb the stillness. He giggled quietly, nervously, then leaped across the floor like a cat to crouch at the body, sniffing. He laughed hysterically.

Ratboy began stammering. 'You . . . killed him.'

All the rage in Rashed was gone. He stood limply, sword dangling in his hand at his side, as he stared down at the headless body. His face looked as white as the snow. Then he looked up to find Teesha watching him.

She wasn't about to let him slip and fall back now.

'Are you sorry?' she asked almost accusingly. 'Do you regret this?'

'It's too late for that now,' Rashed answered. He dropped the sword to clatter on the floor and lifted Teesha to her feet gently with both hands. She said nothing, but kept staring at him, waiting as if she hadn't heard his first answer. Something of his anger came back and the muscles in his jaw tightened.

'No, I'm not sorry,' he added.

She gripped his forearms, or as much of them as her small hands could take in. In the air over Rashed's shoulder, she thought she saw Edwan's wispish form hovering in the rafters.

'We're free,' she whispered.

She had not failed. Corische was dead, and they had no master. They were free. Joy rushed through her, and she wanted to laugh, but she came back to her senses as Rashed pulled away.

He reached up and took the seacoast painting off the wall. 'Everyone gather what you want with you. We leave tonight.'

'Leave?' Ratboy sputtered. He was still standing dumbly as before, staring at Corische's headless body. 'What are you talking about? Where are we going?'

Teesha walked with a smile over to Ratboy, still slightly uncertain on her feet. He stared at her with wide brown eyes. With a gentle touch, she pushed him toward the stairs to their lower chambers for the last time.

'To the sea.'

Edwan jerked away from Teesha's mind, away from memories he could no longer stand to relive. In the silence, neither of them even heard the waves collapsing onto the shore of Miiska.

'Why?' he asked, his empty voice anguished. 'Why show me these ugly visions? Go back before . . . to the tavern.'

'No.'

'To the day we met, to the first time we——'

'No, my love.' She shook her head. 'To understand where you are, you must see where you've been, and not just the sweet parts.'

'I am in torment!' Edwan cried, shaking her completely out of the past and into the present.

'My love,' she whispered, regretting his pain. 'Let's walk among the dark streets and pretend we are high in the north, children again, in distant days.'

'Yes.' He drew near, instantly appeased, and she reached out for his hand. Although she could not grasp it, the cold mist of him settled around her slender fingers.

Ratboy watched a sleeping girl through the loose window shutters of a cottage, her dark hair spread out on the pillow, her breathing light and even. She didn't look anything like the girl he'd ripped and drained not many nights ago, but he felt the taste of blood running on his tongue with the memory. And the merchant on the road, taken so easily.

Who made these absurd rules that killing mortals would not be allowed? Did all of their kind follow such laws? Parko had not.

First there had been Corische enforcing his strict guidelines, desiring power and nobility among mortals. Now there was Rashed dominating every aspect of their existence, Rashed with his disgusting sense of honor, his obsession with safety and mortal trappings. Weren't they

Noble Dead? Wasn't that enough? No undead in his right mind would wish to become a mortal lord, or own a warehouse and earn a mortal living. Lately, Ratboy had begun to suspect Corische and Rashed were the mad ones, the twisted ones, not him, not Parko.

The girl rolled over in her slumber and raised a lovely tanned arm above her head. The movement caused Ratboy to tense, to smell the warm blood beneath her skin.

'What are you watching, my sweet?' a quiet voice said beside him.

He did not jump or even turn to look. It was only Teesha. He pointed through the window.

'Her.'

'It's not wise to feed in their homes. You know this.'

'I know many things. I'm not certain I agree anymore.'

Her hand rose and stroked the back of his hair.

'Shhhhh,' she whispered. 'It's not far to dawn. Come and find easier prey. You must think of our home. You must think of me.'

Closing his eyes at the feel of her touch, Ratboy slipped away from the window. Yes, he'd be cautious for her. But as they turned down the street together, he still remembered the sleeping, tan-armed girl.

8

Four nights later, Magiere stood behind The Sea Lion's bar, feeling a little more comfortable in her daily schedule. Out on the road, she and Leesil had developed a type of routine involving traveling, making camp, planning, manipulating feigned battles, and then beginning the process all over again. These events were interspersed with their experiences in new towns, villages, and Leesil's gambling. Now things were different. Her entire staff stayed up half the night serving guests, then slept late in the mornings. Leesil spent his afternoons working on the roof, while Beth-rae cooked, Caleb cleaned, and Magiere handled supplies, stocked shelves, and kept the house accounts. Chap watched over Rose. They always ate an early supper together before opening for customers. Magiere was continuously clean, warm, and slept in a bed every night.

Physical comfort and a unique sense of structure were not the only aspects of this life which brought her peace. For the first time, she was giving back to a community instead of draining it. The sailors, fisherfolk, and shop-keepers who patronized The Sea Lion enjoyed themselves and had a space of relief from their hard work. It did bother her when Leesil would mention the hushed whispers that often reached his ears about Magiere, 'Hunter of the Dead.' Perhaps she had become a local attraction. She could only guess how such rumors began, although she'd not seen either Welstiel nor the imposing nobleman again. Magiere suspected Leesil might still be drinking himself to sleep some nights, but as long as he stayed sober at the faro table and picked no pockets, she had no complaints.

Beth-rae walked up to the bar, carrying a full tray of empty mugs and looking a bit weary. A few strands of her silver, braided hair hung in loose wisps.

'Four more ales for Constable Ellinwood and his guards,' she said.

Magiere glanced at the table of loud men, but didn't comment while drawing the ale. One customer she could often count on was Ellinwood. Her distaste for the self-important man only grew with familiarity.

She set the mugs back on Beth-rae's tray, and the front door opened, letting in a cool breeze. No one entered, but she saw a head of brilliant red hair in the doorway with a close-trimmed beard of the same flaming color that hid his chin, cheeks, and upper lip. A burly man, perhaps in his late twenties, wearing a leather vest, he stood half in and half out, hesitating. He scanned the room and stopped upon seeing Constable Ellinwood. His jaw tightened, and Magiere knew there would be trouble.

The man stepped in, not bothering to close the door, and strode to Ellinwood's table, glaring down while the constable's ale mug halted in midair, almost to his mouth.

'Can I help you, Brenden?' Ellinwood asked, attempting to make his heavy body sit straighter.

'My sister is dead nearly a week, and you sit drinking with your guards? Is this how you catch a murderer?' the man spit out angrily. 'If so, I could find us a better constable lying in the gutter with a bottle of swill!'

The townsfolk stopped talking, even those at the faro table, and heads turned. Leesil held up one hand toward Chap before the dog moved, motioning him to wait.

Ellinwood's fleshy jowls grew pink. 'The investigation continues, lad. I have found several important facts just today, and now, as any man, I do as I please with my own time.'

'Facts?' Brenden's tone rose to a dangerous level.

The solid muscles of the blacksmith's arm tightened as he leaned on the table, and Magiere judged from his build that he could break Ellinwood's neck without trying. Perhaps his accusations were justified, but she wanted no bloodshed in her tavern. She glanced over at Chap and Leesil again, wondering if she should take action or let Leesil handle it. Her partner was more skilled at managing such situations in a quiet fashion.

'What facts have you found?' the blacksmith continued. 'You slept till midday, then spent the afternoon eating cakes in Karlin's. Now you're here, in your finest velvets, drinking ale with your lackeys. When exactly did you find your new facts?'

Ellinwood's pink tinge deepened, but he was saved from responding when an unshaven guard in a rumpled shirt stood up.

'That'll be enough, blacksmith,' he said. 'Go home.'

He was answered with a resounding *crack* as Brenden's fist connected with his jaw, sending the man tumbling back into another table of patrons. Another guard started to rise, but Brenden grabbed his greasy black hair and slammed the man's head twice against the table before anyone else could move. The guard slumped off the cracked table to the floor, unconscious. Leesil jumped over the faro table as Magiere unsheathed her falchion from under the bar.

'Chap, hold!' Leesil called out. If the dog leaped in, someone would end up bleeding.

Magiere slipped around the bar's front and held her ground for the moment. Leesil could usually stop a fight with few injuries to anyone.

'Gentlemen . . .' Leesil began.

Lost in rage, Brenden swung a backhanded fist at the half-elf, but his blow met empty air. Leesil dropped, hands to the floor, and kicked into the back of Brenden's knee. The blacksmith's large body toppled and a breath later, he found himself pinned, facedown. Leesil sat on his back, with one forearm against the blacksmith's neck and the other pinning his right arm. Although he was much heavier than Leesil, no amount of bucking from Brenden could throw his lithe keeper off. Every time Brenden tried to pull a leg under himself, attempting to get to his knees, Leesil kicked back with his foot in the black-smith's knee, as if he were spurring a horse, and Brenden flattened to the floor again.

'It's all right,' Leesil kept saying. 'It's over.'

The first guard Brenden had hit disentangled himself from the table of patrons that he'd landed on. Blood ran down his jaw and chin from his nostrils and it was obvious Brenden had broken his nose. His hand dropped to the sheathed shortsword on his hip, but then his eyes lifted to see Magiere. Her falchion rested on his shoulder, the sharp edge next to his throat. She said nothing. The guard put his hands up in plain view and stepped slowly back.

Finally, Brenden stopped struggling and lay in a smol-dering, panting heap.

'My friend's going to let you up,' Magiere said to him, not taking her eyes off Ellinwood's guards. 'Then you leave my place, understand?'

'Leave?' Ellinwood puffed. 'He is under arrest for attacking the very men who protect Miiska. He is a criminal.'

While Magiere disagreed, this was none of her concern. She just wanted them all to take it outside.

'He's not a criminal,' Leesil protested. 'Have some pity, you whale!'

One of the guards — not the one with the broken nose — pulled a rope from his belt and crouched down to begin tying Brenden's hands. Leesil reached out to stop him, but Magiere grabbed him by the shoulder. Cursing under his breath, the half-elf stood up and stepped out of the way. When Brenden was roughly jerked to his feet, he glared at Magiere as if she were to blame.

'Don't come back,' she said. 'This is a peaceful tavern.'

'Peace?' Brenden spit out, sorrow outweighing the anger in his voice now. 'How can you talk of peace when you're the one who can stop this killing? No, you hide away, serving ale to the likes of him.' He motioned with his head toward Ellinwood.

'I can't stop anything,' she said, tensing.

The guards dragged Brenden from the tavern.

Leesil walked away without a word and went back to his faro table, but Magiere could see he didn't feel like dealing cards anymore.

Late the next morning, Leesil stood outside Miiska's guardhouse, which also served as a jail, and checked his purse again, somehow hoping the coins within had miraculously multiplied. It had been hard enough to keep his distance from passersby who could have unwittingly aided him with that need, but he'd promised not to lift any more purses now that they had to stay in one place. Upon rising that day, he'd asked Magiere for his month's share of profits in advance. She'd given it to him with some apprehension, probably believing he needed it for a gambling debt. He didn't care what she thought. She'd never understand the truth. He wasn't sure he understood what he was doing anyway.

When he entered the guardhouse, Leesil paused in surprise. He'd hoped to handle things with one of the witless deputy guards, but there was Ellinwood's massive body behind the small table that served as a desk, tucked into the right corner of the room near the front barred window. He was staring intently down at some scribble on a parchment.

Leesil had seen his share of jails, from both sides of a cell door, and this one appeared no different. A few 'wanted' posters were tacked to the walls – those offering a reward or other profit from an arrest – and three cell doors lined the back wall, which was more than enough confinement for a town the size of Miiska.

He swung the front door shut as he stepped over to the cells. At the noise, Ellinwood finally looked up.

'Oh, it's you,' he said with thinly hidden impatience, most likely expecting a formal request for payment regarding the broken tavern table. 'What do you want?'

Leesil peered into the eye-level slots of each door and found Brenden crouched on the bottom bunk of the center cell.

'I'm here to pay the blacksmith's fine,' he answered. 'How much?'

'You want to . . . why would you do that?' The constable looked suspicious.

Leesil shrugged. 'It was either come down here or stay home and work on the roof. Which would you choose?' He paused briefly and repeated, 'How much?'

Ellinwood sat for a moment before answering. 'Six silver pennies, no foreign coin.'

Leesil suppressed the urge to wince. It was an absurd amount for the offense. He only had five and that was a month's estimated share, and well more than a month's wage for many in a small town like Miiska. It seemed the constable made good money by charging outrageous fines – or carried a grudge against the young smith and would make it difficult for anyone to interfere. But Leesil wasn't going to give up so quickly, and he doubted Ellinwood was willing to ignore such easily obtained profit.

'What if I pay you five now and sign a voucher on the other one?' he asked. 'I can pay the balance at the first of next month.'

'I've got the rest,' Brenden said quietly from his cell.

Leesil's head turned to find Brenden's large eyes staring out of the cell's peep slot, his red mane of hair sticking out wild and unkempt around his face. Leesil walked over to the cell door, nodding.

'At least I did,' Brenden continued, 'when I came in.' His gaze shifted to Ellinwood with an accusing glare.

'Well, that should cover it then, eh, Constable?' Leesil added, leaning against the door with his arms crossed.

The constable stared back at them, as if considering

some weighty decision. Then he turned around and picked up a small chest on the floor. Fiddling out a set of keys from under his tunic, he unlocked the chest and took from it a small, char-stained coin pouch. He walked over, unlocked the cell door, and handed the pouch to the blacksmith.

Brenden poured a small assortment of coins from the pouch into Leesil's slender hand, who in turn sifted through the contents until he came up with enough copper coins to make up the difference. Leesil then emptied his own purse to complete the fee.

'Here,' the half-elf said, holding out the coins in his fist. He dropped them into Ellinwood's open palm.

The constable returned to his desk, counting out the amount carefully. He put the coins into the chest, closed and locked it, and then went back to scanning the documents on his table without a word.

Leesil shrugged with disgust and motioned for Brenden to follow him out into the street. People bustled by, heading for the market or off to some other business of the day. A small boy hawked smoke-dried fish biscuits by the near corner. The sun beat down through a sparsely clouded sky.

'I . . . I'll pay you back,' Brenden said under his breath, 'as soon as I can.'

'Oh, that's all right. I don't spend money I can't afford.' Leesil shrugged again. He had food, shelter, and an endless supply of wine. There was nothing more that he needed and little more that he wanted at the moment. 'I'm sorry about last night,' he added.

'Sorry?' Brenden looked away. 'Now you shame me. I heard what you said for me, and you could have set that wolf on me. From the way you put me down, you could have done . . . I guessed you could have done more.'

Leesil began walking, and Brenden fell into step beside him. This blacksmith was a man with a strong sense of fair play. It was odd company for Leesil, after years of less-than-scrupulous ventures with Magiere, or on his own before that. He found it difficult to say anything more now that he'd gone to all this trouble for a stranger.

'What you said to Ellinwood was justified,' Leesil said finally. 'He's done nothing to catch your sister's murderer.'

'I'm not sure he can,' Brenden answered, kicking at some dust. 'I'm not sure anyone can but your partner, and she refuses to help.'

'What are you talking about?' Leesil feigned ignorance, hoping to dismiss what he knew was next on the smith's mind.

'Your partner – hunter of the dead.'

Leesil's stomach growled, but not from hunger. He was beginning to understand Magiere's restless irritation of late.

'You've been listening to too many rumors,' he added.

'Maybe, but *too many* is always the catch,' Brenden countered. 'When it's the same rumor over and over, wherever you go, it's got something of truth behind it.'

'And I find people just like to use their mouths,' Leesil snapped. 'They'll talk up just about anything, including . . . especially what they don't know a whit about.'

'Then why did you come to pay my fines?' Brenden barked back at him.

Leesil had no answer, or at least not one he could put into words. Perhaps Magiere's generosity to Caleb and Beth-rae was contagious. Perhaps, like his partner, he was examining his own past and realizing for the first time how much harm they must have caused swindling village after village. But what possible good could this sudden attack of conscience bring? How could he make amends, any amends? And for all this rather new self-examination, Leesil still considered most people to be mindless cattle who deserved to be cheated by the more intelligent, or wolves who preyed on others through power or wealth. Helping any of them seemed pointless . . . but this blacksmith?

The man had walked into a public tavern and confronted a worthless town constable and demanded justice. Although Leesil tended to circumnavigate problems instead of facing them straight on, he could appreciate bravery when he saw it, and he could respect loyalty to the dead, to those who had no voice.

And for his bravery, Brenden had been called a criminal and locked up in a cell. It wasn't right. Leesil was well aware that his own sense of right and wrong was tenuous at best, but helping Brenden seemed the proper course of action.

The two of them continued walking in silence until they reached the end of the street, where Leesil had to turn down through the middle of town toward the tavern. They both stopped in another uncomfortable pause.

'Don't judge Magiere. You don't know anything about us,' Leesil said more gently. 'Come to The Sea Lion anytime. I'll tell Magiere you're my friend.'

'Am I your friend?' Brenden asked, his tone somewhere between puzzlement and suspicion.

'Why not? I only have two, and one of them is a dog, by the by, not a wolf.' Leesil made a mock face of great seriousness. 'I'm a very particular fellow.'

Brenden slightly smiled, but with a hint of sadness. 'I may stop by . . . more quietly next time.'

They parted. In the empty space between them, a light, brighter than the midday sun, flashed once. A few passersby blinked, turning their heads as if something had been there, then went on their way.

'He was with the blacksmith,' Edwan said in the small sitting room beneath the warehouse. 'I saw him.'

Rashed approached Edwan's visage, not certain why the ghost was so troubled. One minute, he and Teesha had been going over import accounts, and the next, Edwan appeared, rambling about the hunter's half-elf and a blacksmith.

'Slowly,' Rashed ordered. 'What is this about?'

'You need to kill that hunter now,' Edwan said, with emphasized precision in his voice.

'No.' Rashed turned away. Rash actions on top of Ratboy's foolishness would only make them more vulnerable to discovery. 'It's too soon. We will wait until she has lost some of her apprehension.'

'You're wrong. She visited the death place of the girl Ratboy destroyed. I saw her.'

'Why didn't you tell me this earlier?' Rashed asked angrily.

'And today the half-elf, her partner, paid for Brenden's release. They talked together.'

Rashed shook his head and turned to Teesha with a questioning expression.

'Brenden is the dead girl's brother, and the blacksmith in this town,' Teesha said from the couch.

'What?' Rashed turned back on Edwan as if the

agitated spirit had suddenly become the source — rather than messenger — of misfortune. He began pacing again in silence, eyes shifting about without focus as his thoughts worked on themselves.

'She's preparing to hunt, isn't she?' Teesha asked. 'Why else would she be searching for a trail, sending the half-breed to befriend the victim's remaining family?'

Yes, why else would she? Rashed asked himself. Moving this quickly after one murder was dangerous, but that damned Ratboy had left them little choice. If she investigated too far and some connection led back to any of them or the warehouse, there would be little time to prepare. Ratboy had been reckless, and there hadn't been enough time to even clean up after him. It was impossible to guess what clues might have been left at the site of the girl's slaughter.

'We'll have to move against her first,' he said. 'Teesha, stay here, but prepare us to leave if it comes to the worst. Ratboy will come with me.' He raised a hand calmly to her coming objection. 'No, I'll do it quietly myself, and no one will find a body. She'll simply disappear. But I need someone to watch the others, the half-elf and the dog.'

'Then you should take me. I could do better for you than Ratboy.'

'I know you would, but' — he walked over to the couch — 'just stay here.'

'A noble gesture,' Edwan said from the center of the room, 'but I agree. Do be careful, Rashed. It's been a long time since you fought anything stronger than an accounting error. Something unfortunate might happen.'

Rashed did not respond, but he could feel Edwan's

attention upon him like the first glimmer of dawn burning at his skin. He wondered what he had ever done to earn the ghost's venom. It had been Corische who'd falsely accused and beheaded him.

'Yes, you must be cautious,' Teesha agreed, either missing or dismissing the ghost's sarcasm.

Rashed nodded and left to get his sword.

9

Several patrons – mainly young sailors – remained talking and drinking at The Sea Lion until well past midnight. Magiere felt some relief when they finally downed the last of their ale and bid her goodnight. She had set no official closing time, preferring to wait until customers left of their own accord. But tonight had been longer than usual, with less than a handful of hours left until dawn. She was tired, and Leesil had been strangely quiet and distant all night. She overheard one of the fisher-wives gossiping about how the half-elf had bailed the blacksmith out of jail. It surprised her and made her ashamed for her assumption that he'd been gambling on his own time and needed the money for a debt.

Beth-rae sighed deeply. 'I thought those boys would never tire.'

Leesil sat at the end of the bar nearest the door, drinking a cup of red wine. 'Perhaps we ought to start asking people to leave at a reasonable time,' he added.

'You could have gone up to bed,' Magiere said flatly. The last of the faro players had departed hours ago, and, with such peaceful late-night patrons as the young sailors, she wasn't sure why he'd lazed about the bar the rest of the night.

He blinked, then frowned, looking hurt. 'I always help close up.'

Yes, he did, and that wasn't what bothered Magiere.

For all her speculation, she couldn't figure out why he'd spent a month's wage bailing out that headstrong blacksmith and that annoyed her. In fact, it annoyed her enough that she wouldn't give him the satisfaction of asking him.

Chap slept contentedly by the fire, curled in a huge silver ball. With half the lamps and candles in the room snuffed out, the hearth threw its dim red light across the room, reflecting off Leesil's yellow-white hair and smooth skin. It suddenly occurred to Magiere that she really had no idea how old her partner was. With mixed blood, he'd likely live longer than a human, but then she had no idea how long full-blooded elves lived.

'Well, let's clean up then and go to bed,' she said.

'You go on up, Miss,' Caleb said in his perpetually calm voice. 'You've been working harder than anyone. We'll get things closed down.'

She glanced at Leesil, who nodded and stood up.

'Yes, go on, and I'll lend them a hand,' he said. 'I've been sitting long enough.'

The pink tinge of his eyes and almost indiscernible slur in his voice suggested he'd already had more than a cup or two, but she felt too tired to argue and headed for the stairs. Chap awoke and stretched as Leesil went to break up the fire. Caleb and Beth-rae went into the kitchen. All in all, it was a typical late night at the tavern, at least for as long as Magiere had been there.

Inside the darker night of the alley across from The Sea Lion, Ratboy crouched beside Rashed and watched the last glimmers of light in the windows fade out. Rashed stared down hard at him.

'No feeding at all, and no bodies if possible,' Rashed said for the third time. 'Do you understand? Just watch the common room and be ready to assist me if needed. I will enter through an upstairs window and break her neck while she's sleeping. If you have to kill, then so be it – but no noise, no disturbance. We take her body out to sea, and she simply becomes another "disappearance."'

Ratboy's resentment was difficult to hide, as was his discomfort at possibly having to fight the hunter or the dog yet again. At the moment, he couldn't fathom why he hadn't just refused. Even skulking in the night shadows, Rashed looked as resplendent as usual in his dark blue tunic, polished sword gripped in his hand just under the fold of his hooded cloak. His translucent irises seemed to glow softly.

Ratboy liked to pretend that his own shabby, filthy appearance was a conscious choice for hunting. In reality, he knew that no amount of bathing, grooming, or fine clothes would ever bring him close to Rashed's noble appearance. Indeed, if he ever tried, the contrast would be embarrassingly comical, so he hid beneath layers of dirt in an effort to create his own identity. He was never more aware of their unfortunate differences than when the two of them stood so close and alone.

'What about the dog,' he demanded, 'and the half-elf, for that matter? We don't know where anyone is. I could walk into all three of them having late night tea in the kitchen while you're nosing around upstairs. Then what do I do?'

'Don't allow yourself to be seen for one,' Rashed hissed back. 'That's your skill, isn't it – blending into shadows?'

Yes, but Ratboy feared the hunter. He remembered the pain of her blade and the panic as he felt his strength dripping away through gaping wounds until he'd gorged himself. But Rashed didn't care about his feelings. All that mattered to him was that Ratboy do as he was told.

'What if the hunter kills you?' Ratboy whispered. 'You have all the answers. Then what do I do?'

'Don't play the idiot with me.' His companion glared down at him icily. 'No mortal hunter is going to kill me. Now get inside. We have little time, and I won't be caught at sea when the sun rises.'

Ratboy swallowed down the urge to hiss back as he inched to the alley's edge. This was the best time to attack. If all went well, they would catch the household asleep, complete their task, sink the hunter's body in the bay, go back home, and the cursed sun would be halfway to noon before anyone knew something was amiss. Rashed's intelligence was not in question, only his manner. He treated everyone like a servant – except Teesha.

Without another word, the urchin slipped across the street to the corner nearest a front window. Rashed had already tricked Magiere into saying that all the nobleman's friends, as patrons, were welcome. Although her meaning could be ambiguous, the invitation was legitimate. Peering through the shutters, he saw no hint of a light in the dark common room. The fire in the hearth was scattered but still smoldering, embers glowing softly.

Ratboy drew out a shining, thin-bladed dagger and slipped the point between the shutters' edges. He quickly jimmied the inside window latch and silently swung it open. Too easy. He thought a hunter would have had better locks. Ratboy clenched the blade between his teeth as he slid up onto the sill. He didn't plan to lose a second fight if the dog attacked him. He'd cut the beast's throat immediately. Rashed had said 'no noise,' but as for 'no blood,' well, let Rashed try to fight that damn hound. The pompous long-shanks would quickly change his mind.

Testing the air for any scent of the living, Ratboy found the common room was still too rank with the odor of sweat-stained sailors, ale, and burnt meat. No one was at the tables, no one was by the fire. Rashed had probably crossed the roof and slipped inside by now. Perhaps all would go according to Rashed's plan.

Ratboy dropped quietly down on the wooden floor, crouching low and peering over the tabletops across the room. A light shimmer caught in the corner of his vision, and he turned his head, craning his neck.

The silverish hair was light enough to spot in the dark. At the near end of the bar sat the half-elf facing toward the stairs and drinking from a tarnished tin cup. He was about to sip again, then seemed to think better of it and lowered the cup. His hand dropped off the bar.

His head turned, and he looked directly to where Ratboy crouched in the dark.

Ratboy felt his insides roll over. Of course, a half-elf's night vision would nearly match his own. He wondered if he could throw his dagger fast enough to kill the half-blood before any alarm was raised. Then he heard a flutter in the air racing toward him and he ducked back against the wall.

A stiletto struck the tabletop where his head had been, point stuck deep as the blade quivered briefly on impact. An eerie, high-pitched snarl filled the room, emanating from amidst the furniture at the far side of the hearth. The silver hound sprang upon a tabletop, its eyes focused directly on Ratboy.

Rashed sheathed his sword and scaled the inn's wall effortlessly, hardened fingernails clawing into planking cracks and crevasses.

This entire affair was far too rushed, without care, grace, or planning. Given time, he would have visited the inn three or four nights in a row, noting the routines of its inhabitants, who slept in what room and what hour they retired, who locked up at night, who couldn't sleep, and where the hunter kept her sword. He would have learned many things. Now he was forced to enter blindly and seek out his target.

He crept along the roof's edge, looking for a suitable window through which to enter, preferably not the hunter's bedroom window, for fear of waking her and giving her a chance to bolt for the door. Hanging over the edge, he peered through a window where the curtains had not been drawn. The room inside was large enough for a double bed, various chests, and a chair. The empty bed meant someone was still up and about, and he felt an urgency settle upon him. Ratboy had his orders – to be silent and bloodless – but it wouldn't be the first time if he blundered, stumbling upon someone downstairs and awakening the whole household. Then Rashed saw a little blond-haired girl sleeping upon a floor mat at the foot of the bed. By the rhythm of her breathing she was deep in slumber and would not wake at his entrance. She had nothing to fear from him anyway.

He'd never yet found a need to prey upon a child.

The window had no lock, and in seconds, he dropped quietly into the room. He stepped past the child and cracked the bedroom door to peer out. The hall lay empty. There were only two other doors and the staircase downward, so his search would be quick. He stepped out, closing the door behind him.

An unnatural, wailing snarl rose up the stairs from below and crawled over his skin. It was followed by manic snarls and the snap and shatter of wood.

The door at the end of the hall swung open. Rashed froze.

Her hair hung loose around her shoulders, but she was still dressed in breeches and a leather vest. Howls and snarls and the echoes of a wild fight below in the common room were now loud and clear. The hunter's eyes widened.

'You—' she said in surprise.

Before she could finish, Rashed crossed the distance between them and slammed his weight against the door as she tried to shut it. They both tumbled into the room.

Leesil drew his other stiletto out of his sleeve, feeling a rush of shame at being caught so unaware. Half-crouched, he scuttled between the tables and moved roundabout toward the open window. The skulker had gotten all the way into the room before he'd even noticed. Perhaps he was just caught off guard. It couldn't have been the drink.

Chap was in midair, lunging, and the intruder tried to kick the table in front of him out of his way. The dog lost his targeted landing spot and hit the teetering table with his front paws. The angled table legs snapped under the sudden weight, and Chap smashed down upon the intruder in a tumble of shattering wood. The crash and enraged snarls from Chap hammered in Leesil's ears, followed by a pain-filled yelp.

'Chap, back! Get off!' Leesil yelled, pulling aside chairs to reach the skirmish.

The dog did break off, but only because his opponent kicked him, sending the animal spinning across the floor on his back until he toppled two chairs and became entangled in them.

'Stay back!' Leesil ordered the dog, and then he inched toward the window and tried to peer over the slanted top of the table's remains.

The intruder rose up in an unnatural gliding motion. Enough moonlight spilled in between open window shutters to show dark lines running down the side of his face – Chap's claw marks. Leesil stopped when he saw the intruder's features.

It was Ratboy, the dusty beggar from the road outside Miiska. Leesil settled back one step, the stiletto poised and ready.

'Didn't get enough of us the last time?' Leesil asked.

Ratboy put a hand to his cheek, running his fingers along the wounds as if unsure of them. Then he stared at the blood in his hand.

'My . . . face,' Ratboy whispered. The expression of shock and pain washed over him.

His eyes turned as lifeless as a corpse's, and Leesil remembered how the last time this beggar boy had seemed an uncanny creature rather than human – and all the more unsettling for his human appearance. Amidst the clatter of toppled chairs, Chap scrambled to his feet, moving forward for another assault.

'No, Chap,' Leesil snapped, trying to keep Ratboy in sight and still turn his head slightly to see if the dog obeyed.

Ratboy lunged at Leesil with a bloody dagger pointed outward.

Leesil dodged the blade and retreated, baiting his opponent into wild swings. Ratboy was obviously no match for him in a knife fight, but he still remembered their last meeting. The little man-thing had pulled a crossbow quarrel from his own stomach as if it were an annoying sliver. He wasn't going to risk Ratboy getting close enough to grab him. He dodged another wild swing and felt his back rub against the bar's front edge. With a quick hop, he rolled backward over the bar and dropped behind it.

A crossbow hadn't worked the first time, but seeing he had little choice, he grabbed the loaded weapon Magiere kept hidden behind the bar. By the time he lifted it, the creature was in midair – not vaulting but leaping over the bar without touching it. Clutching both stiletto and crossbow, Leesil fired.

The quarrel cracked into Ratboy's forehead above his right eye, and his body flipped backward to smash down on the bar top. The dagger bounced out of his hand on impact, falling to Leesil's side of the bar, but Ratboy tumbled back the other way, flopping to the floor on the far side, out of Leesil's sight.

Leesil leaned forward to peer over the bar, but he couldn't see clearly in the dark. Chap began inching forward from the middle of the room, but Leesil held up a hand to stop him. He was sidling along the bar to move around its end when Chap began to snarl again.

A dirty hand slapped over the bar top from the far side. The bar's wooden edging creaked in that hard grip. Leesil reflexively leaned back against the wine casks lining the back wall.

Ratboy pulled himself up and jerked the quarrel out of his head. Blood ran down across his right eye.

Planning and thinking wasn't usually one of Leesil's strong points, so he did the only thing he could think of.

'Why don't you die already!' he yelled, and swung the crossbow like a club.

The crossbow's center stock smashed into Ratboy's head, and he stumbled a few steps down the bar toward the stairs. Snatching the bar's edge again, the urchin kept himself from falling. He glared at Leesil and moved slowly back toward the half-elf.

'You're going to bleed for me,' he spit out hoarsely.

Just then the curtain in the kitchen doorway was flung aside.

Beth-rae stepped into the room at the bar's far end, behind Ratboy's back, carrying a bucket that slopped full of something. Leesil yelled at her to run, but there was no time. As Ratboy spun about for this new target, Chap charged in to sink his teeth into Ratboy's calf, holding him back. Beth-rae threw the bucket's contents over the struggling intruder in front of her. Before Leesil had time to curse such a futile act, he was halted by Ratboy's scream piercing his ears.

The creature began to thrash, body banging against the bar and nearby chairs as he slapped and tore at his own clothes and skin. His entire body smoked with hissing tendrils of gray mist that rose from his blackening flesh.

Leesil barely caught the distant ring of steel against steel mixed in with Ratboy's screeching. It took him a moment to realize it came from the second floor. He looked to the stairs, and that moment's distraction was too much.

Ratboy took one jerking hop toward Beth-rae, like a hideous smoldering puppet, and struck out at her with one hand. Hooked fingers caught her throat as she tried to back away. Her body spun around, and slammed against the wall behind her. Before she'd even slid to the floor, the howling creature tore through the curtained doorway and into the kitchen. Chap bolted into the kitchen after him.

Leesil hurried to Beth-rae's side as he heard the kitchen's back door smashing open. He crouched down. On the floor, a red-black pool was growing, fed by the gash in her throat. Beth-rae lay motionless, eyes wide. From the tilt of her head, Leesil could see her neck had snapped under the blow. There was nothing he could do for her now.

He dropped the crossbow, readied his remaining stiletto, and headed for the stairs.

'Magiere!' Leesil shouted as he started running.

Magiere scrambled across the bedroom floor and snatched the falchion lying on her small desk.

'Get out!' she shouted from instinct, not expecting the nobleman to obey.

He didn't answer, but lunged and swung hard with

his own sword. She dodged, and his blow landed on the desk. Wood shattered into pieces and the blade's tip embedded in the floor. He jerked it out effortlessly.

No one was that strong. The room felt small with no space for Magiere to maneuver, but then her opponent was also limited. She spun on one knee around the bed's end and onto her feet, her opponent sliding sideways across the floor to match her. In the low lamplight, his eyes were transparent, gazing calmly into hers. Anger overcame fear. Who was this bastard to think he could invade her home – her room?

'Coward,' she snapped at him. Rage grew inside her until it threatened to overcome reason. Her falchion snapped up until it reached the ceiling, and she aimed for his neck, swinging with all the anger she felt. He blocked, but the blow's force made him step back and lose his balance. With both blades still locked, she slammed her free fist into his jaw.

More shocked than hurt, he used his free hand to shove her backward. Magiere toppled onto the bed like a moth he'd swiped aside.

'Hunter,' he said simply and struck down with his long blade again.

She rolled off the bed's far side as the long sword struck her quilt with a flat-sounding swat. There was no room in here to use maneuvers against him. He would kill her by sheer force. That thought would have been enough to terrify anyone, but her rage multiplied so quickly she didn't even try to understand it.

Hatred became strength flowing through her body, making her movements quicker than ever before. Instinctively shifting for small openings, she tried to find some way to get behind him or take him off balance. He kept turning to face her. They shifted back and forth around or across the small room, making flailing slashes at each other. But there was never an opening, never an instant where she could rush the door or duck under his swing to come up on his flank or rear.

Once more shifting to the far side of the bed, she threw herself to roll across it. The nobleman made another dash to follow her across the room. When he did, she stopped short, crouched upon the bed, and struck out with the falchion so fast he didn't have time to block. Boots skidding on the floor, he tried to pull back, his torso leaning away from her swing. The blow missed his collarbone, but sliced a shallow gash down his chest.

'What—'

The rest of his words were lost in a gasping inhale. His wide-eyed gaze shifted to Magiere's sword. As his brow creased in pain, his teeth snapped together hard and clenched. Shock got the better of him, and his grip on his own sword faltered as its point dragged through the debris of the desk.

Magiere couldn't answer him, couldn't remember how to speak. She didn't want to cut him with the blade anymore. She wanted to rip his throat out. The front of her jaws began to ache and would not close completely, as if her teeth had shifted, or grown. Confusion lost her the advantage she'd gained.

When she finally lunged, he had regained his balance, but not his faltering grip on his sword. He released the weapon from his right hand and snatched her sword arm's wrist with his left. Using her weight and momentum, he spun around to slam her against the wall between the door and wardrobe. His now empty right hand clamped around her throat.

She instinctively grabbed his wrist with her free hand. He smashed her sword arm against the side of the wardrobe twice, but Magiere's grip on the weapon wouldn't release

'I don't need a weapon to kill you,' he whispered at her, real emotion leaking into his voice for the first time. 'You need to breathe.'

Her body bucked wildly as she tried to throw him off, but he held like stone, waiting for her to suffocate.

Magiere lost awareness that her breathing had stopped. Loss of air now made room for her to grow, as if the grip on her throat held in her rage, letting it build up inside of her. She stared at him, her eyes unblinking and wide until they began to water.

As the first tear rolled down her cheek, a screaming, wailing cry of pain sounded from below, and the nobleman's head jerked slightly in surprise. Magiere felt his grip on her throat falter only for a moment. She let go of his wrist and grabbed the back of his head, then drove her own head forward and bit into his throat.

She felt the vibration of his panicked shout tingle across her face, as she pressed harder against his cold skin and blood leaked into her mouth. A knot of hunger twisted up suddenly in her stomach. Both his hands came in to push at her head. She pulled her mouth away before he could find his grip, and struck downward with her falchion. This time the blade connected with a solid crack as steel met with bone in his left shoulder.

'Magiere!'

The voice pulled at her from somewhere out of sight and far away – from downstairs.

The nobleman roared and swung with his right fist, even though the movement caused her blade to cut deeper. The blow caught her jaw.

The pain Magiere felt was as far away as the distant voice she'd just heard. The room spun until she saw the floor rushing up to meet her. She fell halfway on her side, and her breath rushed out. The moment that her head bounced off the floor, she thought she heard the sounds of shattering glass and wood. She struggled to sit, walls tilting haphazardly in her sight. She swung her blade blindly around, unable to focus. By the time the room stopped rocking before her eyes, and the pain in her head began to truly register, the room was empty.

Breathing was difficult. Rage and hatred leaked out of her as each breath, suddenly harder than the last, seemed to expel her strength. Her arms and head felt heavy, and she crumpled back to the floor. As she lay there, trying to gasp in air, realization of what she'd just done crept into her awareness.

Not all the blood in her mouth belonged to that hated nobleman, but she had tasted it, tasted his blood. And that memory caused fear to replace lost rage.

Footsteps on the stairs doubled that anxiety – the nobleman. She tightened her grip on the falchion and struggled to pull herself up.

Leesil appeared above her. He dropped to his knees and pulled her upper body into his lap. Relief caused fear to fade at his presence, but for some reason, she didn't want him to see her. She pulled away, covering her face with her free hand.

'Magiere, look at me,' he said. 'Are you all right?'

'It wasn't me,' she whispered, finding her voice. 'It wasn't me.'

'Magiere, please,' he said, his tone desperate. 'Beth-rae is dead, and Chap's badly hurt. I have to get back downstairs. Are you all right?'

Shame, horror, and reality hit her all at once. Why was she hiding from Leesil?

She sat up, Leesil pushing her from behind, and turned to look at him. As she pulled her hand from her face, he grimaced at the sight of blood on her jaw. He reached out to inspect the damage to her lower lip where the nobleman's fist had landed.

Leesil pulled his hand away abruptly and glared at her, as if wary of her presence.

'What?' she asked urgently. 'What is it?'

He hesitated before answering. 'Fangs.'

Night wind blew in from the shattered window frame across the room and stripped the last of anger's heat from Magiere's body.

The scene they found in the common room pressed Leesil down to the point where he was almost unable to perform any more action.

A lit lantern rested on the end of the bar, and Caleb kneeled by Beth-rae's body. He looked up at Leesil in confusion, wanting someone to explain everything away. Chap also sat by the body, whining and pushing at Beth-rae's shoulder with his nose. The fur on his chest was matted with blood, but from the way he moved, it seemed he was not as seriously injured as Leesil had feared.

'I went out for fresh water,' Caleb said numbly. 'I came back and . . .'

'Caleb, I'm so sorry,' Magiere whispered from the base of the stairs.

Magiere still appeared shaken, but at least fully aware of her surroundings. If not for the blood on her chin and the split lip, Leesil would have thought her no more disarrayed than she was after one of their old mock battles played at the expense of frightened villagers.

Beth-rae's throat was jaggedly torn from one side to the other. Leesil knew the weapon had been a dirty fingernail.

'It was him,' he said finally, 'that filthy beggar boy we fought on the road to Miiska.' He didn't look at Magiere as he spoke. 'He attacked us . . . or, actually Chap attacked him, but he climbed through that front window. Beth-rae threw something over him, and he started to scream, and his skin turned black.'

'Garlic water,' Caleb said softly, touching Beth-rae's hair.

'What?' Magiere asked.

'We've been keeping a cask of it in the kitchen,' he answered flatly. 'If you boil garlic for several days in water, it makes a weapon against vampires.'

'Stop it,' Magiere said harshly, stepping closer. 'I don't want to hear it right now. Whatever they wanted, they were just men. Do you understand?'

For the first time since meeting her, Caleb looked at Magiere with something akin to open dislike on his face. He struggled to carefully lift his wife in his arms.

'If you stopped lying to yourself and dealt with the truth, maybe my Beth-rae wouldn't be dead.'

He carried the body through the curtain to the kitchen. Chap followed, still whining.

Magiere slumped down to sit on the bottom stair and covered her eyes with her hands. Strands of her loose, messy hair caught in the drying blood on her chin.

'What's going on?' Leesil asked. 'Do you know?'

'The man at the Vudrask River was the same,' she said quietly.

'What are you talking about?'

'He was the same – pale, bones like rock, too strong – surprised my weapon hurt him. He was the same.'

'You mean the same as the beggar boy on the road, the one in here tonight,' Leesil added, growing more angry. 'Something else you neglected to tell me, yes?'

He took several deep breaths. Shouting at her would do nothing to help the situation, so he turned away. He wanted a drink and walked to the bar, found his old cup, and filled it.

'I can't feel them now,' Magiere said, and Leesil looked up to see her hesitantly running one fingertip across the tops of her teeth, slowly, one by one. She pulled her hand away. 'Maybe you just imagined—'

'I imagined nothing!' Leesil said, his voice growing louder on each word. He slammed the cup down on the bar and walked back to crouch before her. 'This is not just something in your head and certainly not in mine.'

His hand reached up quickly, about to grab her jaw. Magiere started to pull away, but then remained still, staring at him. At first, her features were flat and emotionless at the closeness of his hand, and then they shifted.

The look on her face told Leesil she was defying him to find again what he thought he'd seen.

Leesil moved carefully. Magiere did not open her mouth, but she did not resist as he gently pressed his fingers on her lower jaw to open it. He didn't touch her teeth, because he didn't need to. There was no sign of the elongation of her eyeteeth. Leesil let his hand drop away from her face, but he did not look away.

'We have to inform the constable about the attack,' he said. 'Word is going to spread soon enough about Beth-rae's death.'

Magiere sank back, eyes closing slowly.

'Leesil?' a tiny voice called from the top of the stairs.

Magiere's eyes snapped open. 'Rose?' she said softly, turning to look up.

A small form in a muslin nightdress rubbed her eyes and yawned.

Leesil took the stairs two at a time.

'Where's Grandma and Grandpa?' Rose asked, half awake. Her lower lip quivered slightly. 'I heard noisy things in the dark.'

'You had a bad dream.' Leesil grabbed Rose quickly, but gently, and picked her up, holding her against his shoulder.

'Where's Grandma?'

'People who sleep in my bed never have bad dreams,' he answered. 'It's too big and soft. Would you like to sleep there?'

She blinked again, trying hard to keep her eyes open for the moment. 'Where will you sleep?'

'I'll sit in the chair and watch over you until the sun comes up. All right?'

She smiled, clutching at his hair as she put her head in the crook of his neck. 'Yes. I'm afraid.'

'Don't be.' Before turning toward his room with the weary child, he looked down. Magiere stood at the bottom of the stairs, leaning heavily against the railing for support. His voice was sweet and light as he whispered to the child. 'Everything will be better in the morning,' he lied.

10

Rashed paced inside the cave below his warehouse in nearly panicked agitation. He'd raced back home to find Teesha and Ratboy – assuming that Ratboy would have run home as well – in order to move them someplace safe. The hunter had clearly seen his face, and many people in town knew him or knew of him as the owner of the warehouse. Sunrise was only moments away, and not only was Ratboy still missing, but he'd come back to find Teesha gone as well.

Had she gone looking for them or taken Ratboy to safety herself? Either act was certainly in the realm of Teesha's nature, but he couldn't be certain. Rashed moved toward the lower end of the cave, ready to head back out in search of Teesha, but he could sense the time. After long years in the night, any vampire was fully aware of the time and movement of the unseen sun. Any who failed to build such an awareness had long since burned to ash in the light of day. He knew the sun was cresting the horizon, and so he stopped short of leaving, turning to pace again, back and forth in the dark.

Where was Teesha?

He'd constructed their world carefully in a place where they could exist and thrive, feed judiciously and not worry over being discovered. It was home enough, but not without Teesha. Given time, he'd even hoped

one day she might be free of that specter of a husband
who clung to her in afterlife. If she had gone to find
Ratboy and himself and been burned in the daylight?
Then Ratboy best have burned with her, or Rashed
would tear him apart slowly, piece by piece, over long
blood-starved years, never letting the filthy little wretch
have his second death.

Damn the hunter to eternal torture as well. And what
a fool he'd been himself.

Blood dripped openly from the gaping wound in
Rashed's shoulder, and he could not easily move his left
arm. His collarbone was cleanly broken. The shallow
wound down his chest seeped. Each injury burned as if
he'd been dowsed with some priest's blessed oils. The
wounds weren't healing at all. He remembered Ratboy's
own panic upon returning from the fight on the road
with the hunter, and he knew he would have to feed
soon in order to close his wounds.

He'd told Ratboy 'no noise.' Was that such a difficult concept to understand? In a matter of moments,
he'd lost control of his fight with the hunter, and
Ratboy had managed to alert the entire household.
Now the hunter had confirmation that at least two
undeads inhabited the town. The situation could hardly
be worse.

And what in all the demons of the underworld had
happened to him during the fight itself? The hunter's
sword was magically endowed, if not magically created;
that much was obvious. Where did she get it? Even a
blade that had been warded or arcanely made to battle
the undead should not have prevailed against his open
attack – he was too strong and skilled. This was not

arrogance or pride, but realism. He should have been able to beat her down, if not kill her outright, and been back out the window with the body in a matter of seconds. Instead of tiring, her strength and speed had grown to match his every attack.

And she had bitten him as if she were one of his own kind.

He'd felt the heat of her body, heard the pounding of her heart, and smelled living blood in her veins. She was not a vampire or some other Noble Dead. What had happened? And she had seen his face. It was only a matter of time and questions asked before the hunter connected him to the warehouse.

'We must leave here,' he murmured.

'Rashed!' Teesha's voice called to him from the far side of the cave.

Relief flooded Rashed at the sound of her voice. But when he turned to see her in the dark, stumbling toward him, her face was filled with as much fear as he'd felt when he dove through the inn's window to save his own existence. He ran toward her, and anger returned quickly at what he saw.

Teesha held on to Ratboy's half-conscious form by the back of his shirt collar, dragging him into the cave. She looked exhausted. She'd never had the physical strength with which most Noble Dead were gifted. Perhaps it was a trade-off for her higher ability in thought and dreams that she used to hunt. Even he had sometimes felt the soothing calm wash through him at the sound of her lilting words.

'Someone threw garlic water all over Ratboy,' she said. 'I found him crawling by the sea, using wet sand to scour it off. I had to kill a peddler down by the shore to feed him quickly. Haste would not allow a more discreet hunt, and Ratboy needed a great deal of blood. I buried the body in the sand for now. We just got inside before sunrise, but he's badly hurt.'

By way of answer, Rashed grabbed Ratboy by the front of his shirt and held him off the ground against the dirt wall of the cave. The little urchin's skin was still partially blackened and charred in places, cracking and split. It served him right for his recklessness.

'We're stuck in here now because of you,' Rashed hissed. 'That hunter may come during the day and burn this place around us.'

Ratboy's eyes were mere slits, but hatred glowed out clearly.

'What a pity,' he managed hoarsely.

'I told you "no noise"! You forced me out before my work was finished.' That was only partly true – but Ratboy and Teesha didn't need to know that.

'And who cut through your shoulder?' Ratboy opened his eyes wide in mock surprise. 'Did she hurt you, my dear captain?'

Rashed dropped him and drew his fist back to strike.

Teesha grabbed it. The mere touch of her hands was enough to make him pause.

'This will not help us,' she said. With light pressure he could have easily resisted, Teesha pulled Rashed's arm down. 'We have to get every trap set and hide as deeply as possible.'

Of course, she was correct. There was nowhere to run until nightfall. Now he was the one playing the fool and right in front of her. Ratboy's blundering had undone him in more ways than one. He quickly collected himself.

'Yes, you help Ratboy. I'll set the devices and join you below.'

Her tiny fingers brushed his face as if glad to see him in charge again. 'Let me tend your shoulder.'

'No, it's all right. Just get deeper below.'

Perhaps they would all survive until nightfall.

Leesil and Magiere waited in the common room for Constable Ellinwood to arrive. At sunrise, Leesil had accosted a passing boy on the street and paid the youth to run to the guardhouse with the news of Beth-rae's murder. His initial instinct had been to clean the mess up in the common room, but Magiere stopped him.

'All of this proves we were attacked,' she said.

Everything was left where it had fallen the night before with two exceptions. Caleb had taken Beth-rae's body to the kitchen and had not come out again. And then there was Ratboy's thin-bladed dagger.

Leesil hadn't even remembered it until he'd stepped around to the back of the bar to put away the crossbow, and found it lying on the floor. He quietly picked up the blade out of Magiere's sight.

Ratboy must have used it to trip the latch on the common-room window. The blade was wide and unusually flat, making it thin enough to slip between shutters or into a doorjamb, and the width would provide strength when pushed against any metal hook or latching mechanism. Inspecting the blade, he found it well tended and sharpened, but with an odd shape to its tip. It wasn't overt, and perhaps anyone else wouldn't have noticed, but Leesil had slipped through enough windows in his life to know what he saw.

Near the tip, the edges were no longer straight, but indented slightly. Long use as a tool had worn down the metal and frequent resharpening had produced a slight inward curve in the edge on each side. Ratboy was not a common thief, whatever else he might be, but Leesil could see the beggar boy was practiced at unseen entry. A blade like this was a personal choice, sometimes specially made, and certainly a well-cared-for possession. And yet, Ratboy had obviously not entered the inn to steal anything, and his manner was not that of an assassin – the little creature might be cunning and stealthy to a point, but he had no finesse.

Leesil had serious doubts Ellinwood could even understand such things without them being pointed out blatantly and then explained. And he wasn't even sure how it connected to the more unusual details of last night. If necessary, he'd show the dagger, but for now he tucked it under the back of his shirt. Magiere might not agree with this action, but he would handle that if and when it came up. He stepped around the bar into the open room, surveying the ruins of broken tables and chairs, fresh scars in the bar top, and dried pools of blood.

Magiere's words made sense – everything needed to be left as it was to make Ellinwood believe what had happened, but he hated the thought of doing nothing. The bloodstained floor kept drawing his attention. Why hadn't he initially held his ground and reloaded the crossbow? Why hadn't he rushed the creature as soon as Beth-rae threw the garlic water? The scene played over and over in his mind as he examined every move he could have made differently. Scenarios taught long ago by his mother and father crept back into his conscious thoughts from places where he'd hidden them. He'd made so many mistakes, and now Caleb was a widower and little Rose had no grandmother.

Chap's chest was almost healed, which in itself seemed too much for Leesil to think about, in addition to everything else that made no sense in their lives of late. Magiere's facial wound looked days instead of hours old. Whenever Chap or Magiere fought these strange attackers, they healed with an unnatural quickness. Or had they always been quick to mend? It occurred to him that in their years together he'd never before been in such situations with either of them, so there was no way to be sure. He didn't want to talk about any of it, but how much were they going to tell the constable?

'Magiere?'

'What?'

'Last night . . . your teeth,' he began. 'Do you know what happened?'

She walked closer to him, her black hair still a tangled mess of long waves and strands around her face. Scant light that filtered in through the windows hit her from behind, and the highlights in her hair turned their usual red, almost a blood red, and that comparison made Leesil uneasy. Her expression was earnest, as if she wanted – had been waiting, even – for some reason or moment or encouragement to tell him something.

'I don't know. Not really,' she answered. Her eyes closed tight and she shook her head slowly.

Leesil noted her jaw shift, perhaps as she checked her

teeth with her tongue yet again for the return of what he'd seen there. Her voice dropped low, near a whisper, though there was no one else nearby to hear her.

'I was so angry, worse than I've ever felt in my life. I couldn't think of anything but killing him. I hated him so—'

A knock on the inn's door interrupted her. She frowned in a mix of frustration and distaste, letting out a sigh.

'That must be Ellinwood. Let's get this over with.'

With a quick glance and nod to Magiere, Leesil went to open the door, but to his surprise it was not Constable Ellinwood on the other side but Brenden.

'What are you doing here?' Magiere demanded.

'I told him he could come by,' Leesil interjected, having actually forgotten about it until this moment.

'I heard what happened,' the blacksmith said sadly. 'I came to help.'

Leesil had never seen anyone with such vivid red hair as Brenden, and with his matching beard, he seemed like a broad head of fire in the doorway. His black leather vest was oddly clean for someone who worked with iron and horses all day. Magiere just looked at the blacksmith as if she honestly didn't care whether he stayed or not.

'Ellinwood's useless,' Brenden went on in the same sad voice. 'If you tell him what really happened, he'll bury the case and never discuss it unless you force him to. Nothing will be done.'

'Fine,' Magiere said, turning away. 'Stay if you like, go if you like. We aren't expecting any assistance from the constable anyway. Beth-rae was murdered last night, and the law requires us to inform the authorities.'

Leesil remained quiet through this exchange in the hope that Brenden and Magiere might actually speak to each other, see one another as individuals. The blacksmith was one of the few people in town they'd met so far who was willing to speak about anything related to the attack on the road or what had happened last night. The result of his presence wasn't all Leesil had hoped for, but at least Magiere hadn't ordered him off the premises. Leesil stepped back and urged him inside.

'I'll make us some tea,' he said.

'How's Caleb?' Brenden asked, staring at the blood-stained floor by the bar.

'I don't know. We haven't seen him since just after . . .'

The tavern suddenly felt cold, and the half-elf busied himself by making a fire and boiling water for tea. He could have done it in the kitchen, but he didn't want to leave Magiere. And Caleb was in the kitchen with Beth-rae's body, which Leesil could not bring himself to look at right now.

Somehow the three of them managed to make small talk. Brenden seemed hesitant to question too much concerning the night's events, likely not wanting to wear out his welcome now that he'd regained some acceptance. Magiere avoided giving any complete answers to the few questions ˙asked. Enough of that would be covered all over again once Ellinwood arrived. With Magiere running out of evasive answers and Brenden short on acceptable questions, the room became oppressively quiet until another knock sounded.

'That will be him,' Magiere said with distaste. 'Leesil, can you get the door?'

This time the visitor was indeed Constable Ellinwood, clearing his throat in place of a greeting and looking somewhat put upon in fulfilling his duty. His vast, colorful form filled the doorway like that of an emerald giant gone soft through years of idleness.

'I hear you had some trouble,' he said, his tone that of someone wishing to take command, yet preferring to be somewhere else. Dark circles under his eyes suggested he hadn't slept well, and his fleshy jowls appeared even looser than usual.

'You could say that,' Leesil answered coldly. He turned away without even a gesture for the constable to enter. 'Beth-rae is dead. Some lunatic tore out her throat with his fingernails.'

Ellinwood, entering behind him, sputtered at the bluntness of Leesil's statement. Then he spotted the dark stain on the floor at the bar's far end.

'Where's the body?'

'Caleb took her into the kitchen,' Leesil answered. 'I didn't have the heart to tell him no.'

'Why don't you ask them what happened,' Brenden said, his arms crossed, 'before you start looking for "clues" for something you know nothing about.'

'What's he doing here?' Ellinwood demanded.

'I invited him,' Leesil answered in a half-truth.

Up to this point, Magiere had drifted closer to the fireplace and simply stood by watching and listening. Now she turned away from all three men.

Leesil experienced a wave of pity followed by concern. He had many unanswered questions regarding Magiere, but those could wait until a better time. She was dealing with too much already in too short a space of time. They all were, for that matter. And as much as he wanted answers, he didn't want to see her pushed over the edge any further.

'You start, Leesil,' she said softly. 'Just tell him what you saw.'

Leesil began recounting everything as clearly as possible. For the most part, it sounded like little more than a vicious thief interrupted during a botched robbery – except for the quarrel the beggar boy had pulled out of his own forehead. Strangely enough, Ellinwood did not react to this with more than a raised eyebrow. Then Leesil reached the part where Beth-rae ran in from the kitchen.

'She threw a bucket of water all over him, and he began to smoke.'

'Smoke?' Ellinwood said, shifting his heavy weight to one foot. 'What do you mean?'

'His skin turned black and began to smoke.'

'Garlic water,' Brenden interrupted. 'It's poison to vampires.'

The constable ignored him.

Leesil grew more suspicious. He still didn't accept the idea of vampires, and hadn't actually said or implied any such thing, yet the details were there. Ellinwood did not appear even slightly shocked, neither denying nor accepting Brenden's implied conclusion. Leesil held that thought to himself for the moment.

'Then what happened?' Ellinwood asked.

'He rushed her, struck her, tearing her throat with his fingernails, and breaking her neck,' Leesil continued. 'Then he escaped through the back door in the kitchen.'

A few more questions and answers followed, all of a

similar matter-of-fact and what-happened-next nature, each of which led to no further real exchange of useful information. The constable was casual, almost bored, and always slow to ask his next question. Somewhere along the way, Leesil noted that Ellinwood had not asked about any motivation for the intrusion. The concept of buglary or theft had not even come up. Not that it should have, since it was obviously not a burglary, but the constable hadn't even tried to pass it off as such. When Leesil described the intruder, he did note that Ellinwood fidgeted slightly before resettling into complacency.

It was then Leesil decided he would keep the issue of the dagger to himself. Ellinwood's disinterest was obvious. He was playing his role and giving lip service to his duties – and he was hiding something. Why this was so, Leesil couldn't yet tell, but the dagger might be more useful in his possession than handed over to be stowed away and forgotten.

The constable turned to Magiere.

'And while all this was going on, you were attacked upstairs?' he asked.

'Yes,' she managed to answer. She turned and looked directly at Ellinwood as she spoke. 'He was very tall and striking, with dark hair close cropped and nearly clear eyes with a tint of blue. He was dressed as a nobleman in a deep blue tunic, cloak, and high boots. And he carried a long sword, which he used as if trained and experienced in combat.'

Magiere continued, trying hard to remember more details of her assailant. His expressions and manner of superiority, the way he moved, the way he spoke. Slowly, the constable appeared less bored. His complexion shifted and began turning paler, until his flesh had a sickly white cast to it. Brenden, however, added more wrinkles to his brow, eyes narrowing as if he were trying to focus Magiere's description in his mind and recognition was beginning to settle upon him.

Leesil began to see that Magiere, as well, had caught the fact that Ellinwood had lost his disinterest. And now he looked openly nervous. Magiere grew more intent, turning to questions instead of answers.

'How many men in this town can that describe?' she asked. 'I don't know why that didn't occur to me until now. You must know everyone here, yes? This one was dressed too well for a common ruffian looking for some quick coins in his pocket.'

'He owns Miiska's largest warehouse,' Brenden answered softly. 'I don't know his name, but I've seen—'

'Quiet!' Ellinwood shouted at the blacksmith in a voice that squeaked with strain, surprising them all. 'Keep your foolish conclusions to yourself. There are hundreds of tall, dark-haired men in this town and new ones come in port every day.'

'Hundreds?' Leesil asked, mockingly.

Ellinwood ignored the goad, focusing on Brenden.

'I'll not accuse a respected businessman just to please you!'

'You're a coward,' Brenden said, more in resignation than anger. 'I can't believe what a coward you are.'

'Quiet, both of you!' Magiere snapped, looking more like the caustic tiger Leesil remembered as she stepped between the constable and the blacksmith. Ellinwood backed away, scowling, trying to maintain an air of righteous indignation, but Magiere didn't even notice.

'I'm not reporting this because I expect or desire any help,' she said to him. 'I'm only behaving like a law-abiding citizen. If you want no part of this, you're free to go back to your guardhouse or breakfast or whatever else you do with your mornings.' She turned to Brenden. 'And no one asked for your counsel, blacksmith.'

Ellinwood made no move to continue his investigation, neither inspecting the room nor making any pretense to go survey the body or the second level of the inn. Leesil began to think it was likely that the constable didn't need to do any of those things. The repulsive man probably knew much more than anyone else in this room. Beating the truth out of him was somewhat tempting, but would only add to their troubles. At least for now.

The constable puffed his cheeks out, attempting to gain control of the situation.

'I'll have my men do a sweep of the town, looking for anyone matching the descriptions you've provided. You'll be informed if anything is discovered.'

'Yes, you do that,' Magiere said in dismissal.

After the constable left, the three remaining occupants in the room stood looking at each other.

'I seriously doubt we'll hear anything,' Leesil said. 'Or at least we won't be the first.'

Brenden merely grunted in agreement.

Several tables lay in broken heaps around them, and Leesil remembered they would have to replace Magiere's bedroom door and window. For the time being, he would settle her in his own room, and then bed down himself on the bar or by the fireplace.

'It's not over. We have to hunt them down ourselves,'

Brenden said to Magiere. 'You know that, don't you?'

Oh, by everything holy, was he mad? Annoyance, possibly more than annoyance, hit Leesil for the first time.

'Just leave that alone!' Leesil half shouted before controlling himself. 'She's had enough already for one day.'

'I know,' Magiere answered in a whisper, ignoring Leesil's outburst. 'I know.'

Ratboy believed that vampires fell dormant during the day, like inverted plants or flowers. Of course, he kept this opinion to himself, and would never relate such a fanciful thought in front of Rashed or Teesha.

As the sun rose, he always collapsed into dreamless sleep. But not today. Today.

How long since he'd even considered a term with the word 'day' in it? He could not remember. Lying in his coffin, in the dirt of his homeland, deep in the tunnels under the warehouse, he could not sleep. His body still burned from the garlic water, even though Teesha had fed him, and his spirit burned from Rashed's harsh words.

Would that arrogant sand-spawn ever take responsibility for his own mistakes? Ratboy doubted it. Every action, every decision Rashed made was motivated by his consuming love for Teesha. And what was so comical – so tragic – was that he'd never be able to acknowledge the force that drove him. He played the father and the protector. But he'd never admit anything so pathetic as love, even to himself. Especially to himself.

Not even for Parko.

In the darkness of his coffin, Ratboy allowed his mind to drift back to their journey from Corische's keep. Due to Rashed's foresight, the trip was not uncomfortable.

Rashed packed a large wagon with their coffins, stacked two on two, each carefully covered by a canvas tarp. He also broke into Corische's private quarters and took plenty of money. Ratboy never asked how much, but that was part of Ratboy's past and current dilemma. He always left the details, the planning and the worrying to Rashed. He constantly walked a fine line between hating Rashed and depending on him.

One night on the open road, low growls reached their ears as the wagon approached an overgrown bend in the road. A moment later three half-starved wolves dashed out of the trees and attacked their horses.

Two more wolves leaped up from behind into the wagon, and Parko kicked one away on instinct. More shapes poured out of the forest, and Ratboy realized just how outnumbered they were. He wasn't exactly afraid of wolves, but famine could make these beasts formidable, and their numbers were growing before his eyes.

The horses screamed. He kicked the other wolf out of the wagon and looked around for a weapon. Then the attack stopped.

Teesha was holding the horses' reins, fighting to keep them from running. Rashed was standing in the driver's seat with his eyes closed. He appeared to be whispering, but as close as he was, Ratboy could not hear a sound coming from his lips.

Snarls faded, and the wolves pulled back. A few of them even whined.

One by one they slunk away into the trees.

'What did you do?' Ratboy asked.

Rashed shrugged it off. 'One of my abilities. I don't use it often.'

'You can control the minds of wolves?'

'And sand cats and other predators.'

Ratboy could not control the minds of animal predators. He knew that all Noble Dead developed slightly
different powers and abilities, but why did Rashed seem
to have all the useful ones? It bothered him to depend
so much on Rashed, yet he was forced to trust their
leader, who always knew exactly what to do.

The crux of this dichotomy had occurred on the road
nearly halfway to Miiska.

Before their undead existence began, Parko and
Rashed were the closest of brothers. Ratboy learned this
through snippets of memories that Rashed occasionally
expressed. Parko had been a gentle creature, who needed
the protection of his older brother. And again, although
Rashed did not seem to recognize his own drives,
Ratboy understood that the need to protect was built
into Rashed's nature. However, once their lives as Noble
Dead began, Parko was a completely different person,
savage and often incoherent. He became more and more
difficult to control.

Once they left Gäestev Keep, Rashed's thin hold on
Parko's behavior grew even weaker. Their leader planned
each night's travel carefully and often consulted several
maps he carried. Usually they arrived well before sunrise
at a town or village with an inn. Rashed would pay well
for cellar rooms if they were available, and since he knew
they could never unload the coffins without drawing
attention, he simply had his little 'family' all keep
pouches of dirt with their belongings. Each of them
would sleep with these pouches next to their bodies
until nightfall, when their travels resumed. Rashed

always told a similar story to the innkeepers about how they had traveled all night and needed quiet rest. Teesha would appear to be dainty and exhausted, and Parko and Ratboy played the servants. Although he would never admit it, Ratboy found safety in Rashed's planning and the way he handled both mortals and the mortal world so easily.

Yet something about Parko's wild manner was attractive as well. And Parko hated Rashed's rules that they sleep inside and only feed when absolutely necessary. He rebelled at every opportunity.

One day on the road, they were forced to sleep in an abandoned church. Parko had slipped out of the wagon unseen. Once his absence was discovered, Rashed halted the wagon immediately. He stepped out and glared through the dark, turning slowly, searching. He stopped with his focus directly down the road.

Usually only a master such as Corische could do this to locate a created minion. Perhaps because they had been siblings in life, Rashed could sense Parko's whereabouts. Apparently, his brother had traveled out ahead of them. They would stop at the next village, down the road, to see if he was there.

When they arrived, the village was in a state of hysteria. A small cluster of people was gathered around the open front door of the inn, a few armed men holding them back. Voices were loud and angry, and it was easy enough to overhear that the innkeeper and his wife had been found dead in their beds. Ratboy watched as a guard came running out of the inn and began vomiting in the gutter of the street.

There would be no welcome for strangers in this

village, and Rashed did not even slow the wagon. Once out of sight of the village, he whipped the horses into speed. Daylight was coming.

Although the roadside shrine they found down a side road looked ancient, as if untended and unvisited for years, Rashed clearly did not like the tenuous state of their situation. He raged over the idea of Teesha sleeping somewhere so insecure. When Parko caught up with them just before sunrise, his face and hands were covered in blood, and he no longer cackled and smiled as usual.

Rashed was furious at his brother and actually shouted at him. Parko merely backed into a corner with his pouch of soil, his eyes unblinking as he glared at Rashed. Ratboy suspected Parko had acted from spite, sick of being restrained and forced to continually repress his natural drives and instincts. And Ratboy, as well, wondered what it would be like to let go, to revel in a kill as Parko had done. Parko was still glaring at his brother when Ratboy finally closed his eyes much later and tried to rest.

Teesha kept her own council where Rashed's brother was concerned, but Ratboy could feel tension building in the group. He himself felt torn. At times, he did feel Parko was too wild, but Teesha and Rashed were certainly too tame. Three nights after the inn incident, Rashed stopped the wagon at midnight near a small village so they could hunt. Teesha sat in the wagon for a little while, gazing at trails of smoke rising over the trees from the little huts, her expression wistful.

'Rashed, how far is it to the ocean?' she asked. 'I'm so tired. Will we find our own home soon?'

Rashed was standing on the ground, strapping on his

sword. He quickly climbed back in the wagon and sat beside her.

'We have a long way to travel yet, but we have the maps I took from the keep. Before we sleep in the morning, I'll show you where we are and where the ocean is.' His voice was concerned and tender.

Suddenly Parko howled in rage.

'Home! Ocean!' he shouted. His black eyes turned toward Teesha. 'You!' White flesh seemed stretched over his thin face, and his uncombed hair stood out in several directions. 'No home,' he said. 'Hunt!'

Pain registered on Rashed's face. And it was not lost on Parko, who turned and ran into the forest.

Rashed looked at Ratboy. 'Will you go with him? Make sure he doesn't do anything to endanger the rest of us?'

Their leader rarely *asked* Ratboy for anything. So, Ratboy nodded and slipped into the trees after Parko. Actually, it was a relief to be running through the woods after Parko, leaving Rashed and Teesha in their own private world.

Ratboy reached out with his mind and tried to locate Parko as Rashed had done, but he could sense nothing. Instead, he resorted to mundane methods of tracking. Parko was in such a fit he'd left a trail that was easy to follow. It wasn't long before Ratboy caught up with his charge behind a patch of small trees on the far side of the village. He crouched down beside Parko.

'You see something?' he asked.

'Blood,' Parko answered.

Even at this late hour, a small band of teenage boys was sitting outside what appeared to be a stable. They were laughing and passing a jug among themselves. They had probably stolen some ale or whiskey and were feeling quite rebellious. The sight of them actually brought back memories of the 'life' Ratboy had left far behind, long ago. He'd done the same thing in his youth often enough.

'No, Parko,' he said. 'There are too many, and they're out in the open. One of them would raise an alarm. We'll look elsewhere.'

Parko turned to him.

'You are not Rashed,' he said with surprising clarity. 'We kill. We hunt. We fear no calls to alarm. We fear no boys. No men.' He looked back at the drinking band of teenagers. 'You should not be like Rashed. Drink with me.'

Without another word, he darted from the treeline. Startled, Ratboy watched him move silently and swiftly along the stable's side. Uncertain, Ratboy followed him, until they stopped at the corner.

The boys were almost close enough to touch now. Ratboy could hear every word they were saying, mainly complaints about their fathers, interspersed with laughter and gulps of liquid. He could smell the contents of the jug – whiskey.

In a flash, Parko was gone, and then Ratboy heard laughter silenced as it turned to screams.

Hungry, excited, Ratboy stepped out from the corner of the stable to see three boys lying dead on the ground, their necks broken, and Parko drinking from the throat of a boy with dirty-blond hair. The boy was still alive and flailing his arms in terror.

A short, slightly pudgy boy with dark hair stood

screaming. Why didn't he run? Ratboy felt free. He wasn't like Rashed. He was like Parko, and he grabbed the screaming boy and drove both fangs straight into his neck, closing his teeth over the plump throat until the boy was choked into silence. Fear and blood from his victim seeped into him in equal measures, and he felt euphoric, so alive.

Shouts from deeper voices began sounding down the street. Ratboy drank his fill and then dropped the body to the ground with a thud. He knew he should run. Common sense told him he should run, but he didn't.

Parko finished with the blond boy and laughed.

Instead of dropping the carcass, he began dancing, capering with it. Covered in blood, his black eyes wide, he looked completely mad, but Ratboy didn't care. He laughed as well.

Two grown men with wooden pitchforks came around the corner and halted in shock, then one jabbed his pronged tool at Ratboy. The man looked more frightened than fierce. Ratboy simply feinted around the pitchfork, and tore the man's throat open with his fingernails.

He watched with pleasure as realization, and then horror, dawned on the mortal's face and the pitchfork tumbled from the man's hand as he clutched his gaping wound. Ratboy heard a crack behind him and turned to see Parko dropping the second man's body to the ground.

Parko seemed to be in the mood for breaking necks.

Ratboy wanted to laugh aloud again. They were invincible, free. Why had they ever feared discovery from these mortals?

Then movement caught his eye. Rashed was standing one arm's length away in absolute disbelief. His mouth was even opened slightly.

Euphoria faded. Five dead boys and two men lay on the ground around them. Other villagers must be aware but hiding.

Rashed seemed to search for words. 'What have you done?'

By way of answer, Parko hissed at him like an animal. Rashed closed the distance between them in two steps and swung hard with his fist.

Ratboy had never seen Rashed hit his brother. He didn't think Rashed capable. As the fist connected with his jaw, Parko crumpled and dropped. Parko tried to rise up, and Rashed struck him again, so hard that his brother flew backward and smashed through the outer railing of the stable. Parko lay still and silent in straw and mud.

Rashed grabbed his brother's limp body by the leg, and jerked him out onto the road. Lifting Parko, he slung the unconscious form over his shoulder and glared at Ratboy.

'You come now.'

Ratboy followed without speaking. He was actually frightened, not of Rashed, but what would happen next. When they reached the wagon, Rashed dropped Parko on the ground. Then he climbed into the wagon's back, cut Parko's coffin loose from the others, and shoved it out the back. It thumped and skidded to the ground as Parko began to stir.

Ratboy looked to Teesha, who could sometimes bring reason to such scenes, but she stood silently on the other side of the wagon, watching.

Rashed threw a pouch of money at his brother.

'I am finished with you. You will not travel with us farther. Go down the Feral Path, if that is what you want. Perhaps the mob that village forms will hunt you now instead of us.'

He stepped over the front of the wagon onto its seat and picked up the horses' reins.

'Teesha, get in the wagon.' Then he turned to Ratboy. 'You have a choice. I know the careless abandon of this night was not your doing, but you gave in to him. You either come with us or stay with him. Choose now.'

Parko hissed from his position on the ground, and Ratboy stared at Rashed.

He wasn't good at making his own decisions, and this was the most difficult one he'd ever faced. The idea of staying with Parko and following the Feral Path, slaughtering and drinking blood with no thought to rules, only the hunt – it pulled at him. Desire to throw off all sense of mortal trappings and become the full glory of a predator was difficult to resist.

But Rashed kept them safe and always knew what to do, and Teesha knew how to make a home. Ratboy wasn't ready to give these things up. Not yet. He was afraid to stay alone with Parko. The thought shamed him. He glanced once more at Parko's hissing, writhing form, and then he climbed up into the wagon to sit behind Teesha.

As they pulled away, he did not see Rashed look back once, and he alone watched Parko's pinprick eyes fade in the distance. And for two more nights, Rashed did not speak at all.

Lying in his coffin beneath the warehouse, Ratboy

wondered about the wisdom of the choice he had made back then. He tried to stop thinking, to simply see nothing. After a while, he was finally able to fall dormant.

11

Magiere left her tavern early that afternoon. As she stepped into the street, she noticed a 'Closed' sign hanging on the door, painted in Lèesil's handwriting. Why hadn't she thought of doing that? She gave silent thanks to her partner and walked directly to the nearest inn.

Although Magiere sometimes referred to The Sea Lion as an 'inn,' strictly it was not, since the building had no rooms for lodgers. Perhaps at one time the upper floor had been used for lodgers, the owner residing elsewhere. In truth, Miiska only boasted three actual inns, but a small town such as this had no need of more. Most sailors and bargemen slept on their ships, and she could not see many travelers wanting to come to stay in this out-of-the-way place. Even the scarce peddler, traveling merchant, or farmer from the outlying lands was more likely to camp with his wares in the open market on the north end of town.

This inn was a shabby and run-down establishment with a sparsely furnished common room that smelled of fish and moldy bread. She began asking about Welstiel, describing the strange middle-aged man to a bone-thin woman in a soiled apron, who she assumed was the keeper of the place.

'We got no one here like that,' she said crossly after hearing Magiere out, obviously thinking her time was wasted. 'You try The Velvet Rose. That's where you'll find the likes of him.'

Magiere thanked the crone and left. Everything appeared normal around her. The sun hung like a burning orange ball in the thin haze of high clouds. People talked and laughed and went about their business. Occasionally, a patron of The Sea Lion would wave or call out a greeting, and she would nod or raise her own hand briefly in return. Every now and then, she had the feeling someone was watching her, perhaps whispering with a companion and pointing in her direction. But whenever she turned it was as if no one noticed her at all. The scope of the world had changed, no matter how things appeared. And the only one who seemed to really understand the situation was an overwrought blacksmith with more muscle than brains.

She wanted to talk to Leesil and try to explain the thoughts running through her mind. What if fate or the deities or whatever kept the balance in the world between right and wrong had finally caught up with them – with her? She couldn't imagine what Leesil might think of such a notion. A month ago, he would have laughed and offered her his wine sack. Now their world had altered, and either he was changing with it, or he simply had been hiding aspects of himself. She kept allowing him to handle more and more situations that were basically her responsibility. This morning, he had handled Ellinwood for the most part, and this afternoon he took care of a temporary 'Closed' sign for the tavern door. Now she'd gone out by herself, leaving him behind to comfort Rose and Caleb.

No, she wouldn't burden him with her own deepening

guilt, confusion, and suspicions. He certainly didn't need more to worry about.

But the time had come to take some matters into her own hands. She'd traveled to this town seeking peace, and someone had forced a battle upon her. Brenden was right, and the cards were on her side of the table now.

She walked away from the docks and farther into town. Not many people knew her by sight this far in, and she received no familiar greetings from passersby. She stopped in front of The Velvet Rose. It was quite lovely, reflecting its name even from the outside with red damask curtains peeking through the perfectly tended and whitewashed shutters.

Although her hair was back in its neat braid, she felt underdressed in breeches and boots, muslin shirt and black vest.

A large, mahogany desk waited just inside the entryway. The man behind it struck her as attractive in a strange way, even in her current state of mind. She had seen a few full-blooded elves during her travels, though they were not common in this land. His light brown hair looked as soft as down feathers and hung loose, pushed behind his oblong, pointed ears. But his face was more slender with a narrower chin than her partner's, and his amber-brown eyes and thin eyebrows slanted upward at a more pronounced angle than Leesil's.

When he looked up at her, she could see his skin was a dark, even tan and smoother than any human's she'd ever seen.

'May I help you?' he asked smoothly.

'Yes,' she answered, suddenly unsure of how to proceed, or if she would even be allowed into the place.

'I was hoping to find a friend of mine here, a Welstiel Massing. He's about my height, well dressed, and gray at the temples.'

Without thinking, she motioned to her own temples as if to help the description, then felt foolish for doing so. She hated feeling so nervous and desperate.

'Yes, Master Welstiel currently resides here,' he responded, his tone composed, his speech clear and distinct. 'But he seldom receives guests and never without notifying me first. I am sorry.' He turned back to the parchment on his desk, as if his words were all the dismissal she needed.

'No, I'm the one who's sorry. I may not have an appointment, but he's come to see me several times, and now I am returning his visits.'

The slanted brown eyes flashed back up in surprise.

'Young mistress . . .' he began sternly, and then he paused a moment as if half-remembering some forgotten detail. 'Are you Magiere, the new proprietor of Dunction's?'

'Yes,' she answered cautiously. 'It's called The Sea Lion now.'

'Apologies, please.' He stood up quickly. 'My name is Loni. Master Welstiel did mention your name. I don't know if he's here now, but I will check. Please follow me.'

This elegant elf – who basically functioned as a guard – did not even know if Welstiel was home or not? That seemed odd to Magiere, but she put it aside for the moment.

As they stepped farther into the inn, the place was even more opulent than she expected, with walls painted oyster-shell white. Red carpets, thick enough to sleep on, covered the main floors and hallways, climbing up the staircase at the entryway's far end. Large, dark-toned paintings of battles, seascapes, and tranquil landscapes hung in strategically tasteful places, and the perfect deepest shades of saltwater roses had been chosen for simple and exquisite ivory vases.

'Not bad,' she remarked to Loni. 'You could use a faro table.'

'Well . . .' he said. 'Yes, certainly.'

Magiere almost smiled, knowing his stuffy front was carefully constructed. He was likely as good as Leesil at hand-to-hand encounters, or he wouldn't be working the front of this establishment all by himself. She followed him to the stairs, but rather than going up, he took a key out of his vest pocket and unlocked a door to the side. Opening it, Magiere faced another set of stairs leading downward.

Now came the difficult part. To Welstiel, this abrupt appearance would seem like she'd come to grovel for help. On some level, she suspected he would enjoy this. If there were any other way, any way at all, she would have chosen some other option.

Loni descended, and Magiere followed. At the bottom, they reached a short hallway that led to a single door. Loni rapped gently on the door.

'Sir, if you are in, the young woman is here to see you.'

At first there was no answer. Then Welstiel's distinctive voice said, 'Enter.'

Loni opened the door and stepped back.

Surprised at her own mild anxiety, Magiere swallowed

once and entered the room. The door clicked shut softly behind her, and she heard Loni's soft footsteps retreating back up the stairs. Expecting to find decor which mimicked the wealthy display of the inn's main floor, she was surprised by the room's interior.

Upon a plain table, next to a narrow bed carefully made, rested a frosted-glass globe on an iron pedestal. Within the globe flickered three sparks of light, bright enough to illuminate half the room. One small travel chest sat in the corner and three leather-bound books lay on top of the table. Each book cover was marked in a language she'd never seen before and had a strap and lock holding it closed.

Welstiel sat in a simple wooden chair, reading from a fourth book. He projected such a striking appearance that no one would notice the nearly barren room if they examined him first. His well-tailored and perfectly pressed white shirt and black trousers seemed more a part of him than mere articles of cloth he'd donned. Dark hair was combed back over his ears, exposing the gray-white temples that made him look wise and noble at the same time. And if not for these, the soft light from the orb illuminating his face would make his age difficult to guess. With finely boned hands resting on the book, he seemed unconscious of the missing portion of his finger, even when she glanced down at it.

'How pleasant to see you,' he said, his tone expressing neither pleasure nor wonder at her arrival.

Magiere imagined he fancied himself a rich gentleman who studied ancient lore and magic in his spare time. But why would a nobleman live in these cellar quarters when more suitable comforts were likely to be had upstairs in The Velvet Rose's standard rooms? And if he were such a self-made scholar, what was he doing in a place like Miiska? More likely he was some ne'er-do-well who thought he knew something of the dark half of the world and had simply stumbled across her path by chance. Perhaps he couldn't help her as she hoped.

'I didn't stop by for a social call,' she said abruptly. 'You either know something, or think you do, about the murders and disappearances in this town. My tavern was attacked last night and one of the caretakers is dead.'

He nodded slightly. 'I know. I have heard.'

'Already?'

'Word travels quickly in Miiska, especially if you know what to listen for.'

'Don't play coy with me, Welstiel,' she snapped, stepping farther into the room. 'I'm not in the mood.'

'Then stop denying what your own eyes see and begin accepting reality,' he answered back, just as harshly.

'What does that mean? What does any of this have to do with me?'

He put the book down and leaned forward, pointing at her neck.

'Those amulets hidden beneath your clothes and the falchion you usually carry are telltale signs. If I were a vampire, I'd hunt you down the moment you set foot on my territory.'

She blew a breath out her nose. 'Don't start all that again.'

But her voice pretended a confidence she no longer felt. If she truly believed that nothing unnatural was happening in this town, then why had she come to Welstiel, who spoke of such things?

He studied her face as if it were the cover of one of his books, hoping to catch a hint of what lay behind it.

'You can't escape this. They see you as a hunter and will therefore hunt you first. Take the battle to them.'

She no longer had the strength nor inclination to argue and sat down slowly on the foot of his bed.

'How? How do I find them?'

'Use what is already available to you. Use your dog and the facts you've gathered. Use the skill of your half-elf and the blacksmith's strength.'

'Chap?' she said. 'What can he do?'

'Do not be dense. Let him hunt. Haven't you at least figured that part by now?'

He was mocking her, and she felt a sudden edge of hate for his superior manner. How could he possibly know so many things that she did not?

'If you know so much, then why haven't you hunted these creatures down?'

'Because I am not you,' he answered calmly.

She stood up again, pacing. 'I don't even know where to look. How do I start?'

Without warning, his expression became closed, as if he were a living book suddenly tired of producing information. He got up, went to the door, opened it, and repeated, 'Use the dog.'

Her fear concerning her fate threatened to emerge once more as the tangle of coincidences grew more entwined. How did Chap fit into all this?

Welstiel's opening of the door announced the end of her visit. Besides, he was apparently strong willed, and any further pushing on her part might lead to alienating the only outside source of information she'd found so far. She stepped into the hall and then turned back to him.

'How do I kill them?'

'You already know. You've practiced it for years.'

Without another word, he closed the door.

Magiere made her way quickly back up the stairs, and hurried through the lobby, glancing once at Loni on her way out of the foyer. For all Welstiel's cryptic discussions, only two points truly bothered her. First, to the best of her knowledge, Welstiel had never even seen Chap, but he knew a great deal about the animal. And second, he either knew or pretended to know aspects of her past that she did not. Though that last issue troubled her some, she'd never really cared about her past. There was little worth remembering.

In the years before Leesil, all she had was loneliness, which turned to hardness, which turned to cold hatred of anyone superstitious. A mother she'd never known was long dead, and her father had abandoned her to a life among cruel peasants who punished her for being spawned by him. Why would she want to remember such things? Why would she want to look back? There was nothing worth concern in the past.

As she walked quickly toward home, she noticed the sun had dropped a bit lower. She suddenly felt an urgency to get back to Leesil. For all his cryptic words, Welstiel was right about one thing. They had to give up their defensive position and go after their enemies – and they had only a few hours to prepare before sundown.

Sitting on his bed in his room, in complete solitude, Leesil decided that he hated uncertainty more than anything else, perhaps even more than sobriety. At the moment, he was as sober as a virtuous deity, and that condition gave him clarity – another distasteful state of affairs.

Unlike Magiere, he'd neither bathed nor slept and the odors of blood, smoke, and red wine permeated his nostrils. He knew he should go downstairs and wash, but something kept him here in his room.

Brenden had left the tavern for his home, promising to return soon with appropriate weapons. Caleb had taken Rose into their room several hours ago so he could speak with her. He had closed the door and not come out. Chap still lay by Beth-rae's body, which Caleb had carefully cleaned and laid out in the kitchen in case anyone stopped by to pay respects. And Magiere had disappeared sometime during the afternoon.

Leesil was alone and sober. He was not sure which of those conditions he disliked more.

He went over to a small chest Caleb had given him for storage. Since Constable Ellinwood's examination of the murder scene – or lack of it – Leesil had taken a few private moments to remove Ratboy's dagger from under his clothes, clean Chap's blood from the blade, and store it away. He now pulled it from the chest, careful to grab it by the blade and not the handle. Even while cleaning it, he'd been careful not to wash the handle, for that was the one place he could be certain Ratboy had touched. He would have need of any lingering trace of presence the dusty little invader had left behind.

And once again, uncertainty gnawed at him. Dropping to his knees, he pried up two floorboards that he'd loosened the first night they'd arrived. A long, rectangular box lay inside where he'd hidden it. Even touching the container made him shiver with revulsion, but he never once in his life considered throwing it away. He pulled out the box and opened it.

Inside lay weapons and tools of unmatched elven craftsmanship, given to him by his mother on his seventeenth birthday. They were not what any boy would have wanted as a gift. Two stilettos as thin as darning needles rested beneath a garroting wire with narrow metal handles. Alongside them was a curved blade sharp enough to cut bone with minimal effort. Hidden inside the lid behind a folding cover was a set of thin metal picks that in his hands could unlatch any lock. Just inanimate objects, but the sight of them almost drove him down to the wine barrel and his cup.

He closed his eyes and breathed deep, long, and hard for several moments. Drunk, he was no use to Magiere. But the close proximity of these items and his current sobriety allowed in a rush of memories he'd fought for half his life to keep at bay. Eyes still shut, he could feel the pain.

Rich green shades and the enormous trees of his birthplace appeared. So beautiful. Magiere had never traveled north as far as Doyasag, his place of birth, and he'd never bothered describing it to her. Joining the game with her had been the start of his new life, his erasure of past deeds. He'd left it all behind the night they met.

The fresh smells and scenery of his homeland were merely a painted canvas that hid a mass of power-hungry men who struggled for domination. Instead of being ruled by a king, the country was held by a warlord named Darmouth, who saw treason all around him. Warlords who rule need spies and other hidden servants, and Leesil was fifteen years old and nearly seven years into his training before realizing his father and mother did not simply work for Lord Darmouth. Darmouth owned them.

Leesil's mother's tan skin and golden hair, her exotic elven heritage, made her a useful weapon as she created the illusion of a tall but delicate girl or a rare foreign beauty. His father, for his part, could blend into the shadows as if made of dust in the air, and his passing left no mark and made no sound. They betrayed whomever they were told to betray and killed whomever they were told to assassinate. And they taught Leesil everything they knew. It was the family craft and art, and he was the family's only inheritor.

'We have a tenuous position here, *Lìsill*,' his mother whispered to him late in the night. 'Necessary, highly skilled – and expendable. If we refuse or hesitate, we will be the next ones to die unexplainably in our sleep or be exposed and executed for our crimes. Do you understand, my son? Always nod and do as you are bid.'

No matter what the monetary rewards, Leesil did not possess the temperament required for a life of isolated servitude. Spies and assassins make no friends. His mother must have felt his loneliness. On the day of his fifteenth birth celebration, she presented him with a large, silver-blue puppy that crawled all over him with uncontained wiggles and licked his face. It was the one moment of pure happiness that he could remember.

'This is a special hound,' she said, her graceful hands held outward. 'His great-grandfather protected my people in frightening times long past. He will watch over you.'

That was all she'd ever told him – that he recalled – of Chap or of her homeland, wherever it might have been. And Leesil gave few thoughts to her words at the time. If he hadn't been so happy in that one moment, he might have asked more questions, or even remembered to ask later, but he only cared that some part of his life seemed like other boys'. He had a dog.

When Leesil turned seventeen, his father declared his training finished, or perhaps did so at Lord Darmouth's insistence. His mother presented him with the box filled with all the tools he would need for his duties.

'You are now *anmaglâhk*,' she said, her voice quiet and hollow – a statement of fact filled with no pride.

She seldom spoke her native tongue in all of his life that Leesil remembered. Though he'd learned several of the land's dialects, she never taught him the elven language other than a few words he'd picked up on his own. Once, when he tried to beg her to teach him, she turned coldly angry.

'There will never be a need for you to speak it,' she said.

And as he left her, quick to exit her chamber, he was uncertain of what he saw. As she sat on the window bench, looking out, her face turned away from him, a shudder ran through her body as if she were sobbing silently.

Looking at the box in his hands she had given him as a birthday present, he did not need to ask what the word she had used meant. He knew what he'd become. The same day, he was ordered to assassinate a baron believed to be plotting against Darmouth. The command came from his father.

That night, Leesil scaled the walls of Baron Progae's fortress, slipped past a dozen guards, and climbed down from the tower into the target's bedroom window. He drove a stiletto into the base of the sleeping man's skull, just as his father had shown him, and then slipped out again. No one found the body until nearly noon the next day. What servant would willingly disturb the late sleep of a nobleman?

Progae's lands were confiscated. His wife and daughters driven into the street. Leesil sought out information about the family later. One daughter was taken in as the fourth mistress of a loyal baron. The wife and two youngest daughters starved to death as everyone feared assisting them. Leesil never asked about the families of his victims again. He simply slipped through windows, picked what were often considered unpickable locks, carried out his orders, and never looked back.

At twenty-four, he still looked as young as a human in his late teens. One night Lord Darmouth summoned him personally. Leesil loathed being in his lord's presence, but he never even considered refusing.

'I don't want you to kill this time but gather information,' Darmouth told him through a thick, black beard. 'One of my ministers has given me cause to doubt his true interests. He trains young scribes as a hobby. Your father tells me you speak and write several of our dialects?'

'Yes, my lord,' Leesil answered, despising the brutal hands and unwashed face of the creature who owned his entire family.

'Good. You will live as his student and report to me on his activities, his comments, his daily habits, and so forth.'

Leesil bowed and left.

He was allowed to bring Chap to his new residence, which was a comfort since the dog represented his only link to a life beyond his duties. But the first meeting with Minister Josiah was almost unsettling to him after years of plots, schemes, and silent deaths. A small, white-haired man with violet, laughing eyes, Josiah grasped Leesil's hand in open warmth and friendship. Rather than armor or clothing designed for stealth, the man wore cream-colored robes.

'Come, come, my boy. Lord Darmouth tells me you're a promising student. We'll find you some supper and a warm bed.'

Leesil hesitated. He'd never met anyone like Josiah. The merry minister mistook his pause.

'Not to worry. Your dog is welcome, too. A handsome creature and a bit unusual, as I don't think I've ever seen his kind before. Where did you get him?'

Chap's back now reached a grown man's thigh. His long, silver-blue fur, pale, near-blue eyes, and narrow muzzle often drew compliments from those who saw him. The dog trotted straight up to the old minister and sat, with a switching tail, waiting to be petted. It was the first time Leesil had ever seen Chap do such a thing with anyone but himself and his mother.

Leesil wasn't sure how to answer and tried quickly

to figure out what purpose the question served, what agenda might be hidden behind it.

'My mother,' he finally answered.

Josiah looked up from scratching Chap gently on the head.

'Your mother? Why, I would have thought him to be a father's gift, but no matter' – he laughed softly and smiled – 'a mother's gift is even better.'

With that, the old minister ushered both Leesil and his dog into the house and into his life.

Josiah's loyalties became clear in the days and weeks that followed. He had no intention of creating insurrection, but he had turned his large country estate into a haven for those displaced by Darmouth's continuing civil wars and intrigues. Barracks and small cottages had been built to house refugees. Leesil spent part of his days in lessons with Josiah, and the other part helping to feed or care for the poor. He found the latter acts somewhat futile, since these tragic people would still be poor tomorrow. The poor were poor. The rich were rich. The intelligent and resourceful survived. That was the way of things.

His attitude toward Minister Josiah, however, was quite different. Never given the opportunity to admit or recognize admiration, he did not understand his feelings of protection for the old man. Indeed, he was foolish enough at first to believe he could save himself, save his family, and save Josiah by simply reporting nothing to Lord Darmouth. After all, he disobeyed no orders, refused no tasks, and there was nothing to tell.

'What do you mean, "he's loyal"?' the bearded lord demanded when Leesil had returned once on a 'visit home.'

Leesil stood rigid and attentive in Darmouth's private chambers. Although tired and thirsty from his journey, he was offered neither a chair nor water.

'He bears you no ill will, speaks no treason,' he answered in confusion.

Anger clouded Darmouth's eyes.

'And what of all these peasants flocking to his fields? No other minister gathers armies of the poor. Your father believes you are skilled. Is he wrong?'

Leesil never answered any question before thinking carefully, but now he felt adrift. How could Josiah's act of feeding the poor possibly be construed as treason?

'Is this task beyond you?' Darmouth went on after taking a long drink, draining a pewter goblet filled with wine and then slamming it back on the table.

'No, my lord,' Leesil answered.

'I need evidence, and I need it quickly. His peasant hordes grow. If you can't bring me simple information, I will assume your father is a fool as well and have you both replaced.'

Cold shock washed over Leesil as he realized Lord Darmouth didn't want the truth. He simply wanted something with which to justify Josiah's destruction. If Leesil refused, both he and his father would be replaced, and servants of their kind did not just leave service. At best, they disappeared one night never to be seen again – as the first task of their replacements.

He traveled back north to the warm embrace of his new teacher and ate a supper of roast lamb and fresh peaches while making up stories at the table when Josiah asked all about his visit home.

That night, he slipped downstairs into Josiah's study,

picked a simple lock on the old man's desk, and began reading recent correspondence. He stopped going through the parchments when his gaze scanned a draft of a letter not yet sent.

> *My Dear Sister,*
>   *The situation grows worse with each month, and I fear a loss of both vision and reason in our highest places. I would resign my seat on the council were it not for my work here with those in most need. I pray each dusk for some sign of change with each dawn, for some legitimate change for the better in the command of this land, for a change is needed. These unending civil wars will destroy all of us. . . .*

The letter went on, touching upon Josiah's simple daily routine, queries of family and friends, and other personal topics. It even mentioned a young half-elf as a promising new student. Leesil ignored the rest of the letter. The first paragraph, though not clearly pointing to Lord Darmouth, would be enough for someone like him to justify charges of treason. Leesil shoved the parchment inside his shirt, found Chap, and headed out that night for Darmouth's castle.

Three days later, soldiers swarmed Josiah's estate and arrested him. They dispersed the refugees, killing a handful in the process. After a brief trial by Darmouth's council, composed of ministers now staunchly loyal to their lord as they sat in judgment over one of their own, Josiah was hanged in the castle courtyard for treason. A letter to his sister proved his guilt.

Leesil was well paid for his services and lay in bed

that night shivering, unable to get warm. He tried to focus on loyalty to his parents and not on his own tenuous grasp of Master Josiah's lessons on ethics and morals. Ethics were for those who could afford such luxuries as time for philosophical thought, and morals should be left to clerics and their doctrines. But he had destroyed a man he admired – one who'd cherished a young half-blood stranger in his own house – on the orders of the one man Leesil despised the most.

No, that was no longer correct. He loathed himself even more than Darmouth.

He couldn't stop shaking.

That night, Leesil left behind most of the blood money he'd earned for his parents, knowing they would have need of it once his own disappearance was discovered. He took a few silver coins, his everyday stilettos, his box of tools, and ran south for Stravina with Chap at his side.

For all his training and talent, Leesil found life on the road much harder than he'd imagined. He and Chap hunted for food together and slept outside. And each night, dreams of his past filled the dark behind his closed eyes until he woke before dawn soaked in sweat.

When they reached their first large city, a new possibility occurred to him as he saw a fat purse hanging from the belt of a nobleman.

Picking pockets would be as easy as breathing for him. He cut the purse in a heartbeat and disappeared into a crowd. Half-starved, he went directly to an inn and ordered food. Upon seeing the half-elf's money, the innkeeper smiled.

'You'll be wanting something to wash that down with,' he said.

'Tea will be fine,' Leesil answered.

The innkeeper laughed and brought him a large goblet of red wine. Neither of Leesil's parents ever drank alcohol, so he'd never given it much thought. The path they walked required a keen mind fully alert at all times. The wine tasted good, so he drank it. He ordered another goblet and then another.

That same night he experienced his first wave of numbed forgetfulness, not stirring to a dream until nearly the whole night had passed. The sickness and headache the following morning were a small price to pay for one sound night's sleep – and another, and another.

A new life began for Leesil the Pickpocket, who drank himself into numbed slumber each night. Frequenting taverns and inns and other similar places exposed him to cards and games of chance, and he learned to supplement his light-fingered livelihood with gambling. Of course, it was risky – especially if he were cheating and drinking at the same time. He was actually caught and arrested twice, but neither jail held him for long, even without the tools he'd stored away before going out for the evening's business. Years passed.

He lived nowhere, claimed no one but Chap as a friend, and just as this life was beginning to seem as pointless as his previous one, he saw a tall, young woman with black hair that sparked red in the street lanterns. A strange desire to pick her pocket filled his mind.

It was a bad idea, but he wavered as he tried to walk away. Young women in leather armor who carried swords offered little wealth. And uncommon as they were, they would have to be skilled to survive and might prove more trouble than he wanted should something go wrong. This one's armor was weatherworn and sun bleached, so she was likely not fresh off the farm looking for a life better than marriage and milking the cows. He never approached her type, but the voice in his mind became impossible to ignore, nagging at him over and over and over. . . .

It would be easy. It would be quick. And this one might actually have something worth taking. Silently, he moved up behind her.

She had no visible purse, but carried a large pouch over one shoulder. Carefully matching pace with her, he watched the oversize pouch swing slightly from side to side and out from her back. It was little trouble to time his move. He reached out, poised as the bag bounced quietly against her back, and when it left contact with her body, his hand slipped inside. He was careful not to disturb its swing and rhythm as he fished slowly and carefully about the inside. It bounced twice more against her back without her noticing he was there.

The woman whirled around, grabbing his wrist in the same movement.

'Hey, what are you . . . ?' she started to say.

He could have easily jerked away and run, but her dark eyes caught him. For a blink, she looked enraged, then stood there taking in the sight of him as well. He knew for a fact he'd never seen her before, but for some reason, he didn't run, and she didn't call for the guard. Neither spoke at first.

'You're pretty good,' she said finally.

'Not good enough,' he answered.

That was how he met Magiere and began what he considered to be the third and best of his lives. He didn't exactly remember at what point they came up with his involvement in the 'hunter' game, but Magiere's restrained approval after the first practice run gave him a strange feeling of satisfaction he'd never experienced. After that, he had few responsibilities beyond playing a vampire several times each moon and traveling in Magiere's comfortable, capable company.

Memory ebbed away.

Leesil knelt on the floor of his room, staring at the metal remnants of his first life, the life no one present knew about. How many years had it been? He honestly couldn't remember. And he realized that his once honed and hated skills would now be needed again if he were to help Magiere at all, perhaps for her life's sake.

He snapped the box closed and shoved it inside his shirt. A soft scratching and whining at the door caught his attention.

'Chap?' He walked over and opened the door. 'Come on in, boy.'

Looking down, he saw the dog held a piece of the bloody shawl Caleb had removed from Beth-rae before dressing her for visitors and burial. Chap's transparent blue eyes shone with misery. He whined again and pushed at Leesil's foot with his paw.

Leesil crouched down, examining Chap in confusion. He knew dogs were capable of mourning in a fashion for people they had lost, but Chap had come to him with a specific piece of a dead woman's clothing.

'What is it? What do you want?'

It seemed ridiculous to ask a question of an animal. Then he realized that he didn't need to ask. He knew what the dog wanted. Chap wanted to hunt down Beth-rae's killer.

Footsteps on the stairs made both dog and half-elf look up.

'What's wrong with him?' Magiere asked, stepping off the stairs into the hallway, looking clean, calm, and in charge again.

Leesil ignored the question. 'Where have you been?'

'Getting some answers.' Then she noticed the scrap of cloth in Chap's jaws. Her brow wrinkled in confusion and revulsion. 'Is that Beth-rae's shawl?'

'Yes.' Leesil nodded. 'He carried it up from the kitchen.'

'Did the creature that killed Beth-rae touch it?'

'I don't know, but . . .'

Leesil hesitated. For whatever reason, Magiere was thinking along the same path that had occurred to him. Perhaps it was time to try what he'd had in the back of his mind since he'd first hidden away Ratboy's dagger, deciding not to turn it over to Ellinwood. He returned to his chest and picked up the blade Beth-rae's killer had left behind, careful not to touch the handle and foul any lingering scent.

'Here Chap, try this.'

'Where did you find that?' Magiere snapped at him, reaching out for the blade. 'And why didn't you show it to Ellinwood?'

Leesil pushed her hand away, shaking his head. 'We know that little beggar boy certainly touched this, and Ellinwood doesn't have anyone like Chap.'

'You should have told me,' Magiere said. Following Leesil, she crouched down next to the dog.

'It was a gamble – my gamble,' Leesil answered. 'And what you didn't know, you couldn't be held accountable for.'

He held out the dagger's handle, and Chap eagerly sniffed every inch of it.

'Do you think he can track for us?' Magiere asked.

'I don't know for certain,' Leesil answered. 'But, yes, I think he can.'

She breathed in once. 'Let's get ready as well. We don't have much time.'

Leesil looked at her, puzzled.

'The sun will be setting soon,' was the answer she gave to his unasked question.

Neither one of them said the word 'vampire.' While Magiere went to get her sword, Leesil broke his bedroom chair and fashioned the legs into makeshift stakes. He put them in the sack with his box and headed downstairs to gather further necessities for battle.

For quite a while after Magiere had left him, Welstiel remained sitting in his chair, searching mentally to pinpoint an uninvited presence. He had slowly studied every inch of the room, but so far only books and shelves and his table registered in his sharp eyes.

'I know you are here,' he murmured, more to himself than the presence.

He sensed it. Why was it here, and what did it want? The three sparks of his orb cast a satisfactory amount of illumination. Perhaps more than that was needed.

'Darkness,' Welstiel said, and the orb's sparks immediately extinguished.

With all light gone from the room, he immediately spotted a yellowish glow hovering in the far corner, but only for a moment. It vanished, leaving behind the faint emotional residue of fear and anger.

The possibilities were too varied for comfort in Welstiel's mind. It could have been anything from a spirit to an astral consciousness. But why? He closed his eyes and tried to feel for any kind of trail, any path in the residue of this unseen presence. The traces of fear and anger were gone. The presence had evaporated. He could follow nothing.

Welstiel frowned.

12

Magiere crouched outside the huge shorefront warehouse, Leesil and Brenden beside her. The place appeared almost new, constructed of expensive, solid pine boards.

'Why not just burn it?' Leesil whispered.

'I already told you,' Brenden answered. 'Hundreds of townsfolk make their living from this place in one way or another.'

'Yes, but if we kill the owner, won't that bring about a similar result?' Leesil shifted his weight to get a better hold on the squirming dog. 'Chap, will you stop that?'

Conversing at all was difficult as Leesil was busy holding onto Chap's muzzle and his wildly struggling body.

'Maybe . . .' Brenden hesitated. 'Maybe not. At least their livelihoods might stay intact for a while, if someone else can step in to keep the place running.'

On their way through town, Chap had led them on a wandering course down alleys and side streets, searching the ground with his nose. At the crossing of two roads, he'd lurched back, sneezing as if he'd caught a whiff of something that agitated his senses. He broke into a half-trot, then a full run. All of them were forced to hurry after him, making themselves ridiculously conspicuous. Magiere had cursed herself for not tying a rope around his neck.

Chap ran straight for this warehouse, sniffing the outside floorboards and growling. Welstiel had said to use the dog. If he was correct, then this indeed was the right place. Heavily armed, they now hid behind a stack of crates, deciding on their next course of action and trying to avoid being seen by dockworkers. The sun was low in the sky.

Magiere listened quietly, wishing Leesil and Brenden would stop arguing and let her think. The warehouse seemed a logical place to begin, especially since it matched Brenden's claim that its owner was the one who attacked her. Chap's reaction seemed to confirm their suspicions.

Part of her agreed with Leesil. They ought to just wait until closing time when the workers went home, then pour oil all over the base and set it on fire. Brenden's concern made sense as well. And what if the nobleman and the dirty urchin weren't even inside? What if Chap were only reacting to old or faint residue from either of them passing this way? She had no idea how the dog was able to track these creatures or what was the extent of his abilities.

Yes, finding their prey was the first obstacle to surpass, but once that was accomplished, she and her small group were prepared for fighting undeads, although none of them had used the word. Welstiel had mentioned Brenden's strength. She assumed he meant physical strength, but now she wasn't so sure. Her red-bearded companion crouched calmly, without fear, holding a crossbow in one hand and balancing himself on the packed ground with the other. He'd soaked all his quarrels in garlic water and tucked six roughly sharpened wooden stakes into his belt alongside dangling skins of water. One stake at the center of his back was longer, more like a half-length spear. She didn't know him at all, but was beginning to believe there was more to him than met the eye.

Leesil was now fairly weighted down by a bag tied to his back across his left shoulder. She'd watched him pack and repack it a few times. He had brought a crossbow, several garlic-soaked quarrels, and a long, wooden box. He also filled four small wine flasks with oil, tightly sealed their stoppers, and placed them in the bag, along with a flint. Then he had fashioned two short torches, which he tied to his back as well. She knew he typically carried various stilettos and other bladed weapons somewhere inside his clothes.

She, on the other hand, traveled light, carrying nothing besides her falchion. Her role in this macabre play was to fight Rashed, while the others dealt with the smaller creature called Ratboy, should both their targets be discovered together.

'How are we going to get in?' she asked finally, surveying the warehouse wall up and down. 'We can't exactly walk in the front doors and ask the workers, "By the way, where do your masters sleep?" And I don't fancy trying to enter after dark.'

'There's probably a hidden door in the back wall,' Leesil answered.

She blinked. 'How do you know?'

He hesitated. 'Because I've seen this type of construction before. I'll know what to look for.'

He'd broken into warehouses before? Magiere's curiosity was piqued, but this was not the time or place. 'All right,' she said. 'Stay behind the crates.'

Stacks of wooden crates surrounded this side of the

building, which made it possible to move around to the back without being seen. All the workers were inside and few people wandered about on the pier. Once in position, Leesil passed Chap off to Magiere, who grabbed the dog by the scruff of his neck.

They watched as Leesil's hands moved lightly across the base of the warehouse. Brenden seemed confused and leaned forward.

'What are you looking for? There's no door here.'

Leesil didn't answer and kept moving his fingers across the wood. Magiere began fidgeting after a while, making it harder to keep the dog from doing the same. Her eyes never left Leesil, though they narrowed suspiciously as she tried to figure out what her partner was doing. Finally, Leesil stopped and remained motionless with his hands firmly against one spot. Then his head tilted slightly to one side and his eyes half closed.

Magiere craned her neck, trying to see what Leesil had found. It was just a blank space of wall. Leesil pulled his hands away, but remained crouched as he reached into his sack and pulled out the long box, glancing up at her in concern.

'Do you trust me?' he asked.

The frank question caught her off guard and she hesitated. 'Of course,' she answered.

Long, yellow-white hair fell forward across his face as he leaned down.

'Then don't ask me to explain anything about this.'

When he opened the box, she regretted agreeing to his request.

A wire loop with small steel handles at each end and

two stilettos with blades narrow as knitting needles were the first items she saw. The sight of the wire made her swallow hard. She'd never actually seen such a thing firsthand, but she had once witnessed a criminal executed by strangulation and could guess how the item was used.

The narrow stilettos were another matter. Too slim for any blade-to-blade fighting she could imagine, she couldn't be sure what they would be used for. But looking back to the wire again, she didn't particularly want to know. What she did want to know was how and why Leesil had come by them, and she didn't care for the guesses that flashed through her mind.

The metal of the wire and blades was too pale and bright for common steel. Some other metal had been used, and these were expensive items of a questionable nature no one would buy openly from some weaponsmith. There were only hints of blemishes on the polished blades. Though carefully tended at one time, they had not been taken out for a long while. As much as the items in her companion's possession made Magiere nervous and wary, and even angry, she felt an unexpected wave of anxious concern for Leesil. Pushed aside and hidden, these distasteful possessions had enough meaning for him that he'd kept them shut away for an unknown number of years.

Leesil hesitated, and Magiere saw his back rise and fall in a deep breath before his narrow fingers pressed some hidden spot on the box's inside. He then grabbed the base of the lid near the hinge, and an inner panel folded open to expose a compartment inside the lid itself. Therein, tucked in cloth straps, was an array of shaped wires, long, needle-small hooks, and other similar delicate items crooked, bent, and shaped like a set of tiny tools, the purpose for which she couldn't guess. And again the metal was of a polished silver hue too pale for steel.

'What are those?' Brenden asked.

Leesil ignored him, picking out a thin wire strut that ended in a right-angle turn. The bent end stuck out less than half a fingernail's length and was flattened to be thinner than the longer shaft or handle. He felt carefully around the base of the wooden wall, and then pressed his first finger against a spot that looked exactly like every other place on the vast wall. He attempted to insert the wire directly above his fingernail.

To Magiere's shock, the wire strut's head passed right through the wood, and a panel as wide and tall as her arm slid open.

'Let me go first,' Leesil said. 'There may be traps.'

His body was so tense and face so serious that she hardly recognized him. He knew what he was doing, but somehow to take these actions was a strain on him, as if he forced himself.

Her thoughts stopped and retreated one step. He knew exactly what he was doing. How?

'Leesil . . .'

When he turned, his slanted, amber eyes pleaded with her.

'Trust me,' he said.

He snapped the box shut, slid it back into his sack, and crawled through the secret door. She had little choice but to follow.

★   ★   ★

Once Brenden crawled down the shaft after Magiere and emerged into a plush sitting room, the first thing he noticed was a candle in the shape of a deep, red rose. Wax roses were hardly what he expected. Leesil was already searching the walls and floor by sight and fingertips. Two oil lamps attached to the wall provided small flames of light. Last summer, if someone told Brenden that he'd soon be in the company of a vampire hunter and a professional thief, tracking down the undead murderers of his sister, he would have thought the speaker quite mad. In fact, it really did sound mad, and that thought made the hairs on the back of his neck stand up.

And when he first met Magiere, he had despised her, thinking her a selfish and cold woman, whose only interest was in turning a profit from her tavern. His opinion of Magiere had altered a great deal since then. For all her strength and carefully guarded face, he could see pain and uncertainty buried inside. She did not hide in her tavern because of selfishness but something else, and he did not know her well enough to ask what that was. Now, she had overcome this mysterious obstacle and was standing beside him with a sword, ready to fight and kill or die. He admired her courage, and the clean lines of her features and her long black braid were not lost on him either. Strength, beauty, and fighting ability in the same person seemed a rare combination to him.

Then his thoughts turned back to Eliza, his fragile sister, and the smoldering anger in his chest made him focus on their current goal.

And on this room . . . curved couches upholstered in green velvet, a fine painting of the northern seacoast, braided rugs, and a variety of silver ornaments sitting on polished tables registered in his eyesight all at once. He walked over and picked up a sewing basket. Inside, he found fine needlework. The works-in-progress were more like vivid scenes come to life than mere embroidery. He held a half-finished scrap of muslin that depicted a huge sun surrounded by clouds, setting over the ocean.

Chap was slinking around, sniffing everything and growling softly.

'There's a woman,' Brenden said flatly.

'What?' Magiere appeared somewhat confused by his statement.

'We aren't just dealing with the nobleman and that street urchin. And the things in this room are too personal for a servant. Servants don't sit for hours at needlepoint.'

Leesil stopped his current task of pulling all the rugs up. 'Or maybe one of the men is just artistic with truly fine taste in decor.'

Magiere half-smiled at the flippant comment, and Brenden shook his head. He'd figured out by now that Magiere often hid behind a mask of cold hostility, and Leesil behind his humor, caustic or otherwise. He understood Magiere's defenses, but as much as he'd come to like the half-elf, Leesil's shifts between ill-timed humor and unexpected compassion, between rapid wrestling abilities and now burglary were getting to be quite unnerving.

Leesil examined a clearly visible hatch door in the center of the floor.

'What are you waiting for?' Magiere asked.

'This one is different,' he said almost to himself.

'Whoever put this place together never expected anyone to find that outside entrance, and probably never used it, so there wasn't a real need for active safeguards.' His head rose until his gaze settled upon Magiere. 'We have to go down. I don't know any more about this kind of hunting than you, but I'm sure they'll be sleeping somewhere underground.'

'What do you mean you don't know?' Brenden asked. He looked at Magiere. 'Wasn't this how you earned a living before Miiska?'

The half-elf grinned weakly. 'No time to explain. Both of you stand back.'

Brenden stepped back and then did so again, until his back was nearly against the wall. Leesil slowly walked around the hatch door as if memorizing every part of it. The blacksmith experienced a wave of discomfort after quite a bit of precious time passed and Leesil still continued his study.

'We need to hurry,' Brenden said. 'The sun will be down soon.'

'Daylight won't help us if we're dead,' came Leesil's answer.

A small hole had been cut in one edge of the door to form a simple handle. All one need do was slip his fingers through and lift. Leesil crouched down to dig in his bag, but rather than his box of strange tools, he pulled out a stake.

'Both of you get down behind one of the couches. And hold Chap tight,' he said. 'I'm going to use a stake to open this slightly. When I do, a poisoned needle is going to jab the point. After that, I'll try to lift the door, but there may be further surprises.' He paused. 'I once saw a general rig poison gas to a door like this. If I yell, get into the shaft, no matter what.'

Brenden looked back and forth between his two companions, who were now staring at each other. It was obvious that Leesil was displaying skills and knowledge previously unknown to Magiere. Her expression was more than a little troubled, but she moved back and hid behind a richly upholstered couch. Brenden did the same, peering around one side to watch.

'Be careful,' Magiere called.

'No, really?' Leesil said and gently pushed the stake's point through the opening. A loud *click* followed.

'Got the needle,' he said, and then he flattened himself low to the floor, one leg folded underneath, presumably so he could dive aside if need be. 'Keep your heads down.'

He levered the stake to lift the door's edge, then gave a quick, sharp thrust and pulled back as the hatch flipped open.

A crack sounded out twice from the opening. Well shielded behind the couch, both Brenden and Magiere still ducked quickly in reflex as two crossbow quarrels shot out. The first passed over Leesil, aimed where a person would lean down to pull the door open. The other now protruded from the front of the couch behind which Brenden and Magiere hid. Brenden peered at it over the top of the couch.

'Wait,' Leesil said, holding one hand up. 'I'm not sure that's everything.' He disappeared down the hole.

Magiere didn't do as he bid, but rather crawled around the couch and over to the opening, carefully peeking over the edge. 'What are you doing?'

'Just making sure.' Leesil's voice was mute and dull coming from somewhere below. 'I think you can come down now.'

Brenden joined Magiere, contemplating how to lower Chap, but the dog solved his problem by jumping through and landing next to Leesil. Magiere followed, and the blacksmith went last.

He found himself standing in a narrow tunnel. Always interested in devices and gadgets, he examined the two crossbows sitting in iron supports and carefully aimed upward to the opening.

'It's a simple trick really,' Leesil said. 'You just mount them solidly, load them up, and then run a wire or string from the door to the firing mechanisms.'

'If you two have finished admiring these would-be murder weapons,' Magiere interjected in a low, irritated voice, 'we need to move on. Light a torch.'

Edwan arrived back at the tunnels under the warehouse in a state of agitation. He had listened to every word that passed between the hunter and the stranger who was staying in the cellar rooms of The Velvet Rose. Although he did not fully understand what had taken place, Edwan did comprehend that this hunter was more dangerous than Rashed would acknowledge and that the stranger knew many things about the undead. Also, this stranger was urging the hunter to hunt. Edwan thought back to the night Magiere visited the death place of the blacksmith's sister. The stranger had appeared and talked to her. He called her a *dhampir*. How had he put it . . . ? 'Someone gifted to kill the dead.' The hunter had not been interested in Teesha or

Rashed before that night. Bits of thoughts and connections passed through Edwan's scattered mind. He willed himself to think.

What if this stranger was somehow guiding the hunter's movements? She seemed so proud, yet she sought his guidance.

Edwan knew he must tell Teesha. She would understand what all the words meant — at least the words he could remember. She would know what to do.

He planned on flitting straight to her coffin when he sensed a presence and hesitated . . . no, he sensed more than one presence. Moving on instinct, he floated down a tunnel and came upon the sight of the hunter, her half-elf, the blacksmith, and the dog. They carried torches and weapons and were making their way straight toward the caves where Teesha and Rashed and Ratboy slept. Edwan felt shock and then chastised himself. Of course, they would be here. Did the stranger not tell her to hunt and to use her dog?

Some time ago, Edwan had begged Teesha to move her coffin away from Rashed's, so that he might have a brief span of privacy with her as she retired or when she arose. And she had agreed. Now, he hurried to her. With a bright flash, he appeared visibly in the center of her private underground chamber, frustrated that he lacked the ability to open the lid of her coffin.

'My dear,' he said aloud. 'You must wake up.'

Edwan tried to push his consciousness back to when he'd been alive and could have at least tried to protect her. What would he have done? His thoughts had so long been trapped between the mortal and spirit world, he found it difficult to focus on anything more than the specific details of the moment at hand, let alone a time long gone.

'Teesha.' He attempted using his thoughts this time, allowing his noncorporeal form to pass through the smooth lid of her coffin so that he could see her sleeping face. 'Wake up.'

Her eyes remained closed like a sweet child lost in sleep. Dusk was just beginning. She would awaken soon on her own, but he needed her to rise now.

Edwan drew back out of the chamber into the stone and packed-earth tunnels that Rashed had paid twelve men to dig before the warehouse was built. The job took nearly a year. The men were hired from out of town, and no one ever knew what became of them after they finished their task. The ghost tried desperately to remember any words floating about at that past time. Some areas needed wooden supports – he recalled those words – and the warrior designed a way for one of those places to cave in if intruders passed. Where was that place?

Rapid movement being one of the few gifts left to him, he concentrated upon his presence and vanished.

Leesil kept his equipment bag slung over one shoulder. He held a short torch out in front of him, but wanted his other hand completely free. Chap walked directly behind him, then Magiere, and Brenden brought up the rear, carrying the other torch. He warned both of them not to touch anything, even the walls, unless he told them it was safe.

It had been a long time since he had a reason to locate a sleeping target, and usually the job called for climbing up, not down. Keeping his attention on the task at hand, he moved slowly, examining the floor, walls, and ceiling carefully before stepping forward. He ignored Brenden's continued comments about the need for haste.

He also avoided speaking to or looking at Magiere, which wasn't difficult at this point. Their torches provided the only light source so far down and, after all, he was quite busy.

Chap growled softly, and his eyes grew brighter and even more transparent than usual.

'We're close,' Magiere said. 'I think.'

None of them knew anything about Chap's abilities, but Leesil thought her comment made sense. He cast a glance over his shoulder at her and, in the scant light, something else caught his attention. With all the crawling about, her amulets had fallen out from inside her shirt and hung in plain sight about her neck. The topaz stone was glowing.

'Look,' he said, pointing.

She glanced down and touched it in mild wonder. 'It's not any warmer, just glowing.'

Chap whined.

'Has it ever glowed before?' Leesil asked.

'When I fought that villager at the Vudrask River and . . .' She trailed off, and their eyes locked.

'Maybe you better leave it out,' he said.

'We need to hurry,' Brenden said in clear frustration.

The tunnel was small – barely large enough to stand in – and crudely dug. Leesil could see nothing except the walls, his feet, and a small distance ahead.

'How did they dig this tunnel under the warehouse?' Magiere asked.

'It's been a while, but I remember the construction seemed to take a long time,' Brenden answered. 'Perhaps the tunnel was created first and the warehouse built on top of it?'

That sounded plausible. Leesil saw overhead boards coming up.

'There are wooden supports here,' he said. 'Be careful passing through.'

A small glint low to the floor caught his attention. He stopped, holding up a hand for the others to do the same, and crouched down for a closer look. A small wire ran across the tunnel a hand's breadth above the floor.

'Trip wire,' he said. 'If you look, you'll see it. Step carefully.'

Such things were more of a nuisance to Leesil than an actual danger. His sharp gaze missed nothing, and he'd found his old ways coming back to him naturally, even after many years of trying to forget them. He turned to make sure Chap didn't trip the wire, when a glowing light appeared before him.

Colors solidified in the space of a heartbeat.

Leesil was face-to-face with a beheaded man standing close enough to touch him. The dead man's partially severed head lay at an angle on one shoulder with the stump of his open, bleeding throat exposed. His torso turned sharply, swinging his head in toward Leesil's face as the lips curled into a snarl.

Leesil lurched away from the terrifying sight. But he remembered the trip wire.

His first step was high enough to clear the wire, but his footing slipped as it came down. His trailing foot's heel snagged the wire as he stumbled backward. He instinctively covered his head with his arms.

Two boards pulled loose from above, one of them striking him flatsided as it fell. The roof above him exploded as roots and churning earth gained a life of their own. He tried to see if Magiere was far enough back to escape being buried, but he didn't have time. The pattering dirt and stone falling on him suddenly became a great weight. He was slammed downward, striking the ground with crushing force.

Magiere saw Leesil turn in her direction, then stumble backward down the tunnel, an expression of horror on his face, as if he'd seen something terrible. Almost instantly an avalanche of wood, rock, and sandy soil poured from the tunnel ceiling.

'Leesil!' she screamed, thrusting a hand out to grab him, but Brenden snatched her waist from behind to pull her back.

'No, don't!' he shouted. 'It's too late.'

A cloud of dust enveloped them both, momentarily blinding Magiere.

As rapidly as it had started, the cave-in stopped. Heavy dust still rolled around them in the air, but Magiere could see Chap's tail and haunches and hear him whining. She wiped grime from her eyes with the back of her hand and saw the dog was already digging frantically.

'Get the dog back and take my torch,' Brenden ordered.

There was not enough room in the small tunnel for two people to take action. Brenden was potentially the strongest. Magiere grabbed Chap's haunches and pulled hard and fast.

'Get back, Chap!'

Chap snarled at her viciously, either from her roughness or being stopped in his own desperate labor. Holding the dog, she took the torch from Brenden, who pushed past and began jerking and throwing boards to either side as best he could.

And then, Magiere could do nothing but stand and watch.

She hated having no control. At times, she had cursed the responsibilities that she often placed upon herself. But standing in the tunnel, watching Brenden wildly dig for Leesil, she realized that helpless spectators were worse off than those taking action. Spectators had time to think.

What if Leesil died? What good would fighting for a home and a business be if she had no one to share plans and daily events with? Leesil was the only person with whom she'd ever been able to spend immeasurable amounts of time. What did that say about her? What if he died?

She fought the urge to drop the torch, push Brenden aside and start digging herself. Instead, she held Chap back, not sure if the quiver she felt was in her own body or the vibration of the growling whine coming from the dog. With her other hand, she tried to hold the torch out to the side, giving Brenden light and allowing her to see what was happening.

The tunnel was not completely closed. Debris and earth only blocked it about halfway up. The problem was that Brenden had nowhere to throw the debris he removed. His red-tinged face glistened with exertion, but he never slowed his pace.

'Can you see him?' Magiere asked.

'No, I'm not . . . wait, a foot!'

'Pull! Pull him out.'

She stepped back quickly, dragging Chap with her. Brenden pulled hard, almost backing into her, and a small cloud of dust rose up around them. The dust and her own fear made it seem as if Brenden had created the half-elf from nothing and pulled him into existence.

Now it was her turn. Pressing her back to the wall, she slipped around Brenden and handed him the torch so that she could kneel beside Leesil, putting her ear to his chest, then his mouth.

'He's not breathing.'

Lying there, Leesil looked thinner than ever. His whole body was a single color of earth except where blood from a cut or scrape on face or hand darkened the grime clinging to him. Once, she'd seen her Aunt Bieja save a child, who had fallen into the well, by blowing air into the child's mouth.

Turning her head away from the dust, Magiere took in a deep breath. She pinched Leesil's narrow nose closed with two fingers, sealed his mouth with her own, and breathed out. His chest rose once and then fell still again.

'What are you doing?' Brenden shouted, grabbing her shoulder.

She swung back and struck his arm off of her and repeated her act again. And again. Desperation would not allow her to stop. The fifth time she made his chest rise, he coughed back into her mouth.

Magiere pulled quickly away, watching his face. 'Leesil?'

He lay there motionless. Then he coughed again, dust rising out of his mouth, followed by an audible gasp as he sucked in air. She slumped over him, and relief washed through her.

'Here,' Brenden said, and held out a water skin he pulled from his belt. 'Try to wash out his throat, and then we'll see if any bones are broken.'

Before Magiere could take the water skin, Leesil reached out and grabbed it himself. He took a mouthful, rolled to his side, and spit the water out. Then he tried to sit up.

'I'm all right,' he said hoarsely. He blinked at the dirt still in his eyes. 'Where's the ghost? Is it gone?'

'What ghost?' Magiere asked. Then she ordered him, 'Be still.' Using her fingers, she quickly probed his hands, arms, and legs. 'I don't think he's injured.'

'I'm fine,' Leesil rambled on. 'Where's the damn ghost! I thought he was real . . . but he couldn't be . . . head was cut off.'

Magiere looked back at Brenden. 'We have to turn back. He's hallucinating.'

'No!' Leesil snapped. 'I'm not hallucinating. Oh, forget that. It's too late. If we quit now, they'll know we've been here. How safe will we be at home tonight? How safe will Rose and Caleb be? We have to finish this.'

He was right, and Magiere knew it, but her first instinct was still to get him out of this place. She untucked her shirttail, ripped a piece off, and then poured water from the flask to clean his face and eyes. At first he protested, pushing her hands away, but when she refused to give up, he sat there and let her finish. Small cuts and abrasions marred his tan skin, but none of them looked serious.

'You were lucky,' she said.

'The gods watch over fools,' he answered, trying to smile.

'Oh, shut up,' Magiere snapped, all her panic released in irritation at one of his typically inappropriate remarks.

Brenden shook his head. Magiere knew he thought them both quite odd. She didn't blame him.

'All right, now what?' she asked her partner.

Leesil looked back over his shoulder at the mound of debris choking off half the tunnel's space.

'We'll have to crawl; drag our equipment through,' he answered. 'I think we are getting very close. That ghost must be some sort of guardian.'

He began checking his bag for any broken or ruined equipment. One of the flasks of oil had burst, making the others and his odd box of weapons slippery to handle. Only a small amount soiled his crossbow. He wiped the bow and other items off as best he could with the scrap of Magiere's shirt.

'I lost the torch,' he said. 'We'll have to make do with just one.'

For someone who had almost died, his calm, competent manner both reassured and annoyed Magiere.

'You crawl through and Brenden can hand it to you,' he added. 'But don't move down the tunnel until I'm there ahead of you.'

'Wait,' Brenden said. 'Stand still, Magiere. I brought something for you.' He removed a small flask from the belt at his waist. 'Hold out your arms.'

'What is that?' she asked.

'Garlic water,' he answered. 'I took it from your kitchen. At close quarters, it might help protect you, or at least make those creatures think twice about grappling with you.'

He poured the garlic water all over her arms, shoulders, and back. She found his foresight impressive, but said nothing until he finished.

'Ready?' she asked.

He nodded.

One by one, they crawled through the open space over the cave-in and again began their trek down the tunnel. Perhaps it was her imagination, but Magiere believed Leesil picked up the pace, and although he did check for traps, his examinations were brief.

'I can see an opening,' he said.

A second wave of relief passed through Magiere as they stepped from the tunnel into an underground cavern and once again could stand side by side.

'Over there,' Leesil said, pointing across the cavern.

'What?' Brenden asked.

Leesil moved forward, holding the torch out. He glanced back.

'Coffins.'

Edwan hovered invisibly over Rashed's coffin, torn between joy and frustration. He'd failed in his one chance to make the hunters kill themselves, and now he believed that appearing to them again would only decrease his chance at future shock tactics.

But they had seen the warrior and Ratboy's coffins first, not Teesha's. Let the two of them fight these hunters;

he cared nothing for them. For the moment, his Teesha was safe.

He focused on his own form again and transported to his beloved's tiny cavern.

'Wake up, my sweet,' he whispered. 'Please.'

This time, she stirred.

13

Some vampires rest more deeply than others in their dormant state. Rashed never admitted it to anyone, even Teesha, but he always struggled not to collapse immediately after sunrise, and he remembered little until dusk. Perhaps it was a condition singular to him, having nothing to do with all undeads. He considered this tendency a weakness, but as yet had discovered no remedy.

This time, still lost in sleep, something not unlike a mortal dream touched the edge of his awareness. He felt as if something unseen watched him in the dark. He could see at night better than a mortal, but sight still required some form of light. This was blackness even his gaze couldn't pierce. But he felt that presence in the dark just the same, always moving and shifting, trying to catch him from behind.

So many years had passed since he had thought of dreams. Such visions and concerns were for the living, not the undead. What pulled at him? With a sudden rush of anxiety, the presence in the dark moved inward toward him, and his eyes opened.

Before he could act, his coffin's lid was jerked open from the outside.

Torchlight illuminated the chamber behind a shadowed figure above him, but he could see easily in such light. The hunter stood over him holding a sharpened stake. Her eyes widened slightly. Both of them froze in surprise, and then she thrust downward with the stake.

Snarling more in rage than fear, he grabbed her wrist, the stake's point halting above his chest. Her sleeve and arm were wet, and his hand began to smoke.

Half shouting in pain, Rashed released his grip as he kicked out. His foot struck her lower chest, and she stumbled back. He instantly rolled over the coffin's side to his feet. What had she done?

A pungent smell reached his nose and stung his eyes. Garlic.

He remembered Ratboy's whining about what the old woman in the tavern had done to him. The hunter had doused herself in garlic water.

He could move his left arm a bit, but not enough to use it in fighting, and now his right hand was badly burned as well. The hunter flipped the stake to her left hand and drew her falchion with her right. Rashed reacted immediately, teeth clenching as he pulled his own sword with his burned hand.

She was dusty and grimy, with strands of loose hair sticking to her pale face as if she'd been crawling through dirt, but her expression was hard and angry. She was a hunter, indeed — cold and pitiless, an invader who'd entered his home to kill him and those he cared for. He had not felt true and full hatred since the night he'd taken Corische's head, but it filled him now.

A silver-furred dog howled and snarled wildly from across the cavern, where a red-bearded man held it at bay. Beside them knelt the light-haired half-elf, loading a crossbow.

'Ratboy,' Rashed called. 'Get up!'

The hunter rushed him, swinging the falchion. To his own surprise, he dodged instead of parrying, instinct acting for him. He could not allow that blade to touch him. If he were seriously injured again, he was finished, and there would be no one to protect Teesha. Disarming the hunter was his first and only real priority. He needed to back her into the tunnel where she couldn't swing and his strength might give him an advantage. But the wound in his shoulder from their last battle still burned. Feeling slightly off-balance by his near useless left arm, he gained good footing and charged back at her.

'Yes, my dear,' Edwan said, peering down at Teesha's fluttering eyelids, his head merged through the coffin lid. 'Wake up. We have to flee.'

She wore her velvet gown of deepest red, like rich wine, and her thick curls of chocolate brown spread about the coffin's bed, framing her lovely oval face. He still remembered the first time she had smiled at him. It was one of the few old memories that stayed with him after death.

Like Rashed, Teesha refused to sleep in dirt and spread a white satin comforter over the earth of her homeland. As she sat up and pushed open the coffin's lid, Edwan pulled back out of her way. She blinked at him, and he noted how the pale quilt lining of her resting place made the color of her dress more vivid.

'We have to flee,' he repeated.

'Why?' she asked. 'What is wrong?'

He started to tell her about the stranger at The Velvet Rose, then realized that telling her of that was foolish.

He must tell her about the hunter first, so that she would escape with him. Rashed was fighting the hunter. If fortune was kind, the warrior would be killed and Edwan would have Teesha to himself again.

'The hunter has entered the tunnels,' he said. 'She brought the dog and other mortals and many weapons. We must go.'

Alarm altered Teesha's pretty features. 'Where's Rashed? Didn't you wake him?'

'The hunter found him first, and Ratboy. They can fight her. Come with me, now.'

She quickly climbed out of her coffin and ran into the tunnel toward the warrior's cave.

'No!' Edwan called in shock. He flew past her and stopped directly in her path. 'The hunter is there. You are running toward her. We must escape through the tunnels on the other side.'

'Move, Edwan,' she cried out. 'I have to help Rashed . . . we need him.'

Edwan's shock increased when she ran straight through him. He could not believe this course of events and followed after her in stunned confusion. Sounds of growling and shouting and clanging steel grew louder as they approached Rashed's cave. Teesha stopped, leaning close to the wall of the tunnel at its opening.

Edwan saw Rashed battling the hunter. Every clash and rush of steps moved them both closer to the opening on the far side of the cave. Rashed was trying to back the hunter out into that tunnel. To the far right, just beyond Rashed's resting place, the half-elf and a large red-bearded man, holding the silver hound, were about to open Ratboy's coffin.

Teesha's eyes shifted back and forth between the hunter and her companions.

'Edwan,' she called, 'help Ratboy, now!'

Edwan hovered behind her. She had not even looked at him, just ordered him.

'No.'

Teesha turned back to stare at him in shock. Her mouth opened, but not a word came out. When she looked back into the cave, Rashed had the hunter two steps from the opening. He made a sudden rush forward, trying to close in, slashing down hard with his blade.

The hunter shifted to the right against the cave opening and slashed down on top of Rashed's sword, driving it to the floor. Her other hand, gripping the stake, swung out and struck his wounded shoulder.

The large warrior spun halfway around until his back flattened against the cave wall, his chest fully exposed. At the same time, the upper half of Ratboy's coffin lid shattered outward into the air. The hunter twisted back into the cave, facing Rashed, ready to strike again with the stake.

Before Edwan could say anything more, Teesha launched herself wildly into the cave and leaped on the hunter's back. Edwan's beautiful wife screamed as her arms began to smolder.

Leesil crept closer to the coffin's bottom end, crossbow aimed downward to pin the beggar boy with the first shot. His sack of supplies hung off one hip from the strap slung across to his opposite shoulder. The sound of Magiere's falchion clashing against the nobleman's long sword came from behind him, but he could not turn to look. He would have to trust her to keep her opponent busy, just as she trusted him to get the beggar boy. If either of them failed, the other would end up falling to an attack from behind.

He nodded at Brenden, who simultaneously held the torch and gripped Chap by the scruff of the neck.

'Let go of Chap and pull the lid open,' Leesil said.

Brenden moved to do as he was bid, but before his hand touched wood, the coffin lid's upper half exploded as Ratboy smashed his way out. Startled, Leesil lost his aim and stepped back.

The beggar boy grabbed Brenden's wrist and jerked, hard. The blacksmith stumbled off balance and fell across the bottom half of the coffin, blocking Leesil's line of fire. Chap was forced back as Brenden fell, and the torch in the blacksmith's hand tumbled to the ground. Its light partially blocked by the coffin, shadows leaped upward along the walls in front of Leesil.

Between the sudden shift in light and Brenden's falling body, Leesil lost clear aim at his target. Ratboy curled backward, feet thrusting up above his head as he flipped himself over the coffin's back end. He landed, sitting on the ground.

Leesil tried to set his aim again, but Ratboy kicked out with both feet against the coffin's near end. It slid sharply across the floor, slamming bottom end first into Leesil's legs.

Leesil tried to catch himself with one hand as he fell, and toppled on his side. With the lid's top half shattered, his torso dropped inside the coffin. His clothing snagged on shards of wood, and Ratboy was above him before he could twist over and right himself.

Leesil glimpsed a shadowed and filthy alabaster face with round, red-tinged eyes and openmouthed grin. The teeth, with fangs jutting top and bottom, were yellow. Leesil twisted and ducked his head at a flash of movement.

A clawlike hand slashed down, missing his throat. It caught him across the cheek and mouth. Leesil felt his own blood spatter across his face before feeling the pain.

'No one will recognize your corpse,' Ratboy hissed.

Leesil closed his hands to grip the crossbow, but it was gone – he'd dropped it when he fell. Ratboy's hand flashed up again, and Leesil flinched, one arm raised to shield his head, while grasping at his belt for a stake or stiletto or whatever weapon he could find first.

The face and hand disappeared in a silver-gray flash.

Leesil thrashed his way out of the coffin, rolling over its side, and almost falling on the crossbow he'd dropped upon the ground.

'Shoot!' Brenden shouted, now pulling himself up, a trickle of blood running from a gash in his forehead. 'Shoot him.'

Leesil rolled again into a crouch, with the crossbow at ready, and saw Chap on top of Ratboy. Dog and undead were locked in a thrashing tangle of teeth, limbs, claws, and snarls that moved so quickly Leesil couldn't follow all of it. Chap's fangs snapped and connected over and over, and though Ratboy could not return the same, his claw-hands battered at the dog. Tufts of fur were ripped from Chap's body.

'I can't. I'll hit Chap,' Leesil answered through gritted teeth.

'Fool!' Brenden spit out. He snatched up the torch and flung it skittering across the ground at Ratboy.

'No, don't . . .' Leesil began. He barely had time to see the torch hit Ratboy in the hip. Both dog and undead struggled to get away from the flame.

Out of the corner of his eye, Leesil saw the huge nobleman backing Magiere toward the tunnel opening, the two combatants swinging their blades at each other. Magiere chopped her opponent's sword to the ground and struck his wounded shoulder with her stake. The nobleman spun away along the cave wall, and Magiere pivoted back into the open. Both their faces were distorted with hatred beyond sanity, each having forgotten the existence of anything but the other. Magiere's own features twisted in a silent snarl of exposed fangs as she drew up her falchion to cut the nobleman down.

Leesil started to turn his attention back to his own opponent when a flash of red rushed toward Magiere from behind.

A woman. Brenden had been right.

A mass of brown hair and a red dress enveloped Magiere as the woman leaped upon her back, arms wrapping around Magiere's shoulders and neck. The woman screamed as she began to smoke, burned by the garlic water. Magiere slammed her left elbow back into the woman's side, then, half turning, struck her in the face with her falchion's hilt. The woman toppled backward to the cave floor, and as she fell, Magiere slashed down once with the falchion.

The action cost Magiere the advantage. The nobleman regained his footing and raised his long sword to strike.

Everything else dropped from Leesil's awareness.

He raised the crossbow and fired.

Monster.

The word echoed over and over in Magiere's mind as she slashed and charged and dodged the tall creature in front of her. She was vaguely aware of his physical appearance, his short black hair and clear eyes.

Rashed. She knew that his name was Rashed. The name simply appeared in her mind, but she did not understand how. As her rage and strength increased and her jaw began to hurt, she recognized flashes of images from his mind.

He saw her as a killer, an invader. But she knew what he was.

Monster, she thought again, raising the falchion to strike.

His name didn't matter. His head sliced from his shoulders – that mattered. She was strong, so strong . . . and fast. Her mouth ached, and she couldn't speak.

A shriek sounded in her ears and weight collided with her back and shoulders. Strong, thin arms wrapped around her neck as the wailing voice in her ears turned to a pain-filled scream. Smoke rose around her head, obscuring her vision.

Magiere thrashed backward with her elbow, connecting with a soft torso, and was answered with the pleasing sensation of bones snapping inside flesh. As the arms released, Magiere whirled and slammed her sword hilt at whoever had grabbed her, not even aware if the blow had connected. She only saw billowing red fabric obscured in trails of smoke, and chopped hard at it with the falchion. The blade connected, but she didn't stop to look at her target and turned her head.

Rashed's sword arced down at her. Magiere twisted on instinct, trying to move out of the way.

A crossbow quarrel suddenly sprouted from Rashed's stomach and the path of his blade changed slightly. It passed close by her shoulder and swept outward away from her.

Magiere felt the hate rise up in her like burning elation. She spun back, her sword arm coming up, blade arcing over her head to come down on her prey.

The monster reversed his swing before she'd finished turning.

She felt surprise more than pain as the tip flashed out of sight just below her jaw. Hate and strength spilled out of her at the dull sting in her throat. Wet warmth ran down her body inside her vestment.

Dropping to her knees, she released the stake and grasped her throat. The same warmth ran between her fingers from the side of her neck.

Rashed staggered back one step, pulled the smoking quarrel from his body, then moved forward again, his lips curled in a sneer.

Leesil dropped his gaze long enough to pull another quarrel from its holding place below the crossbow's stock. He couldn't afford to step between those two in their maddened state without being cut down by one or the other, so he readied for another shot. It might not kill the nobleman, but it could slow him enough for Magiere to take the advantage. Fitting it in place, he raised his eyes again as he pulled on the bow string.

Magiere knelt on the ground, hand to her neck. Her face was no longer twisted in rage; rather her brow wrinkled in confusion, eyes wide. Her fingers were already dark with blood.

'Chap!' Leesil screamed, not even looking to see if the dog was free of his opponent. 'Chap, here, get him!'

The nobleman pulled the quarrel from his stomach much in the same manner Leesil had seen Ratboy do on the road to Miiska. Chap rushed by Leesil in a blur. The dog's feet struck the ground only twice before he closed enough to launch himself at the nobleman.

As Leesil turned away, he heard rather than saw Chap connect with the nobleman – snarls, the clattering of metal as a sword tumbled to the ground, followed by a half-intelligible scream of anger. He focused his attention on Ratboy.

Blackened and bleeding, the small undead battered out the last flames from his shabby clothing where Brenden's torch had struck. Brenden was already charging with the longer of his garlic-soaked stakes in both hands. The blacksmith dropped his full weight down onto his smaller opponent and drove the stake through Ratboy's chest.

Ratboy's mouth snapped open to scream, but no sound came out. The undead did not fall limp, or die. He thrashed, striking at Brenden's head and shoulders with one hand while trying to grasp the stake with the other. Even with his size, it was all Brenden could do to keep his small opponent pinned to the ground.

'You missed the heart,' Leesil shouted. Then he whispered, 'We're going to die. . . . We're going to lose this . . . Magiere!'

Everything was falling apart around him. He could grab the falchion and try finishing Ratboy – or the nobleman with Chap's help – but he didn't see how he could get both of them quickly enough. He'd never trained to use a sword. It was not his kind of weapon. And even if he were that lucky, Magiere could die before he got to her.

Leesil reached into his bag, pulled out an oil flask, and smashed it against Ratboy's broken coffin. He had to kick the coffin's base hard, twice, to get it to slide over against the nobleman's own sleeping place, forming a low barrier around the blacksmith and Ratboy struggling on the floor against the cave wall. As he hurdled over the coffins, crossbow still in his other hand, he pulled a stiletto from his sleeve and slashed the remaining waterskins filled with garlic water hanging from the back of Brenden's belt. There was no way he could try a fast use of a stake with Brenden on top of his target, and he hoped luck was with him now.

Water splashed out across both struggling forms on the ground, and Leesil saw the smoke begin to rise. He grabbed Brenden by the shirt and jerked the blacksmith upright with all his strength.

'Get Magiere!' he shouted to Brenden. 'Get her out of here, now!'

Free of the blacksmith's weight, Ratboy clutched with both hands at the stake, off-center through his chest. His body shivered as the garlic water burned into him. Brenden pulled away and hurried off in Magiere's direction.

Leesil grabbed Brenden's torch from the ground in the same hand as his stiletto, and moved outside the coffin barrier. As he turned, Ratboy was climbing to his feet, body still quaking in pain, though the smoke had now dissipated into a thin haze around him. Leesil didn't hesitate. He pointed the crossbow at Ratboy and fired. Then he struck the oil-coated coffin with his torch. The aging wood ignited like a pyre, trapping Ratboy behind. Leesil did not bother to see if his quarrel had struck the charred undead, and threw down the crossbow so he could fumble in the sack for another oil flask.

Across the room, a bloodied Chap tried to corner the disarmed nobleman, or at least force him farther away from the cave opening and Magiere. Chap's strategy against Ratboy had been to knock the undead off his feet and land on top, but even wounded, the nobleman was too large and strong for that ploy. The dog was limited to snapping and biting at the nobleman's legs and hands, doing little more than holding him at bay. And that would not last for long.

Brenden already had Magiere in his arms, having ripped off one of his shirt sleeves to bind her bleeding neck. He grabbed her falchion as he stood up.

'Go, now!' Leesil ordered him, then backed into the tunnel's mouth behind them and smashed another oil flask on the ground. 'Chap, come on!'

Chap snapped at his opponent one last time, then wheeled and headed for the tunnel at full speed. The nobleman was immediately behind the dog, but Chap was too quick. As the dog rushed by into the tunnel, Leesil struck the oil on the floor with his torch and backed hastily into the tunnel. The cave opening went up in flames.

'Run!' Leesil yelled.

Neither Brenden nor Chap needed such coaxing. The blacksmith was well down the tunnel when Leesil caught up to him, Magiere slung over his shoulder and Chap now in the lead. Leesil could see blood already staining Brenden's back from Magiere's wound.

Darkness and dust and fear ran with them.

When they reached the cave-in, Chap crawled immediately through the opening on top of the debris. Brenden crawled through and began pulling Magiere's still form after him. Leesil heard the sound of booted feet coming down the tunnel. He did not have time to wonder how anyone could have gotten through the flames.

'Hurry,' he urged.

Magiere's feet slipped through the opening, and Leesil tossed the torch through and followed as well. Sliding down the other side of the cave-in, he stopped to dig in his sack. He had only one flask of oil left. Picking up the torch, he pulled the flask's stopper with his teeth, spit it aside, and poured half the oil over the boards caught in the debris. He then stuffed his oil-stained sack into the opening and lit it. The gap through which they'd crawled closed in flames.

'That will hold him for a while,' Leesil said, trying not to breathe in smoke, and clutching the remaining half-empty flask. 'Go.'

He barely remembered the rest of the flight down the tunnel, except that every step was another drop of Magiere's blood lost. Brenden moved as fast as he could in the cramped passage, and Chap's increasing pants suggested approaching exhaustion. Leesil kept saying to him, 'Keep going, boy. Just a little farther now.' His own face burned from the cuts Ratboy had dealt him.

When they reached the trapdoor to the decorative

sitting room, Leesil set the torch and half-empty flask on the tunnel floor and grabbed Brenden by the shoulder.

'Give her to me and jump up,' he said. 'You'll have to lift both Chap and her up one at a time.'

Brenden dropped Magiere's feet to the ground, and Leesil caught her limp body, pulling her close. As the strong blacksmith lifted Chap under his arm and climbed the ladder, the dog whimpered softly, but did not struggle.

If there were time, Leesil would have lowered Magiere to the floor, but, instead, he leaned back against the tunnel wall so that he could free one hand to lift her face to his own. Her complexion was almost white, and her wound was still bleeding through the makeshift bandage. He held her tightly against his chest and then tilted his head to place an ear near her mouth.

Her breathing was shallow and short, but he could hear it.

'Is she alive?' Brenden leaned through the opening, reaching down with one hand.

'Yes,' Leesil answered.

'Don't know how, with her neck cut open.'

Leesil pushed Magiere over near the ladder. He lifted one of her arms up until Brenden could grab her by the wrist. Stepping on the first rung, he prepared to lift her as well from below, but as soon as Brenden gripped her vestment with his other hand, he raised her with little effort.

'It'll be all right,' Leesil said to her unconscious form. 'Just don't die on me.'

He grabbed torch and oil and followed up the ladder.

By the time he was out of the tunnel and had kicked the trap-door closed, Brenden had Magiere over his shoulder again.

'Why bring the torch?' Brenden asked. 'We don't need it now.'

Leesil didn't answer. There was no time to argue with the blacksmith over what he planned next. Instead of heading toward the shaft they'd entered through, Leesil walked over and opened the room's main door.

'We can't get Magiere down the shaft, so we're going out the front. This hallway should lead somewhere into the warehouse. Now move.'

Brenden's eyes widened slightly, but then he nodded and headed out the door. Chap followed him.

Leesil hesitated only for a blink. There was no other way to be certain no one followed them, and perhaps he'd get lucky and burn those creatures to death. Either way, he didn't care anymore about the cost of lost livelihoods and merchant tallies – not with what this had cost Magiere.

He sprinkled the oil lightly over the rug and the trap-door. He splashed the couches as well, lit each and the rug, and then ran out the door. He paused in his flight only to splash the walls here and there with a light stain of oil, until the flask ran out. When he reached the enormous warehouse floor, Brenden was waiting for him between the piles of crates arranged for shipping or retrieval by some local merchant.

Leesil glanced quickly around and spotted a stack of cloth bundles. Brenden's eyes opened wide as Leesil set the torch on top of the stack.

'We're out,' Leesil said flatly. 'Let's find a door.'

Brenden looked at the slowly catching cloth and the smoke streaming out of the hallway. 'Over here,' he snapped angrily.

Leesil followed as Brenden led the way to a plain, ordinary-looking door. It was barred from the inside, and so likely not the exit used by the workers leaving at the end of the day. Leesil lifted the bar and threw it aside, kicking the door open.

Once outside, Leesil saw Chap was panting, weak with exhaustion and numerous small wounds. He stooped down and lifted the dog in his arms. Except for his face, Leesil was unhurt but weary. The strength of panic and anger was draining out of him.

'I know little about healing,' Leesil said. 'We have to find them some help quickly.'

Brenden looked at him, sadness and anger trading places across his face. 'My home. You'll all be safer there.'

14

After Brenden laid Magiere on his own bed and covered her with a blanket, his hands began to shake and he could not stop them. Leesil ripped sheets into strips and then attempted to slow the bleeding from Magiere's neck wound by using the strips as bandages. She'd been cut from one side of the neck halfway to the other. Brenden didn't know how or why she was still alive, but he had no doubt she was dying. Did Leesil know?

Chap lay just as still as Magiere, on a rug near the bed, breathing uneasily.

Brenden's small one-room cottage was built out back of his stable and forge. Once, this house had been a warm, comforting place filled with his sister's humming and the smell of baking bread. Eliza had loved candles, and he often brought her wax and oil scents from the market so that she could make her own. She was not beautiful at first sight, a bit on the thin side with plain, mouse-brown hair. But he always knew she'd one day leave him for her own husband. Her beauty was evident in other ways. Her hazel eyes had laughed at his jokes, and she exuded that cheerfulness so many men sought in a woman. She kept the house neat, helped him with work in the shop, and cooked fine meals. What man wouldn't want her? She could not, should not, spend her life caring for an older brother. Though he had no interest in marriage himself, he was well prepared for the day that she would marry and leave him to raise a family of her own.

But that morning, that terrible morning when he found her by the wood stack changed something inside him.

Eliza was small and fragile, not like this fierce woman who now lay dying in his bed. Eliza could not fight for herself, and he'd failed to protect her, even after the news of so many disappearances reached their ears. They liked their home and their smith's business and chose to ignore the whispers and rumors. After all, nothing bad had ever happened to them.

And now she was gone. There would be no husband or children, and he felt no joy from having destroyed her killers. Rather, he sat on his bed, watching a vampire hunter die.

Brenden did not know how to assist, and his hands wouldn't stop shaking. He thought he should feel satisfaction, that a circle had been closed. But he didn't. Nothing about this night was as he had imagined.

The face of the filthy urchin called Ratboy kept flashing in front of him, emaciated and savage. Had this creature been the one to murder his sister? Perhaps it had been the tall one who looked noble. Or maybe the woman. Brenden closed his eyes and then opened them quickly as darkness only made Ratboy's features more clear.

Leesil finished his bandaging and then put his fingers inside Magiere's mouth.

'Her teeth are normal,' he said.

Brenden was confused by the comment. What did that mean?

'She's dying, Leesil. She should have been dead before we left the warehouse.'

The half-elf's head jerked up. 'Are you going to find us some help or not?'

'This is beyond Miiska's healers.'

Leesil sucked in an angry breath. The long scratches on his face hadn't completely stopped bleeding yet.

'She's not going to die. Think! Someone must be able to help her.'

'I can,' a quiet voice said from across the room.

Brenden turned in surprise, fist clenched, expecting to find something had escaped the burning warehouse and tracked them to his home. Instead, an elegant, middle-aged man with white temples stood in the open doorway. The fine fabric of his long cloak suggested wealth and culture.

'Welstiel?' Leesil asked, more a statement than a question. 'Can you help?'

'If you'll do as I say.'

'Anything,' Leesil answered quickly. 'I'll do anything.'

Somewhere outside in the distance, Brenden heard shouts and ringing bells. The townsfolk had been roused with the alarm and would now be scurrying to put out the warehouse fire. He experienced a stab of guilt. Although he agreed with Leesil's decision, many people's lives would be affected for the worse.

Down on the beach, past moonrise, one smooth side of the seashore bank exploded outward, shattering any illusions of peace the night still contained.

Rashed crawled out of the narrow hole, more earth breaking away from its edges as he carefully pulled Teesha after him. Years ago, he'd arranged for this secret tunnel that reached from the caves below the warehouse all the way into one of the caves along the bottom of the sea cliffs. The entrance was quite small and almost completely covered by sand. No one had ever tried entering the cave from the outside, so he'd pushed through the sand barrier from the inside and emerged into open air.

The beach was only a short drop below, but he was injured and nearly exhausted. He held Teesha tightly with his good arm and jumped down, landing on his feet.

'It's all right,' he said, laying her in the sand. 'I'll find blood soon.'

She nodded and even smiled at him, but he knew the slash from Magiere's falchion had frozen Teesha's body from the waist down. A frightening prospect.

He left her there and climbed back up the wall.

'Ratboy, do you need help?'

Only the sound of crawling and digging answered him, and he began pushing more sand out of the way.

Ratboy appeared in the opening, looking so burned, bitten, and pitiful that Rashed assisted him without anger or rebuke. They had both failed to evade or destroy the hunter. Ratboy was not to blame this time.

'Climb onto my back,' Rashed said. 'I'll carry you down.'

Forgoing the usual sarcastic comment, Ratboy quietly grasped Rashed's shoulders with blackened hands, and Rashed descended as quickly as he could to lay his thin comrade beside Teesha.

The sight of Teesha filled him with emotions he could not recognize or explain. Although only her hands and one shoulder were badly burned, the slash on her stomach looked deep and her life-force was leaking away into the sand. Yet she did not complain nor curse him.

'Stay here and be silent,' he said. 'I will return.' He unsheathed his sword and dropped it beside Ratboy. 'For protection.'

Then he headed down the beach toward a mass of ships in the harbor. He no longer cared about sparing the lives of these Miiska mortals and hiding his identity. Such sentiment had gained him nothing in the end. As Rashed approached the harbor, he saw two sailors sitting on a small encrusted log, passing a bottle back and forth. They both looked young and healthy. There was no one else in sight.

Without a sound, Rashed rushed them from the side. Their eyes widened, and he knew himself to appear like some unearthed monster emerged from the depths, with his blood-soaked tunic, useless arm hanging limp, and smoke-streaked face. He struck out with his right fist.

He caught the nearest sailor across the jaw so hard the man fell unconscious, barely breathing. The second one only had time to cry out once and crabstep backward before Rashed grabbed him by the hair and drove both fangs straight into his throat.

Rashed didn't feed like this. He'd never fed like this.

As he held the sailor effortlessly, draining every bit of life he could, strength and power and euphoria filled his being. In a flash of clarity, he felt a glimmer of understanding for Ratboy . . . for Parko. Perhaps feeding could involve more than simply replenishing necessary energies.

He finished and dropped the corpse onto the dune,

leaving it where it lay. Why should he be concerned now? A little fear, a little truth might warn these mortals to leave him and his alone. How many years had he fought, struggled for absolute secrecy, anonymity? This cold woman hunter had destroyed his carefully constructed world. Well, so be it.

He remained still a moment, feeling the life of the sailor washing through his body. Then he focused the flow of life, directed it where it was needed most. The wound on his shoulder began to close, pieces of bone settling together. The burn on his hand lost its sting. Other small injuries would disappear soon, all healed by the life of one insignificant mortal. He grabbed the other, unconscious sailor by the shirt collar and dragged him down the beach. The dead weight of the sailor was nothing to him now.

Fear hit him when he reached Teesha and saw that her eyes were closed. She lay so still. He moved to her side and dropped his burden. Corische once told him that in rare cases vampires could be injured severely enough to slip away into a kind of sleeping undeath. Rashed did not know if this was true, and he did not wish to find out.

'Look at me,' he ordered.

When she didn't respond, he grabbed the sailor's wrist and tore it open with his teeth. Cradling Teesha's head, he pushed the ragged wound into her mouth and let liquid drip across her tongue.

'Drink,' he whispered.

At first she didn't stir, but then strength from the blood must have reached her. The corners of her mouth begin to move, clamping on, drawing down. Forgetting himself, he stroked her hair without thinking, murmuring, 'Good, good,' over and over.

He sat there for a long while, letting her feed, and then his gaze rose to meet with Ratboy's icy stare. Shame touched him. He had two companions and yet only thought of Teesha.

'Wait,' he said to Ratboy. 'I'm coming.'

Gently, he disengaged Teesha's mouth. Her eyes opened in protest, but he could see her wound had already stopped bleeding.

'Ratboy needs to feed as well,' he said, wiping red away from her mouth and laying her head down slowly.

Realization dawned on her face, and she nodded. 'Yes, of course. I'll be all right now.'

He dragged the still-breathing sailor over to Ratboy, whose expression had resumed its usual caustic, angry set.

'Your kindness is touching,' he whispered hoarsely. 'But take care, or the gods of mercy might get jealous.'

'Feed yourself,' Rashed answered, 'so you can help us plan.'

Mild surprise flickered across Ratboy's features. Then he attacked the sailor's throat ravenously.

Rashed turned back to Teesha, who now sat up and surveyed her own state. Her color had returned to its usual shade of pale cream.

'This dress is ruined,' she said. 'It's my favorite.'

He walked over and dropped to the sand beside her.

'Why did you try to jump that hunter from behind? Of all the foolish attacks.'

'I thought to break her neck,' she answered. 'How was I to know she was covered in garlic water?'

Anger began welling up inside him again. 'They burned our home.'

'I wanted to finish her here,' she answered softly, 'but now I think we should all leave this place.'

He couldn't believe her words. 'No, that hunter dies. She began this battle. We won't crawl away in the night.'

'Teesha's right,' Ratboy said. The sailor lay dead at his side. 'We can't stay here. The town probably believes us dead anyway. Let us remain dead. Or perhaps you'd rather add resurrection from the ashes to your accomplishments.'

Rashed jumped to his feet. These two did not fully grasp the situation.

'We have nowhere to sleep tonight. The earth from our homelands was in our coffins.'

A glowing light appeared before him, and its colors solidified into the tragic form of Edwan.

'Undead superstitions!' he said in open contempt.

Rashed always sensed dislike, even distrust, from Edwan, but something was different now. There was something harder in the ghost's hollow voice.

'What do you mean, my love?' Teesha asked.

Rashed heard discomfort and coolness in her tone. What had happened between the two of them?

Edwan turned. 'I mean, my *dear*, that you do not need to sleep in the earth from your homeland. That is a peasants' tale spun so many times even your kind believes in it. I am not the only disembodied in this world. I talk to the dead. With the little I can grasp I know this, trust me.'

Ratboy crawled to his feet. His burns weren't completely healed, but he seemed a good deal improved.

'You're certain?' he asked earnestly.

'Yes,' Edwan answered without looking at him.

Rashed leaned over and pulled Teesha to her feet. The thought of sleeping anywhere besides his own coffin unnerved him, but he hid his feelings for the others' sake.

'I know a safe place then, somewhere I go to think.' He looked at Edwan. 'I cut that hunter's throat deeply. She may be dead, but we have no way of knowing. Can you find out?'

Edwan hovered, glowering at him. 'Whatever you ask, my lord.'

He vanished.

'We have to rest and feed again – and heal,' Rashed said to his companions. 'If the hunter lives, next time she'll be the one caught sleeping.'

Welstiel remained standing in the doorway of Brenden's home, and Leesil decided not to ask him to come closer. Whatever he had to say, he could say it from a distance.

As he took in the man's calm, cold stare, Leesil began to hate his own ignorance even more. Magiere's breathing was broken, shallow, and irregular, and her flesh was whiter than sun-bleached parchment. He didn't know how to save her and yet loathed the prospect of letting Welstiel even this near Magiere. The strange man's striking countenance and elegant clothes did not fool Leesil. Welstiel was not to be trusted.

'What do I do?' Leesil asked finally.

'Feed her your blood,' Welstiel answered simply.

Of all the instructions Leesil expected, this was not one of them, and he found himself stunned speechless.

'What are you talking about?' the blacksmith asked, and his face reddened with anger.

'She is a *dhampir*, the child of a vampire, born to hunt and destroy the undead. She shares some of their weaknesses and their strengths. Though she is mortal, and from such a wound she will die without the blood of another mortal.' Welstiel gazed at Leesil. 'And who cares for her but you?'

'You're mad!' the half-elf spit out angrily. 'Mad as the warlord of my homeland.'

'Then you have nothing to lose by feeding her your blood and, if not, you can sit and watch her perish. I believe you said you would do anything.'

Leesil looked down at Magiere. The bandages were soaked through and the pillow was already damp with her blood. If only she would open her eyes and laugh at him, curse him, berate him as a fool for wanting to believe Welstiel. But her eyes remained closed, and he could no longer hear her breathing.

'I hate you for making me do this,' Leesil said to Welstiel in a low, clear voice. 'She'll hate you even more.' And he jerked a stiletto from his sleeve.

'Leesil, don't!' Brenden cried out. 'Don't listen to him. This cannot help her.'

'Get back!' Leesil warned the blacksmith.

'You must do one more thing,' Welstiel said, as if Brenden were not there. 'Pull out the bone and tin amulet and place the bone side against her skin. The bone must have contact with her skin.'

'Why?' Leesil asked.

'You don't have time. Do as I instruct.'

The half-elf lifted his leg across Magiere's stomach

and straddled her body. The straw mattress shifted slightly and sagged as he moved, but he was careful not to put any of his weight on her. He pulled the amulet out from inside her shirt and turned it over, placing the bone side against the hollow of her throat. He noticed the topaz stone was still glowing. Then he leaned near her face.

In one motion, he sliced across the inside of his wrist, dropped the blade, and used his good hand to cradle her head. Even tainted by smoke and dirt, her hair felt oddly soft.

Blood spilled down the side of her face as he used the hand with the slit wrist to pull her mouth open. He forgot about Welstiel and Brenden's presence and pressed his slashed wrist between her teeth.

'Try,' he whispered. 'Just try.'

At first his blood just trickled into her limp mouth, some of it spilling to the side and down her jaw and then down her neck. It soaked into the linen bandage to mix with her own.

She stirred once, and then without warning, one of her hands latched on to his arm, forcing his wrist deeper into her mouth. He hadn't anticipated the prospect of pain, and her sudden flash of great strength caught him off guard.

A too-hot sensation, like being burned from the inside out, caused him to instinctively want to jerk his arm away, but he held fast and let her continue feeding on him. It was disturbing, but enthralling – the wet soft-ness of her mouth around the sharpness of her teeth connecting with his flesh. Her body shuddered and tigh-tened beneath him. He experienced fear, anger, pain, and sorrow all at once, but couldn't be sure the feelings were all his own. She was so close, right beneath him, so near that everything he felt could have risen from her right into him.

Her breathing became stronger and deeper, and he felt suddenly tired and warm at the same time.

The pain began to fade, and all he sensed now was how close she was, the feel of her mouth on his arm and his hand in her hair, her breath warm on his face. His head dropped until their brows touched.

Magiere's dark eyes opened wide, the irises fully black without color, and she did not appear to recognize him. Her other hand grasped his shoulder and drew him down until his body pressed against hers. He wanted her to keep feeding, until he knew for certain she would live.

To keep feeding.

Her face grew dim in front of him – shadows darker – fading.

Then she was holding him up, with both hands gripping his shoulders. His bleeding wrist dropped limp across her chest. In her open mouth he could see blood-smeared fangs, but her eyes – still all-black irises – were wide with sudden fear and confusion. The amulet fell from the hollow of her throat and dangled against the pillow on its chain.

'No . . . keep feeding,' Leesil whispered. He felt so tired that it was hard to speak. 'You need my blood.'

From somewhere distant he heard shouting, someone shouting at him, but it didn't matter.

'Stop it! Enough.'

Leesil felt himself pulled from Magiere's embrace, saw her face seem to fall away from him. There was rage in her eyes, as she pulled at his shirt, trying to bring him back to her. He raised one hand and tried to reach for her.

Then she was gone from his sight.

Brenden was in front of him now, shaking him. 'That's enough! Do you hear me?'

Even in Leesil's current state, he could see Brenden's red face turning pale. The fear in his expression was followed by disgust, then by horror, and then sorrow. Why should he be sorry?

Leesil slowly became aware that he was standing up against the wall beyond the foot of the bed, Brenden pinning him in place. One of his own hands was pushing feebly against the large man's chest, trying to drive him off. The other, its wrist smeared with his own blood and Magiere's saliva, was outstretched toward the bed. Magiere, now crouched on the bed, snarled once at the blacksmith, but her eyes were on Leesil. As he looked at her, he felt a sudden wave of anguish for abandoning her there. Everything around him was blurred and faint but her.

She looked at him with hunger, then her mouth slowly closed. Black irises shrank, and Leesil noticed their color for the first time that he could remember. They were a deep brown, as rich as the soil of his homeland. Her gaze shifted to his outstretched hand and its bleeding wrist.

'Leesil?' Magiere pulled back, shrinking away from him across the bed into the corner against the wall. She huddled there, trembling, and could not take her gaze off his wrist until he finally lowered his arm.

'Good,' another voice said. 'Good lad.'

Leesil rolled his head toward the sound of that voice, and found Welstiel still standing in the cottage doorway. The man pulled a small jar from the pocket of his cloak and tossed it to Brenden. The blacksmith released one grip on Leesil's shoulders and caught the jar with his large hand.

'Put this salve on his face and wrist, and on the *majayhì's* wounds,' Welstiel told Brenden. 'They will both heal faster. Have them eat as much meat, cheese, and fruit as you can get over the next few days, and make sure the half-elf has no wine or ale. It will only thin his blood, and the *dhampir* may need him.'

Leesil suddenly felt tired and ill. What had he just done? The sensation of Magiere's mouth on his arm still lingered and he tried to speak.

'What's a *majay-hì?*' he managed to whisper.

Welstiel watched Magiere for a long moment, and then looked at Leesil.

'The dog. It's the elven name for your dog.'

Leesil realized he was now sitting on the floor, Brenden having lowered him. He turned his head toward the bed again.

Magiere sat up in confusion now. Her hands came up to her throat, and when she felt the bandages there, she began pulling them off. Her fingers moved slowly over the exposed skin. Though there was blood still caked around her neck, Leesil could see no sign of the wound except a thin red line across her skin.

She looked at Leesil, then down at his wrist where Brenden was smearing the salve from the jar. Her fingers touched the side of her mouth, feeling a wet smear. Again, her expression changed to fear.

'What did you do?' she asked. 'Leesil, what have you done?'

Leesil turned to Brenden. 'Food. Go. Get us some food. I'll see to Chap.'

As if unable to endure any more of the scene, Brenden let go of Leesil, and stormed out the door. Welstiel was already gone. No one had noticed him leave.

Using his hands to push himself up, Leesil stood and tottered once but remained on his feet. With the exception of Chap, he and Magiere were alone.

'What did you do?' she repeated.

'You were dying. I did what he told me to.'

She took in the sight of his face and wrist with greater comprehension. 'You're hurt.'

'It's nothing. I can bandage myself.'

Memories seemed to be returning, and she touched her throat again. 'I was fighting. He cut me and then . . . what happened?'

The full weight and length of the tale was more than Leesil could manage. It overwhelmed him. Standing became even more of an effort.

'Such a long story,' he whispered. 'Too long for tonight.'

She turned away from him. She appeared weak and pale, but otherwise all right. Slowly, she climbed off the bed, but did not approach him. How much did she remember of his feeding her? He wanted her to remember all of it.

She began pacing. Glancing at his wrist again, her expression turned to . . . embarrassment. Is that what she felt?

'I can't . . . I can't be here,' she said. 'If you are all right . . . and Chap?'

He felt too empty to argue. 'I'll take care of him.'

No coaxing was needed. Magiere picked her falchion off the floor where Brenden had dropped it, but she neither touched nor took any of the other weapons or supplies lying about. Her long legs strode for the door, and she fled Brenden's home as a prisoner flees a cage.

Leesil managed to walk over and retrieve the jar of salve. He knelt beside his dog, applying thick ointment to Chap's wounds. But Chap continued to sleep deeply.

For the first time in years, Leesil felt alone.

Some months ago, while walking through the forest, Rashed had come across a small ship run aground in a narrow inlet. Brush and trees now covered part of the outer hull, and he found no sign that anyone had been inside the ship for years.

'We should be safe here,' he said.

He went through the motions of settling Teesha and Ratboy inside, and then went back out to check for any places where a patch of daylight might shine through and burn them when the sun rose. These actions were his duty, his role in their family. But visions of fire and tunnels collapsing filled him with silent rage. There wasn't even a blanket for Teesha to rest on. The thought troubled him. He should have a blanket for her.

All of her scrolls and books and dresses and embroidery were gone. He knew she'd never complain. She'd never say a word, but he felt almost overwhelmed by a sense of loss.

'Come and lie down,' she said from the hatch doorway.

'I told you to stay inside,' he answered, but he quickly went to the hatch and followed her down below deck.

Ratboy was already asleep on the floor. There were no bunks. Teesha lay down in the ship's wooden belly as well and reached out her hand toward Rashed, inviting him to join her. He stretched out beside her, but did not touch her. He rarely touched her unless it was necessary. It wasn't that he considered her too precious or too fragile. But even in life, he believed a warrior should not practice affection. It seemed like a weakness. As if once that flood-gate opened, it would be impossible to stop, and then he would lose all strength. He needed his strength.

He didn't mind when she touched him though. Not at all.

Chocolate brown curls fell across her tiny face as she rolled onto her back.

'Sleep,' he said.

Her rose candles were gone, too.

Rashed's mind moved back to the first time she saw Miiska and the delight on her face. They had been trav-eling for weeks on end, searching for someplace she might call home. He never told her how difficult their journey was for him. Guilt over Corische's death haunted him. Guilt over his abandonment of Parko haunted him. He hated being out in the open so much, always moving down strange roads. But he also remembered what Teesha had done to the keep, what a comfortable and beautiful place she had created from an empty stone dwelling. He wanted that again. She reminded him of life, of being part of the living.

Perhaps he was caught between two worlds, but so was she, and on some level, so was Ratboy, or the young urchin would have followed Parko.

Once they reached the coast, he thought the journey

would soon be over, but none of the towns they passed through felt right to her. They were either too big or too small or too loud or too strange compared to what she had known in her life. When they reached Miiska one night, she climbed out of the wagon and ran down the shore a little way, then back to him, and smiled.

'This is the place,' she said. 'This is our home.'

Relief filled him, and the next night, he began to work. Money was no issue. Corische's wealth was in the wagon. Building Teesha a home, creating a place in the world for his small family eased the guilt. He convinced himself that he had done the right thing, was doing the right thing. He laid down laws and expected Ratboy to follow his orders. Here, the keep lord and his rule of the land did not protect them. They had no legal protection beyond that of ordinary citizens, and if they wanted to remain in this home, secrecy was essential.

'No bodies,' he stated flatly.

For the most part, Ratboy obeyed, but like Parko, he too felt the pull of the Feral Path, and there had been mistakes. Rather than drive Ratboy out, Rashed simply made a deal – an expensive deal – with the town constable. Distasteful but necessary.

Teesha had once again made their home comfortable and beautiful. And now it was gone.

He was lying on the deck of an abandoned ship without even a blanket to cover her.

'You'll never be able to rest if you don't stop thinking,' she whispered through the fading darkness.

'All our money was in the warehouse,' he answered. 'I don't know how bad the damage is yet, but we may be coinless.'

'That doesn't matter. You always find a way to fix everything. Now rest.'

She reached out and placed her small hand on his chest.

He closed his eyes and allowed her hand to remain.

15

When dawn broke, Leesil picked up Chap and carried him home. Although the dog was half awake by then, he seemed so sick and weak that Leesil wanted to get him to his favorite spot by The Sea Lion's huge hearth. Brenden's house felt cold and unfamiliar.

He saw almost no one on the short walk home and wondered briefly where most of the shopkeepers were. The answer came when he saw the smoke still rising into the air over the town from down near the docks. Much of the town must have been up half the night controlling the fire. He purposely took a route through town that would pass nowhere near the ruined warehouse.

Entering the tavern's common room, Leesil almost sighed in relief when he saw it was empty. He couldn't face dealing with Caleb or Rose at present and fervently hoped they would both sleep the morning away. The fire was low but smoldering, and everything about the dimly lit room filled Leesil with a certainty that this world still made sense – from the oak bar to the faded chairs to his faro table.

Feeling exhausted from having carried Chap halfway across town, Leesil now trembled under the hound's weight. The half-elf knew he lacked strength due to blood loss and the previous night's events. Even the food Brenden had brought him didn't seem to bring much of his strength back. The blacksmith had left again shortly afterward.

Nearly panting from exertion, he stumbled over and laid Chap on a small rug near the fire. Most of the dog's wounds were messy but superficial.

He stroked his dog's velvet ears. 'I'm going to heat some water, and I'll be right back.'

Chap just whined and tried to lick his hand.

Then the commotion started.

At first, he only heard a dull roar coming from outside. He started for the window to look out, and the strange resonance suddenly turned into the sound of shouting voices very near the tavern. He changed directions and went to open the door. Several images hit him at once.

Brenden's broad, leather-clad back was within arm's reach. The blacksmith was holding off a large crowd led by Constable Ellinwood. The constable's round face was pink tinged with rage.

'How dare you interfere with my duties!' he roared.

'You haven't done your duty in years,' Brenden spit back.

'What is going on?' Leesil asked in amazement.

Brenden glanced back at him. 'I'm sorry. I couldn't keep them away.' He crossed his arms and turned back to the constable. 'But I'll keep them out.'

The blacksmith looked haggard and worn, still filthy from crawling through the warehouse tunnels. Among the crowd of about twenty people, Leesil spotted three city guards. What fresh horror was this? Some perverse god seemed to think he needed yet another trial.

'Brenden here has admitted that you and he and your partner burned down Miiska's finest warehouse,' Ellinwood said, stabbing a thick finger in Leesil's direction. 'Do you have any idea what you've done?'

Realization hit Leesil like a rock.

'Oh, the warehouse. Is that what this is about? You should be grateful. Your town is much safer now.'

'Grateful?' a middle-aged man at the front of the crowd sputtered in disbelief. 'Where will I work? How will I feed my children?'

Although he felt pity for these dockworkers, Leesil's ability to weather any strong emotion was completely spent. He had no wish to continue this pointless conversation.

'If the owner of the warehouse wishes to make a formal complaint, let him talk to the constable,' he said. 'I've got a sick dog to tend.'

'You killed the owner!' Ellinwood shouted. 'You and your partner are both under arrest. The blacksmith, too.'

Brenden's crossed arms tightened, and Leesil wondered why Brenden hadn't been arrested already. Then he noticed the guards were hanging back, not even attempting to get close to Brenden, and Ellinwood's expression seemed close to hysteria.

Using clear, precise words, Brenden said loudly, 'The owner was sleeping in a coffin, in the dirt of his homeland, so far beneath ground that we had to crawl down a tunnel to reach him.'

Fear and discomfort silenced angry murmurs among the crowd. Brenden stepped forward, backing Ellinwood away.

'If anyone doubts that this town was plagued by the undead,' Brenden called out, 'he can go dig up my sister and see what was done to her. Thieves and murderers don't leave teeth marks. They don't drink blood.'

By this point, he was standing among the crowd.

'This coward you call a constable has known of these creatures for years, and he's done nothing to protect you! The warehouse may be gone, but at least your children are safe. You should be thanking this man behind me. You should be thanking that woman.' He pointed past the crowd.

When Leesil looked beyond the dockworkers, he saw Magiere standing alone in the street. He'd never seen her resemble a warrior so vividly. Tall and lithe in her leather armor, with her falchion hanging casually from her waist, she stared at the mass of people through haunted eyes. Grime and smoke streaked her cheeks and hands. A thin red line stood out on her throat.

No one spoke. Then one of the guards, with a cold look on his face, stepped away from the crowd, walking toward her.

Leesil watched Magiere closely. There was no way he could get through the crowd to her in time if this guard tried to take out his anger on her, and she'd been through too much.

The young guard stepped up to her. Everyone in the street became silent, waiting to see what would happen. He just stood there quietly, looking her in the face.

'My brother disappeared two years ago,' he said. 'I'm not arresting anybody.'

He said nothing more, but turned and walked away. The other two guards paused, and then followed him.

Ellinwood puffed three breaths, and Leesil knew the constable had lost his hold. If his guards refused to take action, he himself was useless. But why was Ellinwood so angry? He wasn't posturing here for the benefit of pretending to do his job. And the fleshy beast certainly did not care about any of Miiska's working-class families. So what caused this surge of venom over the lost warehouse?

Magiere moved straight through the crowd. Leesil quickly stepped aside to let her in. She didn't speak.

Brenden was still bristling at the constable. Leesil faced the dockworkers and shook his head.

'Go home, please. If you want ale or a game of cards, we open at dusk.' He glanced at Ellinwood. 'Cheer yourself. There's nothing for you to hide from now.'

The first stab of real pleasure he'd experienced in days washed over him as half the crowd regarded their constable with open disgust. People began to break off and walk away. Ellinwood, however, wasn't finished.

'Amends will be made,' he said, in the most serious voice Leesil had ever heard him use. 'If I have to confiscate your bank notes and sell this tavern and the smithy to do it.'

Brenden's fury increased, and Leesil feared his friend might attack the frustrated and equally enraged Ellinwood.

'Don't kill him,' the half-elf said tiredly. 'Or you really will be arrested, and I don't have a copper left to bail you out.'

Dry humor was the only tool he had left, but it worked. Brenden held his ground, relaxing slightly.

'You do what you have to,' Leesil told the constable. 'But I somehow doubt the town council will allow you to sell anything that belongs to us over this.'

Ellinwood looked shocked at these words, and Leesil decided the conversation was over. He reached out for Brenden's arm and pulled him into the tavern, leaving Ellinwood and the few remaining townsfolk out in the street. He then placed a wooden bar in the door's metal bracket.

'Let him knock if he wants to.' But no sound came.

Inside, the common room was empty. Magiere must have gone upstairs. He and Brenden were alone.

'Someone needs to clean out those claw marks on your face,' Brenden said matter-of-factly. 'They're going to scar as it is.'

Leesil sighed and ignored the comment. 'How did that rabble get started?'

'I went to see the warehouse, to make sure it collapsed. When Ellinwood and his men showed up, the dock-workers started demanding action. I tried to be honest about what happened, about why you did what you did, but they just wanted someone to blame. He used you and Magiere as scapegoats, got everyone worked up. I couldn't stop them before they reached the tavern.'

Leesil stoked the fire. Well, at least Brenden was still on their side. Considering how he'd reacted the night before, a change in his loyalties would not have surprised Leesil.

'Brenden, will you tend to Chap while I check on Magiere?'

His friend paused uncertainly. 'What is she?'

'I don't know. I truly don't, and neither does she.'

'She seems so much like a woman. I'd even thought about . . .' His words trailed off. 'But now I just don't know what to think.'

Leesil felt his body stiffen. What was Brenden saying? Had he considered courting Magiere? As if that were possible. As if Magiere would court anyone. Leesil suddenly felt an unfriendly urge to make Brenden leave.

He calmed himself and realized how foolish he was being. Brenden was his friend, and he didn't have many of those.

Instead of its usual fiery red, the large man's beard was black-brown with dirt and dust, and Leesil knew how tired he must be. The half-elf didn't like leaving him to care for the dog, but Magiere was back and he had to see her.

'Will you see to Chap?' he asked again.

The blacksmith nodded. As Brenden began heating water, Leesil went up to Magiere's room, stood outside the still half-broken door, and knocked once.

'It's me. I'm coming in.'

She sat on her bed in silence, head down, hair hanging forward. Not excited at the prospect of honest conversation, he remained standing in the doorway for the moment.

'What's done is done. Come to the kitchen with me. We've got to get started cleaning ourselves up and taking stock of each other's wounds. It's impossible to gauge injuries under all this dirt.'

'I don't have any wounds,' she answered quietly. 'I only had one, and you healed it.'

Exhausted or not, he wasn't getting out of this.

'Magiere, they're dead. I burned that warehouse over their heads and it collapsed. Whatever happens to you only happens when you're fighting undeads, and they're gone now. It's over.'

Her head lifted. 'Your face. Look what they did to your face.'

'Don't worry. I'll still be pretty.'

She didn't smile. 'You have to tell me what happened.'

He stood straight and tried to exude an unbendable resolve.

'Brenden's downstairs. You come to the kitchen with me so we can get cleaned up. Then we make tea and breakfast. While we're eating, I'll tell you everything. Bargain?'

She started to argue and then stood up. 'All right.'

'Grab that dressing gown,' he said. 'Those pants you're wearing are so torn and dirty even I want to burn them – and you're the fussy one.'

Although distressed by Leesil's insistence that they clean up and eat before talking, Magiere later admitted to herself that his instincts were right. Once she'd washed, braided her hair, and donned the thick, warm dressing gown, she made tea and sliced some bread, while he scrubbed his own soot away. These simple activities gave her time to collect herself, to feel more sound and capable of facing what they might tell her.

She'd had blood all over her last night and not all of it was her own. Her stomach had felt rock hard as she wandered alone in the hours before dawn.

Thinking about how much blood he'd lost for her last night, she found cold mutton and cheese for Leesil. Then she carefully cleaned the angry scratches on his face and applied the ointment Welstiel had supplied. Sitting on a stool, softly smearing medicine on his skin, she began to feel more like herself again. She felt better just doing something, anything, for him. He would have some scars, but he was right, and his narrow features would still be handsome.

During this process, Brenden came in to tend himself,

and the three of them made no references to the night before until they were all comfortably seated around a table in the common room. The tea tasted good, and she was thirsty.

She finished one cup and poured another before asking, 'Are you going to start talking?'

So far, she and Brenden had managed to avoid speaking to each other, but his questioning, sidelong glances were difficult to miss.

Leesil swallowed a mouthful of mutton. 'How much do you remember?' he asked.

'I see bits and pieces of the fight, but the last clear memory I have is jerking Rashed's coffin lid open.' Both her companions shifted in their seats at the mention of the undead's name. 'That is his name,' she insisted. 'He must have told me.'

Leesil sipped his hot tea. She noticed the skin on his face looked less jagged and swollen. Perhaps the ointment would diminish any scars.

'After that,' he said somewhat matter-of-factly, 'Ratboy smashed through his coffin lid from the inside.'

He went on for a long time recounting the chain of events. She knew he wasn't one to tell well-ordered stories in this manner, and she appreciated his concentration and use of detail. But she became – and remained – embarrassed from the point where Brenden had to carry her out all the way to the part when Welstiel showed up. Brenden glanced away as Leesil faltered. There was little mention of specifically what happened when he had fed her.

'I didn't know what else to do,' he said. 'You were dying.'

Leesil had fed her his own blood, and the act some-how saved her life. She did not know how to respond to his sacrifice. Brief memory flashes came unbidden, of his fingers gently moving on the back of her head, of his wrist in her mouth, of his strength supporting both their bodies close together until that strength passed into her.

'You breathed for me and brought me back after that cave-in,' he said. 'I don't see the difference.'

But Magiere found his comment too simple. Everyone alive needed to breathe. They did not need to feed on blood to survive. What exactly was she?

'There's something else,' Leesil added. 'But I don't know what it means.' He pointed to her neck. 'Welstiel had me pull out one of your amulets and lay the bone side against your skin. Do have any idea why?'

Further confused, she shook her head. 'No, I don't. He seems to know much more than we do. But he also talks in circles and how much can we believe? You said he used the word "*dhampir*." He said that once before when I was standing at the spot where . . .' She looked at Brenden. 'Where Eliza died.'

'A *dhampir* is the offspring of a vampire and a mortal,' Brenden finally spoke. 'But they are only a legend, a folk-tale. My mother's people are from the far north, and her mother was a village wisewoman, a practitioner of hedge magic, rural spellcraft, and the like. I've heard some things about the undead, and they cannot create or conceive children. Such an offspring would be impossible.'

'Then how do you explain my healed throat?' Magiere asked, not really wanting an answer. 'My weapon? The amulets? The things that happen to me when I'm fighting Rashed?'

'Well, we can't believe everything Welstiel says,' Leesil put in. 'He called Chap a *majay-hì*, and I know that's ridiculous.'

'Why? What does it mean?' Brenden asked.

'I know little of the elven tongue, but I've been thinking about it. I think it means something like "magic hound." Well, probably more like "fay hound." But the fay and nature spirits I've read of weren't exactly pleasant creatures. No, Welstiel may know more than we do, and he may be useful in some ways, but he's either mad or just as superstitious as the villagers of Stravina.'

'You can't deny there's something special about Chap,' Magiere whispered. 'He's different, like me, whenever he fights one of those . . .' She trailed off.

Leesil grew thoughtful. 'I've been wondering about that. My mother said something to me once about Chap being bred to protect. Perhaps undeads were more plentiful in the distant past, and my mother's people tried to breed a line of hounds capable of fighting such monsters.'

Magiere looked up at him, and blinked in surprise. It had been a long time since Leesil had said anything of his past, and he never spoke of his family.

'Did you know your mother?'

He stiffened. 'Yes.'

A knock sounded at the door.

'Oh, for the love of drunkards,' Leesil exclaimed. 'Brenden, if Ellinwood is still trying to arrest us, I give you permission to kill him.'

Brenden got up with a scowl and went to open the door, but it was not Ellinwood who waited outside. On the other side of the door stood a teenage girl Magiere didn't know and a boy who looked vaguely familiar.

'Geoffry?' Leesil said. 'What are you doing here?'

Then Magiere placed the young man. He was the son of Karlin, the baker.

'Hello, Brenden,' the girl said, holding out a green pouch. 'We brought payment for the hunter.'

The girl was perhaps fifteen, with large eyes, a pleasant face, and one missing front tooth. She had an odd manner of speech Magiere had never heard.

'I heard you was with 'em,' she added. 'I always thought you was brave.'

'This is Aria,' Brenden said by way of introduction. 'Her family moved here from the east a few years back. She was a friend of Eliza's.'

Aria stepped into the common room and looked around. Geoffry followed.

'My father collected payment,' he said, 'and he sent us here.'

At first, Magiere didn't understand. Then she studied the pouch Aria handed to her, and her stomach lurched. They were paying her for killing Miiska's undead.

'Take it, Miss,' Geoffry prompted. 'It's real money, not just trinkets or food. We know you don't work cheap. The constable may be a fool, but lots of folks here are thankful.'

'This is a nice place,' Aria said, touching the oak bar. 'I never been in here.'

Magiere tried to stand up, but couldn't. She dropped the pouch on the table and pushed it quickly across toward Aria.

'Take those coins and give them back to everyone who contributed. We didn't do any of this for money.'

Aria and Geoffry stared at her in confusion, even

disappointment. Perhaps they had asked for the honor of bringing the hunter her fee. Magiere could imagine where the money had come from. Visions of bakers and fishmongers and now out-of-work warehouse laborers pooling their last pennies rushed into her mind.

She felt sick and her breakfast threatened to come up. This was like a nightmare from which she couldn't awaken. The past kept tracking her down to repeat itself over and over.

Brenden politely rushed the young visitors out. Magiere heard phrases and bits of kind words like 'appreciate' and 'thank your father' and 'the hunter is tired.' But once Aria and Geoffry had been bundled off down the street, he turned to her in puzzlement.

'They were just trying to thank you. And it isn't as if such gratitude is unfamiliar. You and Leesil have destroyed undeads and taken payment many times before.'

Magiere turned away from him. She couldn't help it, and she looked to her partner for some kind of response, any kind. Leesil drained his teacup, walked behind the bar and filled it with red wine.

'Of course,' he said. 'Many times.'

16

At a loss for what to do, Ellinwood left The Sea Lion and hurried home to The Velvet Rose. He needed to think, and he thought best at home.

Once safely ensconced inside his plush rooms with the door closed, he allowed panic to set in. What was he going to do? His first thought was to sell the lovely furnishings all around him. But then he remembered that he did not own them. It was all property of The Velvet Rose. He owned little besides the expensive clothes on his body, the clothing in his wardrobe, a sword that he'd never actually used, and a few personal items such as silver combs and crystal cologne bottles.

Rashed was gone, and there would be no more profits coming in from the warehouse trade.

The constable's own image stared back at him from the oval, silver-framed mirror, and a portion of the panic faded. He cut a fine figure in his green velvet. Of course, some people thought him too large, but the thin were always intimidated by men of stature. He had dominated Miiska for years. He could weather this current situation.

Walking over to the cherry wood wardrobe, he unlocked the top drawer and looked inside. Rashed had not left him coinless, and he had not spent all of his profits. Indeed, if he rationed money for his opiate and spiced whiskey slightly, he could keep himself in comfort for perhaps half a year.

Then a thought struck him. His arrangement with Rashed was not so unique. After all, as Miiska's constable, he knew many things. He had recently discovered that the wife of Miiska's leading merchant was betraying him with a caravan master who came through town six times a year. How much would she be willing to pay to keep her secret? And Devon, one of the council members, had used a large sum of the town's community funds from taxes to pay off a gambling debt not long ago.

Ellinwood's mind began to race. There was no need for fear. When powerful people had secrets, they would pay handsomely for silence. He knew exactly what to do.

But not yet.

First he would change tactics in this Magiere situation and praise her. He would offer her his full support, now that there was nothing left to do, and win back the trust and loyalty of his guards. At the moment, his position was somewhat tenuous. He would become the ideal constable for several months – before taking any action toward quiet extortion. In the end, very little would have to change in his game besides the names of the players.

Feeling safer and more content, he opened the bottom drawer of his wardrobe and removed the opiate and spiced whiskey. He'd never indulged in the morning before, but today was special. He needed comfort.

Soon his crystal-stemmed goblet was filled, and he sat comfortably in his chair to sip.

The entire day passed quickly.

*　　*　　*

Teesha stirred first that night and sat up with an odd sense of disorientation. Then visions from the night before flooded her mind, and she remembered Rashed settling her in the belly of the old ship.

He lay asleep on the floor next to her. She touched his shoulder.

'Rashed, wake up.'

His transparent eyes opened. Just a brief flicker of confusion passed across his perfect features, so quickly she almost didn't notice, and then he, too, sat up, looking like a competent commander again. She'd done well to choose him as the champion of her small family. But he could be so strong-willed. How ironic that such a trait was his only true weakness. Now she faced the difficult task of manipulating him into flight again. It hadn't been easy the first time.

'How do you feel?' he asked.

'I could use a needle and thread.' She smiled at him.

He never smiled back, but she knew pleasantries on her part always put him at ease. And somehow she gained strange comfort from comforting him.

She examined their surroundings, feeling more aware than she had last night. Apparently, Rashed had come across this abandoned ship one night while exploring. The crew must not have been able to free it, because they simply left it behind, and now trees, shrubs, and moss almost hid its existence entirely. The boards of the deck were old but intact, and no light peeked through to burn them. It was as safe a place as she possibly could have expected.

Rashed walked over and shook Ratboy. 'Wake up. We have to go.'

Of the three of them, Ratboy still seemed the weakest and least healed. Though most of the dog's bites were closed, a mix of fire and garlic water had taken their toll. He would need to feed again soon.

'Where are we going?' Teesha asked Rashed.

'Back to the warehouse.'

'What? Why?'

'Because we have nothing, and we don't know if it burned down completely,' he said. 'What if the dockworkers put the fire out? Not one of us could blend into a crowd safely like this. We need clothes and weapons. Everything was in the warehouse.'

She shook her head. 'It's too dangerous. There may be guards investigating. We should just leave tonight. I know it's risky, but we can feed while traveling and steal what we need along the way. After passing through a few households, we should be adequately, if not well, set up.'

Ratboy struggled to his feet. 'I agree.'

'Guards are nothing to us,' Rashed said.

'If we disappear, the town will think us dead,' Teesha insisted. 'The hunter will leave us alone.'

For the first time in her memory, Rashed snapped at her in anger. 'She'll only stop hunting us if she's lying in a grave!'

Even Ratboy seemed stunned by this outburst and shifted uncomfortably. Rashed pushed open the hatch door.

'Come. We've got to see what happened to the warehouse.'

Teesha wasn't angry. She could never feel anger toward Rashed, but his manner unsettled her. She wanted him out of this town and away from the hunter. She never wanted that hunter's blade near him again.

The three of them should just quietly leave. That was the logical course of action. But he was in charge, and she had certainly helped to place him in that position.

With little choice, she and Ratboy followed him outside.

While feeling any sort of sympathy for Rashed seemed impossible to Ratboy, as they all stood staring at the burned remains of what had once been home, he dimly realized that he felt only a small portion of anger and loss compared to the tall warrior who looked on without expression.

There was nothing left. The three of them were now hidden from sight by a huge half-charred crate, but the warehouse structure itself had burned from the inside out, allowing heavy support beams to collapse inward. The tunnels below were probably nonexistent now. Had Rashed not planned that secret tunnel to the beach, they would all be lying crushed under a pile of dirt and beams. Or burned to ash as well.

And therein rested Ratboy's dilemma.

Everything inside Ratboy screamed that Teesha was right. They should leave Miiska tonight and take their chances on the road, killing and resupplying along the way. However, as much as he loathed Rashed's arrogant manner, the self-proclaimed leader of their group was always one step ahead when it came to survival.

The question here was one of motivation. Rashed claimed that lasting safety could only be achieved by destroying the hunter. If this were true, then Ratboy would stay and fight. But tonight, Rashed appeared less rational than usual. In fact, he seemed to be functioning from a standpoint of pure revenge. Vengeance was a luxury. Ratboy had no interest in luxuries.

And what exactly was driving Teesha toward flight? Was it a sensible desire for survival or some perverse wish to keep Rashed from further combat with that hunter? He sometimes believed that he understood her a great deal more than Rashed did. Their leader viewed Teesha as a lovely creature to be protected, as the fragile heart of this little family. Ratboy knew she possessed the ability to care, even to love, but she had always been ruled by her own drives and desires, and she knew how to work Rashed like her own personal, life-size toy soldier.

But lately her actions were difficult to gauge. He suspected her feelings for Rashed were beginning to outweigh her own survival instincts.

And for all his resentment of Rashed, Ratboy did acknowledge his uses. And Ratboy certainly knew he didn't want to be alone. But problem solving wasn't one of his strengths. He wanted to follow the course of action that would stop this hunter's vendetta and allow them to continue existing. But which course was that? Flight or fight?

Cool air blew in from the sea, causing piles of dust from the blackened wreckage to rise and drift away.

'Oh, Rashed,' Teesha said in genuine regret while examining the remnants of their home, 'I'm so sorry.'

She walked over and gently touched his shoulder in comfort. He did not move or acknowledge her.

'Well, we aren't going to find anything of value here,' Ratboy said sensibly. 'Do we feed, run, or start tracking the hunters? I say we should all agree on our next move before doing anything.'

Teesha smiled at him gratefully. Her concern for Rashed's state of mind was becoming obvious. Actually, Ratboy was growing worried as well.

'You're both fools if you look to him for decisions,' a hollow voice said.

Edwan appeared near Teesha in his usual horrific state. Although Ratboy wasn't exactly unnerved by the ghost's macabre appearance, he'd never learned to regard Edwan as anything but an erratically useful aberration.

This was a night of new expressions. Teesha almost frowned.

'My dear,' she said to Edwan. 'We are in a rather bad way tonight. I wish you would attempt to be helpful.'

'That hunter is not a charlatan,' he answered angrily, his long, yellow hair moving as his severed head jerked toward his wife. 'She's a *dhampir*, born to hunt and kill your kind. You will not defeat her. If you stay here, you will all die a true death and join me.'

Rashed finally turned away from the burned warehouse. 'How do you know this?' he asked of the ghost. 'Every time we talk, you have more tragic or critical news to share.'

'There is a stranger living at The Velvet Rose. He knows many things. I heard him tell her.' Edwan's words faltered slightly, and Ratboy knew communication on a physical level was becoming more difficult for the ghost with each passing season. 'He's strong – not like the others. Something about him . . .'

'So how badly injured is the hunter?' Rashed asked bluntly.

'Not at all,' Edwan answered. 'The half-elf fed her his blood, and she healed like one of you.'

Rashed shook his head almost sadly.

'Long years in this physical realm are affecting you. *Dhampirs* only exist in stories. Offspring of a mortal and vampire? Our kind cannot procreate. You know that.'

Ratboy wasn't so certain. 'Corische used to talk to me sometimes when he fell into black moods, and his favorite subject was always our strengths and weaknesses and abilities. He told me once that it takes our bodies a bit of time to completely alter. I don't know why. But he said that in the first days after being turned, it was still possible for an undead to conceive or create a child.'

'This is pointless.' Rashed waved him away like an annoying insect. 'If she is something beyond human, then the need to kill her is increased not reduced.'

'Well then, my *lord*,' Ratboy drawled, 'perhaps we ought to try a different tactic. The two of us would have killed her last night were it not for the half-elf, the blacksmith, and that damned dog. No one else in this town will help her. If we rob her of any present assistance, she will be alone.'

Teesha nodded, her face intense. Ratboy could just glimpse her smooth, white stomach through the rip in her red gown.

'Yes, Rashed,' she said. 'If we kill her friends first and then destroy her, will you take us away from here? We can rebuild someplace else?'

His voice softened, and he stepped over to stand behind her petite form. 'Of course. We can't stay in Miiska.'

'One on one is the only way,' Ratboy put in. 'Less chance of being seen.'

'All right then,' Teesha said, almost happily. 'I will take the blacksmith . . . no, Edwan, don't be concerned. He lives in solitude. I will sing him to sweet sleep before he even knows what's happening.'

'I'll take the half-elf,' Ratboy said in resignation. 'I can use the dog to lure him off by himself. Although to deal with the dog, I may have to use something vile and mortal like a crossbow.' He smiled. 'Or maybe an ax.'

'You're both certain?' Rashed asked. 'I know they're just mortals, but don't try anything unless you can each draw the blacksmith and half-elf off by themselves.'

'Don't be so protective,' Teesha answered. 'I know how to control a mortal.'

That much was true, Ratboy mused. She knew how to control immortals as well.

Rashed wanted the hunter's blood tonight, but Ratboy could tell this new plan made sense.

'Decided then,' the tall undead said, more to himself than anyone. 'Her friends die now, and we'll track her down tomorrow. Then we'll be free to go.'

Edwan watched this entire exchange in silence, but his form was exuding a cold that even bothered Ratboy – who never felt the cold.

'And what will you be doing while the two of them are out murdering this hunter's followers?' the ghost asked Rashed.

Rashed stepped back in calm determination. The sea wind blew against his torn tunic. 'There's only one hole in the belly of that ship. Otherwise, it's intact. I'm going to try to repair it and push it off the ground.'

* * *

At first, Magiere found the thought of serving customers at The Sea Lion that night to be absurd. She could not believe Leesil had made a public announcement that they would be open for business.

Caleb quickly put together a simple mutton soup, and Leesil bought bread from Karlin's bakeshop. They tried to lay the convalescing Chap on Leesil's bed and close the bedroom door, but he whined and pawed at the door so much that Magiere relented and brought him back downstairs. All his wounds were nearly healed, but he still moved slowly and carefully. As long as he lay quietly by the fire and pretended to keep watch, he could stay in the common room with everyone else.

Once people began arriving to drink ale and talk, her spirits lifted slightly. Leesil's instincts were correct yet again. The inn was transformed into a place of life, food, and chatter. She'd spent too much time with death lately.

Her clientele was slightly altered. Fewer dockworkers came, but more shopkeepers and market-dwellers walked through the door and shouted greetings. Of course, she could always count on a variety of sailors. Several fishermen's wives made a fuss over Leesil's face, and he in turn soaked up the attention like a dry sea sponge.

Magiere poured tankards of ale and goblets of wine, the new glass goblets purchased as a gift by some of the local folk. Leesil helped Caleb serve soup until the supper crowd was sated, and then he started up a loud faro game. Too loud for her tastes, perhaps, but half the room alternated in and out of players' positions, the other half shouting or cursing at the luck of the cards.

Something in the air felt almost like a harvest celebration. Although Magiere could not take part, an expected – but not entirely unwanted – feeling of satisfaction began pushing away the guilt and horror she'd experienced earlier when Geoffry and Aria tried to pay her. Miiska was her home now. Intentionally or not, she and Leesil had actually done something to protect it.

This thought forced her gaze from the ale cask to the only person in the room not celebrating: Brenden.

He'd stayed all day on the pretense of helping get the tavern set up, but she had a feeling he simply didn't want to go home. Now he sat alone, drinking, occasionally smiling and nodding when someone else spoke to him. But the moment he was left in solitude again, she saw a deep sadness settle back over him. He was clean now, wearing a long-sleeved white shirt and brown breeches. Without his blacksmith's leather, he looked more vulnerable somehow. Magiere wanted to comfort him, but she didn't know how.

She herself was wearing the tight-laced, dark blue dress Aunt Bieja had given her so many years ago. As Leesil had pointed out that morning, her usual clothes were ruined beyond repair. She ordered a new set from Baltzar, a local tailor, but for now, the dress would have to do. Besides, the sight of it made Leesil smile. She owed him that much at least, and tried to return his pleased glances. Still, when she looked at him, the half memory of his pale skin and bleeding arm would rush back to her.

The door opened again. Karlin the baker, Geoffry, and Aria all swept in with a chorus of 'hellos' and laughter. Both young people went to watch the faro table, and Karlin practically danced over to the bar.

'You look lovely,' he said, smiling.

'So do you,' she joked.

'Pour me an enormous tankard of ale. I rarely drink, but tonight is different.'

'And why is that?' she asked, wondering if she wanted to broach the subject at all.

'You know good and well. Our town is safe. The streets are safe. Our children are safe. I think I'll drink till dawn.'

Much as Magiere's thoughts still wandered to dark places, the jolly baker's mood was infectious.

'I'm going to need a steady supply of bread if you can manage,' she said. 'At least for a while.'

He nodded, his plump face glowing.

'I have a better idea. Aria's father is the local cobbler. He does a good business, but there are five children in the family, and they can only assist him so much. The girl's a fine cook. I thought you might want to employ her now that . . . well, now that Beth-rae is gone.'

Magiere realized that one of the things she liked about Karlin was his ability to discuss the truth without ever seeming crude or unfeeling.

'Is she interested?'

'Yes, we spoke of such an arrangement on the way over.'

Magiere nodded. 'I'll speak with her later.' She paused and tried to seem lighthearted. 'Why don't you go visit with Brenden? I see he's sitting alone.'

Karlin picked up his tankard. 'I'll just do that.'

And so the night went on.

The townsfolk of Miiska stayed late. Magiere had not spoken to Caleb of any matters beyond business. She felt shame that Beth-rae's body had been taken from the kitchen and buried at some point during the past two days, but she didn't know where or when. She would have to ask later, when a proper moment allowed. She would take Leesil, and they would pay their final respects. He needed to do this as much or more than she did. And she would see to it that flowers were placed regularly at the grave.

Little Rose was sitting by Chap near the fire. She appeared wide awake, wearing her usual muslin dress. Her long, blond curls hung in an uncombed mess. Magiere didn't have the heart to send her up to bed.

Sometime, past the heart of the night, when only a few patrons remained, Leesil stood up and announced it was time to close. His actions surprised her slightly, but she agreed and helped him to good-naturedly usher the last celebrators out – all except Brenden.

'What a night,' the half-elf exclaimed as he closed the door. 'I'm ready to drop.'

The huge common room felt empty and too quiet now. Magiere heard the fire crackling, and she turned to see Rose lying asleep on the braid rug beside Chap, the dog with his nose pushed warmly into the back of the child's neck. She almost went to wake her, then thought better of it. Let the child rest there. Leesil could carry her upstairs later.

Brenden got to his feet. 'Well, I should be going, too. You all need your sleep.'

'I'll walk you home,' Leesil said. 'Just let me put the cards away. You should see the profits, Magiere. Everyone was in such a good mood that I fleeced them a little.'

'I thought you were tired,' Brenden said. 'You don't need to walk with me.'

'The air will do me good. It's a bit stuffy in here.'

Magiere knew Leesil too well to believe he wanted some night air. He must have been watching Brenden's mood as well.

'You both go on,' she said. 'We'll clean up in the morning.'

Brenden looked at her helplessly, as if he wanted to say something, but then he turned and stepped out the door.

As Leesil followed the blacksmith, he paused at the door. 'I won't be long,' he said.

Magiere merely nodded, and closed the door. Then she was alone with Caleb.

She found the old man in the kitchen, quietly washing the stew pot.

'Just leave that,' she said. 'Should I carry Rose up for you?'

'No, Miss,' he responded. His expression was always so calm and composed. 'I can bring her. You should get some rest.'

'Are you all right?' she asked, with an unusual desire for a real answer.

'I will be,' he said. 'You know most of the townsfolk are grateful, don't you? No matter what the cost.'

'Yes, grateful,' she repeated. 'The desperate are always grateful.'

He looked at her quizzically, but did not speak.

'How many people knew, really knew their town was a home for a band of undeads?' she asked him. 'And how did they know? How did you know?'

Again, he seemed further puzzled by her words. 'People don't simply disappear without a trace in a town the size of Miiska, especially people like my daughter and Master Dunction. Before you came, a body with holes in the neck or throat would be found now and then. It didn't happen often. Sometimes a season or two would pass between such happenings. But word traveled quickly. I think most of the townsfolk believed something unnatural plagued us. Wasn't that the way with most villages you served in the past?'

The clean lines of his aging, questioning face pulled at her heart. She'd never had a father to speak with, and a desire to tell Caleb everything suddenly gripped her. But she knew doing so would only hurt him further. His wife was dead, and he believed her sacrifice had been made to help the great 'hunter of the undead.' He needed to believe that Beth-rae's life was worthy of sacrifice for the freedom of Miiska, so that no one else had to endure the disappearance of a daughter or the loss of a spouse. Magiere would not be so selfish as to destroy his illusion in order to ease her own conscience.

'Yes,' she said. 'But for me, this is over, Caleb. I just want to run the tavern with you and Leesil now.'

A mild gust of air hit them both as the kitchen door banged open against the wall.

'Over?' a near-angry voice said from the doorway. 'And why exactly do you think that?'

Welstiel stepped in like some lord invading a peasant's home on his lands. Dressed and groomed, as always, his striking countenance was concerned, almost agitated.

'Caleb,' Magiere said. 'You take Rose and go upstairs.'

The old man hesitated, but then he left the kitchen.

'What are you doing here?' she demanded of her new visitor.

Somehow, this seemed an odd place for a conversation with Welstiel, standing among pots, pans, and dried onions hanging on the walls. Though they had spoken in Brenden's yard, in her mind, she now saw him always as part of his eccentric room at The Velvet Rose, surrounded by his books and orbs. Only two small candles and one lamp illuminated the kitchen. The white patches at his temples stood out vividly.

'I'm wondering if you're truly as much of a fool as all the other simpletons in this town,' he answered, voice deep and hard. 'I expected that you would be planning your next steps, yet you served ale all night, celebrating some illusory victory.'

'What are you talking about?' she asked. 'I'm tired of your little half-mysteries and concealing observations.'

'How could you possibly assume the vampires here have been destroyed? Have you seen bodies? Have you counted those destroyed?'

A cold trickle of fear ran down her spine.

'Leesil burned the warehouse, and it caved in. Nothing could survive that.'

'You are a *dhampir*!' he said angrily. 'You received a fatal wound last night, but now you stand here, whole again. Their bodies heal even faster than yours. They are like the black roaches beneath these floorboards.' He stepped closer. 'Imagine what they can endure.'

Magiere leaned over and gripped the aging oak table that Beth-rae had once chopped vegetables on. She felt fatigue weigh her down until she had to sit on the stool. This could not be happening. It should all be over with.

'I may not have seen any bodies, but you haven't seen any undeads roaming the streets either. Have you?'

The flesh of his cheekbones pulled back. 'Look to your friends.'

He turned and quickly disappeared out the door into the darkness.

'Wait!' Magiere shouted.

She ran after him through the kitchen door, but the backside of the tavern that faced the forest between the building and the sea was empty. In a moment of crystal clarity, only one thought registered.

'Leesil.'

Magiere bolted back through the kitchen to the bar and grabbed her falchion.

As Brenden and Leesil walked down the streets of Miiska in silence, Brenden marveled at what a mass of contradictions this half-elf was: one moment a cold-hearted fighter and the next a mother hen. Leesil wore a green scarf tied around his head which covered the slight points of his ears. He now resembled a slender human with slightly slanted, amber-brown eyes. Brenden wondered about the scarf.

'Why do you sometimes wear that?' he asked, motioning toward Leesil's head.

'Wear what?' the half-elf said. Then he touched his forehead. 'Oh, that. I used to wear it all the time. When Magiere and I were on the ga . . . when we were hunting, we didn't like calling attention to ourselves. She thought it best to blend in until we'd decided to take on a job. There aren't too many of my kind in or around Stravina, so I kept my ears covered. It doesn't matter here, but old habits die hard. Besides, it keeps my hair out of my face.'

They talked of such simple, small things along the way. Except for a few drunken sailors, and a guard here and there openly patrolling the streets, no one else was about. Soon enough, the two of them approached Brenden's home.

Leesil finally asked, 'Are you all right?'

Answering such a question was difficult for Brenden, but he had no wish to hurt his friend.

'After my sister's death, I was so enraged by Ellinwood's conduct that anger consumed me. Then you came. While we were searching, fighting, seeking revenge, I had a sense of purpose. Now that it's all over, I feel like I should bury Eliza . . . begin to mourn. But she's already in her grave. I don't know what to do.'

Leesil nodded. 'I know. I think I've known all day.' He paused. 'Listen to me. Tomorrow, you'll get up and go visit Eliza and say good-bye. Then you'll come here, open the smith's shop and work all day. At night, you'll come to The Sea Lion, have supper, and talk to friends. I swear that after a few such days, the world will begin to make sense again.'

Brenden choked once and looked away.

'Thank you,' he said, needing to say something, anything. 'I'll see you tomorrow night.'

The half-elf was already walking away down the street, as if he too felt a loss of appropriate words.

'If you run out of horses to shoe, you can help me fix that damned roof.'

Brenden watched his friend's long-legged strides until Leesil turned a corner, and then he went inside his small empty cottage. Only sparse furniture and decor remained, as he had bundled all of Eliza's things and stored them away. Such items were too painful to see every day. A candle she made last summer rested on the table, but he didn't light it, preferring to undress in the dark. As he began untucking his shirt, beautiful strains of a wordless song drifted in the window and filled his ears.

Was someone outside singing?

He walked to the back window and looked out. Standing next to the woodpile was a young woman in a torn, velvet dress. Soft curls the color of deep Portsmith coffee hung to her small waist. She seemed vaguely familiar. Such sweet music floated from her tiny mouth. Something told him to stay in the house, but an irresistible urgency and longing pulled at him. He stepped out the back door and off the porch into the yard.

Slowly approaching this serene visage, he saw her white hands were those of a child. Yet the tight-laced bodice of her gown and rounded breasts proved her a woman. He could not tell how old she was with her doll-like face.

'Are you lost?' he asked. 'Do you need help?'

She stopped singing and smiled. 'I am lost and alone. See the sadness in my eyes.'

He looked into her dark, oval eyes and forgot where he was. He forgot his name.

'Come sit with me,' she pleaded.

He crouched down beside her and leaned against the woodpile. Her delicate bone structure made him afraid to touch her, but she laid her head against his shoulder in contentment.

'So gentle,' she whispered. 'You would never hurt me, would you?'

'No,' he answered. 'I would never hurt you.'

Her face turned up toward his, and her hand touched the back of his hair.

'Yes, you would.'

A grip of solid bone restrained him, and she bit down hard on his throat.

No, she wasn't biting him, but kissing him, and he wanted her to go on. He relaxed in her arms, letting her do as she wished.

Then he closed his eyelids and sank down into her embrace.

Ratboy had not stopped thinking about the slim, tan-armed girl for days. He remembered standing outside her window, watching her sleep, drinking in her scent when Teesha had pulled him away. Now, he found himself standing outside her window again.

Rashed would want him to feed, heal, and grow strong again before attacking the half-elf and the dog. He was certain of it. This time there could be no failure, so he should be at his peak of strength and reeking of fresh blood.

The girl had long, tan hair to match her arms. When she rolled over in her sleep, he caught a whiff of clean muslin mixed with lavender soap, and he could wait no longer.

He rarely exercised any of his mental ability beyond making some of his mortal victims forgetful. Why should he? They were killers, not tricksters, but at times he admired, even quietly envied, Teesha's ease of hunting. And weren't they going to rid themselves of this hunter and begin traveling again? Perhaps he should practice his abilities and improve them. Teesha's concern for Rashed was beginning to outweigh her concern for him. Maybe it always had and he'd simply never realized. Ratboy would never be Rashed. But he had other gifts, other skills. He should develop them and impress her along the road. The thought made him smile.

At the same time, he felt an uncontrollable desire to possess this tan-haired girl, to touch her skin, to feed on her life. And he needed to be at full strength.

'Come,' he whispered.

She opened her eyes, and he projected a thought into her mind. There was something important outside. She must get up and find it. Perhaps she was dreaming? But in the dream she still needed to see what waited.

Rising, she hurried to the window and looked out. Upon seeing nothing, she leaned the upper half of her body over the edge.

Ratboy grabbed her shoulders protruding through the window and pulled her outside. She did not scream, but blinked at him in mild surprise.

He did not want to frighten her, so he kept projecting the idea that she was lost in a dream. She didn't struggle in his arms, but rather examined him curiously through slightly slanted, brown eyes. An alien sense of excitement passed through him. He took his time, experiencing the scent of lavender soap in the crook of her neck mingling with the barest hint of dried fish on her hands. His fingers brushed the softness of her hair and the smoothness of her arms.

Then he pushed her slowly to the ground and used his teeth to puncture the wellspring in the base of her throat, all the while continuing to calm her with the power of his mind.

Her slender hands instinctively pushed once against his shoulders, but the moment passed, and he felt her gripping his shirt.

Power and unbelievable strength flowed into him. Domination through blind fear was one thing, but this was something else, something he and Parko had never talked about.

He drank until her heart stopped beating.

She was only a shell now, and he left her body where it lay, feeling some regret that the moment was over. Somehow, he knew Rashed didn't care about secrecy anymore.

Thoughts of the half-elf and the dog moved to the front of his awareness. Weapons? Shouldn't he find some weapons? No, his burned flesh was healing rapidly, and he had never felt stronger. No mortal trappings were necessary. He slipped down the near-deserted Miiska streets toward The Sea Lion.

Upon reaching it, he jerked one of the common room's shutters off. The dog lay alone in the large room, resting by the hearth.

'Here, puppy, puppy,' he sang. What had that half-elf called him — Chap? 'Here, Chap.'

Chap's great, wolflike head snapped up in what Ratboy swore was disbelief. Then, as Ratboy anticipated, the dog's lips curled up in a hate-filled snarl, and he launched himself toward the window. Loud high-pitched wails burst from his long mouth.

Ratboy smiled. He bolted for the outskirts of town and the tree line.

★   ★   ★

Magiere ran down the near-black streets toward Brenden's shop until her lungs threatened to burst. Her long dress kept catching at her legs, but she pulled it up with her free hand and kept running.

What if Welstiel were right?

Truth hurt more than the exerted ache in her chest. How could she simply assume all danger had passed because Leesil and Brenden believed the burning warehouse had caved in the tunnels? She ignored the pain in her legs and ran on, falchion in hand.

As the smith's shop came into sight, she called out, 'Leesil!' not caring whom she woke up.

The front door was closed. She pounded on it.

'Leesil! Brenden?'

No one answered, and she tried to open it. The door was unlocked.

Magiere shoved it open and stepped inside, but there was no one at home in the small one-room cottage. Maybe Leesil and Brenden hadn't gone directly to the blacksmith's house. What if Leesil had tried to cheer his friend by hunting up a late game of cards somewhere else?

Yes, she comforted herself. Leesil had taken Brenden somewhere else, and they were probably both sitting in some decrepit little inn playing faro. But her hopes were hysterical attempts to create personal security, and she knew it. Aunt Bieja always said, 'We mustn't worry until we have something to be worried about.'

No, Leesil had said he wouldn't be long.

When she walked past the back window, a flash of white caught her eye. She turned and saw Brenden's shirt. He was lying near the woodpile, not far from the fading stains of Eliza's blood.

'No!'

She rushed out the back door and into the yard, dropping to the ground at the blacksmith's side. His flesh was alabaster, contrasting with the dark red of his torn throat. She crouched down in front of him. His expression was not horrible, but more peaceful than any she'd ever seen on his face. Bright red hair stood out starkly against wan skin.

There was little blood on the ground, as whatever had ripped his throat open had carefully consumed every drop. She tried to let the sight sink in, to allow it inside where she could properly absorb and deal with it. But she couldn't.

Brenden was the only truly brave member of this town, the only one to help her and Leesil. And what had his bravery purchased? What did standing by them bring him? It had brought him death.

She reached out with her free hand and touched his beard. Her hand moved down to his throat, where her fingertips pressed against the side as if to feel the blood pumping. Nothing. She already knew he was dead, and her actions futile, but now she was one of the desperate, and she was paying a price.

Magiere remembered him standing in front of the tavern door that morning, blocking Ellinwood's entrance, protecting her home.

'I'm sorry,' she whispered to him. 'I'm so sorry for everything.'

Welstiel was right. She should have made sure. She should have searched for the bodies and never stopped until she made sure those vampires were truly dead. She had let Leesil and Brenden just walk out into the night air. This was her fault.

She dropped her falchion and gripped her own knees, rocking back and forth. It was too much.

Too much.

In the distance, an eerie keening wail broke through her inaction.

Magiere grabbed her falchion off the ground and ran out into the street near the front of Brenden's stables and forge.

Chap's cry sounded out again. Chap was hunting.

'Leesil.'

17

After Leesil left Brenden, he started for The Sea Lion, then changed his mind. Sounds of the sea called him, and he wanted a bit more time to himself before going home, so he walked toward Miiska's waterfront instead of taking the streets back to the tavern.

Pity for Brenden occupied his thoughts, but he was also troubled by the realization that he wanted to tell his friend the truth – well, maybe not the entire truth, just the part about how he and Magiere had earned a living for several years. How would Brenden react when he realized he'd risked his life hunting undeads with two people who probably knew less about it than he did?

Then again, they had been successful and everyone in their group survived. Perhaps the truth didn't matter.

Before him, gravelly sand and water stretched up along the forested shore and to the docks farther down. The sea lapping gently in and out on the beach was strangely comforting in moonlight.

Leesil tried to push aside any troubles that did not require immediate attention and focus on the moment at hand. Of course, some memories, old and deep, haunted him no matter what, but tonight the beach was peaceful, Magiere was alive, and Brenden might finally be able to mourn and someday recover from the loss of his sister. And Chap was on the mend. What more could he ask of life?

He strolled down the shoreline at a steady pace, and soon he found himself thinking about the tavern roof and getting an advance from Magiere for some new clothes. She needed some as well. Had she mentioned something about already ordering a new shirt? Maybe she had.

Magiere.

He tried hard not to think of the previous night, and found himself testing the bandage around his wrist. He felt the lingering ghost of her lips and teeth on his arm.

Leesil shook himself. It wasn't bad enough that the whole event had been macabre and grotesque – it was somehow alluring. Or perhaps that was just because of her and not what had happened, what he'd been forced to do not to lose her.

A small wave lapped near his feet and then a high-pitched wail exploded near the tree line. He froze.

Impossible.

It was impossible for Chap to be hunting. That cry he had only used when pursuing vampires. There was nothing left to hunt.

Leesil bolted down the beach toward the docks.

'Chap!' he yelled. 'Hold! Wait for me.'

The small bay grew deeper as he approached the docks, and the beach disappeared into the water until only rock and earth slanted sharply up to the edge of town. He climbed the rough embankment and kept going, not even pausing at the burned remains of the warehouse. When he reached a point where The Sea Lion was just up ahead, he stopped to listen.

Leesil turned slowly around, waiting to hear Chap's howl again. When it came, the eerie sound was out in the trees beyond the tavern and the south end of town. He bolted again, not bothering to wonder what he would do when he caught up.

'Chap!' he shouted while still in motion. 'You stop. I mean it!'

The dog's cry stopped briefly, but Leesil couldn't tell if this had anything to do with his orders or not. As suddenly as it stopped, the wail burst out again, but it changed directions.

Leesil stopped in a small clearing, panting among the giant firs and brush, in almost total darkness. Though the moon was bright, it did not penetrate the forest completely. He forced himself to stand still and just listen. The howls were growing quickly louder, now separated by barks and snarls. Then he realized that Chap – or whatever the dog pursued – was coming directly toward him.

Almost too late, Leesil dropped and tried to roll as a blurred form flew at him from nowhere, striking him hard across the jaw. Dazed and gasping for breath, he looked around wildly, still not sure what had hit him.

'Why don't you run?' a faintly familiar voice asked with gleeful intent. 'Run and I'll catch you again.'

Despite severe dizziness, fear caused Leesil to push himself upward and see the creature taunting him: a dirty, brown urchin with a skeletal face and torn clothing.

Ratboy.

'How?' he tried to whisper, but his mouth wouldn't work.

With unnatural quickness, Ratboy dropped to a crouch as if he wanted to talk. He half smiled, but the gesture did nothing to ease Leesil's panic.

'You know,' Ratboy said, 'I've never been one to play with my food, but now I feel like taking my time.' His smile faded. 'Where's your oil? Your stakes? Your hunter?'

Leesil tried to swallow, to think. In one flick he could have a stiletto in each hand. Would such weapons help him? Could he even get close to this . . . this thing that moved faster than he could see?

Chap's voice grew closer, and Leesil willed him to hurry. How had this creature survived the fire?

Ratboy's face caught and held Leesil's attention for a blink of time. So human, so young and lean and sharp like his body. Brown eyes glared, shining with the emotions of hate and triumph. Leesil had to remind himself that he wasn't facing an unkempt teenage boy.

Where was Chap?

'Perhaps we could call this a draw?' Leesil joked to buy time. 'I promise not to hurt you.'

'Oh, but I want to hurt you.'

Ratboy jumped up and kicked him in the ribcage hard enough to flip him over onto his back. A loud crack resonated through Leesil's body, and he felt at least two of his ribs snap. For a moment, the pain blinded him.

And then, like a song cut short, the eerie baying stopped, as if Chap had disappeared.

Ratboy's head swiveled toward the trees and back again.

'Is that what you were waiting for, the dog? I'm strong enough for him now, too, but my pretty partner must have finished with your blacksmith and come to assist me. I do apologize.'

He leaned down and grabbed Leesil by the shirt.

As Ratboy pulled him to his feet, Leesil curled his hands and flicked open the holding straps of the sheaths on his forearms. Stilettos dropped out of his sleeves into each hand.

He slammed both hilt-deep into Ratboy's sides.

'One good . . . turn for another,' he gasped out and then wrenched both hilts down.

Ratboy's mouth dropped open at the sound of his own ribs snapping. One of the stiletto hilts came away in Leesil's hand, its blade breaking off inside the vampire's body.

Without exerting himself, Ratboy flung the half-elf through the air.

Leesil's body glanced off a tree trunk into a low branch. His impact severed the branch, and he fell hard to the forest floor.

Choking, fighting for air, half-blinded by pain, Leesil clutched the broken piece of wood and held on tight.

Magiere cursed her long skirt as she ran into the forest, following the sound of Chap's voice. Catching on brush and hitting her ankles, the heavy fabric slowed her pace.

Something told her not to cry out, not to call for the dog.

Who murdered Brenden? How many of the vampires had escaped Leesil's fire? Why had they lured Chap into the forest? If they wanted to kill the dog, they could have done it while he slept alone by the tavern's fire.

The dog's cry suddenly stopped. So did she.

Two breaths later, the wail burst out of the night

again, and she could tell Chap had changed directions. He was chasing something through the trees. Or was something leading him?

She realized that crashing through the forest like a wounded bear would only give her away, so she gathered her skirt in one hand, clutched her falchion in the other, and moved more carefully through the trees.

Damn Welstiel. How had he known? Leesil was neither careless nor foolish, and he'd been certain nothing could survive the burning collapse of that warehouse. The brush was dense around her, and she stepped cautiously over bushes and through damp nettles.

Chap's voice was closer now. An odd relief grew inside her that she would see him within a wail or two. Then, like a bird shot in flight, his death song ended. It did not return.

Throwing caution aside, Magiere ran in the direction of his last cry. Falling into a small clear patch, she scarcely believed the sight.

A lovely young woman with dark brown curls and a torn red dress stood calmly, holding one hand out, speaking soft words. An arm's length away from her, Chap stood quivering and trembling. He growled, but his voice and expression lacked conviction. If he'd been a human, Magiere would have called him 'confused.'

'It's all right, my sweet,' the woman said, her tiny, pale hand offering him a caress. 'Come and sit with me here. You are very special.'

Both dog and woman were so intent upon each other that neither noticed Magiere's entrance – though it could hardly be called a quiet one.

'Chap!' she snapped. 'Get away from her.'

Both sets of eyes turned in her direction, and the haze left Chap's expression. He shook his head and charged to her side. He whined, pacing back and forth around her and watching the small woman in red.

'Is that how you killed Brenden?' Magiere asked, falchion pointing at the woman. 'You used some trick?'

The woman smiled, and Magiere felt its power like a physical blow. Small white teeth flashed from a face so gentle and innocent and warm that she might have been the source of love.

'You need to talk,' she said. 'To tell someone your troubles. I know these things. You've lost your friend . . . Leesil? Is that his name? Come sit with me, and I will listen. Tell me everything and then perhaps we can find him together.'

On a starkly conscious level, Magiere desired nothing more than to sink down beside this woman and pour out the last twenty years of her life. But she did not. Rage swelled up inside her, and fangs began to grow inside her mouth with a sharp, but now familiar, speed.

'That won't work,' she half whispered. 'Not on me.' She stepped closer. 'Are you armed? For your sake, I hope so.'

Images from the woman's mind floated into Magiere's. Teesha. This woman's name was Teesha.

'I think not,' Teesha answered calmly. 'Why should I when I have a swordsman?'

'I don't see him here,' Magiere replied, but banter grew difficult, and she feared losing control.

There was no rage or lust for revenge or madness in Teesha's eyes. Everything she did, everything she said, was calculated. Magiere hesitated, uncertain. This creature's powers were different from Rashed's or Ratboy's.

Chap growled low, and Magiere clung to rational thought. Teesha backed slowly toward the tree line. This vampire was afraid.

'You didn't think I'd be here, did you?' Magiere asked. 'Or you would have come prepared.' The truth became clear. This was all some plan to remove Leesil and Brenden. 'I can kill you, and you can't stop me.'

She stepped forward to swing, but the ground where Teesha stood was vacant. A rapidly fleeing voice echoed through the trees.

'You'll have to find me first.'

Magiere pursued. Behind her, Chap whined and then began barking loudly. She stopped and turned. Chap remained standing tensely in the clearing, barking at her, and Magiere's thoughts cleared again.

This undead woman was trying to draw her away from the real reason she'd come out here.

Wiping savage thoughts from her mind, Magiere ran back to Chap. 'Go, I'll follow.'

Chap turned and sprinted off into the forest.

Still panting, Leesil clutched the broken branch and forced himself to wait, to play the lame bird luring the fox in. If he attacked out of desperation, he would die.

Ratboy's pleasure and confidence were now marred. The blades thrust through his sides couldn't have hurt him much, but he was now openly angry. And that might make him careless again. He looked less human now and more like a filthy, feral creature.

'This is so much fun,' he spit out, but there was less

laughter in his voice than before. 'I might even bring you home – except I have no home. Do you remember Rashed? Tall, dark-haired, dead eyes, big sword? Yes, I bet he'd love a word with you. That warehouse meant a lot to him, you know, more than simply a business. It represented freedom and his ability to exist in your world. Can your small mind understand such ideas?'

Leesil's chest hurt so badly that every breath cost effort, but he regained his composure and tried to appear restful. Pulling himself up, he flopped back to lean against the tree.

'If you'd stop your senseless chatter, we could go and meet him now,' Leesil said. 'I doubt he'd take this long to kill me.'

Any remaining glee on Ratboy's face now faded. 'Do you wish death?'

'Anything is better than listening to you.'

Leesil tensed, anticipating a rapid lunge. When it came in a blur of movement, he fell back into the past and became a product of his parents' teachings, someone able to set aside pain, someone able to strike a focal point with fluid second nature and the right amount of force. His hand thrust out of its own accord just before Ratboy's hands could reach him.

The sharp, jagged end of the branch burrowed into the center of Ratboy's chest before either of them could grasp what had happened. A small spray of warm, black-red blood spattered Leesil's jaw and ear as he tried to roll out of the way.

Ratboy screamed in shock and what sounded like fear. The undead stumbled back, wildly clawing at the branch in his chest.

'Leesil! Where are you?'

Those words had come from out of the forest, not from the beggar boy's gaping mouth.

Magiere was somewhere in the trees. Relief flooded Leesil's mouth like water, but he found shouting impossible.

'Here,' he tried to call. 'I'm here.'

One of Ratboy's hands found its way around the branch, and he pulled it out. But he behaved nothing like he had when he'd pulled a crossbow quarrel from his body. He was choking, and blood poured, rather than leaked, from his body. He alternately gagged and whimpered, pressing both hands over the hole in his chest.

'I hit your heart, didn't I?' Leesil managed to whisper. 'I didn't pierce it completely, but I hit it. What happens when you bleed out? Will you fall limp, too weak to move, and lie in fear till the sun rises?'

Ratboy gargled spitting sounds and stared at him in panic. Approaching footsteps could be heard, and Chap's growls. The undead made a limping run for the trees away from the approaching sounds.

Ratboy disappeared through one side of the clearing as Chap burst through from the other. Magiere was close behind the dog. Through a haze of exhaustion, Leesil felt a tongue licking his face and Magiere's hands on him, searching for injury.

'Are you cut?' she asked. Then she asked louder again when he didn't answer immediately, 'Are you cut?'

'Go after him,' he whispered. 'Hurry.'

'No, I'm getting you home.'

'Brenden,' he said. 'We have to warn him.'

She offered him neither comfort nor sympathy, but

he heard the edge of hysterical sorrow in her voice. 'Brenden's dead.'

The underbrush grew thicker as Ratboy approached the small inlet river which hid the landlocked boat. Pain such as mortals feel did not plague him, but fear and exhaustion as he'd never known slowed his pace. All he could think of was Rashed and the boat and finding help. His lifeblood – taken from the tan-armed girl – covered every leaf and nettle he passed over. He had no idea how large the hole in his chest might be, but the entire front of his shirt was soaked.

How? How had the mortal half-elf injured him again?

Ratboy used the trees to support himself as he lurched forward, desperate to find his own kind, no longer caring about pride nor the shame of needing assistance.

Through the dense, deep green around him, the smell of life hit his nostrils. He tensed in confusion, and then an unfortunate deer hopped almost directly in front of him. Large, liquid eyes and a flash of white tail registered in his vision, and he rushed forward on instinct, screaming out in desperation as he grabbed the creature by the head and bit into its neck.

The deer kicked hard and dragged him a short way, but the terror of true death coming for him made his strength maniacal. He hung on with his arms and rolled his body, pulling the beast over to the ground. The animal weakened and began to grow limp in his arms. Feeding on animals was a pale shadow in comparison to people. An animal's life energy did not fill him with satisfaction or contentment, but it still offered life and healing. He released the animal as it died.

Panic subsided. The opening in his chest closed just enough for his own bleeding to stop. He left the deer where it lay, its eyes wide open, and headed for the boat again.

Now that true death was not imminent, his state of mind changed. He was uncomfortable and embarrassed by his previous fear – and his need for Rashed. Undeads lived in each other's company out of choice, not need.

The wild, clean life force of the deer flowed through him, unfettered by the complexity of relationships and emotional attachments. He felt the heart of the forest beat inside his ears, even though his own stopped beating many years ago. Wolves howled and an owl hooted.

Did he wish to hide inside the belly of a boat for weeks while Rashed forced them all to sail until settling in a new town – but just like this one? Would they build another warehouse and pretend to live as mortals?

Ratboy slowed his pace. He looked down at his chest and then ripped off what was left of his shirt. Torn flesh met his inspection. The blood of a mortal would finish healing him. Again, he wondered about the best course of action.

Teesha had wanted to flee.

Rashed wanted to stay and fight.

Both their motivations were becoming clear. Rashed wanted revenge and to make certain Teesha would be permanently safe from the hunter. Teesha just wanted to keep Rashed away from that hunter. But what about him? What about Ratboy? Did he matter to them at all? He had stayed with them all these years because he'd never really liked living alone, but standing there in the forest, looking at his wounded chest, he wondered if he hadn't been alone the whole time.

'Do not be one of them,' a mad but familiar voice breathed in his ear.

He cast about wildly, but saw no one. He knew the voice. Unbidden, images of Parko danced in the darkness, and he longed for the freedom to hunt and kill and feed as the need drove him.

The white face and feral laugh of his old companion followed when he started moving again. And where was Parko's body now? At the bottom of a river because some hunter put it there – the same one who now hunted him.

He heard the sound of a hammer pounding on wood and moved up quietly behind a tree. The mild inlet river gushed softly as it flowed past, and Rashed stood not far away with his own shirt off, attempting to repair the hole in the boat's hull.

Rashed's white skin was the only unnatural element of his appearance. The heavy bones of his bare shoulders and the practiced swing of his mallet seemed completely human, completely mortal. Other tools and boards lay on the ground, waiting to be used.

'Is he a true Noble Dead?' Parko's dead voice whispered in Ratboy's ear.

'No.' Ratboy shook his head. He stepped back, realizing the futility of Rashed's actions, the pointless danger of remaining to fight this hunter, the regret of leaving Teesha behind.

There was no indecision, no real turmoil inside him anymore. He wasn't going back. The forest called him.

He could kill along the way, steal clothes from his victims, and be true to his own nature.

One last pang of longing passed through him as he thought again of Teesha. Then he disappeared into the trees . . . heading north.

Even though the hole in the ship's hull was small, Rashed was beginning to realize he'd never be able to mend it himself without proper supplies – and even then it would take several nights to make her sea-worthy. He'd ripped some boards from the deck and attempted to use them for hull repairs. At first the work pleased him, as it gave him something constructive to do and reminded him that he indeed controlled his own fate. Now he decided a different course of escape might be in order. If they could travel by road at night to the next town along the coastline, he could buy them passage on a ship.

He frowned. That would take money. He had counted on being able to delay concern over finances.

His thoughts turned to Teesha.

Her method of hunting did not give him cause to worry, but he still glanced backward occasionally, wishing she would appear.

Often given to admiring aesthetics, he could not help noticing the beauty and variety of forest life growing on and around the boat. Vines of purple and white, bell-shaped flowers hung down from the bow and the stern, connecting to heavy fir trees and wild lilac bushes. Even in the moonlight, glowing blankets of light green moss covered many tree trunks and roots like soft carpets. The thought of fleeing such a place only fueled his anger toward the hunter who had desecrated his current existence.

'You could have been a carpenter,' said a sweet voice behind him.

He turned to see Teesha inspecting his work, which he hardly thought worthy of praise. With her dark curls falling like a blanket around her petite face and shoulders, the glorious colors of nature faded in his estimation. Nothing compared to her.

'Is the blacksmith dead?' he asked flatly, not mentioning his relief at her return.

'Yes . . .'

Something was wrong. He lowered his mallet and walked to her.

'What is it? Did the half-elf escape Ratboy?'

Teesha raised her chin to look him full in the face.

'I think Ratboy has left us. I felt his separation.'

Rashed didn't understand, but he knew Teesha's mental abilities surpassed his own. 'What do you mean?'

She reached out to touch his arm. Earlier, he'd removed his torn tunic to work with greater freedom, and the sensation of her fingers on his bare skin made him tremble.

'He is gone,' she said simply. 'He has followed Parko onto the Feral Path.'

A sense of loss hit Rashed. It was not so much because he cared for or missed Ratboy, but more that his safe world was unraveling around him and he could not seem to rewind the skein.

But that which mattered most still stood by his side, still needed his protection. If he were capable, he would have embraced Teesha tightly and whispered comfort in her ear.

He was not. Instead, he turned halfway toward the boat and said, 'So there are only two of us now?'

'And Edwan.'

Yes, Edwan. Why did he always forget the ghost? 'Of course,' he said.

Teesha hesitated. 'We still have one another. Perhaps we should see Ratboy's decision as a sign. Perhaps we, too, should forget everything here and slip away.'

For a brief moment, Rashed wavered. Teesha was safe. She was with him. Perhaps they could just leave this place and disappear into the night. But then an image of the hunter flashed in his thoughts, as well as the memories of himself pulling Teesha through collapsing tunnels while his home burned over his head.

'No, that hunter dies. Then we leave. I'll kill her myself tomorrow night. You will stay here. I won't be long. I can't take the chance that she'll follow us.' He gestured toward the boat. 'This is not repairable with the tools and supplies I have, but I promise we'll leave here soon. I have an errand to take care of tonight. We'll need money for traveling.'

She dropped her gaze and her usual facade of casual charm.

'All right,' she said quietly, 'but I want you to know that I'm afraid, and very little in this world frightens me.'

The urge – and the inability – to comfort her became physically painful. 'I won't let anything hurt you.'

'That isn't what I'm afraid of.'

Rashed waited outside The Velvet Rose until a tall, richly dressed patron exited the inn. Stepping from the shadows of a side alley, Rashed punched the man in the face hard enough to drop him. He stole the man's purse and then his cloak. Rashed quickly donned the cloak, making sure its hood completely hid his face. Even at this late hour, The Velvet Rose could sometimes teem with life and he did not want to be recognized.

Upon entering The Velvet Rose, he only saw three people: a maid, another patron preparing to depart, and Loni, the elf who functioned as a polite proprietor and guard. His mental abilities could handle all three. Casting out with this mind, Rashed projected a suggestion that they should ignore him, that he belonged here. Teesha was better at this, but Rashed knew how to use his abilities when necessary.

Once past the foyer and the front desk, he walked up the stairs and knocked on Ellinwood's door. There was no answer but he could sense the constable's presence inside.

He reached down and turned the knob. It wasn't locked. At his previous visit, the constable had made him welcome, so he was able to walk right in.

Upon entering, he saw Ellinwood's enormous form half lying in a damask-covered chair. The flesh around his partially open eyes was puffy and tinged with a pinkish-red hue. Drool ran down one corner of his mouth and dribbled into a wet pool on the neck of his green tunic. On the table next to him sat an empty, long-stemmed crystal glass, an urn, and a bottle of amber liquid. Rashed walked over and looked in the urn. He knew of yellow opiate. In his soldiering days in the Suman empire, he'd seen enough of it in the back-alley bars and dens where the desperate gathered to sate their needs. He'd long suspected Ellinwood spent his profits on some addiction, but he'd never cared enough to seek an answer.

Disgust filled Rashed. Why should anyone mourn for these mortals when they so frequently chose to destroy themselves? And Suman opiate was dangerous. It consumed those enslaved to it. The constable would soon do anything to acquire more.

'Wake up,' Rashed ordered.

Ellinwood's eyes fluttered several times before opening completely. He was dazed and incoherent at first. Then his expression cleared. As the sight of Rashed registered, confusion was replaced by shock.

'Ras . . . ?' he managed to say.

He tried to sit up, but the soft muscles of his massive body would not cooperate. Without his hat, his brown hair was visible, sticking to his skull in lank, unwashed strings.

'Yes, I'm here,' Rashed said quietly. 'You are not dreaming. I need money.'

Gaining more control over his body, Ellinwood now sat straight.

'You came here for money? How did you escape the warehouse? That hunter's partner burned it to the ground.'

'We lost everything,' Rashed said, ignoring his question. 'I need to take Teesha away from here. I believe you can spare a bit of wealth, considering what we have been paying you.'

He could almost see the thoughts in Ellinwood's mind passing across the man's swollen face. Anxiety was followed by alarm, and then by cunning, and finally, the constable smiled.

'You don't think I would keep any of my silver here?' His gaze shifted unconsciously to the top of the wardrobe and then quickly back to Rashed. 'Some light-fingered maid might steal it.'

Rashed did not have time for games, and disgust for this greedy man was turning to hatred. He changed tactics and focused psychically.

'You are in danger,' he said. 'I've come to take you to safety. Gather your money. Gather what you need and follow me.'

Ellinwood's already weak mind, further dulled with opiate and whiskey, was easy to overcome. He suddenly believed himself to be in danger from an outside source and that Rashed was his protector.

'Yes, yes,' he said, fumbling in panic to get to his feet. 'I won't be long.'

'We'll go to the docks,' Rashed said. 'You will be safe there.'

'Safe,' Ellinwood repeated.

He hurried to the wardrobe, unlocked the top drawer, and pulled out several heavy pouches that jingled in his hands.

'Give me the coins for safekeeping,' Rashed said. 'I will guard them for you.'

The constable handed him the pouches. Rashed tied them to his belt and pulled the cloak around himself again.

They walked down the stairs together, and this time, Rashed simply hid beneath his hood as they passed Loni. The constable lived there. No one would question him leaving with a companion. The two of them traveled quickly through the quiet town to the shore, and Rashed moved out to stand on the wooden planks at the end of a dock.

'Here,' he said. 'You will be safe here.'

Ellinwood joined him. His weight caused the boards to creak.

'Safe,' he said again, smiling.

Rashed could not believe how easy the man's mind was to control. It took little effort at all, and controlling the perceptions of another while feeding suggested thoughts was normally a great effort for him. He reached out with both hands and grasped Ellinwood's fleshy face. Then he jerked hard to the left, snapping the constable's neck. His victim felt no pain, but was simply rendered lifeless.

Rather than attempting to hold the heavy body up, he allowed it to fall backward off the long dock. No one would hear it hit the water. It might wash out to sea, and it might wash up on the shore. If someone discovered it, they would see red-pouched eyes and later find the yellow powder in his room. Either way, by the time he was found, Rashed planned to be long gone.

The thought of Teesha alone at the boat made him anxious, and he left the docks quickly, fingering the pouches on his belt, not giving Ellinwood's place of death a backward glance.

18

Magiere knelt upon the floor and bandaged Leesil's ribs as best she could, while the half-elf sat numbly on the side of his bed. According to Caleb, Miiska had possessed a competent healer until the previous winter. The healer's wife suffered from a breathing illness, and he'd taken her south to a drier climate. Caleb said the few others in town who claimed to be healers were probably less skilled than Magiere herself at dealing with cracked bones, and the last knowledgeable herbalist was Brenden's mother, who died years ago.

Although alarmed that Leesil was injured again so soon, Magiere felt a guilty sense of purpose for the task of tending him. It gave her an activity to focus on. Leesil had not spoken a word since hearing of Brenden's death and stared at the wall of his bedroom while she used torn sheets to wrap his broken ribs. His jaw was now several shades of purple and yellow. Some of Welstiel's salve remained, and she carefully applied it to his face.

Chap paced about the room. Twice, he came over and shoved his wet nose into Leesil's dangling hand, who did not respond.

'You'll heal,' Magiere said finally.

'Will I?' he answered.

'Yes, you will.'

He was quiet for a while and then drew air in through his mouth, wincing slightly.

'I thought they were gone, Magiere. I swear to all the gods that I thought them dead.'

'I know. We all did. It isn't your fault.'

Magiere remembered how in the beginning she'd been desperate to avoid becoming embroiled in all of this. How foolish. There was no way to avoid it. There never had been. And now these undead creatures would not rest until she and any near her were dead and buried in a local graveyard.

'I won't pretend to understand how you feel, but the worst is yet to come,' she said, and her voice failed her for a moment. 'I need you. Are you up to making a defense plan with me?'

He blinked in sadness. 'I honestly don't know.'

She got up from the floor and sat beside him on the bed.

This was a pleasant room. The mattress was stuffed with feathers, not straw, and everything smelled of Leesil, a mix of earth and spices. There was also a slight musty smell, and she knew his bedding had not been aired since Beth-rae's death. A small table and one chair were in the corner, but with the exception of a fat, white candle, the table was bare. For the most part, his room was neat and spare. Although he had the ability to go through money at an amazing rate, material objects held little interest for him.

Magiere still wore her blue dress, but the skirt was now torn and muddied. The faded cotton shirt she'd pulled off him and dropped on the floor was stained and torn beyond repair.

'We're going through a lot of clothes,' she said, more to break the silence than for any other reason.

Leesil did not respond for a long while, then finally looked at her.

'I know.' He nodded. 'I was thinking about that earlier tonight . . . seems like a long time ago. Everything was different.'

'The three of us aren't enough to deal with this,' she urged, now that she had his attention again. 'We need help from the townsfolk, as much as we can get. I don't know how to manipulate people, and you do.' She paused and added in apology, 'I mean that as a compliment.'

He didn't even pretend to bristle or take offense. His lack of reaction was beginning to gnaw at her insides. How much spirit did he have left?

'What do you want me to do?' he asked.

Magiere took a deep breath, slowly and quietly, trying not to let him see her own unease.

'Get some rest first,' she answered, standing up. 'I'll call for a town meeting downstairs later in the day. When it's time, I'll come for you. I need you to convince these people that we need their help. I have to face Rashed myself, but we need to lay a trap and that is going to take numbers. Once we get these creatures in the open, inside of town, they can't be allowed to get out again. Does that make sense?'

'Yes.' He nodded again, and she put her hand carefully against his back and helped him lie down.

Magiere pushed white-blond hair back out of his eyes and noted again how the long scratches on his face didn't really mar his narrow features. Before their arrival in Miiska, she'd never realized just how much she liked his face.

'What are you going to do now?' he asked.

She attempted a half-smile. 'I'm going to make you some soup, and hopefully not poison you in the process.'

Something in her words or manner shook him from his passive state, and he grabbed her hand. The strength in his grip surprised her. It almost hurt.

'I'm not a coward,' he said. 'You know that, don't you?'

'Of course,' she said. 'Don't be a fool.'

'There are ships leaving dock all the time. Nobody would even notice if you and I and Chap slipped out of here. We could be halfway down the coast in a few days and start over someplace else.'

The thought of flight had never occurred to her, and she did consider Leesil's words briefly. Sailing away from all this, the three of them intact and alive, was suddenly enticing. The mere thought of it brought a feeling of release that washed through her. They had enough money to start a new life and leave this horror to the people of Miiska.

But faces and names kept surfacing in her mind. Bethrae. Brenden. Eliza.

And all the others they'd heard of. The town's main warehouse was now gone, and so many lives were now affected.

'No,' she said. 'We can't just leave. If we do, everything we've done here would be for nothing. Everyone who has died will have died for nothing. We have to finish this.'

Leesil looked away.

'And this is our home,' she went on, urging him to understand. 'I've never had a home. Have you?'

Resignation cleared some of the sorrow from Leesil's

expression. He let go of her hand and relaxed against his pillow.

'No, not really. You and that dog and this broken-down tavern are the most I've ever had.'

Magiere started for the door. 'I'm going to make soup. You rest.'

Before she stepped in the hallway, he called out softly, 'I want to bury Brenden.'

She didn't answer.

Later that morning, Magiere made large pots of tea and opened a cask of good ale, while Caleb left to call a town meeting. He promised to speak to as many people as possible. By midday, when he returned, Caleb had learned a number of important revelations that he reported to Magiere.

First, the bodies of two sailors were found dead on the beach. One's throat was literally torn open. The other was found up shore, closer to Miiska. His wrist and throat were punctured. Although no one spoke of it, Caleb said both bodies were so pale that the cause of their deaths left little to mystery.

Secondly, he told her Constable Ellinwood had vanished. One of Ellinwood's guards had gone to notify him after the bodies of the sailors were discovered. His office was empty, and so were his rooms at The Velvet Rose. According to rumors – which Caleb heard through friends among the guards – nothing in either place appeared to have been packed or removed. An urn of yellow powder and a bottle of whiskey were found near a used glass, though no one seemed to know the nature of the strange powder. Loni reported that Ellinwood had left with a companion quite late in the night, or perhaps quite early in the morning, and had not returned. The constable simply disappeared.

Magiere puzzled over this. Where had he gone? In spite of the man's possessions being left behind, Magiere certainly considered Ellinwood capable of flight.

'Are the guards still looking for him?' she asked. 'Perhaps he simply spent the night with a lady friend?'

Caleb nodded. 'Yes, they've combed Miiska. No one has seen him since last night.'

It was likely something would turn up sooner or later, and Magiere had other worries. Although the constable's disappearance was puzzling, she didn't exactly find it unwelcome. Convincing the townsfolk they must defend themselves might be even easier for Leesil with their authority figurehead unexplainably missing.

The last bit of news Caleb related bothered Magiere for several reasons. Apparently, he'd asked several of the market shopkeepers to carry Brenden's body into The Sea Lion's kitchen for visitation before burial.

'He has no family left,' Caleb said. 'This is a decent act.'

Of course, it was decent. She had no argument with that. But was it wise? Leesil's current state of mind was fragile enough without Brenden's dead body lying on the kitchen table. And she mourned for Brenden, too. He was a brave man who would still be alive were it not for her. But he was beyond help now. She had to protect the living.

However, Caleb did not ask her permission. He simply announced his decision and let the matter drop. She decided to do the same.

'How soon can we expect people to arrive for the meeting?' she asked.

'Any time now.'

When she looked at him, it seemed his walk was a little more stooped and his hair a little more gray than when she had met him. Poor man. So much had happened in the past few days.

'Where's Rose?' she asked.

'I think she's sitting with Leesil. I'd better get them.'

'No, I'll do it. Why don't you find some tea mugs?'

For some reason, she didn't want Caleb to know how badly Leesil was injured. The half-elf couldn't even walk without help.

She jogged up the stairs and found Rose sitting next to him on his bed, showing him some pictures she'd drawn with charcoal on old paper. The scene struck her as too calm, too normal for their present circumstances.

'I like the one with the flowers,' he said.

Rose's muslin dress was clean, but no one had bothered to brush her hair since Beth-rae's death. It was beginning to look quite tangled. Her small face glowed with a rosy tinge. In the way of children, she accepted change and appeared to be turning to Leesil for company. The purple color of his jaw was nearly black in hue, and although the scratches on his face were healing, the savage nature behind those long claw marks was obvious.

Magiere wavered. Perhaps she should keep him up here and try to convince the townsfolk herself. But he was the talker, not her.

'Are you ready?' Magiere asked quietly.

'Yes, just help me up.'

'Come on, Rose,' Magiere said. 'We're going downstairs. You can sit with Chap by the fire.'

By the guarded wince he made, she knew the effort to stand caused Leesil more pain than he would ever admit. She pulled his arm over her shoulder and supported him as best she could.

'I know you're injured,' she said, 'but try to hurry. I want to get you settled in a chair before anyone arrives. Do you have any ideas yet?'

'Yes,' he answered. 'I know what to do.'

Not long after that, Leesil found himself in a chair by the fire, feigning comfort. He did not blame Magiere for pulling him downstairs like this to face a mass of townspeople. On the contrary, he admired her strength and clarity of thought. But at least three of his ribs were broken, and he feared that when Ratboy had thrown him against the fir tree, the action caused more damage than simply bruising his back. Sitting up was agony.

Forty men and women from Miiska were now gathered in the common room of The Sea Lion. Leesil knew Magiere had hoped for more, but forty were better than none and almost overfilled the room. Caleb served tea and Magiere served thick, nut-brown ale to those who wanted it. The whole affair appeared more like an afternoon party than a discussion of survival.

His partner walked over to him and leaned down. She was still wearing the torn blue dress, carrying a tray of ale mugs, and her hair had pulled loose from its braid. She hardly fit the image of a warrior.

'I'm going to force them to admit what we are facing, and then you explain the plan,' she whispered.

The plan? Didn't a plan usually involve careful thought and discussion? But he did not have the luxury of time. What he basically had to do was sell these people on the idea that if they wished to be saved, they would have to help save themselves.

Magiere turned to face the crowd. Karlin, the baker, and his son, Geoffry, sat directly in front of her.

'Yesterday,' she began, 'many of you donated coins to pay me and my partner for ridding this town of a nest of vampires.'

Several people flinched or gasped slightly at the use of the word 'vampires' out loud. One of them was Thomas, the candle maker. Magiere pointed at him.

'That reaction is part of your problem,' she said. 'You all know what's been going on or you wouldn't be here. But no one is willing to even openly talk about it, much less take matters into his own hands.'

'Mistress Magiere,' Karlin stammered. 'Perhaps this isn't the best way to—'

'Yes, it is,' she cut him off. 'Why did you all try to pay me? Because you know exactly what's going on. Many of the bodies you've found were buried pale and bloodless. Some of you even carried Brenden's body here today. And you saw his throat.' She glanced at Leesil and back to Karlin. 'These killers are not natural, and cannot be destroyed by natural means, but Leesil and I can't do this alone.'

Thomas was staring at her. 'What exactly do you propose?'

She motioned to Leesil. 'Let him explain.'

As he took in the hopeful, yet doubtful expressions on the faces of Miiska's shopkeepers, fishermen, and dockworkers, Leesil realized he'd have to make them trust him first. He'd have to do anything, say anything to win their confidence. Humor had served him best in this regard. He smiled weakly for effect.

'I know I'm not as pretty as usual,' he said wryly. 'But I've fought the same undead four times now and neither of us seems able to win.'

His jovial manner caused some people to relax visibly.

'None of you know Magiere or me very well,' he went on, 'but I do want you to know I've been trained in both defensive and offensive battle strategy. I was once a personal counselor to a warlord in the east, near my homeland.'

If he'd told them exactly who the warlord was, the mere mention of Darmouth's name would have won them over. But he couldn't risk becoming a legend or having word of his location reach the wrong ears. And in turn, have that someone reveal exactly who and what he had actually been in that life.

'Magiere and I now believe all three undeads escaped the fire,' he said. 'We saw the female, called Teesha, and the one who resembles a street urchin, called Ratboy, last night. The warehouse owner, who some of you know, is their leader, and we should act on the belief that he wasn't destroyed.'

'Are you saying you want us to fight these creatures?' asked a dockworker he didn't know.

'Not exactly. Magiere and Chap will do most of the fighting. What I want you to do is establish a perimeter around the tavern. The vampires seem determined to kill the three of us, so we're going to be the bait to lure them in. If enough of you can shoot crossbow quarrels soaked in garlic, it might wear them down, or at least prevent them from escaping. We're going to lay a trap.' He paused, and then added reluctantly, 'And we may have to burn a few buildings down.'

This comment brought murmurs and outright curses of disbelief from a number of those present. Leesil's voice gained strength.

'What good will those buildings be if the people of Miiska keep vanishing? You want safety? You want this problem solved? If that is your desire, then you must not only defend yourselves, you must help us carry out an attack that will finish this once and for all. I have a plan, but it's useless until I know there are enough people here with the courage to help me carry it out. I need to know first if you'll help yourselves.'

He couldn't imagine what Magiere was thinking, as he was hardly playing the role of her drunken partner these days and now sounded more like some world-weary military commander.

'I'll help,' Karlin said instantly.

'Me too,' said Geoffry.

But the rest of the crowd spoke in low voices to each other or just muttered in discomfort. Whatever their expectations for this meeting, being asked to battle vampires wasn't on the list.

Leesil did not expect to win them easily, and he was about to speak again when the door to the common room burst open. The man who stumbled through it looked vaguely familiar, and then Leesil realized it was one of the guards who'd arrested Brenden that very first night the blacksmith came to the tavern to question Ellinwood. In fact, it was the guard who had tied

Brenden's hands behind his back. He was panting hysterically, and his eyes were wild.

'Darien, what's wrong?' a young fisherwife asked, jumping to her feet and running to him.

'Korina's dead,' he breathed. 'I stood watch all night at the guard house. When I got home, I found her outside our window. . . . Her throat's torn open.'

He stopped talking and began to sob without sound.

'Who's Korina?' Leesil asked, even though the question hardly mattered.

'His wife,' Karlin said flatly. 'They'd only been married since winter.'

Gripping the table before him, Leesil somehow managed to stand.

'These creatures are growing bolder. Magiere and I can't do this alone.'

Several dockworkers crowded in around Karlin. Not pleased but resigned, one of them said, 'Tell us what to do.'

Sometime before sunset, Magiere stood in the street outside of The Velvet Rose, hesitant to go inside. She would rather have fought Rashed ten times than ask Welstiel for help again, but too many people depended on her now.

The lovely brocade curtains and white shutters seemed a travesty now. This pretty facade seemed to reinforce the notion that Miiska was safe and no unnatural beasts dug tunnels beneath it or fed on its people at night.

No one who lived here would think of helping her destroy vampires, much less admit the truth . . . except for Welstiel. But how much help was he? She'd grown tired of his cryptic advice by their second meeting. She needed specific information regarding the weaknesses of her enemies. Perhaps she never expected Leesil to win help from the common folk of Miiska. Though not exactly eloquent, his words were powerful and direct and convincing. He'd almost made *her* believe that part about him serving a warlord.

'Well, he's done it now,' she said aloud to herself.

Back at The Sea Lion, he was overseeing preparations for an attack. Such work was his domain, although she had no idea how he managed to stay on his feet. Her task was more personal, more private. She required more information about herself and about finding an effective method to destroy Rashed.

In addition, she needed more help than a few untrained shopkeepers and laborers could offer, and sitting at a desk just inside the door of The Velvet Rose was someone she'd like on her side.

Loni, the handsome elven proprietor, raised his head as she entered and stunned her with an expression of relief.

'Magiere,' he said instantly as if she were an acquaintance. 'Master Welstiel is expecting you. Please come this way.'

She stopped. 'He's expecting me?'

'Yes, yes, he's asked about your arrival several times,' he answered in near annoyance, as if any delay was too much. 'Please follow me.'

When he stood up, she noticed he was about the same height and build as her. He wore a plain, but well-made, white cotton shirt and a thick pair of black breeches. He seemed most eager to assist her and bring her down to Welstiel. Since he was being so obliging, a thought occurred.

'Loni, may I borrow some clothes?' she asked tiredly. 'If you wish, I'll pay for them.'

There was no time for a tailor, and she couldn't fight Rashed in this dress. Expecting Loni to give her a befuddled stare, she silently thanked him as he merely glanced up and down at her tattered clothing in comprehension.

'Of course,' he said. 'I'll have them ready before you leave.'

He knew what was happening, she thought. Or at least he knew something critical was happening, and that his honored guest was waiting to see Magiere, the legendary hunter of the dead. Her falchion was hanging on her hip, and he did not ask her to remove it.

Loni led the way through The Velvet Rose's opulent main room, past the paintings and blooming flowers, and down the stairs to Welstiel's room.

He knocked lightly. 'She's arrived, sir.'

Without waiting for an answer, he opened the door and ushered her inside, closing it quietly behind her.

Welstiel sat in the same chair as before, but he seemed to be brooding rather than reading this time. The room had not changed. However, his expression actually flickered in surprise at the sight of her. Not that she cared what he thought, but she knew her appearance was that of a barmaid who'd been rolled in the hay.

'How long since you've slept?' he asked.

'I don't remember. I didn't come here to discuss my sleeping habits.'

She'd never noticed how black his eyebrows were before. They contrasted sharply with the white patches at his temples.

'Why did you come here?' he asked, without moving from his chair.

'I thought there might be a slight chance you'd actually offer some help instead of your usual riddles.'

The absence of windows and the unnatural light from Welstiel's glowing orb now unnerved her slightly.

'I heard a rumor. Of course, I'm sure it's just a rumor,' he said, 'that you had enlisted some of the fishermen and dockworkers.'

'It's no rumor.'

He stood up, and his tranquil face showed a hint of anger.

'Send them home. All of them. You are *dhampir*. Involving commoners will only cause chaos. This whole affair should have been finished days ago.'

Magiere crossed her arms. 'Fine, then you and Loni carve some stakes and come fight with me.'

Welstiel's flicker of anger disappeared, and he smiled.

'I'm afraid that isn't possible, my dear. I once thought you clever, but perhaps you still don't understand. *You* are the *dhampir*. Your purpose, your existence, revolves around destroying the undead.'

A mix of fury and frustration filled her, and on impulse, she drew her sword.

'I'm so tired of your games! If you know half as much as you pretend to, then spit it out now.'

His dark eyes looked down to the falchion's edge and back up again.

'Can you feel the rage building? Every time you

battle one of these vermin, does your strength not grow?' His tone dropped low. 'Have you ever heard a foolish old saying that evil can only be conquered by good? It's a lie. Evil can only be conquered by evil. These bloodthirsty creatures are unnatural and have no place in the land of the living. However, one of them must have been wise enough, unselfish enough, to create you.'

She lowered her sword. 'What does that mean?'

Welstiel stepped a little closer.

'I have studied the ways of vampires at length. In the first days after being turned, it is still possible for one of them to create a child. One of your parents, probably your father, was undead. Half of you belongs to the dark world, a negative state of existence that needs to draw in and consume life in order to exist. But your mortal side is stronger. In *dhampirs*, this imbalance creates a hatred for their own unnatural half that they cannot control. By drawing on the powers of their black side, they become the only living weapon capable of battling and defeating vampires. Do you understand now?'

His words cut like a blade. She did not want to believe him, but could not deny recent events.

'How did you know, about me, I mean? How can you tell?'

He pointed to the leather thong and chain just visible around her neck. 'Those amulets, hiding inside your dress. Who gave them to you?'

She paused and several pieces of the puzzle began to shift reluctantly into place.

'My father, or so I was told. He left the armor and

the falchion as well. But if he were a vampire, why would he create me and then leave me weapons to destroy his own kind?'

Welstiel's hand impulsively reached out and then it stopped. Perhaps he sensed the sorrow she felt. 'Sit down,' he said.

She didn't move.

'Some vampires revel in their existence. They welcome it,' he said, 'but others are sometimes created against their will. I believe it is possible for a vampire to hate its own kind.'

He seemed to be speaking with candor, and Magiere did not know whether to be grateful or regretful. She'd spent her life blotting out her past as thoroughly as she could. As it was, there was so little of it worth remembering. Her father abandoned her and her mother was dead. Both gone from her life before she was old enough to even remember their faces. At times, she had even envied Leesil for knowing who he was and who he came from, even if he was reluctant to speak of it. Now this arrogant madman believed she was born of the same kind of creature as the ones she'd been trying to destroy ever since arriving in this town.

She didn't want to share such thoughts with Welstiel, but he seemed to know more of her than anyone. If he was right, or even partially so, then somewhere in this world her father might still . . . exist.

'You think my father was turned against his will, and he made me as some kind of weapon?'

'It is possible.'

'Then why would he leave me? He left me in a village of superstitious peasants who hated the sight of me.' She would never cry, had never cried, but her voice broke slightly. 'Why would he do that?'

'I do not know,' Welstiel answered. 'Perhaps to make you strong.'

She studied his face and the intelligence in his eyes. 'How do you know any of these things? Tell me, please.'

He paused. 'I study and I observe, and I've traveled many places. I heard a hunter of the dead was coming to live in Miiska, and I had to see for myself. The first time I saw you, I knew. Do you remember? You were in the tavern, wearing that dress, although it was in much better condition, and you tucked those amulets out of sight.'

'Yes,' she said. 'I remember.'

'Sit.' He gestured to the end of the small bed.

This time she obeyed. He pointed again at the neck-line of her dress.

'Have you figured these out yet?' he asked.

She looked down, but did not pull her amulets into view.

'I'm not sure. The topaz seems to glow when I'm near a vampire.'

He nodded. 'Yes, like the dog, it is an alarm, of sorts. It senses the presence of negative existence. The bone amulet is different. I've read of this, but yours is the first one I have seen. Undeads who feed on blood are actually feeding on the life force. They are an empty vessel that constantly needs to be refilled. A negative life force, if you will. Consuming life maintains their existence and causes them to heal so easily.

'However, you are still a living being,' he went on. 'This bone was endowed, enchanted, so that contact with a living being allows that mortal being to also absorb the life force and use it in the same way as the Noble Dead. The only living creature I know of who can consume blood the way you have already done is a *dhampir*. That amulet allows such an act to become more than feeding on blood; it allows that feeding to become the consuming of life energies directly.'

'Where would something like that come from?' she asked.

He frowned. 'You said your father left it for you. I don't have all the answers. But if I could do what you can, I would not be sitting here chatting with me. I would be preparing to fight.'

'I'm still losing every time I fight Rashed. How do I win?' she asked.

'Don't resist yourself. Become one of them. That is why they fear you, because you can use all of their strengths against them. Fight without conscience or morality. Use every one of your gifts.'

His advice was not what she wanted to hear. And she suddenly felt some anger toward him for being honest, as if blaming the messenger would bring comfort. She knew she should not blame him. But being in the same room with him was difficult now. She stood up and walked to the door.

'I won't see you again,' she said. 'After tonight there won't be a need.'

19

Wearing black breeches, a white shirt, and a snug-fitting leather vest that Loni had provided, Magiere found movement easier without her heavy skirt. When he offered, she'd allowed him to call the housemaid to comb out her hair and bind it back with a leather thong into a long tail. She found this was actually more comfortable than a braid.

His offer did not seem familiar but rather a contribution to what he either knew or suspected she was doing for his town – the act of an ally rather than a friend. After dressing, she started to tuck her amulets inside the shirt and then stopped, leaving them to dangle loosely in plain view. Perhaps the topaz stone could help warn her.

Just past sundown, Magiere walked home through the streets of Miiska. Her armor waited at The Sea Lion, but other than this, she felt ready for whatever lay ahead.

Someday, she would turn to dealing with what lay behind her in the past she'd ignored for so long.

Stands of garlic hung in every window she passed. How many times had she walked through a village decorated with garlic bulbs, some still with leaves and flowers attached?

Was she seeking redemption or forgiveness? And from whom? Why had Leesil's suggestion of flight never occurred to her?

The street was barren and abandoned. In the years of travel with Leesil, the village paths and town streets had always been empty before they 'performed.' Those with no intention of fighting, believing openly in the threat, now hid inside their homes. She couldn't blame them. When she reached The Sea Lion, she went around back and approached the kitchen door. It was ajar, and a bizarre sight greeted her.

Brenden's cleanly dressed body lay stretched out on the table. He was clad in a green tunic, dark breeches, and polished boots. The tunic's collar covered his throat. Near the end of the table, Leesil sat on a stool, soaking quarrels in a large bucket of brown water. He moved slowly, as if each small effort hurt him. The bandages around his ribcage hung loose.

'You should be in bed,' she said from the doorway.

He managed a smile. 'You'll get no argument from me, but we've got a long night ahead.'

She came in to stand by the table, looking down at Brenden's closed eyes.

'It's like he's asleep,' she said, 'as though he'd been peeling potatoes for a party and stretched out to nod off on the table.'

She had no time to properly mourn Brenden, but his pale skin and endless slumber did not allow neglect.

'I know,' Leesil answered. 'It was a macabre sight. There were near a dozen people in here all working with me. I kept trying to ignore him as he lay there, but then I had to send the townsfolk to their places, and for quite a while, it's just been me and him. I actually talked to him, chastising him for sleeping on the job. Sounds crazy, yes?'

Magiere touched Brenden's stiff shoulder. 'No, it doesn't. I never thanked him for carrying me out of those tunnels.'

'He didn't expect thanks – not from us.'

All the pots and pans were scattered about, some full of garlic water, some empty.

She sighed. 'I have to get my armor. Are we ready?'

'Yes, I think so. Oh, there was a hidden cellar beneath the floor of the stable just up the road from us. I've had Rose and the other children moved there . . . as many of the youngest that could fit.'

'Good, where are you going to be?'

'With Karlin and our so-called "archers." They'll need direction when the fighting starts.'

Magiere blinked. 'Leesil, you can barely walk.'

'I'll be all right. Caleb made me chew some foul-smelling bark that deadens pain. Tasted even worse than it smelled. I only need to make it through the next few hours.'

Every instinct told her that she should track him and knock him out cold from behind. She could hide him below the stable with Rose. But he was right. The others would need direction and someone with clear wits to hold them together. Half of them would probably run at the first sight of Rashed.

Leesil was so calm, and he'd put up with so much.

'Be careful,' she said simply.

'You, too.'

When Rashed woke, his senses told him sunset had long passed. The hull floor felt hard. He turned over and pushed himself up. He was alone.

'Teesha?' He scrambled to his feet, instantly awake. 'Teesha?' he called louder.

Crawling through the trapdoor to the boat's deck, he cast out with his thoughts for any trace of her presence. He'd never been able to sense another of his own kind, except his brother, Parko, but he tried it just the same. Only the background tingle of forest life answered him.

Caution abandoned, Rashed dropped to the shore, calling aloud and not caring who heard him. 'Teesha!'

'She's gone,' a hollow voice whispered.

The tragic visage of Edwan materialized beside him. Although Rashed could not help feeling some pity for the ghost, he disliked having to speak with Teesha's dead husband. Worry now overrode such personal distaste.

'Where?' he asked.

'Into town, to defend you.' Edwan sneered in open hatred, the twist of his mouth awkward looking on his tilted head.

A jolt ran through Rashed. At first, he did not recognize the sensation, smothered in astonishment as it was. Then it cleared, and he could feel the fear.

'Why didn't you stop her?' he demanded.

'Me? Stop her?' Edwan's transparent features were vacant, not from lack of feeling, but from anger and hate turned bitterly cold. 'She listens to no one but you, cares for no one but you. Did you see her shed sorrow over Ratboy's departure?'

Rashed bit back a retort, suddenly pitying Edwan. He regretted Corische's act of executing a helpless bartender, but such sentiments were trivial – a mere shadow compared to Teesha's safety.

'Where has she gone?' he asked with as much calm as he could feign.

For the first time in Rashed's memory, Edwan's manner altered to one of obvious desperation. His long yellow hair seemed to float on an invisible wind, and his voice pleaded.

'Listen to me. That hunter is not mortal. Do you understand? She is half Noble Dead – half of your kind.' He faltered. 'Teesha cares nothing for revenge. Find her and leave this place, please. I have never asked you for anything and never expected anything. I ask this of you now.'

Rashed crossed his arms in frustration.

'Edwan,' he tried to sound patient, 'I can not. If I leave that hunter alive, we will never be safe.'

'I think . . . I was wrong about the hunter's intentions!' the ghost cried. 'She was counseled by the stranger living in the cellar of The Velvet Rose. And now you and she are caught up in playing some tit-for-tat game of revenge. Someone else has been urging her on and, in turn, you keep coming back to her. You are each blindly convinced the other is an enemy seeking a battle. Can you not see that? Find Teesha and take her away. No one will follow.'

Rashed strapped on his long sword, picked up an unlit torch he'd prepared the night before, and then waved one hand in dismissal. 'Go. You are no help to me.'

As soon as the words left his mouth, the ghost's form began slowly spinning around, its image warping in the air with frustration. At first, Rashed thought the spirit was trying to do something, use some new ability never before displayed. The whirl of mist continued, and it became clear to Rashed that the ghost was merely entangled in its own rage and helplessness.

'You are a fool!' Edwan cried.

Rashed left him there and ran into the woods, leaving the boat and all his tools behind. Dark trees around him pulsed with life, and near the edge of the forest, he stopped and closed his eyes, seeking outward. Although Teesha's mental abilities were more defined than his, he possessed a few strong talents that he'd rarely used. His own thoughts were now stained with the sensations of a hunt – urgency, the smell of a prey's trail tainted with fear, the rush of hunger as the chase closed, and all the other things that called to a predator.

From far away, a sound reached his ears. It was so distant and faint that no one else might have noticed it among the soft night noises.

A wolf let go a long, throated howl.

'Children of the hunt,' he whispered, concentrating. 'Come now.'

Leesil leaned against the front wall of a candle maker's shop just across the street from the tavern. He wondered how much longer he could stay on his feet.

Karlin the baker stood nearby, anxiously peering this way and that. Leesil tried to hide his own physical condition as well as he could. The pain in his chest and back had long since spread to a numb rebellion throughout his whole body. He feared his legs would buckle and betray him, but he had to keep going.

Magiere was inside the tavern, donning her armor while he carried out his part of the plan. Sensible in its simplicity, it entailed arming the townsfolk with bows, if possible, and pitchforks and shovels when necessary. He'd placed most of them on watch inside homes, shacks, and small buildings in a perimeter around The Sea Lion, as too many on the roofs or outside would give them away. He'd wanted to prepare a firetrap ahead of time, but rejected the idea as too easy for the enemy to spot. Instead, he had women armed with dry boards, flasks of oil, and flint with makeshift lines of tinder and wood between buildings, ready to be ignited quickly if needed.

The whole point was to keep the vampires inside the perimeter and not allow them to escape once they entered. He had no idea what more these creatures were capable of, but hoped he'd already seen all they could do. There were childhood tales he remembered of undeads that flew or transformed into beasts large and small. He said nothing of this to the townsfolk.

To their advantage, four of Ellinwood's patrol guards – Darien among them – had offered their help. Leesil had positioned them in an old storehouse close to the tavern. Two of them were even properly armed and looked capable of hard fighting. Perhaps, like Darien, they had lost loved ones, or they were just disconcerted by Ellinwood's disappearance and looking for leadership. Leesil didn't care which. He was just slightly relieved to have anyone besides bakers, weavers, townsfolk, and merchants to hold things together.

Strangely enough, his right hand and most dependable 'soldier' was Karlin. The man's resourcefulness was astonishing. Between Karlin's ability to organize a band of frightened laborers and find a wealth of tools to serve as weapons, Leesil could not have managed without him. Now the two of them moved to stand outside the tavern, occasionally seeing one of the townsfolk peering out a window.

'Everyone ready?' Leesil asked, not remembering until too late that he'd already asked this same question twice before.

Karlin nodded, and for a moment he reminded Leesil of Brenden. Although he was beardless, the baker's solid, yet massive, form and matter-of-fact countenance were familiar. He was also considerate of others and had brought Leesil a heavy, dark blue shirt which hid the half-elf's injuries and helped him blend into the night. Leesil tied his hair under a long black scarf, the last wrap of which he pulled across his face, leaving only his eyes exposed. He could vanish into the night shadows if need be.

'What if one escapes from the tavern and Magiere can't kill it?' Karlin asked, voicing doubts for the first time now that they were alone.

'I've told the archers and the guards in that storehouse to inflict any harm possible.' Leesil lifted his hand and held up an ax. 'If they can even stun it, I think I can take its head off.'

Karlin flinched, biting his lower lip.

'It may sound grisly,' Leesil admitted, 'but what it would do if it escaped would be far worse.'

'I'm not questioning you,' Karlin answered softly. 'You and Magiere have more courage than I can imagine.'

'And Brenden.'

'Yes,' the baker said, nodding. 'And Brenden.'

Leesil recalled his first proposal that morning, that he and Magiere find a ship or boat and disappear. If Karlin knew that, he wouldn't think so highly of his present company.

'We should keep out of sight for now,' Leesil said. 'Everyone knows what to do. I want to stay close to the tavern. With the guards on the seaside, we stay in this shack, landside. If need arises, we'll be able to close in.'

Karlin nodded. For some unsettling reason, Leesil thought of his own beautiful mother and the green trees of his homeland. They were bare in the winter and lush in the spring, so unlike these cold firs and evergreens around him now that never changed. Of all the places where, and for all the reasons why, he thought he would die, defending a small coastal town of common folk from undeads was not among the possibilities he'd ever imagined. But then again, perhaps Karlin and these laborers had nothing to do with his efforts. Of the faces pushing to the forefront of his mind, only one truly mattered – one with smooth, pale skin, a serious expression, and thick black hair that shimmered red in the light.

Teesha never spoke of nor consciously acknowledged several senses she'd developed after Corische turned her. She considered a heightened sense of smell, attuned to all the small and tedious odors constantly present, to be unladylike. Nevertheless, as she slipped into Miiska and approached Magiere's tavern, the *smell* of the town was wrong. Scents of perspiration from fear and nervous exhaustion hit her and continued to grow the closer she drew to The Sea Lion. The strength of it contradicted the quiet of the empty streets.

Casting out with her mind, she absorbed a jumble of thoughts carried on the presence of life in the town.

I'm thirsty.

Where's Mother?

Joshua always teases me because I'm short.

I'm going to marry Leesil when I grow up.

Mustn't let 'em escape Magiere.

What simpletons these mortals were. Then she caught a flash of thoughts joined in a cluster. Frightened, but simple and clear.

Children. Where were they?

Turning in the night air with eyes half closed, she felt for their origin, as if the cluster of thoughts were a breeze she could feel upon her face and judge its direction.

Moving quietly along the sides of buildings, Teesha stopped when the wash of thoughts across her became strong and near. She found herself facing the end of one of the main streets toward a stable in the lower half of town not far from the tavern. On the roof, she could make out two adult men crouched or sitting. She felt the tension in them, and it was easy enough to send them a tingle of apprehension that made both turn toward the shoreline, as if unsure whether they had heard something. She slipped silently across the road to the wall of the stable.

Teesha lingered on the outside, carefully separating the patterns until she could identify at least ten . . . no, twelve young minds somewhere within. She was about to step in and seek them out, then stopped.

Empty streets smothered in fear.

Children hidden away.

Two guards on the roof.

They had laid a trap in the town.

She slipped inside the stable's door. Upon her entrance, a large bay gelding threw his head and snorted. Entering his thoughts, she calmed him.

'Shhhh, sweet beast,' she crooned softly to the horse. 'The night is when you sleep.'

The gelding quieted, pawed once at his stall floor, and settled with eyelids drooping.

Teesha sensed that one of the smaller girls missed her mother terribly. Looking about, all she could see were two bales of hay, straw scattered thickly across the floor, a few broken pitchforks, and the one horse in its stall. The other five stalls proved empty. She looked about once more, then stood motionless.

'Murika,' she called in a gentle voice. 'Where are you?'

Silence followed and then, 'Mama? I'm down here.'

Down. They hid somewhere below.

She searched the floor, pulling aside the straw as quietly as she could, and finally found a trapdoor. Fairly well-crafted, it was disguised with a layer of dirt beneath the scattered straw. It opened easily, and peering down, she found a huddle of small children, all looking back up at her with curious stares. Not one was above eight years old.

Teesha smiled warmly.

'Well, hello,' she said. 'What are you doing?'

'Hiding,' a green-eyed boy of about six answered. 'You should hide too. Something bad is going to happen, and we have to be quiet.'

'You're not being quiet,' scolded a smaller girl to his right.

Teesha nodded in agreement and then sent out the mental suggestion that this event was only a dream. 'I'll be very quiet, too. Now tell me, which one of you wants to marry Leesil?'

A lovely girl of about five years old stood up. Although

her hair was badly in need of a brushing, creamy skin and tiny features marked her as a future beauty. Even her miniature hands were already dainty and fine.

'I'm Rose.'

Teesha's smile blossomed. 'Well, he sent me to find you. Come, dear.'

Little Rose hurried over without question and held up her hands. Teesha grasped them and lifted her out of the hiding hole. As Teesha carried her from the stable, she felt the softness of the girl's muslin dress and the warmth of the small body beneath the cloth. No one on the roof saw them leave.

The streets were almost black this far from the center of town. Teesha flitted from the deeper shadows of the buildings, working her way out back to move along the shore side of town. She occasionally caught the presence or thoughts of a fear-filled person hiding somewhere nearby. And though she could not see them, as with the guards on the roof of the stable, it was easy enough to push their thoughts and drive their attention away from her path. She dashed quickly across the last open space and around to the backside of The Sea Lion.

Teesha shifted Rose to sit on her hip and wrapped one arm around the child's waist.

'Hang on to my neck, dear,' she murmured. 'We're going to climb up the building and then crawl through your window.'

'I like your dress. I always wanted a red dress,' Rose answered.

'Well, then you should have one, as red as they come. Now take hold of my neck.'

Scaling the tavern was a simple matter for Teesha. She

cradled Rose carefully while entering through a broken upstairs bedroom window.

'This isn't my room,' Rose said matter-of-factly. 'It's Magiere's.'

'Really?' Teesha answered. 'How nice.'

She had no idea how long it would take Rashed to wake and begin his attack. His only real weakness was an uneven dormant pattern. But now, the purpose of the moment began to play on her. Carrying Rose to the far side of the room, she set the child on the floor in direct line of sight with the open door. She then knelt down.

'Look at me,' she said.

Oval brown eyes obediently moved to Teesha's face – which shifted instantly to a grimace of fangs and glimmering translucent eyes drawn wide with hunger.

'Scream,' she ordered.

Rose screamed.

Sword in hand, Magiere crouched behind the bar, peering out a small hole she'd gouged through its wall. Rashed would likely want to trap her upstairs again, where she had less room to swing her falchion and he could better use his size and strength. As it was, he'd probably search the entire upper floor before coming down, and from her current position, she could watch him descend. If he got close enough to her hiding place, she might be able to take his head off in a moment of surprise. Chap sat beside her, occasionally pushing his nose against her arm but otherwise obediently silent. She no longer doubted anything strange or uncanny he appeared to do. His calm state told her they still had time left to wait.

Then Chap jumped to his feet, growling softly, his attention focused upward.

'Shhhh, don't give us away,' she whispered.

She knew he wouldn't, but felt a need to remind him. All the two of them had to do was wait for Rashed to finish his search and come down the stairs. The wooden boards beneath her knees were attached to her home, to her business, and she would defend them. She leaned closer to the hole and peered toward the stairs.

Noticing soft light reflecting off the wood near her face, she glanced down. Her topaz stone was glowing. Chap whined almost pitifully, and Magiere was about to tell him to be quiet again, when a scream rang out from upstairs — female, high pitched, and terrified. A child's voice.

Magiere knew the voice. It was Rose's.

Chap rounded the bar toward the stairs before she could respond, forcing her to follow.

'Wait!' she ordered in a loud whisper.

He stopped, growling low, body trembling.

Magiere had counted on meeting Rashed in an open fight. She had felt his thoughts in the cave below the warehouse. Monster or not, she'd felt his perverted warrior's sense that would bid him to attack alone. Would Rashed use a child as bait? Such an act seemed out of character. She joined Chap at the foot of the stairs.

Rose screamed again and didn't stop this time. Magiere grabbed the scruff of Chap's neck.

'Slowly,' she said. 'Keep a sharp watch.'

She hated allowing herself to be lured into a trap, but there was no choice. Rose was in danger.

Staying alert, they crept up the stairs toward the sound

of Rose's cries. Not running to help her became more difficult with each step. Nearer the top, she could tell the sound came from her own room. She peered quickly around the wall's edge with one eye, then pulled back. The door was wide open.

'Get Rose,' Magiere whispered. 'Do you understand? I'll fight. You just get Rose.'

Chap stuck his head out around the top of the stairs toward the door, then back toward Magiere, and he growled.

Magiere stepped into the hallway to see Rose sitting on the floor of her room, crying loudly. She appeared unhurt, but tears streaked her face, and she was so frightened that Magiere struggled not to simply run in and grab her. Otherwise, the room, what she could see of it, appeared empty.

'Come here,' she whispered, hoping Rose might be able to run out on her own. 'Come out of there, now.'

Rose only shook and cried harder.

Magiere stepped forward cautiously, Chap inching along close at her side. As she approached the doorway, she leaned her back near the right wall and, stepping sideways along it, watched the left side of the room come into view around the doorjamb. She held out her hand to Chap, motioning him to wait. When her shoulder brushed the doorjamb, the whole room was in view.

It was empty, wind blowing through the still-broken window where Rashed had crashed outward several nights before. She relaxed slightly, and reached out her hand to Rose.

Rose's eyes turned upward.

Magiere ducked as a hand slashed down from above

the door. Fingernails raked her throat in a wild attempt at a grip as a body landed on her back, driving her down on one knee. Rose's cries turned to hysterical screams, mixing with Chap's snarls.

The hand grasping her jaw still fought for a grip, and if it managed one, it would most likely snap her neck. Strength and rage welled up in Magiere, but this time she knew it would come, and so it did not overwhelm her.

She pushed off from her folded legs, curling her head and shoulders down, and turning in mid dive until her back and her attacker led the slide across the floor. When she collided with the nearest bedpost, the attacker was caught between the post and her own back.

The bed lurched and the hand across Magiere's jaw lost its grip entirely.

Magiere rammed her elbow backward. The point of it connected with her attacker's torso, and she was able to scramble away, spinning around on hands and knees to hold the falchion at guard in front of her.

As in the forest the night before, just the sight of Teesha caused Magiere to hesitate. Everything about this exquisite creature seemed like a dream, unreal. But the scratches on Magiere's throat felt real enough, reminding her of the danger.

Teesha was on her feet instantly, and Magiere lunged, driving her around the bed's end and across the small room. Magiere shifted in the other direction across the side of the bed, ready to cut through lithe woman's back if she tried for the window.

'Now, Chap!'

Teesha froze as Chap rushed in, gripped the back of

Rose's muslin dress with his teeth, and dragged the screaming child into the hallway out of sight.

Open, honest emotion shone off Teesha's fine features – hatred.

'You thought to break my neck when I entered?' Magiere asked. 'Do you have another idea now?'

'I can move faster than you. I won't let you hurt him again.'

Magiere experienced an unwanted moment of hesitation. The uncontrollable fury she normally dealt with when facing these creatures seemed weak.

She looked at Teesha's brown curls and red gown and small waist. There was no sword in Teesha's hand. She simply appeared to be a lovely young woman. Enraged, but not a monster. And even though Magiere knew better, Teesha's appearance affected her, as did the small woman's words. This creature was trying to protect its . . . partner, companion . . . mate?

'I never wanted this battle,' Magiere said, not quite sure why she spoke. 'He started this.'

'Rashed? No, you began this.'

'It was him, and Ratboy, who broke into my home and killed Rose's grandmother.'

'After you befriended the blacksmith, sniffing about his sister's death place, asking questions. Lie to yourself if you want, but not to me. You've been hunting us since the day you arrived.'

Confusion threatened Magiere. Is that what they thought, that she'd come here to hunt them?

'No, Teesha. I never—'

'You're tired,' Teesha said, her voice melting from cold anger to sweet comfort. 'I can see it in your face. And no wonder, after what you have been through these past nights. Poor thing.'

Warmth and sympathy swirled inside Magiere's mind.

'Life isn't easy for your kind,' the compassionate voice said softly. 'No, it's just as hard as ours. Always in motion, alert, waiting and watching. Sit with me, share with me. I will listen. I will understand.'

Magiere once saw a tapestry of a sea nymph on the wall of an expensive inn. The tapestry was so well executed that she remembered standing for a long time and examining every detail. The portrayal was so alive as the nymph's arms reached outward in welcome, abundant dark hair falling to her waist, stray damp curls clinging to narrow cheeks.

Teesha sat before her on the rocks, droplets of seawater clinging to the bare skin of her cheeks and throat. Did she wear a red dress? Did the smooth white of her stomach show through a jagged rip in the cloth? The compassionate eyes looked at Magiere. Arms stretched out to invite her.

All she had to do was lower her sword and lay her head on the nymph's shoulder. Teesha would understand. No one in Magiere's life had ever held her, comforted her, that she remembered. Not friends . . . there had been no friends . . . not family, not even Aunt Bieja.

Leesil. He had done this once, one long night on the road, or had it been twice? Had it really happened at all?

Magiere stepped forward and was rewarded with a grateful smile.

'Tell me everything,' Teesha whispered. 'I will care for you. I will take your sorrows and drain them away.'

Her fingers brushed Magiere's chin and moved up to stroke her temple.

Chap growled from the open doorway.

Teesha's attention flickered briefly toward the dog.

The nymph faded from Magiere's visions. There was only the woman, the creature. Teesha. Magiere back-stepped once as her sword arm pulled up and swung level.

Teesha's focus shifted instantly back to Magiere.

Realization didn't dawn on Magiere until she found herself looking down at the red-clad body lying limp across her bed. The head still rocked on the floor where it had fallen, neck stump dripping dark fluid onto the floor and into its disheveled hair. The eyes were locked wide, but the pale face was blank of expression.

Instead of triumph, loss and regret hit Magiere. Two single tears slipped out, not at the death of this creature so much as the death of the illusion Teesha had painted in her mind.

Chap sniffed at the head, then barked low and soft.

'Take Rose back to the stable and protect the children,' she ordered him.

He looked up at her with a low whine of obvious disagreement.

'Do it!' she said.

Chap hesitated briefly, then left the room.

Magiere stood there for a long time. Finally, she picked up Teesha's head by its hair and walked back downstairs.

20

Leesil waited tensely inside the shack with no idea the battle had already begun. The dwelling he crouched inside was not a home. Barely large enough for Karlin and himself to hide in, it must have once been a kind of toolshed. Now only spiders and a broken rake inhabited the place.

'It's well past sundown,' Karlin whispered. 'Shouldn't something have happened?'

'I don't know,' Leesil answered honestly. 'If they've discovered we're prepared, they may wait a long time.'

'People will already be shaking from fear. Much longer, and they'll be exhausted.'

'Exactly. Hence, the waiting if they know something is happening.'

Leesil peered out a crack in the door, hoping to see something, anything, when he heard Rose scream. The sound shot through him like an arrow, and he burst out into the street without thinking.

'Rose?' he called and started for the stable up the street.

Another scream rang out, and in confusion, he turned toward the tavern. Karlin now stood beside him.

More screams echoed through the town around him.

Turning, he saw two dockworkers run from their hiding places in panic. Snarls and growls followed frightened cries, and Leesil stood dumbfounded, not knowing what he should do.

Wolves.

Long-legged, enraged animals were running in the streets and attacking Miiska's citizens. Some were even jumping through windows. Geoffry, Karlin's son, was holding off an enormous black beast with a makeshift spear. Leesil dropped his ax, grabbed Karlin's crossbow out of the man's hands, and fired, catching the wolf through the throat.

'Get off the ground!' he yelled.

The streets turned to chaos. His simple but well-laid plan shattered into pieces as more canine creatures appeared from around side streets to savagely rout his people from their hiding places. Thoughts of undeads disappeared as weapons and terror shifted toward new targets.

The wolves were not starving, mangy beasts. They appeared to be healthy timber wolves, except they had gone mad and were attacking anything human that moved. He and Magiere had some experience with wolves on the open road in Stravina, but he'd never known one to attack a person, unless famine or disease drove it to desperate action. Wolves avoided areas where people settled. But now, these tall, gray-and-black furred creatures ran down and savaged random citizens. Screams and snarls filled the night air.

'Leesil!' Karlin shouted. 'The tavern's on fire.'

Rashed sent the wolves ahead, following rapidly through the trees toward Miiska. This time it would be the hunter who was caught off guard, distracted by carnage, and he would be the one with well-prepared forces. While he did not consider wolves to be complex creatures, they became quite single-minded when he set them to a task for which they were suited. With one thought image, he showed them that task, ordering them to attack and kill anything that moved. They obeyed.

Reaching the edge of town, he strode in without hesitation, carrying a burning torch in one hand and his sword in the other. There was no time or need to hide in shadows now.

He felt no satisfaction when the screaming began. Random violence was distasteful and lacked honor. Even killing to feed was a foolish act that raised suspicion and depleted the local food supply. But the hunter had retreated to hide among the townspeople, so the town itself must be otherwise occupied for him to pull her into the open and finish this conflict. The hunter had forced him to this slaughter.

The closer he drew to the tavern, the more people ran out of nearby buildings, and this puzzled him. Few mortals made their homes near the docks or as far south in the town as The Sea Lion. He saw armed men jumping off roofs to either save those on the ground or escape from a wolf that had found its way up.

Magiere, the spineless hunter, had set a trap, hiding behind simple townsfolk and laborers. The thought angered him.

No one noticed him as he strode purposefully toward the tavern. In fact, only when the dwelling was directly in his sight did one person even try to stop him. A young town guard was aiming a crossbow at a wolf across the street when he saw Rashed and started slightly. Instead of shooting at the wolf, he aimed at Rashed and fired.

At full strength and concentration, the Noble Dead simply caught the quarrel in mid-air and tossed it aside.

The young guard's eyes widened, and he ran away.

Rashed did not follow. Instead, he walked up to The Sea Lion, kicked a few boards at its base loose, and thrust the torch's head in among them. The tavern's wood was old and dry, and burst into flames. He quickly repeated this act on each side of the building, leaving the back until last, after which he threw the torch through the upper window of what he knew was her bedroom. Then he returned to the front to wait for Magiere. She was inside. He could feel her presence after so many close encounters. He watched the door and windows for any glimpse of her.

At first he saw nothing. Then a flicker of movement passed by the small window to the left of the front door. His eyes focused between the door and main window of the common room, one of its shutters torn off and lying on the ground.

Magiere stepped into plain view through the larger window.

He was not surprised by her sudden appearance, but rather by her composure. Hair pulled back and armor cleaned, her expression was calm. She appeared fresh and rested, not like someone who'd been fighting night after night. The fire was spreading and devouring the tavern, but neither that nor the battle in the streets affected her. Why didn't she run out?

They stood, staring at each other. She gripped her falchion in one hand and kept the other hand hidden behind her.

Without a word, she lifted her concealed hand. For

a moment, Rashed could not see what she held through the fire's glare and the dark inside the tavern. A distinct shape dangled down from brown strands of hair clenched in her fist.

Teesha's head.

Leesil's body no longer functioned as he wished, and desperation ran out of him in sweat that chilled on his skin in the cool night air. He'd worked his way through the turmoil, trying to drive off beasts assaulting people in the street, and now found himself near the shore, with the docks to the north of him and the near side of the tavern just to the south. Everything had deteriorated into confusion. Then Karlin shouted at him.

The Sea Lion was on fire.

Two bodies with torn throats lay between him and the burning tavern. In his present condition, he could not help Magiere fight, even if he could get to her. Staying on his feet was becoming more difficult with each passing moment.

Leesil looked frantically around, but saw no one he could call to assist with putting out the fire. Of the few people still standing, most were running or fighting for their lives. Should he try to organize some semblance of a retreat? If so, how?

From around the back of the tavern came Chap, lunging hard with legs bent as he used shoulders and haunches to struggle forward as quickly as he could. Cloth was clamped between his teeth as he dragged something across the ground away from the fire.

If Chap had come from the tavern, then Magiere was still inside. Why wasn't the dog in there helping her?

'Chap,' Leesil called. 'Here, boy.'

Leesil dropped the empty crossbow and leaned against the buildings as he struggled forward.

A building-and-a-half away from the tavern now, Chap spotted Leesil and stopped, letting go of his burden. The dog then ran back and forth and around whatever he'd been dragging, barking loudly and unwilling to leave it. When Leesil reached Chap's side, he understood.

Rose's half-conscious form lay on the ground. This was why Chap had left Magiere's side.

'It's all right,' he said.

Crouching down, he caught himself from falling with one hand on the ground. Rose lifted her head, face tear streaked.

'Leesil!' she cried, reaching out her hands.

That was good. If she could still talk and move, then whatever had happened, it had likely not caused her any lasting harm. He doubted he could get to Magiere, and the townsfolk were now beyond his help. But he could save Rose.

The dog whined and licked his face. Rose crawled to her feet and grabbed his neck, hanging on tightly. Her slight weight hurt his ribs and back.

'Can you walk?' he panted. 'I can't carry you.'

She seemed confused, then nodded in comprehension. 'Yes, I can.'

'Take me to the stable, to the other children,' he said.

For one so young and frightened, she grasped his meaning quickly. Leading him by the hand, she hurried toward the stable, moving faster than he could and attempting to pull him along. Chap ranged alongside, ears pricked up at the sights and sounds of people fighting off wolves somewhere down the side streets. The night grew darker as they moved farther from the burning tavern. Leesil ignored everything but the need to keep moving. When they reached the stable door, he managed to jerk it open and then froze.

Two large wolves – one dusty black and the other gray – loped about inside, sniffing and pawing through the floor straw, searching for a way to get to what they smelled below. The children. Both of them lifted their heads and two sets of yellow eyes locked on the new arrivals.

The black wolf snarled, and Chap charged. Furred bodies collided.

'Rose, get up on the hay!' Leesil shouted, casting around for anything to use as a weapon. Every pitchfork and shovel had been cleaned out by the townsfolk earlier that day.

Rose scrambled as high as she could up the loose pile of hay strewn around two stacked bales. Chap and the black wolf rolled across the wooden floor like coiling snakes.

Leesil saw the gray wolf's sharp fangs and tensing muscles as it lunged two steps toward him and attacked. Fear and instinct took over, driving his actions.

One arm shot up to guard his head and throat, as his other swung down hard to his side in a flicking motion. The strap that held his stiletto in place snapped free and the hilt dropped into his hand. The wolf's teeth snapped closed around his raised arm.

When the animal's forepaws hit his chest, he felt his broken ribs stab deeper into his body, stopping his breath. He let the wolf's weight topple them both to the floor.

The impact sent another shock of pain through his body.

In the same fluid movement with which he'd once pinned Brenden to the tavern floor, he rolled with the wolf's weight, pushing its jaws upward with his forearm to trap its head against the floor. With the last inertia of his roll, he rammed the stiletto down through the animal's eye.

There was a crunch as the blade tip broke through bone and passed into the skull. The furred body spasmed once, then ceased moving. Leesil flopped over to the floor and tried to get air back into his lungs again.

Chap snapped and battered with his paws again and again at the other wolf, the two of them twisting and turning about each other. Leesil tried to move, to help, but nothing happened. His breath came in short sucking gasps that hurt so badly he wanted to stop breathing altogether.

There was no sound from the children below. Either blind fear or good sense had kept them from giving their position away.

Chap caught his opponent's front leg and bit down. A loud snap and a yelp announced the end of the fight, and Leesil felt one small moment of pride. Stout Chap had been running down undeads. Dealing with a mere wolf was only a matter of moments.

The wounded animal stumbled out the stable doors on three legs, moving as fast as it was able. Chap let it go and reached Leesil about the same time that Rose climbed down from the hay.

'Get below,' Leesil whispered. 'You have to hide with the others.'

Rose didn't move. She wouldn't leave him.

'Listen to me—' he hissed in anger, but he didn't finish before darkness filled his head, and he dropped limp and unconscious.

When Magiere held Teesha's head up, she expected to see rage and thirst for vengeance color Rashed's face. With the growing flames between them, she anticipated the satisfaction of driving him to wild action.

At first, absolute incomprehension registered in his crystalline eyes – then horror – and finally something between fear and pain.

'Teesha?' he mouthed as a question, though Magiere could not hear his voice over the sound of the fire.

Magiere felt an unexpected and unwanted sensation of guilt, but swallowed it down.

'Here I am,' she called, determined to finish what *he* had started. 'Why don't you come take my head?'

He could not have heard her either, but at those words he cried out incoherently and came crashing through the window, the base of the wall below it giving way before his legs. Burning boards dropped around him, and he gripped his long sword as if it were the only thing that mattered.

Still Magiere felt nothing she expected. Sorrow danced around the edge of his cry, not rage.

'Coward!' he managed to yell before swinging so hard that Magiere dropped Teesha's head and jumped back instead of blocking. His attack now stirred the power and anger she longed for.

With Teesha, she had controlled that rage and how it affected her actions, and she believed she could have done so even now. But she didn't want to, and she let it take her, rushing through her body. The sharpness inside of her mouth was welcome, no longer unsettling. To destroy him, she would become him – one of his kind.

The common room had always felt large and open before, but standing inside the growing fire and forced to back away from Rashed, Magiere suddenly felt trapped in too small a space. His physical presence felt too close, too immediate.

Rashed positioned himself between her and the open wall, standing his ground, waiting. She hated him for the murdering monster that he was, but admired his strategy in the midst of all this madness. He wasn't going to let her out. Whether he killed her with a sword or forced her to burn in the fire didn't matter. Before long, the second floor would cave in.

If that was his plan, then let him try. This time, she charged.

Steel clanked on steel, and Magiere forgot Rashed's grief at seeing Teesha's severed head.

Every move he made was familiar, as if she could feel his intent before the action. They each swung and blocked and swung again. Somewhere in the back of her thoughts a voice whispered that if they didn't run from the tavern soon, they would both burn to death. Did that matter? It didn't seem to matter to him. No, and nothing mattered to her but cleaving Rashed's head from his body.

Heat from the inferno around them caused her to choke, and the flames grew hotter and higher. His blade nearly caught her shoulder as she gulped in scorching air. He jerked his sword up and left himself wide open while attempting to cleave her skull. Instead of opting for a sane, defensive move, she thrust upward, aiming for his stomach.

'You fools!' someone shrieked.

The unexpected cry startled both of them and each missed their blow. Even through the smoke and fire, Magiere clearly saw a horrible visage that disrupted her bloodlust.

Floating over Teesha's head was the ghost of a nearly beheaded man, his long yellow hair hanging from his tilted head. Magiere had thought nothing could shock her anymore, but even in her rage the bright hues of his open throat pulled her attention, flames flickering through his transparent body.

'You fools!' he repeated. His face exuded all the rage and venom she'd expected in Rashed's.

'Get away, Edwan,' Rashed shouted over the fire. 'Vengeance is beyond you.'

'Vengeance?' the ghost answered in disbelief. 'You murdered her. You and your pride. Can't either of you see what's happening? Did either of you want this?' He drifted down to kneel near Teesha's severed head, his face weeping, but without tears. 'You slew my Teesha.'

Magiere stumbled once. Nothing made sense. No action seemed correct. The heat inside her began to fade and, instead, she felt the bright flames around searing her flesh. Her leather armor smoldered in several places.

When she looked back to Rashed, she saw the tavern stairs behind him and realized they had maneuvered completely around each other. Her back was now to the opening in the front wall where he'd crashed through moments earlier.

Magiere backed up hesitantly.

'No!' Rashed shouted, flames reflecting off his hard crystal eyes.

An ear-splitting crack sounded overhead. Magiere's gaze turned up briefly. The upper floor began to give way. The desire to survive won out.

She turned and dove through the jagged opening in the wall, shielding her face with one arm. Fresh air from the open street flooded inside her as she rolled once across the ground and came up to look back into the flames.

A heavy beam wider than his chest pinned Rashed to the floor, and he lay completely engulfed in flames, fighting to get up. His thrashing limbs were like waving branches of fire. Over the blaze's roar, she couldn't hear anything, and wondered if he was screaming.

The beheaded figure flitted about the room, in and out of the flames devouring Rashed. The ghost appeared to be laughing.

Magiere staggered back a few paces more and sank to the ground. She watched Rashed's writhing, burning form until he stopped moving. Then the entire upstairs floor caved in. Sparks flew like a thousand fireflies into the night air.

Aside from all the methods she had learned from villagers' folklore and legends, she thought burning an undead's body completely to ash was as good as any other way to destroy it.

Where was her earthen jar to trap his spirit now? Where were the peasants to sigh in relief? How brave, how very brave she was to have leaped away and watched her enemy become trapped under a flaming crossbeam.

The topaz amulet around her neck glowed steadily.

A light brighter than the flames flashed beside her and the horrible visage of the beheaded man appeared close to her face. She cried out and fell backward.

'Over, over, over,' the thing sang while floating in the air above her, its severed head close enough for her to see every minute detail. 'Over, over, over, over . . .'

The light of him began to dim, and he faded until only the night and the flames of the tavern remained. Magiere half lay on the ground, numb inside as she watched the burning building for any sign of Rashed.

There was nothing but fire and smoke in the dark.

21

The first return of emotion fluttered inside Magiere when she saw Leesil open his eyes. He lay on the ground beside her, out in the street. There were fresh teeth marks on his left arm below the ones she'd given him two nights before. His face was pale, but he was breathing without too much discomfort that she could see. He blinked twice from the light of a torch stuck in the ground nearby.

'Is it morning?' he rasped.

'Almost,' she answered. 'Soon.'

Leesil scowled, and that brought Magiere more comfort. Irritation and a foul mood meant he would probably be all right.

'Are we alive?' he asked.

'Yes.'

'Good . . . nobody should feel this bad if they're dead.'

Magiere sighed, releasing all the anxiety and tension she'd not even been aware was locked inside her. She sat gazing at what had been The Sea Lion. Separated as it was from the buildings nearby, the fire had not spread beyond the tavern.

As Leesil gained some awareness, he lifted his head enough to see the smoldering remains of their home, groaned, and then raised his hands slightly in resignation. When his hands flopped back down, his face winced from pain, and then he tried cradling his injured arm.

'Don't move,' she said. 'I got you out of the stable, but after that, I thought it best to keep you still.'

He half rocked on his back and tried to pull off the wool cloak she'd covered him with, but he only managed to rumple it to one side. She pulled the cloak back up into place again.

Streaks of light now stretched out over the trees to the east, gilding a few white clouds high in the sky. Around them, people still tended the injured or helped them off the streets. Karlin's voice rose occasionally above the general noise as he suggested how to best treat an injury or who might need to be carried. Some members of their little army who hadn't been seriously injured conversed in low voices and patted each other on the shoulder.

Magiere had her own injured to care for, but there wasn't much she could offer Leesil, besides time and rest. Once she'd gotten him out of the stable, she laid him flat and kept him warm. Karlin had told her they were setting up the bakery as a hospice. Although, like Caleb, he didn't think much of Miiska's current healers, he had several people trying to locate one.

'Where'd you find me?' Leesil asked. 'The last thing I remember is killing a wolf.'

'Apparently, the children dragged you down into their hiding place. Chap was still sitting on the trapdoor, keeping guard when I arrived.' She paused. 'They're good children. Resourceful. These people are worth trying to save.'

'Where's Chap now?'

'Geoffry took Rose to the bakery. I sent Chap with them.'

'Is Rashed—'

'Gone.' Her tone became flat and empty. 'I watched him burn.'

She couldn't muster any joy, but Leesil didn't seem to notice. Just when she thought he'd be able to rest and heal, something new managed to beat him down yet again. But not anymore.

That thought brought some comfort again. At least this spiral of success and failure was truly over.

'Nothing happened like I thought it would,' she said.

Leesil was about to answer when Karlin walked over to check on him. Though dirty and exhausted, the baker appeared unhurt. 'Ah, you're awake. I'm so glad. We'll get you somewhere more comfortable as soon as possible.'

'What about the rest?' Leesil asked with effort.

'Only five deaths,' Karlin replied. Despite the phrase, his tone held enough sorrow for ten times as many. 'I'm already trying to arrange visitation ceremonies before burial . . . when people are ready to face it.'

'Brenden's body burned with the tavern,' Leesil realized. Then he seemed unable to continue with the thought. 'I never planned on fighting wolves.'

'No one did. It's not your fault.' Karlin's brows knitted. 'The moment the tavern collapsed, they all fled back into the forest, as if Rashed lost his hold on them.'

'He did,' Magiere confirmed quietly.

Leesil lay back and stared up at the sky. 'Well, we're homeless . . . again. All that fighting, and we lost the main thing we'd been fighting for.'

'Did we?' Magiere asked.

Again, Karlin frowned, his round cheeks wrinkling slightly. 'Heal up and rebuild.'

'What?' Magiere stared at him incredulously. 'How, and with what? We don't even have a place to live in the meantime.'

Karlin knelt and pointed at the smoldering tavern.

'The land plot is still yours. And the payment the shopkeepers tried to give you is still sitting in my kitchen. Those coins will buy supplies to get started. We'll work in the evenings and at week's end. Some of the stonework in the kitchen, and fireplace, might not even need to be replaced. It may take a moon or two, but I think enough folks will be willing to help.'

Magiere couldn't respond. Karlin did not seem to see himself as unselfish or astounding. The whole resolution seemed so simple, so clear to him.

'Brenden's home is empty now,' he chatted on. 'It may seem a bit odd at first, but he'd want you there until we've got The Sea Lion rebuilt. There's grain and fire-wood already stored at the place, and the rest can be dealt with along the way.'

He talked as if Magiere and Leesil's current situation were commonplace, and a bit of planning and polish would fix everything. Magiere wasn't nearly so certain.

She looked down at her partner, whose amber eyes were still fixed on the sky. His hands trembled slightly. She carefully touched him on the shoulder to return his attention.

'What do you think?' she asked.

He nodded once without speaking.

'Done then,' Karlin said, and he stood up. 'Ah, here come Caleb and Darien with a door.'

His words confused Magiere, and she looked over to see Caleb and Darien, the guard, lifting a fisherman with a bleeding thigh onto a door they were using as a stretcher.

'I'll send them for Leesil next,' Karlin said. 'We don't want to jar his ribs again.'

The portly baker walked away with purpose, calling out instructions along his way. Magiere smelled smoke from the embers mixed with salt from the ocean. She looked down at Leesil.

'I'll be right back,' she said, getting up.

Leaving her partner's side, she walked to the crumbled remains of The Sea Lion. She stepped into its black and slightly smoldering cinders, her boots growing warm but not hot. Pulling her falchion, she used it to dig about in the debris until it clanked against something in the ashes. She cleared some of the ash, uncovered Rashed's longsword, and used her own blade to lift it out into plain sight.

She flipped Rashed's sword out onto the bare ground and stepped out after it, again finding herself unable to feel triumphant. The ash of Rashed and Teesha's bones had mingled with that of her home.

A gust of cool air blew in from the sea. As it filled her lungs with its freshness, she watched it swirl and carry off traces of ash in its passing. This place, this town, was home now, and perhaps that much, at least, felt certain. And Leesil was alive to share it. In a few days, mortals would clear all this away and rebuild over Rashed and Teesha's graves.

She glanced back at the half-elf, his head rolled to one side to watch her intently.

'Keep the sword,' he said. 'Hang it over the new hearth.'

'As a trophy?' she asked.

'As redemption. We did do something good here – something real. You know that, don't you?'

When had Leesil grown wise?

'I won't be able to offer much help with the rebuilding. I barely faked my way through running a tavern,' she said. 'What am I going to do for the next moon?'

His narrow eyebrows arched. 'Why, play nursemaid to me, of course. Not a bad job.'

'Oh, shut up.'

She turned away as if continuing to sift through the ashes, hiding the near smile she tried to suppress. No, it would not be a bad job at all.

Epilogue

Late the following night on the north edge of Miiska, at the entrance to Belaski's long coastal road, Welstiel Massing sat on his bay gelding in the darkness. The horse trembled and shied away at his touch, but it would obey. He turned for one final look at the sleepy town. Everything he needed was packed into his saddlebags.

He felt no regret at leaving, for he had no attachments to sever here. His work was done. In this place, Magiere had come as far as he could compel her along the path he had set. Setting events in motion had been easy enough, once her banker in Bela informed him that Magiere was looking to buy a tavern. There had been time enough to meet the owner of The Sea Lion, Dunction, remove him, and quietly assist her behind the scenes with the actual purchase. The banker was glad for his commission and the ease of the transaction.

Pitting Rashed and Magiere against each other had been equally simple. *Dhampir* and vampire – from all he had learned over the years, their natural state was to be at each other's throats. All he needed to do was raise her awareness of her true nature, carefully, just a bit at a time.

Miiska was now cleansed, and Magiere's self-awareness awakened. This place served no more useful purpose. The next stage in her development now had to be planned, and she still had far to go before she would be of real use to him.

'Until we meet again, Magiere,' he whispered.

He reined his horse around and began his journey up the dark road.

Look out for . . .

THIEF OF LIVES

The sequel to *Dhampir*

by
Barb and J. C. Hendee

www.orbitbooks.co.uk